# Love Comes to Paradise

# Love Comes to Paradise

## MARY ELLIS

HARVEST HOUSE PUBLISHERS
EUGENE, OREGON

Scripture verses are taken from the *Holy Bible,* New Living Translation, copyright © 1996, 2004. Used by permission of Tyndale House Publishers, Inc., Wheaton, IL 60189 USA. All rights reserved. Verses are also taken from the King James Version of the Bible.

*Cover by Garborg Design Works, Savage, Minnesota*

*Cover photos © Chris Garborg; Bigstock / Volohatiuk*

**LOVE COMES TO PARADISE**
Copyright © 2013 by Mary Ellis
Published by Harvest House Publishers
Eugene, Oregon 97402
www.harvesthousepublishers.com

Library of Congress Cataloging-in-Publication Data
Ellis, Mary,
Love comes to Paradise / Mary Ellis.
    p. cm. — (New beginnings series ; bk. 2)
 ISBN 978-0-7369-3867-9 (pbk.)
 ISBN 978-0-7369-4300-0 (eBook)
1. Young women—Fiction. 2. Life change events—Fiction. 3. Reputation—Fiction.
4. Triangles (Interpersonal relations)—Fiction. 5. Amish—Fiction. 6. Missouri—Fiction.
I. Title.
PS3626.E36L68 2013
813'.6—dc22

                                                                2012031186

# THERE IS A FOUNTAIN
William Cowper, lyrics 1771

*There is a fountain filled with blood*
*Drawn from Immanuel's veins*
*And sinners plunged beneath that flood*
*Lose all their guilty stains.*

*The dying thief rejoiced to see*
*That fountain in his day*
*And there may I, though vile as he,*
*Wash all my sins away.*

*Dear dying Lamb, thy precious blood*
*Shall never lose its power*
*Till all the ransomed church of God*
*Be saved, to sin no more.*

*Ever since by faith, I saw the stream*
*Thy flowing wounds supply*
*Redeeming love has been my theme*
*And shall be till I die.*

*When this poor lisping, stammering tongue*
*Lies silent in the grave*
*Then in a nobler, sweeter song*
*I'll sing thy power to save.*

*On that day a fountain will be opened for the dynasty of David*
*and for the people of Jerusalem,*
*a fountain to cleanse them from all their sins and impurity.*

ZECHARIAH 13:1

# ACKNOWLEDGMENTS

Thanks to Robert Tucker of the Taylor House Inn in Columbia, Missouri, for providing a fabulous place to stay.

Thanks to Kay and Judy, sisters from Higbee, along with patrons of Crossroads Restaurant in Sturgeon, Missouri, for answering my endless questions.

Thanks to Rosanna Coblentz of the Old Order Amish for the delicious recipes.

Thanks to my agent, Mary Sue Seymour, who had faith in me from the beginning; to my lovely proofreader, Joycelyn Sullivan; and to my pastor, Daniel Jarvis, for his inspiring, "fiery" sermons.

Thanks to my editor, Kim Moore, and the wonderful staff at Harvest House Publishers.

Finally, thanks to the charming Old Order Amish of Randolph, Audrain, and Boone Counties who allowed me to peek into their lives. Although those counties are real, Paradise, Missouri, is a fictional town.

# ONE

*There is a fountain filled with blood*

$A$re you lost, miss? This is the bus to Columbia."

Nora King almost jumped out of her high-top shoes. She turned to find a kind ebony face inches from her own.

"I don't think I am. Do you mean Columbia, Missouri?" She shifted the heavy duffel bag to her other hand.

The bus driver chuckled, revealing several gold teeth. "It's the only one we've got. You're a long way from South Carolina. Want me to stow your bag in the underbelly, or do you want it in the overhead?"

The question dumbfounded Nora as people jostled past on both sides. "I'm not sure," she murmured. In fact, she wasn't sure of much since leaving Maine. Who would have thought it would be so hard to get to Missouri? It certainly hadn't been such an ordeal to travel from Lancaster County, Pennsylvania, to Harmony, Maine, last year.

The bus driver straightened after stowing several suitcases into a large compartment above the wheels.

"It's a little more than two hours to Columbia from here, St. Louis." He pointed at the ground, in case she truly was lost. "Is there anything you will need from your bag during the drive? Snacks, reading material, personal items?"

"*Jah*...I mean, yes." Nora flushed as she lapsed into her *Deutsch* dialect. "Sorry, I'm Amish."

He offered another magnificent smile. "That much I figured out on my own. Because your bag isn't too large and you'll need things, feel free to stow it in the rack above your head. But you'll want to climb on up and find a seat. It's time to go." The driver gestured toward the steps and then resumed packing luggage into the compartment.

Nora had no idea why she was acting so uncertain of herself. She'd ridden plenty of buses in her lifetime—just not on any this side of the Mississippi River. She was in the West and in the new home state of Elam Detweiler. That thought left her weak in the knees. Nevertheless, she joined the queue boarding the bus in the St. Louis terminal and started the second-to-last leg of her journey. Soon she was inside the vehicle and looking for a seat.

"Nora? Nora King?" An unfamiliar female voice sang out.

Nora gazed over a sea of English faces, yet none seemed particularly interested in her.

"Back here, Nora." A small hand waved in the air, midway down the aisle.

Nora inched her way forward, careful not to bump anyone with her overstuffed bag. Her sister Amy had sewed her several dresses, along with lots of white prayer *kapps,* and then bought her brand-new underwear. Nora should have brought a bigger suitcase. After hefting up her bag and jamming it between two others, she looked into the blue eyes of the person calling her name—a pretty girl around her own age.

"You're A-Amish," she stammered.

"I am. Did you think you would be the only one on board?" The girl became even prettier when she smiled. "Sit here with me and stop blocking the aisle." She patted the vinyl seat beside her.

Acutely aware people were growing impatient behind her, Nora did as she was told. "*Danki*, I will."

"I'm Violet, and I'm your official welcome-to-Missouri committee. My mother and me, that is." She hooked a thumb toward the rear of the bus. "My *mamm* moved to another seat so you and I could get acquainted during the ride." Violet straightened her apron over her dress with an expression of joy with her idea.

Nora peeked over the seat. Two rows back a sweet-faced woman lifted her hand in a wave. She appeared old enough to be the girl's *grossmammi*, not her mother. "*Danki* for saving a seat and for the welcome, but how did you know I would take this bus?"

"Our meeting was arranged by Emily Gingerich, sister of Sally Detweiler, sister-in-law to your sister Amy Detweiler. Hmm, does that make Sally your sister-in-law too? I don't know how that works, but it doesn't really matter because you're here now, and soon we'll be in Columbia. My father arranged for a hired van to take us the rest of the way to Paradise."

Nora blinked like an owl, bewildered despite Violet's detailed explanation. "I see," she said unconvincingly.

"Forgive me for chattering like a magpie. My *daed* says I run off at the mouth to make up for the fact I can't run around." She laughed without restraint.

"I don't mind. Talk all you want. But are running or jogging frowned upon in your local *Ordnung*?" Nora was eager to learn the rules and regulations after her experience in the ultraconservative district of Harmony, Maine.

"Goodness, no. You can run until you drop over with a side-stitch if you like. But I can't due to bum legs." She patted her dress where her kneecaps would be. "I fell from the barn loft when I was four years old. I'd sneaked up the ladder when my sister wasn't looking, even though my parents had warned me a hundred times to stay away from it."

"Oh, my. You're lucky you weren't killed." Nora noticed with pleasure that Violet's dress was a soft shade of sea blue. The Harmony *Ordnung* had allowed only dark or dull colors: navy, black, brown, or olive green.

"That's the truth. I don't have to stay in a wheelchair all the time. I can hobble around on crutches, but I tire out quickly."

"At least a wheelchair is more comfortable than the hard, backless benches at the preaching services. And you'll always have a place to sit at social events."

Violet threw her head back and laughed. Her freckles seemed to dance across her nose. "You have a great attitude! You're not uncomfortable with me being handicapped?"

Nora stared at her as the bus pulled out of the depot. "Of course not. What difference does it make whether or not you can run? I can always push your wheelchair fast if you need to get some place in a hurry."

Without warning, Violet threw both arms around Nora and squeezed. "You and I might end up being good friends."

A perfect stranger until ten minutes ago.

An expression of affection from a human being other than her sister Amy.

"That would be nice. I don't have any friends in Missouri. I only had two in Maine, and I didn't have many in Lancaster, either." Nora smoothed out the wrinkles in her mud-brown dress, wishing she'd worn one of the new ones.

Violet's eyes rounded. "You lived in Lancaster? I've heard stories about how crowded that county has become. Many Old Order folks have resettled here because they couldn't find affordable farmland to buy in Pennsylvania."

Nora's stomach lurched, and it had nothing to do with the bus gaining speed on the freeway entrance ramp. "Please don't tell me that where I'm headed has only a dozen families and a town the size of a postage stamp. There were just a couple hundred Amish people in three communities in the entire state of Maine."

"You're moving to a place you know nothing about?" Violet drew back, clucking her tongue. "There are nine thousand Amish in Missouri in thirty-eight settlements and at least ninety districts. Does *that* brighten your day a bit? The city of Columbia is only an hour away with beautiful parks and nature areas and a super-duper mall." She leaned over conspiratorially. "But don't tell my *daed* that *mamm* and I went there twice after doctors' appointments. We didn't buy anything except for a giant pretzel. We just looked around at the stuff *Englischers* spend their hard-earned money on. My father has no use for English malls, but I think they are quite fun."

Grinning, Nora relaxed against the headrest. She liked Violet already. "Harmony would be nice if I were ready to marry and raise a family, like my sister Amy. But for a single woman, not wanting to settle down yet, it was deader than an anthill in January."

"In that case you'll like Paradise. We have almost forty Amish businesses in town and spread throughout the county. Lots of bakeries; mercantiles; doll shops; and quilt, craft, and antique stores, as well as manly businesses such as lumberyards, feed-and-seed stores, leather tanners, and carriage shops. You'll have no trouble finding a job." Violet dug a package of crackers from her purse and offered some to her companion.

Nora took one to calm her queasy stomach. "You mean your *Ordnung* permits women to work?"

"Of course women are allowed to work. Where did you say you came from? Maine or Mars?"

Nora choked on a bite of cracker. "The two were pretty much

the same thing," she said after a sip of water. "Women were forbidden to take jobs outside their homes."

"Usually women here quit work once they marry and the *bopplin* start arriving, but until then people will scratch their heads or shake a stick if you sit around the house twiddling your thumbs." She leaned over to whisper into Nora's ear. "Don't you love that quaint expression, 'start arriving,' as though babies take the Greyhound to the Columbia depot, call for the hired van, and show up with a fully packed diaper bag?"

Nora snickered. "It does paint a different picture than a mother in hours of painful labor." She pulled another cracker from Violet's pack. "I'm glad Paradise isn't as stodgy as Harmony. There was little to do, especially during the winter, with few social events other than singings. And the church singings were for *everybody*, not just young single people. And there was no *rumschpringe.*"

Violet's hand, holding the last cracker, halted midway to her mouth. "You're pulling my pinned-together leg, right? No *rumschpringe?*"

"I assure you, I don't joke about the district I used to live in. The Amish there are very conservative and tolerate no running-around time."

"How on earth do folks court, marry, and then add to the rapidly growing Amish population? Or are you saying most Harmonians live and die lonesome, celibate lives?"

Nora smiled at that. "People still manage to meet and fall in love, in spite of the incredible obstacles placed in their path." She gazed out the opposite window as memories of tall, handsome Lewis Miller flitted through her mind. She could easily have fallen in love with him if not for the monotony of central Maine...and if the irresistible, black-eyed, wild-as-an-eagle Elam Detweiler hadn't changed everything for her. She shook off thoughts of both men and turned back to her companion. "Do you know Emily

Gingerich—Sally Detweiler's sister? I will be staying with her, at least for a while, but we have never met."

"Of course I know her. Paradise may be larger than Harmony, but we have plenty of social occasions to meet one another. Besides, Emily owns Grain of Life Bakery." Violet lowered her voice. "That is the best bakery in town, but don't tell my *mamm* I said that. One of her *schwestern* owns another of the shops."

"So far you've shared with me one secret to keep from your father and another from your mother, Violet. We just met today. For all you know, I could be the world's biggest blabbermouth."

"You don't appear to be, and I'm a good judge of character." Violet studied Nora with narrowed eyes, not the least bit nervous. "Tell me, are you up to the challenge, Nora, to not divulge the confidences you've heard today?"

"You bet I am. It's been a long time since anybody trusted me." She sighed, remembering Elam and his secrets.

Violet reached down to rub her leg, generating a metal-against-metal sound. "My leg braces itch like crazy sometimes." She winced, as though her scratching had touched a sore spot. "And now that you're privy to several of my dark secrets, you must confess one of yours."

Nora's head snapped around. "What do you mean? What makes you think I have any?"

"Come on. My legs may not be perfect, but there's nothing wrong with my mind. You just moved halfway across the country to a town that's a complete mystery and are staying with a couple you've never laid eyes on. I smell a secret as strong as cheese left out in the sun." Her eyes practically bored holes through Nora. "Don't you trust me?"

Typical of her impetuous personality, it took Nora no time to decide. Something about Violet appealed to her enormously. She wanted nothing to nip their friendship in the bud.

"I fell in love in Harmony with the wrong sort of man," she whispered. "I don't know if he plans to stay Amish, and he doesn't even know I'm coming. But when he left Maine, he said he was heading to Paradise. So I pointed myself in the same direction." Nora leaned back in her seat. "Now you know *my* secret."

Violet stared at her, wide-eyed. "That is the most romantic thing I've ever heard in my life. I will take your secret to my grave if need be."

And if her expression of awe could be trusted as an indicator, Nora had just made a new best friend.

❧

"I'm coming," called Emily from the hallway. She pulled off her apron, tossed it on the counter, and swept open the kitchen door. Before her stood a small woman, not more than a girl, really, in a dusty cape and wrinkled brown dress. Her clothes looked too big for her, as though they were cut from a pattern meant for someone else. But she had the prettiest green eyes Emily had ever seen.

"Mrs. Gingerich?" the girl asked, peering up through thick dark lashes. "I'm Nora King, Amy Detweiler's sister. I've come from Maine."

"Thank goodness. For a moment I feared you were here to sell me a new set of pots and pans or some of those English cosmetics." Emily grabbed her sleeve and pulled her into the kitchen.

Nora waved at the hired van idling in the driveway as she passed through the doorway. "No, ma'am. I hope my arrival hasn't come at an inopportune time." She clutched a large duffel bag with both hands, gazing out from inside a huge outer bonnet.

"I was joking, Nora. Please make yourself at home. I expected you today and hoped you would enjoy the company of Violet and Rosanna on the ride from St. Louis. Isn't that Violet a hoot? She never fails to make me smile within five minutes of being in the same room with her."

Nora removed her cloak and the hideous bonnet, and then she hung them both on a peg. "She seems nice and is really quite funny. *Danki* for arranging them to meet me. I was a bit discombobulated in St. Louis." She stood behind a chair as though waiting for a certain sign or signal.

"Sit. Take a load off. They travel to Columbia once a month for physical therapy and twice a year for a specialist's reevaluation of Violet's legs. The doctors want to keep them as strong as possible because she insists on using crutches whenever she can." Emily filled the kettle and placed it on the stove. "We'll have tea and cookies. Dinner will be in an hour or so."

Nora sat and folded her hands like a schoolgirl awaiting an assignment or admonishment.

Emily smiled encouragingly at her. "Unless you're starving now, in which case, I'll make you a sandwich."

"No, ma'am, tea will be fine. I can wait until supper." Nora remained very still, as though too frightened to move.

"Please, no more ma'ams. My name is Emily." Without the bonnet, the girl had delicate, small-boned features. Wisps of strawberry blond hair escaped her prayer *kapp* and framed her face. "Are you *sure* you're the Nora King my sister wrote to me about? Or have I admitted an imposter into my house?"

Nora paled significantly. "I am she, although I have no identification. Shall I describe Sally's home or her two sons, Aden and Jeremiah?"

Emily placed some oatmeal cookies on a plate and sat down across from the scared rabbit. "Because I haven't met my nephews yet, nor have I ever been to Sally's home in Maine, I'll take your word for it. And I'll stop teasing until we get to know each other better." She filled two mugs with hot water and tea bags. "Welcome to our home, Nora. My husband and I are happy to have you, and we hope you'll soon like our humble part of the world."

"Everyone has better senses of humor here." Nora took a cookie from the plate to nibble. "I'm afraid I lost mine when I left Pennsylvania."

Her earnestness tugged on Emily's heartstrings. "Sally told me about what happened to your parents in a letter. You have my deepest sympathy. A woman is never prepared to lose her *mamm*, even if she's seventy years old. At your tender age, the loss must be especially painful."

"I try to focus on the future instead of the past. I did too much staring out the window and crying in Harmony. I'm eager to make a new beginning in Paradise."

"Then you've come to the right place. The Amish population of Missouri has tripled in the last twenty years. Folks move here from all over—Ohio, Indiana, and Illinois. We still have cheap land, and farming is what ninety-nine percent of us do."

Nora gasped. "That's not like Pennsylvania at all. Most folks there have had to learn a trade or start a business."

Emily stirred sugar into her tea. "Well, my *ehemann* is actually part of the one percent. His brothers work their family's land, but Jonas started a lumberyard. It does fairly well, selling to Amish and English, if you'll forgive me for some prideful bragging."

"I will forgive just about anything if I can have another cookie. These are delicious." A dimple formed in Nora's cheek, the first sign her shyness may be ebbing.

Emily pushed the plate across the table. "Eat to your heart's content. You can stand to gain a few pounds, whereas I cannot." She gently slapped one rounded hip. "Didn't my sister feed you while you lived there?"

"Sally certainly tried to, but I get migraines from time to time. They take my appetite away for days."

"Migraines can be triggered by stress. I aim to see you relaxed and not worrying so much."

Nora reached for another cookie and consumed it in three bites. "Was your Old Order district formed by people moving here from Pennsylvania?"

"No, we were settled sixty years ago by a group who came from Iowa."

"Iowa? Where is that?"

Emily smiled. "And to think you traveled all the way from practically the Atlantic Ocean. The Lord be praised! He pities those with a poor knowledge of geography."

"I prayed plenty on the way here. I took the Downeaster train from Portland to Boston; the Lake Shore Limited from Boston to Chicago; and then I caught the Texas Eagle to St. Louis. I tried to learn the layout of my country along the way. What are the states near Missouri?" As she asked, her face reflected the innocent, curious expression of a child.

"Iowa is to the north, Kansas is to the west, Arkansas is due south, and Illinois lies to the east. A corner of our state touches both Kentucky and Tennessee. A long time ago I pronounced our southern neighbor as 'Ar-kansas,' so it rhymed with our western neighbor, but one day an *Englischer* in my shop corrected me. She whispered the correct pronunciation softly so I wouldn't be embarrassed. But what's to be ashamed of? I had never heard anybody say the word before."

Both of them laughed.

"These Iowa Amish…do you think they are similar to the Maine districts?" asked Nora, taking another cookie.

Emily realized where her guest's queries were headed. "Sally wrote to me about Harmony's no-*rumschpringe* policy. And about the fact you haven't been baptized yet. I assured her no one would pressure you to commit to the Amish church until you're ready."

Nora released an audible breath of air, relaxing for the first time since her arrival. "I'm happy to hear that. It wasn't so much that they pressured me to be baptized, but every time I turned around I was breaking another rule. Truly, Harmony was too small to be my cup of tea." She drained the contents of her mug and set it back on the table. "Violet mentioned that your bishop allows social events for young people, regular-type courting, and jobs outside the home for unmarried women. That sounds more like what I'm used to after being raised in Lancaster County."

Emily considered her reply before speaking. Should she mention that their district might soon become far less liberal if one of their ministers got his way? She glanced at Nora and quickly decided to hold off on full disclosure. The woman had just arrived in a strange land where she knew no one.

"We're more liberal than the districts near Seymour, Missouri. But why don't you wait to learn all the details? Let me show you to your room. You can bring up your bag and unpack."

Nora rose gracefully to her feet. "Will I share the room with your daughter? Sally didn't mention whether you had *kinner*."

"We haven't been blessed...yet." Emily hoped her greatest sorrow wasn't obvious as she walked toward the doorway.

"*Danki* for opening your home to me, Emily." Nora followed on her heels. "I so wanted to move here after Sally described her childhood and *rumschpringe* while courting Thomas."

"*Jah*, but I wish he hadn't taken my sister so far away. At least she's happy in Maine, so that's what counts." Emily led the way up to the bedrooms and chose her words for the second delicate topic in almost the same number of minutes. "Sally mentioned her brother-in-law's relocation had something to do with *your* coming to Missouri." Emily opened the door to the guest room, which would be Nora's for as long as she wanted it.

She walked straight to the blanket chest and deposited her bag. "Partially, I suppose. Elam and I became friends when I lived in

Harmony. But it really was Sally's description of Paradise that fascinated me." Nora smiled with genuine warmth. "The fact her kin still lived here helped me decide because I didn't want to return to Pennsylvania. I hope to run into Elam if he's around. He mentioned taking a grand tour in his new car. He even planned to see the Ozark Mountains, wherever they are."

"He brought a car?" asked Emily, shaking her head. "The Ozarks are in Arkansas, to the south. A cousin said Elam is living somewhere in the county, but he hasn't shown his face here at our home…or at a preaching service yet, I might add." She fluffed both of the pillows. "You'll find him, I suppose, if it's meant to be."

Emily walked to the door. "You have time to unpack and take a nap before dinner. Come down about five o'clock. I wound the clock on your bedside table."

Nora hurried toward her hostess and embraced her shyly. "Thank you. I am so grateful to you."

"There's nothing wrong with making a fresh start." Emily hugged the thin woman, patting her back.

*Who has made her afraid of her own shadow? Thomas Detweiler seemed like a good man when he took away Sally five years ago. What has gone on in my sister's home?*

એન્ડ

"Giddy up there, Nell. I can walk faster than you're pulling this buggy." Solomon Trask shook the reins above the mare's back, but he did not slap them down. No sense in startling the old girl. She was probably enjoying the warm April sunshine on her flanks, the sweet smell of apple blossoms tickling her nose, and the absence of traffic on the county road—increasingly rare for Saturdays.

The horse dutifully picked up the pace to a *tad* quicker than he could walk.

Solomon tilted his head back, letting the sunshine reach his face beneath his hat brim. How he loved the spring! Overhead, songbirds filled the crystalline blue sky with their music, red-tailed hawks soared on wind currents, and waterfowl crossed the Great Plains back to Canada. Life was good. The Lord had richly blessed him with a *fraa* and five fine *kinner,* including three boys who had built their homes nearby. His sons had taken over farm duties so he could minister to the district, keeping the members on the straight-and-narrow path. If he failed in his responsibilities, the Lord might not continue to bless their growing community.

Since the drawing that had made him one of two district ministers for life, he had endeavored to adhere to the Bible. God hadn't provided His holy Book as mere suggestions or helpful advice. His Word was law, and only through strict adherence could a man find direction in this life and salvation for the next.

A hollow, uncomfortable rumble in his belly reminded Solomon it had been hours since lunch, and at this pace it would be hours before supper. Should he stop to buy a dozen cookies at the next farm—one of the district's three bakeries? After all, his wife would appreciate an extra pie or two in case she hadn't found time to bake.

It wasn't long before he turned off the main road. Pricking up her ears, Nell trotted up the drive as though oats and a good rubdown waited up ahead.

However, she hadn't heard the whinny of another horse but the sound of a car radio. Loud, discordant music blared from a pickup truck parked in the side yard of the Morganstein farm. Solomon climbed slowly from the buggy and tied the reins to a hitching post. As usual, his back spasmed from sitting too long.

"*Guder nachmittag,* Minister," greeted one of the Morganstein sons.

"Good afternoon to you. Would you bring my mare a bucket of water and maybe a little grain?"

The boy nodded and scampered off as Solomon trudged past

the truck. He headed toward Levi's leather shop, an outbuilding that had become popular on Fridays and Saturdays with English tourists. Solomon hadn't gone twenty paces when a sight stopped him in his tracks. Two of Levi's sons, both in their late teens, were talking with two English girls of around the same age. Doubtless, the girls belonged to the red truck. One was swigging soda from a bottle, while the other moved her body suggestively to the beat of the infernal music. Solomon's gut twisted into a knot. Both girls wore shorts far above their knees and tops that didn't cover their stomachs. He approached the foursome with building ire.

Luke Morganstein spotted him and spoke first. "Hullo, Minister Trask. My dad's in his shop and my mother is in the house."

Solomon noticed the boy spoke in English, not their dialect of German. He addressed the *Englischers*. "Where are *your* parents?"

The taller of the two girls smiled brightly. "My dad's buying a new jacket. You guys make the best leather stuff in the state. And my mom's over there checking out free-range chickens. She loves the idea of no cages and will buy every last egg available."

Solomon's eyes followed the girl's long purple fingernail in the direction it pointed. The sight made his jaw drop. A middle-aged woman in a sweatshirt and tight blue jeans focused her camera, snapping pictures of the youngest Morganstein child, a girl of around three years old. The woman was actually posing the child by the henhouse. Bile inched up his throat, souring his mouth.

Sol turned to the teenagers. "Go back to your truck, turn off that loud music, and stay there if you don't have additional clothes to put on."

The pair stared, blinked, and then bolted down the drive. The Morganstein sons vanished into the barn before Solomon could take two steps toward the chicken coop.

"Stop that," he said. He hadn't raised his voice, but the woman froze and then turned like a cornered animal.

"Stop what?" she asked, glancing around nervously.

"Do not take pictures of our people. They are graven images and are forbidden."

She blushed to deep crimson. "I'm sorry. I didn't know that. What about the chickens and goats. Can I photograph them?" She sounded utterly sincere.

Solomon sighed. "Yes, animals and buildings are fine. Good day to you."

He picked up the little girl and strode toward the house. Dealing with *Englischers* wasn't his calling, but dealing with members of his congregation was. He opened the back door without knocking, a common practice among the Amish, and stepped into an overly warm kitchen.

"*Guder nachmittag*, Sol," greeted Sarah Morganstein. "You look hot. How about a cool drink of water?"

After he had set the child down, she scampered for her mother's skirt.

"*Jah*, that would be *gut*," he said, breathing in and out as he tried to control his temper.

Sarah handed him a glass filled to the brim. "I suppose you heard from the deacon that Levi worked on the Sabbath. He hadn't intended to, and it was only one time, but he had to fill a large order of leather chaps on a tight deadline. Of course, the deacon stopped by that particular Sunday and found Levi in his shop." She tugged on her dangling *kapp* ribbons. "He's mighty sorry and told Jonas he would never do it again."

The glass of water almost slipped from Sol's sweaty fingers as he sorted out the new information, although he had no idea what "chaps" were. "No, I hadn't heard. I wanted to say your sons are cavorting with half-dressed English girls and a woman was taking photographs of your little one." He spoke in a raspy whisper.

Sarah blanched as she drew her daughter to her side. "I didn't know about the pictures. The tourists buy much from Levi and the bakery, helping pay the medical bills from my last surgery. But I'll keep a better eye on little Josie and my boys."

"See that you do." Solomon drained the glass and handed it back to her. "Tell your *ehemann* he broke the Fourth Commandment and must confess on his knees on Sunday." Then he marched from the house to his buggy without buying pies or speaking to Levi.

This wasn't the first time he suspected district members were doing things they shouldn't on the Lord's Day. He would take the matter up with the entire congregation—and the sooner the better—before things spiraled out of control.

# TWO

*Drawn from Immanuel's veins*

## Thursday

Nora pulled down the window shade and let it go with a snap. It flapped around the roller several times before coming to rest. The houses in Paradise had shades instead of heavy, wind-blocking burlap curtains like in Harmony. It was only one of the many differences. She opened her window to gaze out on her favorite bit of change thus far. Spring arrived earlier in Missouri than in Maine. Seeds had not only been sown, but many tiny sprouts had already pushed their green heads above the rich brown earth. Jonas said they would plant soybeans next week, which preferred warmer soil than corn. And here in Paradise, farmers cut hay four times compared to three in Harmony during the best of years.

Supper with the Gingerichs certainly differed from meals with the Detweilers. Although Nora had grown fond of Sally, she usually threw dinner together at the last minute, with some food still raw and some quite overcooked. Emily Gingerich ran her kitchen with flawless efficiency, making any task look easy. Although she had no toddlers underfoot the way Sally did, Emily worked outside the home and yet managed to juggle cooking, baking, and housecleaning effortlessly.

"Nora, did you forget what day this is?" A voice carried up the steps, piercing her woolgathering.

"I certainly did not!" Nora hollered. She shut her window against the breeze, put on a fresh *kapp*, and smoothed the winkles from her new dress. The fabric was the shade of ripe peaches... what a joy after the drab attire of Maine, even for unbaptized women. Downstairs in the kitchen she found Emily filling two travel mugs with coffee and milk.

"*Guder mariye*," greeted Nora. "Am I late?"

"Not at all. Today the bakery will be open from ten o'clock until six, but we're going in early for training. Not that there's much to learn. As long as you can make change and know how to smile, you'll do fine." Emily offered her one of the mugs.

Nora sipped the strong hot brew. "I'm grateful for the job. It would have been enough just to have a bed to sleep in and a meal or two each day."

Emily winked one brown eye. "I plan to work you like a draft horse. You'll earn that soft feather mattress, hand-stuffed by Jonas, and my delicious, *gourmet* cuisine."

"I promise to try my best."

"Who could ask for more?" Emily handed Nora a small basket of blueberry muffins. "Let's be off."

"Are these what we're selling today?"

Emily burst into laughter as they left the house and marched toward the road. "Goodness, no. Those are for us to eat while we walk to work. Jonas dropped off what I baked yesterday on his way to the lumberyard."

"Good idea. I was afraid to eat one if this was all we had." Nora bit into a warm muffin.

"Most of today's customers will be Amish. Many of the elderly have discovered they don't like to bake much anymore. Tomorrow we're open from one until seven, mainly seeing *Englischers*. Poor Jonas must eat a late supper those days."

"English tourists?" Nora tried matching her pace to Emily's but practically had to run. She sipped coffee while nibbling her muffin and dribbled both down her dress.

"No, mainly locals from Randolph and Audrain Counties. Lots of folks around here get Friday afternoons off." Emily devoured her breakfast without losing a crumb. "The tourists come on Saturdays when we're open from eight to six. I have to shoo them away with my broom or they would chat all day, but I'm usually down to bare shelves by then anyway. More and more tourists discover us and tell their friends. Every Amish business I know increases sales each month." Emily paused on the side of the road. "I'm glad to hire you, Nora, because I really can use your help. If you're any good, I'll pay a small salary starting next month."

Nora pressed a hand to her chest, relieved they had stopped. "Oh, no. I couldn't accept pay," she said, panting. "I'll gladly work in exchange for room and board. Besides, I inherited money when my sisters and I sold our parents' farm. I can write to the banker in Lancaster if I need more than what I brought along."

Emily resumed her brisk walking. "You missed the key word in my offer—a *small* salary. What I had in mind will barely buy a latte or ice cream cone when you go to town on your day off." She drained her coffee mug without breaking stride.

"In that case I accept your terms, should you deem my work worthy." Nora took another muffin from the basket. "And if these are typical of your bakery's products, I understand why your business is booming."

"You're good for building my confidence but bad for my prideful soul." Emily stopped in the mown weeds a second time. "Why are you breathing like that? We're not walking that fast."

"I'm out of shape, I suppose," Nora said, gasping a little.

"The next time Violet sees her therapist in Columbia, maybe I'll send you to a doctor for a checkup. You might have asthma and those Lancaster County folks never figured it out."

Nora brightened with the prospect of seeing Violet again. "All right, as long as I pay the doctor bill. I won't be a financial burden on you and Jonas."

"Just wait to see how hard I work you, Miss Draft Horse. Anyway, if we grow too rich from my husband's lumberyard and my bakery, it'll be harder to get into heaven. Scripture says so."

"How much farther?" Nora asked as they turned the corner onto a busier highway. The rest of the muffin crumbled between her fingers.

"This is Y road. It's much better-traveled than our township lane. We have another half mile to the bakery."

Nora attempted to hide her breathlessness. "What does the L stand for?"

Emily glanced sideways. "It doesn't stand for anything. Letters are for paved county roads and numbers are for townships, like our one hundred sixteen. They're described as all-weather surfaces, but they're really not much more than hard-packed dirt."

Blessedly, Nora didn't need to speak for the rest of the hike. When they rounded the next bend, she saw the sign for Grain of Life Bakery and clapped her hands. "It's adorable, Emily."

The white one-story building was the size of a pioneer's log cabin with a green metal roof, screened windows that opened cottage-style, flowers and shrubs in tidy beds, and a pea gravel path leading to a parking lot. A hitching area had water troughs, a pump well, and picnic tables for warm-weather socializing.

"We'll see if you still find it adorable at day's end," Emily said as she unlocked the door and waved her in.

Nora stepped inside and pivoted in the center of the room.

There were four sets of carved wooden shelves to hold bakery items, along with a glass-enclosed display case. On the counter sat an old-fashioned cash register, an order pad, and a cup of pens. A gleaming table stood against one wall with shelves of baking ingredients above and below. The opposite wall had metal racks filled with boxes, bags, and canisters of supplies.

"Jonas bought me that display case last year. It has propane-powered refrigeration so I can sell cream pies in the summer. One of our ministers still grumbles about what a vain, fancy extravagance it is for an Amish bakery, but every now and then he buys a coconut cream pie for his youngest daughter."

Nora walked to the back wall of the shop. "That is the biggest oven I've ever seen." She ran her hand over the black enamel stove.

"Wood-fired heat adds better flavor to bread than my propane oven at home. I still use it throughout the summer, even though it generates quite a bit of heat, but I keep the windows open." Emily pointed at a functional skylight in the ceiling. "Today we'll bake four kinds of bread, mix up batches of homemade trail mix, and make egg noodles. Tomorrow we'll do six kinds of pie. While I get firewood and stoke up the stove with kindling, you unload what I baked yesterday. Jonas stacked the tubs on the back steps. Clean the shelves with Windex and paper towels and arrange the cookies and turnovers nicely in the display case." Without further explanation, she bustled outside.

Nora sent up a prayer the moment the door closed. *Thank You, Lord, for bringing me here. Help me to learn quickly before Emily loses patience.*

Soon they flipped the window sign from "Closed" to "Open" and Nora's first day of employment officially began. Between waiting on customers, kneading bread dough, and mixing granola with nuts and raisins, they barely had time to eat lunch—a jar of spreadable cheese with thick slices of multigrain bread. Nora had never stood on her feet so long at one time, yet she felt exhilarated instead of exhausted. She loved meeting customers and introduced herself to everyone who entered. However, around four that afternoon a man wandered in who required no introduction. When the tiny bell above the door jangled, Nora looked up to meet the dark eyes of Elam Detweiler.

At that moment her heart skipped a beat inside her chest.

"Nora King," he murmured. "A little bird told me you had arrived. I thought they were crazy, but here you are…in the flesh." He sauntered to the counter, still as tall and powerfully built as she remembered.

"Elam!" she gasped. "What a surprise."

"Why would that be? I told you I was moving to Paradise." He flashed a toothy grin. "You're a sight for sore eyes." His gaze traveled slowly from her *kapp* to her toes.

As the door swung open, Emily carried in another load of wood. She stopped her in her tracks.

"You must be Emily Gingerich," said Elam. He lifted the brim of his ball cap.

"And you must be Elam Detweiler. I'd heard you were in town. Funny how you haven't come to see us yet." Her voice held little enthusiasm.

He scratched his stubbly chin and leaned both elbows on the countertop. "I truly should have, considering we're practically family, your sister marrying my brother and all."

Emily dumped the firewood into a metal box next to the stove and washed her hands at the sink. "Something tells me you'll be dropping by on a regular basis now," she said over her shoulder.

Nora turned a shade to match her dress. *Folks in Paradise sure say whatever comes to mind.*

Elam raised his eyebrows. "You heard Nora and I were friends back in Harmony?"

Drying her hands, Emily walked to Nora's side. "Sally might have mentioned as much."

Suddenly Nora felt invisible and uncomfortable. "I'm working here, Elam, so did you come in to buy something?" His close proximity combined with Emily hovering like a hawk made her uncomfortable.

"I did. Let me see." He stepped back to read the sign on the wall. "Molasses crinkles; chocolate chip, oatmeal raisin, and peanut butter cookies; pumpkin whoopie pies...yummy. Has Emily taught you to bake yet? If my memory serves, you couldn't bake a chicken already dressed, stuffed, and sitting on the counter." Elam hooked his thumbs in the pockets of his pants. Although his shirt was Plain, the tight Levis were not.

"It's my first day, but I'm a quick study when I want to be." Nora placed her hands on her hips and glared, while Emily picked up a ball of bread dough. She kneaded with far more energy than she had exhibited earlier.

Elam read aloud the other hand-painted sign. "We use only natural sweeteners, such as honey and maple syrup, and add no hydrogenated shortening. Our wheat is locally ground, and our eggs come from free-range, organically fed hens." He strolled back to the counter. "If the weather weren't so balmy here, I'd swear I was back with those health nuts of central Maine."

"Whereas you're just a non-healthy, garden-variety type of nut." Nora spoke without thinking.

"I think we'll overlook the must-be-friendly-to-customers rule this one time," said Emily from the table.

Elam grinned, bringing deep dimples to his cheeks. "A point scored for Miss King."

The bell signaled the arrival of another customer. "Have you made your selection, Mr. Detweiler?" Nora asked, crossing her arms. Honey was no sweeter than the tone of her question.

"Yes. I'll take a dozen peanut butter cookies and all the chocolate chip you have left." He pulled a twenty from his wallet.

Nora bagged his purchase, handed him his change, and turned to the elderly customer with no further eye contact with him. And that was a good thing. Seeing Elam resurrected every fantasy she thought she had buried when he packed up and left in the dead of night all those months ago. Those tender emotions turned out to be much closer to the surface than she would have imagined. Funny things could happen when a woman came face-to-face with her heart's desire.

❧

Elam Detweiler sat in his car with the radio on and the windows down, smoking what he hoped was his last cigarette of the day. Nasty habit, smoking, and also expensive. He'd promised himself he would quit when he arrived in Missouri. But here he was, still fouling his body in the land of milk and honey. Maybe the possibility of getting friendly with pretty Nora King would provide the necessary motivation.

He'd been parked across the road waiting for the green-eyed beauty to finish work for two hours. He'd read every magazine from his backseat stash and devoured an entire dozen cookies. It was the only food he'd eaten all day, but he had never followed a balanced diet. Just when his patience ran out, Elam saw the door to Grain of Life open and the reason for his delay step into the sunshine. Without hesitation, he popped a breath mint into his mouth and bolted across the road.

"I thought you'd never get off work," he said once he reached her side.

She startled, as though he'd crept up on her. "What are you doing here? I thought you left hours ago." Wisps of russet hair blew loose from her *kapp*.

"I waited to talk to you. How about a lift back to the Gingerichs'? I assume that's where you're living." He bobbed his head toward his car. "Remember the Chevy? You were instrumental during its purchase, and I still owe you a favor for that one."

She focused across the street. "Yes you do. How was the drive? Did you have any trouble coming from the East Coast?"

"Not a bit. She's good on gas too. How about a ride to judge for yourself?"

Nora buttoned her cloak over her pretty peach-colored dress despite the warm temperatures. "No, thank you. As I just arrived, I prefer to stay out of trouble for a while."

"What do you mean?"

"Being seen accepting a ride from a strange man? I'll walk." She stepped around him and headed toward the corner.

"Give me a minute to lock my car and I'll walk with you." Elam sprinted across the road, but she didn't wait. He had to run a ways to catch up to her.

"Whew, slow down. What's the big hurry, Nora? You didn't find me all that strange back in Maine. Why don't we take it easy and catch up on the news?" He took hold of her elbow.

She slowed her pace but shook off his hand. "Strange, as in folks around here don't know you...or me, for that matter." She met his gaze and held it for a long moment. "I *am* glad to see you, Elam. I hoped we would run into each other."

"That's good to hear, since I'm the reason you moved to Missouri, right?" He shuffled through the weeds to give her the smooth shoulder of the road.

Nora blushed. "Don't flatter yourself. I was intrigued by Sally's stories of Paradise, the same as you."

"Sure. I didn't mean to imply anything else." He pulled her off the pavement as a truck passed too close for comfort. "Why don't we go for coffee or a bite to eat? I'll jog back for my car."

Nora shrugged away a second time. "No, Elam. I left work early to start supper at home. Emily will be leaving within the hour, so I want to have the pork chops in the oven." She stopped walking and looked at him with an earnest expression on her face. "I don't know where or how you're living—whether Amish or English—but I plan to get off on the right foot with the Gingerichs. I was in hot water more often than not in Harmony."

Elam felt a surge of irritation. "You blame *me* for your troubles with my brothers?"

She shook her head, sending her *kapp* strings flying. "*Nein*. I blame only myself. I made no attempt to get along with people… to fit in in Maine." She turned her face skyward and breathed in the crisp spring air. "So far, I really like it here. I'm going to take things slow and think before I act." She laughed with the wonderful musical sound he remembered. "Because traveling was such an ordeal, I'm in no hurry to pack my bag and move back."

They continued walking side by side.

"You don't want to be friends with me anymore, Miss King? I'm a memory from the past better off forgotten?"

"Good grief, Elam. Don't go all dramatic. Can't we be friends in an Amish sort of way? Or have you completely jumped the fence?"

He whistled through his teeth. "I have not. I'm still walking the tightrope between two cultures, never a man who made up his mind quickly." He pulled her to a stop. When she faced him, he lifted her chin with one finger. "Maybe a woman like you can help me make the big decision." Her creamy skin, soft rosy lips, and sparkling eyes nearly stole his breath.

For a moment it seemed she stopped breathing. Then she said, "I'll give it my best shot, but right now I need to start supper." She stepped away again, out of reach, heading toward home.

"Wait a minute. I have a favor to ask if we're still friends."

"What is it?" She turned, shielding her eyes from the sun.

"I haven't found a job yet, and I'm running low on cash. I'm thinking of showing up at Gingerich Lumberyard tomorrow to fill out an application. Would you put in a good word for me?"

She hesitated only a moment. "Sure, why not? You have lumber experience from the north woods of Maine. I'll talk to Jonas tonight at supper."

Elam breathed easier. He hated asking a woman—any woman—to help him find a job, but an empty belly and an almost empty gas tank drove a man to new lows. Who would have thought *Englischers* wouldn't hire without job references? He dared not list his last logging crew because the boss fired him for fighting. And his Plain brethren didn't want to employ a man who hadn't committed to the faith.

"Thanks, Nora. If I don't find a job soon I'll be evicted. Now I owe you three favors."

She grinned. "You're welcome. We can't have you sleeping in your fancy car, no matter how much you love your Chevy. I'll walk the rest of the way alone so you can start back. Good luck tomorrow." Without another word, she took off running.

Elam stared after her until she disappeared from view.

*You have no idea how close I am to living in my car, sweet Nora.*

❧

Jonas Gingerich drove home from the lumberyard humming an old hymn, one of his *mamm*'s favorites. He'd been able to leave work on time for a change because no last-minute customers arrived just before closing. Mostly, Plain folk dropped by to purchase split rails to replace rotted fencing, two-by-fours to frame new barn stalls, or sheets of plywood for chicken coop roofs. Many drove flatbed wagons or borrowed their neighbor's if they didn't own one. One customer ordered wood for a new barn to be erected next month. Amish workers would load the order onto a truck trailer to be driven by an English employee. Some orders were too heavy for a team of draft horses. Jonas would pass along a modest delivery charge to the customer, not much more than the cost of diesel fuel. He had no desire to get rich, only to make a modest living for Emily...and any *kinner* the Lord might someday bless them with.

He was a patient man. Contented people usually were. He had the love of a good *fraa*, work he enjoyed, and a position as the district deacon to keep him close to his faith. He seldom passed an evening without spending time in prayer or reading his Bible to Emily. Now a shy young woman had joined their household. Maybe Sally sent Nora south to fatten the girl up or to put color into her pale face, but for whatever the reason, Jonas welcomed the extra help for his wife. Her bakery grew more popular with each passing month, and he hated her toiling over that wood-burning oven alone.

Jonas lifted his hand to wave at least a dozen times on the way home. As the deacon, everyone knew him or would soon meet him. The number of Amish in Randolph County was increasing rapidly as new people arrived from every direction. Most newcomers adjusted easily to their *Ordnung*—the rules governing an Amish community. Plain folks were taught obedience and submission to God's will at an early age, so seldom did the bishop encounter anyone resistant to change.

*"Why do you all dress alike?"*

*"Why do your houses look so similar?"*

*Englischers* who had been taught uniqueness and independence couldn't understand the concept that no one individual was more special or should be singled out over any other. All were equal in the eyes of the Lord. Only Jonas's choice of careers differed from his brothers. Whereas they loved the feel of dirt between their fingers and enjoyed growing food to sustain their families, he loved the hum of diesel-powered band saws, the smell of sweet pine sawdust, and building kitchen cabinets during the slow winter months.

When he entered his kitchen, after rubbing down, feeding, and watering his horse, Jonas nearly jumped a foot into the air. Nora stood at the sink, peeling and slicing potatoes.

"Hello, Jonas," she said. "Did you forget about me?"

"I didn't expect to see anyone. If I get home on time, I usually read Scripture for an hour before my *fraa* arrives." He hung his hat and coat on a peg.

"She let me go early to start supper. How about a cup of coffee? I made a fresh pot."

"That's *gut*, but I'll get it myself. I don't allow anyone to wait on me except for my wife." He laughed at his favorite joke.

"Emily says *you're* the helpful, indulgent one in the family." Nora dumped potatoes into a pot of water.

"I suppose we do tend to pamper each other." Jonas took a sip of strong, black coffee. "This will taste good after my shower, *danki*." He was halfway to the bathroom before she called to him.

"Jonas, may I speak with you a moment?" Nora set the pot on a burner and then dried her hands. "You own Gingerich Lumber, *jah*?"

"That's correct." He swallowed another gulp.

"That means you have say-so in the hiring and firing?"

"Don't tell me Emily fired you on your very first day. She usually shows more patience than that."

Nora smiled after a moment's pause. "Not to my knowledge. I believe my position is still intact." She picked up the coffeepot to top off his mug and then her own. "An old friend from Maine stopped by the bakery today. He's out of work and needs a job." She leaned against the counter, reluctant to meet his eye.

Jonas stroked his beard. "A friend has already found you in Paradise?"

"I was quite surprised when he walked through the door of Grain of Life to buy cookies. Two types in fact."

"Tell him to stop by and fill out an application for the next time there's an opening." Assuming the matter was finished, Jonas strode to the doorway, eager for a muscle-relaxing hot shower.

"But he needs employment now," she persisted, her voice following him. "Isn't there some way you can use him? He worked hard with lumber back in Maine. At least that's what I heard from Thomas Detweiler."

"Who is this old friend?" Jonas turned back to their houseguest, curious.

"Elam Detweiler." Nora wrapped both hands around her mug.

He tried to recall what Emily had mentioned about her sister's brother-in-law. Something about him still being on *rumschpringe* and unable to commit. But as half of Jonas's employees were English, that wouldn't be a problem. "He lives here now, in Missouri?" The question probably was superfluous but he asked it anyway.

"*Jah*, but if he doesn't find work soon he may become homeless." Her green eyes grew very large.

Jonas had never heard of a homeless Amish person, and so he had no choice but to grant her request. "Tell him to come to my office. I'll hire him for a trial period. If he works hard, then the position will become permanent. But if you'll excuse me, Nora, I want to finish my shower before Emily gets home."

"*Danki,* Jonas." She turned back to the stove, smiling brightly.

As he left the room, he had the strangest feeling Nora had asked her question just now *because* Emily wasn't home yet.

# THREE

*And sinners plunged beneath that flood*

Most women weren't so eager to get to work, but most women weren't Nora King. She couldn't wait until she flipped the sign to "Open" and slipped on a clean apron. It was her third day of employment. She may have sore feet, but she now slept like a baby and hadn't suffered a single migraine since arriving in Missouri.

Besides, today was Saturday—the bakery's day for tourists. Nora loved to see what English women wore to sightsee, shop, and run errands. She also hoped she would have her first date with Elam that night. Just thinking about him sent shivers of anticipation up her spine. When he had touched her face, she almost came out of her shoes.

*"Maybe a woman like you can help me make the big decision."* What had he meant by that? How could she influence his choice to remain Amish or turn English? Could he possibly be in love with her?

Nora set kindling atop newspaper and lit a fire in the stove. Just now she had no time to contemplate the affections of Elam Detweiler. Emily had sent her to the shop early to start baking, using the written recipes and explicit instructions left on the table last night. She would arrive in the buggy later after she stopped at the home of Violet Trask. Apparently, Emily and Violet's mother were friends. When Emily arrived, Nora would have an answer to the note she had written to Violet.

After applying for a job at the lumberyard, Elam stopped at the bakery yesterday and brought her flowers from the grocery store. Jonas had hired him, giving him the position of pulling morning orders. Because he had a driver's license, Elam would also fill in making truck deliveries. While Nora's face had been buried in the bouquet, Elam had asked her out. At first she declined, but then she reconsidered when she heard it would be an Amish social event. What better way to meet other young people than at a cookout and volleyball game? She'd agreed with one condition.

Now her entire future hinged on her new friend, Violet.

Just as Nora slid a second batch of cookies into the oven and started rolling out a third, a breathless Emily entered through the back door.

"Whew, it's warm already. I tied the mare to a tree away from the road on the longest rope we own. She should graze contentedly for a few hours." Emily hurried to the cupboard to change her apron.

"Well, what did she say?"

"Can't a woman wash her hands first?" Emily rolled up her sleeves, while Nora took several deep breaths to tamp down her impatience.

Finally Emily joined her at the work table. "Violet would love to go the cookout so you're not alone with Elam. She can be ready at six o'clock." Emily nudged Nora to the side and selected a ball of dough from the bowl. "Are you sure you want to go out with him even with Violet along?"

Nora opened the enamel oven door to peek at the cookies. "*Jah*, he and I are old friends. This way I can meet folks and make new friends in the district. And, if Elam picks us up, Violet won't suffer from a jarring buggy ride. Her leg braces become uncomfortable when she's cramped for long periods."

"Elam has no business driving a car." Emily issued a dismissive snort.

"He won't buy a horse and buggy until he's baptized." Nora carefully removed the pan of molasses crinkles with a pot holder.

"What if he never joins the church?"

"By then I will have met other men to court." Nora angled a smile in Emily's direction. But in her heart, she couldn't imagine any man in her life but Elam. "Did you say six o'clock?" she asked, trying to remember Violet's message.

"*Jah*, don't worry. You may drive the buggy home at four. I don't mind walking. Then you'll have plenty of time to shower and dress."

*If your mare were a race horse*, she thought. "Excuse me a minute." Nora slipped outside and pulled her cell phone from an apron pocket. She kept it charged up in the barn. Jonas ran the generator every other day to charge his phone for business purposes. She dialed the number Elam had given her, left a message, and then returned to baking cookies with a grin.

"Cell phones are only for emergencies," said Emily, furrowing her brow. She held the rolling pin aloft as though a club.

"I'll keep that in mind, I promise. Please don't whack me with that thing. It would have been rude not to tell Elam my answer and have him drive over for no reason."

"Sorry." Emily lowered the rolling pin. "I haven't whacked anybody in years. Just don't whip out that phone and call for a pizza if they run out of food tonight."

Nora relaxed as the bell signaled their first customer, avoiding more questions about her date. With the steady stream of people and plenty of baking, the day passed quickly. Soon she and Emily's slow-but-steady horse were on their way home. Before she had a chance to fully dry her hair, Elam pulled into the driveway.

Nora pinned her damp hair under her *kapp* and answered the door on the second knock. "My, you look almost Amish."

"Thank you, I think." Elam entered the kitchen with his usual swagger. "I would have brought flowers, but you got some yesterday. It'll be a while until my next payday."

She stared at his appearance—Plain shirt and trousers, suspenders, straw hat, and work boots. And he had shaved every bit of stubble from his face and chin. She'd never seen him clean shaven.

He noticed her appraisal. "I didn't want to make trouble for you, Miss King, since we're both new. First impressions mean a lot. Ready to go?"

"I am." She grabbed her purse and a basket of cookies she had brought home from the bakery. "We'll have plenty of time to pick up the friend I told you about. Here's her address and directions." She dug a piece of paper from her bag.

Elam accepted it without much enthusiasm. "No problem. I know women worry about their reputations. I'm glad men don't have to concern themselves." He opened the door and offered an elbow.

Nora ignored his arm and walked toward the car as though she were Cinderella from her childhood picture book. "No hanging on to each other. That's one of my rules."

He followed at a leisurely pace. "Like I said, no sweat."

And apparently Violet joining them wasn't a problem. Elam entertained both of them with amusing tales all the way to the social. "And you should have seen my friends' faces when I showed up in Pennsylvania driving a car. One of my cousins asked if I stole it and if the sheriff's department was in hot pursuit."

Violet laughed. "They probably watched for flashing lights and blaring sirens during the entire visit."

"How long did you stay in Mount Joy?" asked Nora, feeling a pang of homesickness for her sisters and grandparents back in Pennsylvania.

"About a month. That was enough of a taste. It's sure more crowded and more expensive than I remembered. A man could go through plenty of money eating out in Lancaster."

"It's a good thing there are no restaurants in Paradise. A person won't go broke at the local diner in Sturgeon." Violet glanced at Nora over her shoulder.

"You said a mouthful, Miss Trask." Elam took another cookie from Violet's basket. "And these are the best I've ever tasted."

"What about Nora's?" Violet sounded nervous as she fidgeted on the seat. Nora had insisted Violet sit up front because the backseat would be difficult with leg braces and crutches.

"Those would be the best molasses cookies I've ever tasted." Elam met Nora's eye in the rearview mirror as she leaned forward.

"You could get hired as a diplomat if the job at Gingerich Lumber doesn't work out."

"The lumberyard will work out just fine." He winked at her as they pulled up the stone driveway of the hosting family. Buggies were lined up in the grass on both sides. His would be the sole car. Elam parked as close to the picnic tables as possible, jumped out, and then ran to the passenger side. "Your amusement awaits, ladies," he said, offering Violet a hand.

"Are you sure you don't need your wheelchair?" whispered Nora. Rosanna Trask had insisted on stowing it in the trunk.

"Absolutely not. I'm headed to those seats there." She pointed with one of her crutches. "Go take a stroll with Elam. I'll be fine."

"No, we're sticking together." Nora moved at Violet's pace across the lawn, but Elam had to keep stopping while they caught up. Long legs were a problem she did not have. After Violet lowered herself to a bench, Nora took both baskets of cookies from Elam. "Try to stay out of trouble while I take these to the buffet table."

"You are truly a nice person, putting up with the extra work." Elam materialized at her side.

Nora frowned. "What extra work? Violet is a sweetheart. I'm lucky to have her friendship. Besides, she needs to get out more."

Shouts from the volleyball game drew their attention. They paused in the grass to watch the spirited competition for a few minutes. "Care to play, Nora?" he asked. "I see you wore appropriate shoes."

He pointed at the scuffed sneakers she'd brought from Pennsylvania, which she hadn't worn even once in Maine. "I don't intend to sweat after standing near a hot oven all day. You go ahead while Violet and I judge whether you're any good. You'd better score plenty of points, Mr. Detweiler."

"Your wish is my command." Elam swept off his hat and bowed low.

Nora caught a faint scent of spicy aftershave and noticed he'd tied his long hair back with a thin strip of leather. But he still hadn't cut a fringe of Amish bangs. After delivering their cookies, she returned to Violet with her heart pounding and her palms clammy. Why did he affect her so? His presence made her giddy and nervous at the same time.

*"I'm the reason you moved to Missouri, right?"*

She had avoided answering his question truthfully. He *was* the reason she came to Missouri. Whether that decision had been wise or foolish remained to be seen.

"A penny for your thoughts," said Violet as Nora sat down.

"I'm thinking I'm hungry already. Let's hope this game is worth postponing supper for." They shifted the bench to improve their view as Elam took a spot on the disadvantaged side—the one with more females. To their amazement, he blocked serves, scored points, and assisted weak hits that otherwise wouldn't have cleared the net. His months spent logging timber, after years of farming, had made him muscular and agile. Warmth began to slowly build in Nora's belly as she watched him bend and stretch—sensations totally inappropriate for a first date.

After twenty minutes of the game, Nora scrambled to her feet. "Let's eat. Shall I fix your plate and carry it back?"

Violet shook her head. "No way. You'll probably load me up with succotash and pickled beets like my *mamm*. Because my parents aren't around, I want nothing but burgers and junk food." She hobbled to the buffet, surprisingly adept with her crutches.

"In that case, no health food for either of us." Nora carried their plates while Violet loaded them up with an assortment of treats.

They had only taken their first bite when Elam appeared. "Save me a seat with you two lovelies. I'm always ready to eat." He sprinted toward the barn.

"Something or *someone* must be more fascinating than a volleyball game." Violet winked at Nora before attacking a pile of potato chips.

"Apparently so." As other people joined their table, Nora worried what subjects Elam might bring up in conversation. She hoped he wouldn't reveal her missteps back in Harmony. But when he returned with a plate piled high, he concentrated on eating, not revealing secrets from Nora's past.

Violet nudged her under the table. "When do you suppose he ate last?" she whispered.

Nora giggled behind her hamburger, but her laughter faded as she watched him. He devoured the meal as though starving. He'd joked about being close to eviction. Could he also be out of grocery money? Is so, why had he bought all of those cookies at Grain of Life? She waited until he finished his meal before asking the questions she'd been holding in since he came to the bakery. "Where else did you stop after leaving Lancaster?"

Elam dabbed his mouth with a napkin and crumpled it into a

ball. "I saw sights you would have loved, Miss King. I left the freeway at Wheeling, West Virginia, and followed a road along the
Ohio River. It was slow going even in a car, but I saw such beautiful countryside. Lush, green, and fertile—the river must overflow
often enough to deposit nutrients back into the bottomlands."

"Spoken like a true farmer." The young man across the table
raised his soda can in salute.

"Former farmer," he said, stretching out his hand. "Elam
Detweiler."

"Josh Shelter." The two men shook hands.

"Where did you sleep along the way?" asked Violet. "In hotels?"

"Couldn't afford them, but there were town parks along the
river. I would spread my sleeping bag under the stars, right on the
grassy levee. And if you looked hungry enough, *Englischers* would
share their picnic supper."

Nora felt pity for a man forced to rely on handouts from strangers. But Elam viewed the trip as some grand adventure—anything
different equaled something desirable.

"It took me three days to reach Maysville, Kentucky, where
the road left the river and ventured inland." Elam closed his eyes
as though reliving a pleasant memory. "But before I did, I saw an
old-time paddle wheel boat bound for Cincinnati. I would love to
ride on one before they fall into the scrap heap."

"Lots of Plain folks have settled in Kentucky," interjected the
man who had introduced himself as Josh.

"That's true. I drove through several communities. Each district pointed me in the direction of the next—with free food and
haylofts or back porches to sleep on." Elam drained his glass of
iced tea and rose to his feet with the grace of a bobcat. "Why don't
I bring back a plate of desserts to share? You're in for a treat if you
sample either Nora's or Violet's cookies." He directed this praise
toward Josh.

Nora stared as he walked away, his back muscles bunching under the thin cotton of his shirt. What a different experience his trip had been compared to her cross-country bus ride. What would it be like to be married to such an adventurous man? Suddenly, the sharp sting of a pinch grabbed her attention. "Ouch!" Nora complained, rubbing her arm.

"I said, how do you like your new job at the bakery?" whispered Violet in her ear. "Don't worry. He's coming back. You won't die of loneliness."

Nora blushed but managed to smile. Violet's humor was hard to resist. "I love working there. I'm learning things my mother never managed to teach me despite her best attempts. And I see interesting people every day. You have no idea what bizarre clothes *Englischers* find fashionable." She clucked her tongue.

Violet slumped dramatically onto her elbows. "You lucky dog. I would love working where I get to meet folks. *Mamm* thinks quilt-making should be enough to keep me busy." She pulled a frightful expression.

"Emily could still use more help, in my opinion. We're busy as hornets the entire time we're open. Should I ask her about hiring you? I could pick you up in the buggy on my way to work. Then I wouldn't have to walk, which would please me greatly." Nora cracked her knuckles.

"You are an absolute angel sent from heaven, but give me time to soften up my *daed* first." Violet threw her arms around Nora and kissed her cheek with a loud smack.

Everyone either laughed or looked mortified. Such displays of affection among the Amish were rare.

"We'll see if you say that after Emily works you like a draft horse."

❧

The next morning Solomon Trask walked to the front of his congregation prepared to do battle…or at least convince his district of the dangers of outside influences. He had witnessed first-hand what happened when a Plain family relied too heavily on money from tourists.

Young men with lust in their hearts ogling underdressed women?

A wife and mother too busy baking sweets for her shop to properly watch her *kinner*?

And Levi—a man familiar with Scripture—working on the Sabbath to produce overpriced leather goods? The memory soured Sol's stomach but fortified his resolve.

"Let us turn to the book of Genesis for today's lesson," he said, opening his Bible. He'd planned to begin reading in chapter six but reconsidered and set the book down. "I shall paraphrase the story of Noah so my message is clear to everyone." He waited to speak until he had full attention. "As time went on, the world became filled with evil. Man's imagination only worked in evil ways. The Lord regretted ever creating humankind. He decided to destroy all living creatures except for one man and his family who had found favor with Him.

"He ordered Noah to build an enormous ark of gopher wood with many rooms, seal it with pitch, and then fill it with a male and female of every species. Noah was also to supply the ark with enough food to sustain them. Two by two the animals entered the ark along with Noah's wife, sons, and their wives. Then the Lord sent a great flood to destroy all life on earth.

"Finally, the sun shone again and the waters began to recede. Noah was patient aboard the ark. He sent out a raven and then a dove to gauge the progress of the earth becoming habitable again. When the dove returned no more, Noah knew it was time to let down the ramp."

Solomon looked over both sides of benches. Everyone seemed

enthralled with his sermon. "And God told Noah to go forth with his family and the creatures. To be fruitful and multiply in the clean, new world." He walked to the table where he'd laid his Bible and placed his hand atop the worn cover. Then Solomon lifted his chin and steeled his gaze at the district members. "Look around our community, state, and country. Does not the world grow more mean-spirited, more evil with each passing year? Aren't hearts hardening to the sorrows of others? Don't we often turn away rather than correct the wrongdoings we witness?"

He scanned the people, not letting his focus fall on anyone in particular. "Don't we allow outside influences into our lives that corrupt our families? We welcome English tourists because they bring the dollars necessary to pay taxes, medical bills, and repair our farms, but what are we trading in return for these comforts?" Solomon's demeanor grew serious. "We should examine our consciences carefully before we encourage additional intrusion into our Plain lifestyle." His voice rose steadily in increments.

Several men and many women shifted uncomfortably on the benches. His message seemed to have pierced their hearts. He hoped there would be no more ignoring the Fourth Commandment—working on the Sabbath—in his community. "Let us bow our heads," he murmured.

Solomon prayed for the people he loved that they wouldn't end up like the neighbors of Noah. When he sat down, the preaching service continued with singing and then another sermon delivered by the bishop. He felt he had served his Lord well.

After church concluded, he watched his *fraa* wheel his younger daughter out into the sunshine. Both of their faces glowed with renewed faith. Those sweet, dear women would never find themselves on the wrong side of God's favor. Several men waited to speak with Solomon about questions regarding taxes. When the minister finally put on his black hat and left the Yoders' outbuilding, he spotted his wife and daughter under a Sycamore tree. They weren't chatting with his married *kinner* as usual, but with Deacon Jonas and his wife, Emily. A skinny girl hovered over Violet's wheelchair.

"*Daed*," exclaimed Violet. "I thought you would never finish up. This is my new friend, Nora King, who moved here from Maine." Violet clutched the girl's hand.

"How do you do, miss?" asked Solomon, tipping his hat. "Welcome to Paradise. Are you kin to the Gingerichs?"

The girl identified as Nora stared at him mutely, as though a second head sat on his shoulders.

Violet shook Nora's arm. "Don't look so frightened. My father won't bite."

Solomon watched the girl's mouth open, yet not a single sound came forth. Either she'd been struck deaf during the last ten minutes, or their newest arrival had been rendered speechless by his sermon.

Emily slipped her arm around Nora's waist. "Nora is related by marriage to my sister. She's quite shy around strangers, but given time she will soon talk your ear off like most young women." Emily could feel Nora shrinking inside her shoes.

"Why don't you all come to our house this afternoon for a visit?" asked Violet, struggling to stand from her chair.

Her mother forced her down with a firm hand. "Please do." Rosanna gazed at Emily. "It'll only be cold sandwiches and tea, but we could put our chairs in the shade. We get a nice breeze from the west most afternoons." She kept a hand on her daughter's shoulder.

Emily rubbed the bridge of her nose. "I've had a sinus headache for two days, so I think Jonas and I will rest at home today. But there's no reason Nora can't take the buggy to your place. She knows the way from last night." Emily heard an indistinguishable squeak come from the mouse on her right but ignored it. "We'll be off then," she said cheerily. "*Guder nachmittag*, Solomon, Rosanna. Expect Nora later with one of my peach pies."

Emily grabbed Nora's hand and pulled her to the parking area while Jonas hitched up their horse. Once inside the enclosed buggy and rolling away from the hosts' farm, Emily turned to Nora in the backseat. "What got into you? You acted as though Minister Trask was a rabid dog with huge snapping teeth."

Nora leaned between them. "Didn't you find him scary, talking about God drowning everybody but a handful in a big flood?"

"It's all in Scripture." Jonas steered the horse onto the shoulder to let a car pass by. "We have nothing to fear as long as we walk with God."

"Nothing to fear?" squawked Nora. "The minister just said he witnesses plenty of sin in this district caused by *Englischers*."

Emily exchanged a glance with her husband, but Jonas had a quick reply. "Solomon wasn't blaming the English for Amish sin. He pointed out what *could* happen if we ignore God's words and satisfy our worldly desires. It was a cautionary message, not a judgment of our English friends and neighbors."

Nora didn't seem remotely convinced. "All I know is that I had to pinch myself to make sure I wasn't still in Harmony with their strict *Ordnung* and rigid thinking."

"You find adherence to God's Word rigid?" Jonas's question was no louder than a whisper, but it carried the weight of a draft horse.

"No, *mir leid*," she apologized. "I'm just flustered by Minister Trask. I can't believe he's Violet's father. When she talked about him on the ride from St. Louis, she never mentioned he was a preacher with a voice that could echo across the Mississippi River. According to her, she has him wrapped around her little finger."

Emily laughed in spite of herself. "Sol does sound like a preacher from olden days, no? But Violet wasn't exaggerating. That stern man absolutely dotes on his *fraa* and *dochder*. You'll see for your-self when you visit this afternoon."

"Must I go? What if I say the wrong thing and make him angry?" A look of pure panic filled her face.

"I thought you liked Violet, or weren't you sincere about that?" asked Emily.

Nora wasted no time responding. "I like her very much. She's the first woman in a long time I can be friends with, maybe in my entire life." She placed her hand on Emily's shoulder.

"Then you must swallow your fear and go see her. If you value her friendship, there's no way to avoid her father."

Nora settled back on the seat, lost in thought. She remained quiet for the rest of the way home. While Jonas harnessed a fresh horse to the buggy, she washed her hands and face and Emily set a pie into a basket.

Picking up the wicker handles, Nora smiled tentatively. "I'm off. If I don't return, tell my family back in Lancaster that I love them."

Emily waited until she was halfway down the walk before deliv-ering her final words of advice. "Remember, Solomon is a man of God," she called. "I doubt he'll cut you into little pieces to use as fish bait."

Nora climbed into the buggy and waved feebly. She drove off at a snail's pace, not in any hurry to see if the minister was planning a Monday fishing trip or not.

"That was rather merciless of you, *fraa*," said Jonas, entering the kitchen.

"*Ach*, I thought you were still in the barn." Emily knew that wasn't much of an excuse.

"Fish bait. Where do you get such notions?" He buzzed a kiss across her *kapp*, a sure indicator he wasn't angry, and hung up his coat.

"Perhaps a little teasing might reduce some of the girl's stress. Did you see the look on her face after preaching?"

Jonas nodded his head. "Sol's sermon hit a chord with many folks, not just with our houseguest." He poured a mug of cold coffee, his Sunday staple. "Much contained in the early books of the Old Testament is hard to comprehend. A God who would destroy every man, woman, child, animal, and bird, except for a chosen few? But there it is in black and white, English or High German, either way you choose to read it."

Emily felt an involuntary shiver snake up her spine. "Is that why the Lord hasn't blessed us, Jonas? Because of our sins? Because we have fallen short of His expectations?" A lump rose up her throat.

He turned around. "What are you talking about?"

"We have no *kinner*. No sons or daughters to carry on after we're gone. Will your bloodline and name be continued only by your *bruders*?" She hated the shrill tone in her voice.

Jonas wrapped his arms around her. "Emily, bloodlines and names aren't important to me. Anyway, where is your faith? Didn't God bring Elizabeth and Zacharias a child in their later years after her fertile time was long past?"

She spoke into the soft fabric of his shirt. "I doubt if God considers us as worthy as the parents of John the Baptist."

"It will happen in God's own time. Don't lose hope. We're not too old yet. If it be His will, we'll have children on His timetable. But if He chooses for us to remain childless, we can still lead productive lives of service to our community and church. We have been blessed with much. And I thank God for you each day." Jonas kissed her lightly on the forehead.

What could she say after that? She loved her *ehemann* with her whole heart, but didn't every woman harbor passion to be a mother? "Let's have a sandwich. Then I think I'll lay down for a nap on the sofa. My attitude will improve greatly after food and a little rest."

Jonas grinned and sauntered away to wash up.

Emily forced away her selfish thoughts, for they indeed revealed a lack of faith.

# FOUR

*Lose all their guilty stains*

Solomon let his youngest child jabber until she ran out of air. Emily Gingerich must have had Violet in mind when she referred to young women who could talk your ear off. Not that he minded. It was good to see his daughter so excited.

"She traveled all the way here from the Atlantic Ocean *by herself*," Violet emphasized. "Her sister got married and stayed in central Maine, but they're from Lancaster County originally. Oh, *mamm* and *daed*, her parents died in a horrible house fire. Her two younger sisters remained in Pennsylvania with their grandparents."

"Nora told you all this during the bus ride from the doctor's office?" asked Rosanna. She sat between Violet and Sol. He had ordered the buggy extra wide so neither woman would have to crawl into the backseat.

"*Nein*. She told me Saturday night at the cookout, while her friend from Harmony played in the volleyball game."

"She didn't want to play?"

"I told her I wouldn't mind if she did, but she said she preferred talking with me to smacking at a silly white ball." Violet beamed with pleasure. "Those were her exact words."

"It's too warm to run around in the hot sun." Rosanna wiped her brow with her hanky.

On and on Violet rambled, filling in every known detail about the life and history on her new friend. For some reason the girls had taken to each other instantly, even though Violet usually kept her distance from people her own age. She preferred *kinner* and the elderly—those who posed no threat to the impenetrable protective wall she maintained. She suspected any attention or kindness to be a form of pity and wouldn't tolerate it. Somehow Nora King had passed Violet's mysterious unwritten set of rules for potential friends with flying colors.

"Are Nora and the volleyball player a courting couple?" asked Sol, peering over his spectacles.

"If they are, one would never guess. She refused to leave my side the whole evening. I told her I was a grown woman with bad legs, not a toddler learning to walk. No one needed to watch me. But it did no good. When we moved down to the bonfire, she shared a bench with me instead of Elam. But he was busy making new friends among the young men of the district. You should have heard his stories about camping on his way from Pennsylvania. Because he's still on *rumschpringe*, he drove a car and accepted handouts of food like a skinny stray dog that wanders up your drive." Violet shook her head. "It takes all kinds, no?"

Sol opened his mouth to ask more about the cross-country camper when Violet launched into more background on her favorite topic, Nora King. "Did you know that women, even single gals, aren't allowed to work in Harmony, Maine? They can only sew or bake at home and then consign the items to markets and stores."

Solomon waved a car around the buggy that had slowed to a

crawl. "Sounds like wise counsel from their elders and ministerial brethren to me. Women don't need to be exposed to every temptation and evil running rampant in the world."

"Oh, Papa." Violet purred like a cat. "What evil will Nora encounter working for Emily in her bakery? Rolling and cutting out cookies, kneading bread dough, and filling piecrusts with fruit preserves doesn't sound very dangerous to a person's soul."

"Violet," he admonished. "Don't make light of serious matters, such as where a person will spend eternity."

"I'm not at all," she said, swiveling to face him. "I just believe a woman's hands shouldn't be idle. And what better way to stay busy than creating good food to eat?" Violet patted Rosanna's knee. "*Mamm* tends house so well she scarcely needs my help."

"Turning our conversation back to a more suitable subject for the Sabbath, what did you two think of my sermon?" Solomon pulled hard on the reins as they started the last half mile to their house downhill. If left unchecked, the mare would run pell-mell to her bucket of oats.

"Papa," said Violet, sounding shocked. "If I didn't know you better, I would think you were fishing for a prideful compliment."

Sol flushed to his hairline. "You *do* know better than that, daughter. But from all the talk of long-distance travelers and employment opportunities for women, maybe you napped during my sermon."

"Never. I loved the story of Noah and his ark filled with animals. Amazing how God kept the lions from eating the antelopes and zebras! And how Noah trusted a dove to let him know when it was safe to get off the boat. Birds have brains the size of peas."

Before he had a chance to interrupt, Violet changed her tack. "But God rewarded faithful Noah with a new world, free of those sinful people. He and his offspring were given a chance to make things right."

"Many were moved by your warning, Solomon," added his *fraa*, finally able to get a word in edgewise. "They will be careful not to let dealings with the English influence their lives."

"We should have almost no dealings with them, other than lending a hand to neighbors in need." But Solomon soon lost his audience as he drove the buggy toward the barn. Rosanna got out as soon as they stopped and then helped Violet down.

Violet, as usual, refused her chair and hobbled toward the house on crutches. "Let's set up our cold lunch on the picnic table so everything will be ready when Nora arrives. I do hope there's enough potato salad left from yesterday and some of the pumpkin bread Kathryn made. *Mamm,* could we sweeten the iced tea with honey?"

"It's still the Lord's Day, young lady," thundered Sol.

"Papa, it wasn't *our* industry that created the honey, but the bees'. God will have to hold them accountable." She resumed her labored walk up to the house while he drove the horse and buggy into the barn.

*Papa.* How many times had he requested she use the simple word *daed* to address him? But Violet complied only for a short while and then returned to her favorite term of endearment. He'd finally given in. Now hearing the word warmed his heart. Violet had been a gift to them—a late-in-life baby when their older *kinner* were teenagers. And what a joy she was.

By the time he unhitched and rubbed down his horse, the women had set out sandwiches, salads, and cool drinks for the meal. He noticed Violet had trimmed crusts from the bread and decorated the salad with flower petals. Her fancy ideas came from magazines in doctors' offices. Once she fixed twice-baked potatoes, even though the first baking had been sufficient. Violet apparently intended to sit in her wheelchair shooing flies until the anticipated guest arrived. Luckily for hunger's sake, they didn't have to wait long. The skinny girl with the baggy dress drove up the lane, set the brake, and hopped down just as his son arrived from the adjacent farm.

"Ah, Irvin. Please tend to the young woman's horse and then have some lunch." Sol would be able to remain in the shade.

"Thanks, *daed*, I will. My family is off visiting without me today."

"Nora, you made it!" Violet's exclamation belied the fact the Gingerichs lived less than two miles away.

"I have." Nora walked through the clover with hands clutching a basket. "*Guder nachmittag*, Minister and Mrs. Trask. Emily sent you a peach pie for later."

"*Welcum*. And it's Rosanna and Minister Sol. We're glad you could come. Why not wash in the kitchen and then join us out here?" Violet's mother pointed to the seat next to her daughter as Nora headed toward the house.

Sol never heard so much formality in his life at an Amish meal. Who did the women think had arrived, the Queen of England or a new transplant from the East? Violet was already piling sandwiches, potato salad, and sweets onto Nora's plate. Solomon almost objected, but then he remembered her skinny frame. *If she can eat all that, so be it.*

As soon as his son sat down they bowed their heads in silent prayer. Sol took a tiny portion and ate at a snail's pace to be certain there would be enough. He was curious about the young woman who had tragically lost her parents and then chose to leave her remaining family behind. And while her sister had married Sally Detweiler's brother-in-law in Maine, the Gingerichs were shirttail relations at best. Unfortunately, Violet managed to monopolize conversation with gossip overheard at the cookout as to who was courting whom. Rosanna seemed fascinated, while Nora nodded her head politely and nibbled like a mouse. However, every now and then she stole a nervous glance in his direction as though wary of any sudden move. She was terrified of him for some reason. Perhaps preachers of the East neglected to mention the fate of those who broke God's laws. A little fear went a long way in modifying behavior.

He wouldn't press the newcomer for answers to his questions or information about her past. Frankly, Solomon was pleased Violet finally had a friend. Humans required companionship, and his *dochder* spent too much time with Rosanna and himself. He would be patient. If this Nora King had hidden secrets, they would eventually be revealed. In the meantime, Sol whispered a silent prayer of thanks. It had been a long time since Violet had been this happy.

*꙰*

The following Friday Nora wished she had used the past week altering dresses instead of fretting over her second date with Elam. Although they were the soft shades of blue, green, and rose she preferred over matronly drab browns and grays, every one of them was too big on her.

A pink or green feed sack was still a feed sack.

This would be their first date by themselves because Violet refused to tag along, as she called it. She planned to drive herself to the singing or ask a brother to take her. She insisted Nora spend time alone with the love of her life—Violet's term for Elam.

*Was* he the one for her? Nora didn't know, but she worried too much about his wayward lifestyle to pine when he wasn't around. Maybe tonight would clarify a few things once and for all. Because Violet wouldn't accompany them, Nora decided they would walk to the singing. Cars were still forbidden in Old Order districts, *rumschpringe* or not. Elam reluctantly agreed, but it came as no surprise when he arrived in a horse and buggy at the appointed hour.

"Looks like you might stay Amish after all," Nora said, stepping onto the porch.

"Whoa," he said, probably to both her and the horse. "Don't jump to conclusions. I borrowed the rig. And, Cinderella, the carriage must be returned by midnight or it'll turn into a pumpkin." Elam threw the reins over the post and strolled up the walkway, looking more handsome than any man had a right to. He wore a pressed white shirt, black pants, clean boots, and a straw hat. All good. But the day-old beard and long hair tucked behind his ears weren't so good.

Nora flashed a smile. "I'll probably have had enough of you by midnight, Elam Detweiler, and be ready to come home." For some reason, she couldn't control her tongue around him. Perhaps it covered up her nervousness. She felt like a side of beef hanging at the butcher shop, hoping to be chosen by the next hungry family.

"Ready to go?" he asked, unaffected by her sarcasm.

"As much as I ever will be." Declining his assistance, she stepped into the one-seat buggy and placed her dessert between them as a barrier.

"What's in the basket? More molasses crinkles, I hope." He lifted the checkered cloth.

She batted away his hand. "Nope. I baked fruit tarts in peach, pear, and apple just to be different. No sampling ahead of time." She sat as far from him as the small buggy would allow.

"I wouldn't have you any other way. Different is what makes you interesting, Miss King." With a slap of the reins, the buggy lurched toward the road.

For the next thirty minutes, he continued his saga across the United States. "Folks can keep their mountains. They're pretty enough, but traveling through them takes forever and burns up lots of gas. Up and down, around and around—getting nowhere fast. A person can drive all day and barely advance a hundred miles." He held the reins loosely between two fingers.

"Be thankful you weren't in one of these." She patted the wooden bench.

"You said a mouthful with those rosy-pink lips." He winked mischievously. "I drove through the Alleghenies getting out of Pennsylvania, never realizing how close the mountains are to Lancaster County. The map didn't bother to say what the mountains of eastern Kentucky were called. The No Name Mountains, I suppose. By the time I found the Ozarks of Arkansas, I was plum worn-out and ready for flatland." Elam gazed off into cornfields stretching as far as the eye could see. "You can actually get from here…" he slapped his kneecap, "to there without going in endless circles." Unexpectedly, he patted her leg when he enunciated the word "there."

Nora gasped and shifted away. "Don't get fresh with me."

"What's gotten into you, girl?" His forehead wrinkled with confusion. "You liked me back in Harmony. You even let me kiss you once or twice. Now you treat me as though I have hoof-and-mouth disease." He watched her from the corner of his eye. "Honest, Nora, I've had all my shots."

"That's good to hear. I was particularly afraid of rabies." She scooted back an inch. "And I still like you well enough, Elam, but I plan to take things slow. What good would it do to fall head over heels in love? You might decide to turn English and head to Denver or Topeka." She couldn't believe she had just expressed her deepest, darkest fear so blithely. But why not? Better to find out now where she stood rather than later.

His laughter was a rich, throaty sound. "Gals sure do love to worry." He patted her knee a second time. "If I were to go anywhere, it would be to California to see that bridge made of gold. But for now I'm done traveling." He met and held her gaze. "You got me a job at Gingerich Lumber, and I like it there. The salary's good too. One of these days I'll have to pay back those favors I owe you." He parked at the end of a long line of buggies, got out, and tied the horse to a round stanchion of hay. She descended from her side, bringing the dessert with her.

As they walked to the barn in silence, her brain struggled to process his remarks. "Goodness, they've already started," she said. "I can hear folks singing." Nora hated drawing attention by arriving late.

Elam paused in the barn doorway. "I see room on the girl's side. You go on in."

Her head jerked up. "Aren't you coming?"

"*Nein*. People will be glad if I don't because I sing like a braying mule. I'll sharpen two sticks to cook hot dogs and marshmallows and wait for you by the fire." Before she could object, he disappeared into the shadows.

"Nora, sit here," called Violet, oblivious to the fact they were in the middle of a song.

Nora slipped onto the bench, grateful for a familiar face. Both sides of the table were crowded. For a long while she concentrated on staying in tune and following along in the *Ausbund*. She'd almost forgotten her unsociable date when Violet whispered to her between songs.

"Your beau is shy, no? Don't worry. I'm leaving after the singing. He'll have you all to himself on the log." Violet giggled like a child.

"He's not as shy as you think. There's no reason for you to leave." Nora remembered the futility of arguing as Violet rolled her eyes.

When the crowd filed out afterward to the refreshments or down to the fire, Violet limped away toward the buggies. "Wait!" called Nora. "At least let me fix a plate of snacks for the ride home."

Violet had already reached Irvin's buggy by the time Nora caught up to her. "Go find your Elam, but don't do anything I wouldn't do." Violet winced in pain as her brother helped her up.

Nora handed Violet the plate, and for a moment she considered climbing in beside her friend. "That only rules out skydiving and bareback horseracing. I'll talk to you soon." She waved as the Trask buggy rolled away and then walked in the direction of shooting sparks and billowing smoke, forcing away thoughts of the house fire that claimed her parents' lives.

Elam waited on a bench made for two, holding sharpened willow branches. "Hot dogs or marshmallows?" he asked with eyes particularly bright and shiny.

"Hot dog, please." Nora sat and smoothed the folds of her skirt.

"A good choice. I've already eaten two and I'm about to roast a third. Should I cook yours or do you wish to be independent?"

"By all means, singe your eyebrows on my behalf," she murmured.

"Who needs eyebrows anyway?" Elam crouched low by the fire, twirling the sticks expertly to cook both sides evenly. The man was no novice with campfire cooking.

Nora fixed plates with buns and condiments. On her way back to the fire something niggled at the back of her mind beside the noxious smell of the wood smoke. She'd detected an odd odor on his breath, stronger than hot dogs, mustard, and sweet pickle relish.

"Here we are—burned to perfection." He slid one hot dog onto each bun and plopped down on the bench.

*Burned to perfection?* Nora lowered herself to the bench, feeling faint. She couldn't look at the charred food, let alone eat it.

Unaware of her distress, Elam forgot about his own meal for a moment. "Did I mention I crossed the Mississippi River on a car ferry? I found it on a map and thought it would be another new experience. That ferry dipped and rocked in the strong current." His hand undulated before her face. "It was miraculous the motor didn't conk out, leaving us floating like a fishing bobber down to New Orleans."

"Where exactly is New Orleans?"

Elam was talking louder than necessary and gesturing wildly. "It's a city in Louisiana where the mighty Mississippi dumps into the Gulf of Mexico. Someday I'll visit there if a pretty gal doesn't make an honest man out of me first. If that happens, I'll be working at that lumberyard until I'm a white-haired old *grossdawdi*." He waved the pointed stick dangerously through the air.

Nora might have wondered who this *fraa* would be, giving him *kinner* and *kinskind*. She might even have pictured herself in that role, rocking on a porch with a *boppli* in her lap. But unfortunately the other guests at the bonfire were staring at them—at Elam in particular. She jumped to her feet and spoke softly. "Would you walk me to the buggy, please? I'd like to get my shawl."

Elam blinked, struggling to focus. "Sure thing. I can eat this along the way. By the time we get back, we can roast our marshmallows." He picked up his cold hot dog.

Nora smiled and nodded politely at the circle of youths and then strode into the enveloping darkness. Elam bounced at her side like a puppy released from its crate. After devouring the hot dog in four bites, he licked mustard from his fingers.

No one had ever accused her of being a genius, but truly she should have figured out what had triggered his change in behavior. The realization struck her like a whack to the head. "Have you been drinking?" she hissed.

"Maybe I enjoyed a few beers while waiting for that off-key singing to finish. But I saved a cold one for you. It's hidden under the seat."

She glanced around to make sure no one overheard him. "I wish you wouldn't have done such a thing on only our second outing in the district." Nora stepped into the buggy for privacy.

Elam sprang up beside her from the other side. "Do you really care what these hayseeds think of us?" His tone was soft, almost soothing. He settled his muscular arm on the back of the seat.

"Well, *jah*, I do. I like it here, and thought I'd made *that* crystal clear." She sounded like a cat cornered by an aggressive stray Tom.

"Relax, sweet thing. No one at the bonfire suspects a thing. They were too busy chowing down and making moon-eyes at each other."

"I wouldn't be so sure about that. Remember when you joined your family for dinner while my Aunt Prudence was visiting?" Nora reached for her shawl as a chill permeated her bones. "You thought yourself subtle and clever, but your *bruder* figured out you were drunk. As I recall, that's when Thomas delivered his ultimatum—shape up or pack up." She wrapped herself in her warm covering as though in a cocoon.

Elam slumped against the wood. "You wound me with your sharp tongue. And I thought we were friends."

She refused to take the bait and ignored his mesmerizingly dark eyes. "We are, Elam. That's why I'm pointing out the slippery slope you're on. Wouldn't a friend mention that a high speed freight train were coming if you stopped on railroad tracks?"

He was slow to smile. "Before I left Maine, I left a message for you. I told your sister to tell you to be adventurous and not let Harmony moss grow up your backside. Here you are, Nora King, in Paradise. And you want to wear a straightjacket like everybody else?"

She had no reply to that...because on some level he was correct. The serenade of crickets and tree frogs rose to a din while she tried to organize her thoughts. "I wanted a change and so I came. But I don't wish to date if you continue to drink. That doesn't lead anywhere good." Memories of her aunt, abused by a drunken spouse, fortified her convictions.

"I remember you had insisted on trying the stuff and willingly drank a beer. In fact, you drank two."

"One and a half, and only because I was curious and angry with the world. I paid the price the next day and never plan to touch the stuff again." She crossed her arms and drew an imaginary line in the sand. "So you'll have to choose between us."

His arm dropped from the back of the seat to her shoulders. "Easy decision. I pick you, sweet thing. I'm already in trouble with the family I'm living with. They threatened to evict me when they found my bottle of vodka, even though I'm caught up with the rent." He pulled off his hat and ran a hand through his thick, glossy hair. "And they intend to tell the bishop, even though I haven't been baptized yet. They said I'm still part of the district."

Nora shivered, despite the warm shawl. On the one hand, she was ecstatic he would give up alcohol for her sake, but on the other, she was unnerved that the ministerial brethren had found out about his nasty habit. The beginnings of a headache pulsed at her temples. *What did* mamm *used to say about the company a person keeps?* She didn't want to be branded a troublemaker in such a nice community.

"Ready to walk back and roast marshmallows now?" he asked.

"*Nein.* Let's head for home. Tomorrow is a workday for both of us. Besides, you need to return the buggy before it turns into a pumpkin.

He sighed wearily and released the brake. "As you wish, Cinderella."

❧

The next day Emily watched Nora from her end of the long trestle table. The girl was cutting out sugar cookies, which would be baked, frosted, and then sprinkled with colored sugar. "How many have you done so far?"

"Six dozen. I'll use purple on this batch because English *kinner* seem to love that color." Nora focused on her work, looking paler than usual.

"You look tired. Didn't you sleep well?"

"Well enough."

"You didn't stay long on your date last night. How did things go?" Emily pinched up the edges of another piecrust to hold the fruit filling.

"Okay, I suppose." Nora wielded the frosting spatula with precision. "What kind of pies are you making? I hope more apple walnut. Those and the blueberry are so popular."

"Those two, plus pumpkin and sweet potato. Why didn't Elam come in the house when he brought you home? I hope he's not avoiding us."

"I mentioned the bakery would be open today, so he probably figured you went to bed early." Nora slid the next pan of cookies into the oven. "Should I mix up bread dough, or did you bake enough loaves last night?"

"We have plenty of bread. From the way you keep changing the subject, I take it you don't want to discuss last night's date."

"There's not much to tell. We attended a singing, cooked hot dogs over the bonfire, and came home. We're not officially courting. Not yet, anyway." Nora started a pot of coffee on the stove.

"I'm not your *mamm*, and even if I were, it still wouldn't be my business." Emily was hoping for a reaction but waited in vain.

After a minute of frosting cookies, Nora glanced up. "There is something we can talk about…how busy your shop is. We barely have a chance to sit down the entire time we're open." She selected a horrid shade of purple sprinkles from the assortment on a shelf.

"Are you angling for a raise already? It's only been a couple of weeks—"

"Goodness no, but I would like you to consider adding another employee. She'll work hard, and she's good with people—especially children—and I can pick her up so she'll never be late to work." Nora's pretty green eyes pleaded more than her words.

"Who is this rare person, and why doesn't she already have a job?" Emily rose from her perch on a tall stool.

"Violet Trask."

Emily stepped back from the table and burst out laughing. "You're joking, right? Minister Sol would never allow his daughter to work in a hot bakery all day waiting on customers. She would be worn out by lunchtime. Her legs are weak."

"Violet wants to work with people and promises to stay in her chair the whole time. She could run the cash register, keep inventory, and would require very little pay."

Emily dumped a quart of blanched berries into her pie shell. "It would be good for her, but her *daed* is very protective because she constantly pushes the limits of her disability."

"If Minister Sol agrees, do you?" Nora glanced at the clock and walked to the sign in the window. The moment she switched "Closed" to "Open," they heard the stomp of feet on the steps. "See what I mean? Business keeps improving every day."

Emily shrugged her shoulders, relenting. "Sure, why not? Because I know exactly what Solomon will say to this harebrained idea."

"I can't wait to tell her." Nora swept open the door to a pack of tourists, from age eighty down to eight months.

"Hello, we're the Monroes from Columbia," said a pretty woman carrying a baby. "We heard this is the best bakery in Amish country."

*Amish country? Have we broken away from Missouri and the United States?* But to the family, Emily voiced a warm welcome. "Come in. I hope you see something you like."

The woman set her baby carrier on the glass countertop while making her selections from the displays. Another little girl with long pigtails, purple trousers, and a pink shirt with mermaids clung to her side. Emily peered at the infant—a boy, judging by the blue clothing. He laughed and chortled as though having great fun. His tiny fists opened and closed as though he just discovered how hands operated. She pulled back the lightweight cover to better view his perfect face. His downy hair was soft brown, while his hazel eyes sparkled with delight.

"That's our little Adam," said another woman—his grandmother, judging by her age. "Can you say hello to the nice Amish lady?" Granny chucked him under the chin.

Emily offered her finger, which the baby clutched eagerly. She pulled back a moment before he inserted it into his mouth.

"He was quite a surprise. My daughter wanted to wait longer between kids, but Mother Nature, or I should say God, had other plans." The grandmother smoothed the soft skin of his forehead.

"He's a fine boy," murmured Emily. She stepped away, her heart aching.

"Mommy, I want some purple cookies," said the little girl wearing mermaids.

"We'll have a dozen of the purple sugar cookies, a loaf of multigrain bread, and six peach tarts." The English woman pulled out her wallet with a smile.

"My assistant chose well with frosting colors this morning." Emily boxed up the sweets while Nora rang up the purchase. "Please come back and visit us soon," she said, handing the woman her change. But for the rest of the day and for most of the night when sleep refused to come, Emily's thoughts circled in her head.

*God brought that English woman another child before she was ready, but He won't even bring me one, though I've been ready for years. There must be a reason I can't seem to find favor for this longing in my heart.*

# FIVE

*The dying thief rejoiced to see*

When Jonas returned from tending to their horses, milk cow, and hens, Emily had their Sunday breakfast waiting on the table. She arranged red raspberries into a smiley face atop his cold cereal.

"Look at that. My cornflakes appear to be in a good mood." Jonas admired her handiwork on his way to the sink.

"And why shouldn't they be? It's a beautiful morning in May. The sun is shining and we have nothing to do today but rest and give thanks. I love Sundays." Emily filled two mugs with coffee and carried them to the table.

He took his first long sip before breaking the news. "I hope this won't ruin your day, but I wish to drive over to the Trasks'. I left a note in Sol's mailbox on my way home from work yesterday that we would come for lunch."

Emily stopped eating and stared at her husband. "Why today? Can't you discuss district business during the week?"

"It's not district business so much as I want to change his mind. And I could use your help."

"You would need the army Joshua took to Jericho to change Solomon Trask's mind. What concerns you, *ehemann*?"

"His low opinion of English tourists. I want to point out the advantages so he'll have a different perspective. And what better person for this than the owner of the best bakery in Amish country?" He dug into his fruit and cereal.

"I imagine Nora told you that. She used my growing popularity to convince me to hire Violet. The girl wants to get out of the house in the worst way."

"*Ach*, one more thing to talk about, but only if Sol brings it up. Perhaps Violet hasn't summoned the courage to broach the subject yet with her *daed*." Jonas looked around. "Where is Nora, anyway? I didn't see her outside."

"I let her sleep in. She's been working very hard at the shop. I don't think she's used to physical labor."

"You'd better wake her up. I want to leave by eleven, and she takes more long baths than anyone I know." He stood, lifted his bowl to drink the milk, and grabbed his mug. "If you need me, I'll be in the front room. I want to finish reading the book of Genesis before meeting with Minister Sol."

Emily called up the steps, and a few minutes later a sleepy-eyed Nora appeared in the kitchen doorway. "*Mir leid*," she apologized. "Did you need me this morning?"

"Not at all, but I thought you might want time to get ready. We're going to see Minister Trask and his family."

"Today? But it's a non-preaching Sunday—a good day to sit on the porch reading and writing letters to my family." Nora didn't try to hide her disappointment.

"Jonas plans to speak of the merits of tourism with Sol. At least you'll be able to see your friend."

Nora's smile was small but genuine. "*Jah*, that will be nice. I have much to tell her. Maybe I can take her for a long walk in her wheelchair, far away from the serious discussions." She poured a tall glass of milk.

"Or maybe Violet will use the opportunity to ask Sol's permission to work with us."

If the girl had been pale before, she turned as white as her beverage now. "One can only hope for the best." Nora slumped into a chair and reached for the cornflakes. When she climbed into the buggy two hours later, Emily noticed that she had selected her black Sunday dress. All three of them remained quiet during the ride as each formulated arguments, defenses, or a strategy for evasion, as the case may be.

But when Sol marched down the steps, he greeted them with a cordial smile. "Good afternoon Deacon, Emily."

"Afternoon, Solomon." Jonas shook hands with a far more solemn expression.

"*Welcum*, Nora. Violet will be glad you came." When Sol lifted his hat, his silky white hair blew wildly around his head.

"*Danki*, Minister Sol," murmured Nora. "We brought pies, but we didn't bake today—never on the Sabbath. We made them yesterday." She wavered on her feet as though the wind might blow her over.

"That's *gut* to hear, but I would have assumed as much. Let's sit on the porch in the rockers. They're more comfortable than the plastic lawn chairs Rosanna insisted on buying in Columbia." Solomon led the way to the front of the house. "Why don't you go inside, Nora? I believe you'll find my *dochder* upstairs. She wants to show you her room, although it looks like most Plain bedrooms— a bed, blanket chest, bureau, and writing desk." He lowered himself into a rocker, while Emily and Jonas selected rockers on either side. Nora wasted no time disappearing into the house, nearly bowling over Violet's mother in the doorway.

"Whew, that was a close call." Rosanna set down a tray of

refreshments. "Here is some lemonade and sandwiches." She took the lawn chair facing them.

"In your note you said you had a matter to discuss." Sol spoke to Jonas.

"I wanted to express my opinion of conducting business with the English. I've had good experiences with them, Sol, and certainly not the road-to-ruin encounter you described in last Sunday's sermon."

The minister had a ready reply. "Your lumberyard deals with English locals, not tourists. People who have lived as our friends and neighbors in Randolph and Audrain Counties for years. Generally, they respect our ways, as I hope we show respect for theirs. I believe most of them wouldn't dream of snapping photos of our *kinner* or showing up at our homes half naked."

Emily blanched with his choice of words. What had happened at the Morgansteins' farm to have him so rattled?

Jonas began to rock. "That might be true, but we do get some tourists. I have found them curious but never rude. And I feel the same about my English employees." He leaned forward to peer around the minister. "Emily gets plenty of tourists at her bakery. What say you, *fraa,* on the matter?"

Sol focused his deeply lined, heavy-lidded eyes on her. Briefly, Emily considered bolting up the stairs to find Violet and Nora, despite how cowardly that would be. Instead, she said, "*Jah,* I must agree with Jonas. Most of our Saturday business is tourists, and they seldom present any problem. Oh, except for wishing to pay with credit cards instead of cash or check and asking if we have regular bathrooms or use outhouses. And once a tourist dumped out his car ashtray into my parking lot. It took me a while to clean up the mess."

Jonas scooted his chair forward to catch her eye. "But do they negatively affect your Plain lifestyle?"

"*Nein*. If anything, I breathe a sigh of relief when they get in their cars and drive away. They're always in such a hurry and worried about inconsequential things, such as whether there's butter or margarine in the piecrust. They make me glad I was born Amish." She realized too late she wasn't helping her husband's argument.

Solomon rocked and stroked his beard, reflecting on what Emily said.

Jonas coughed to clear his throat. "Let's not forget many people in the community who depend on tourist income to pay taxes and medical bills. We've had several crop failures in the past few years, and Amish folks still must pay unto Caesar that which is Caesar's."

The minister stopped rocking. "I am well aware, Deacon, as to the financial needs of this district, the number of crop failures, and what Scripture says about paying our obligations." His words were as brittle as icicles in the dead of January. "Encouraging tourism is something new to Paradise, promoted mainly by the local chamber of commerce to help English businesses such as restaurants and gas stations. But Plain folk have managed to survive without selling crafts and quilts to outsiders. I'm sure if we polled the brethren of Pennsylvania about their current opinion of tourism, they might have a different attitude than yours. There's no doubt it changed Lancaster lives and not for the good."

"How about something to drink?" asked Rosanna, lifting the tray to within easy reach of her guests.

Emily took a glass of lemonade and sipped from it. Poor Jonas. He resembled a chastised dog after chewing up the master's shoe. But he certainly didn't crawl beneath the bed to hide.

"Your reference about Noah last Sunday implied the English were evil," he said in a voice louder than necessary.

Sol shook his head back and forth, sending his hair flying. "I implied no such thing. Scripture speaks of people who practiced evil ways and turned their backs on God. My fear is that our *own* people will lose the straight and narrow path." His tone matched Jonas's.

"Anyone care for a bite to eat?" Rosanna hoisted the plate of sandwiches, bound and determined to break the tension on the porch.

"They look delicious," murmured Emily, accepting a ham-and-cheese. She was the only one to do so.

"I beg your pardon, Minister," conceded Jonas. "I misinterpreted whom you referred to in your message. But this morning, I studied the first book of the Bible. You omitted a key part of the story."

The minister's watery blue eyes bulged, while Emily and Rosanna stared at Jonas. "What passage would that be?" Solomon asked.

"Noah built an altar to the Lord and offered burnt offerings." Jonas sounded as though he'd memorized the words. "When God smelled Noah's offering, He established a covenant with Noah and his descendants never to destroy all living things again. He promised not to send another great flood." Jonas clenched his chair's armrests. "I think the district will be heartened to hear the rest of the story."

"And I believe you, Jonas Gingerich, should read the last chapter of the Bible before you grow too *heartened*, as you call it." Solomon didn't shout nor did he shake his fist, but his rage was apparent from the top of his head down to his boot heels.

Emily had never heard Jonas—or anyone else for that matter—tell a minister what he should or shouldn't preach. She placed her sandwich back on the plate, uneaten. Her appetite had vanished, along with oxygen on the porch and her husband's good sense.

❧

"Please, Emily, let's all have a sandwich since my *fraa* went to the trouble of fixing them."

Solomon watched the deacon's wife pick up the same ham-and-cheese with a shaking hand. She nibbled off a corner. He also took a sandwich, even though he would probably choke on it. Anger was hard to purge once it seized hold of a man. And Solomon was experiencing a boatload of anger.

How dare Jonas question his teaching and authority? The man was a deacon, not a preacher. Sol couldn't refute that God established a covenant with Noah, but his flock would be better served if they concentrated on *avoiding* God's wrath in the first place.

"I think I'll eat mine on the ride home." Jonas stacked two sandwiches on a paper napkin. "*Danki,* Rosanna. I've taken up enough of your Sunday afternoon." He stood abruptly as did Emily, still nibbling her bread crust.

"Just as well, because I need to drive out to the Petersheims' this afternoon," Sol said. "The bishop asked me to speak to a young man who rents a room from them. He's apparently exercising his *rumschpringe* in a fashion annoying to his hosts." He stood and pushed back his chair.

"Good day to you then. I'll call Nora." Jonas marched into the house, Emily following on his heels. "Nora," he called at the bottom of the steps. "It's time for us to leave."

Violet wheeled herself to the upstairs landing. "Why so soon?" she asked. "We haven't eaten yet. What about those pies you brought?"

"Your father has another appointment." Jonas smiled up at Violet. "If you send Nora down I'll let you keep the pies. Tell her we'll be at the buggy." Jonas and Emily left through the kitchen door without a parting word.

Sol waited until the door closed to address Rosanna. "This is what happens when a man spends too much time with the English.

He is full of insolence and argumentativeness, as though an *opinion* counted in matters of scriptural doctrine and the *Ordnung*. Did God take a vote among His children regarding their destiny?"

"Oh, dear, the meeting didn't go well." Rosanna peeked out the window, wringing her hands while watching the Gingerichs head to the paddock for their horse.

"It went as well as Jonas should have predicted," thundered Sol. He didn't know why he spoke loudly, as only he and his *fraa* remained in the room.

Except for one tiny mouse. "Excuse me, Minister Trask." The voice came from behind.

They stood in the doorway, blocking Nora's route of escape. "Take a sandwich for the ride home," said Rosanna. She thrust the plate at the girl.

As Sol moved back, Nora grabbed one and bolted out the door. She didn't stop running until she disappeared into the backseat of Jonas's buggy.

"Papa, what happened? Did you men have a fight while Nora and I were visiting?" Sol's daughter struggled into the room on crutches. She headed toward the first-floor wheelchair in the corner, panting from exertion. Beads of sweat formed on her forehead.

"Jonas and I didn't have a fight. We had a minor disagreement about the content of Sunday's sermon." Sol reached for a glass of lemonade, his mouth suddenly dry as dust.

Violet lowered herself into the chair and leaned her crutches against the wall. "If it was so minor, why did the Gingerichs take off in a hurry before we even had lunch?"

"We all had sandwiches, even Nora." Rosanna wrapped her hands in her apron as though they were wet. "No one was ready for pie. Are you hungry?" She carried the tray across the room to her daughter.

Violet rolled her eyes and then rolled her chair toward the back hall. "I should have known better than to expect a straight answer from my parents."

Sol clenched down on his molars. "Some things are not your business, even if you are twenty years old. That conversation was between the deacon and myself. And your mother asked you a question, young lady." He pulled the lapels of his *mustfa* vest.

Violet pivoted around. "Beg your pardon, *mamm*. No, *danki*. I put a snack of cheese and crackers with sliced peaches on the porch for us. I'd better eat that before the dog runs off with it." She smiled at Rosanna, but Sol spotted tears on Violet's face.

How he hated to see his daughter upset. Closing his eyes, Sol searched for some semblance of peace but found none. He lifted his felt hat and Sunday coat from the peg. "I'm on my way to the Petersheims' to do what they asked. I'll return as soon as I can, *fraa*." He took a sandwich from Rosanna's plate and headed out the door.

During the drive to the neighboring farm, he mulled over his conversation with Jonas. There wasn't anything else he could have said. The deacon's don't-worry-everything-will-be-fine attitude would lead to nothing but condemnation for the congregation. Unfortunately, nothing improved his mood once he reached the Petersheim homestead. Ruth and James hurried out to his buggy before he even set the brake.

"*Guder nachmittag*, Solomon," greeted James. "We were expecting the bishop."

"Because I live closer, he asked me to come. If my warning doesn't do the trick, he'll step in as the person of authority." Sol climbed down stiffly.

"Shall I turn your horse into the corral?" James pulled on his suspenders.

"*Nein*. Just tie up my rig in the shade and perhaps bring her a bucket of water. This shouldn't take long."

"How about something to eat?" asked Ruth.

"*Danki,* but I ate a sandwich along the way. Rosanna has pie for me when I get home." Sol handed James the reins. "Tell me the problem."

"Our boarder, Elam Detweiler, is tinkering with his car behind the barn. We told him to keep the vehicle out of sight."

"You said he was drinking in your home?"

Ruth nodded, growing very pale. "*Jah.* When I ran the dry mop under his bed on cleaning day, out rolled a bottle of vodka—half gone."

"I confronted him," interjected James. "And he admitted it was his, but he said that because he hadn't joined the church, he didn't feel it was our concern." The farmer looked more confused than angry. "It's very much our concern. We have young ones to worry about."

"I will deal with this." Without further discussion, Sol marched to meet Nora's friend—the same friend who had taken Violet to a cookout. He proved easy enough to locate.

A tall, muscular man of around twenty-two was bent under the hood of a red car. He wore Amish pants and shirt, but not the dressy black clothes for Sundays. And his long hair was tied in a ponytail similar to those worn by English teenagers.

Sol reached the side of the vehicle without the man raising his head. He cleared his throat. "I am Minister Solomon Trask."

Elam peered up with a black smudge on his chin. "How ya doing? I met your daughter Violet. She's real nice." He resumed banging under the hood with a wrench. "Say, do you know anything about engines? A guy where I work said my car burns oil. I added another quart, but I'd like to fix what's wrong. Burning oil can get expensive in a hurry." He whacked another part with the tool.

"I certainly don't know anything about engines," said Sol, indignantly. "And this car is one of the matters we need to discuss, if I can have your full attention."

Elam straightened his back, laying down the wrench. His pleasant expression faded rapidly as he wiped his hands on a rag. "I'm on *rumschpringe*. I haven't joined the district yet."

"I understand, but even so you aren't to drive this car to Amish social gatherings. And because Gingerich Lumber is owned by our deacon, I'd prefer you not use it to get to work either."

Elam tipped his head back and massaged the muscles of his neck. "The lumberyard is too far away to reach by six o'clock. That's my starting time. Besides, I don't have money to buy a rig right now. I just caught up with the rent I owed." He trained his coal-black eyes on the minister.

Sol considered for a moment. "All right, you may use it for work until your baptism. But the Petersheims said you have been drinking. They have every right to expect abstinence in their home." He narrowed his eyes into a glare.

"*Jah*, I expected as much. I won't drink anymore on their property." The young man turned his attention back to the mysterious machinery under the hood.

His response wasn't remotely satisfactory to Solomon. "We prefer little to no alcohol use among members. If you're planning on remaining here, I suggest you get used to that rule now. And in the meantime, I don't want you ever driving my daughter Violet anywhere. I won't have her life endangered." Sol considered adding "or her friend, Nora King, either" to his demand, but he knew he didn't have the right. He waited for Elam to nod or somehow acknowledge agreement, but he continued to bang away on the engine instead.

So Solomon set his hat on his head and turned on his heel, close to losing his temper for the second time that day.

๛

"Am I walking too fast?" asked Emily.

That was the third time she had asked the same question, so Nora responded with her third matching reply. "No, this speed is good exercise for me." She struggled to keep up with her boss. Nora loved her job…except for the walk to work three days a week.

*If Emily suspects her pace is too fast, why doesn't she just slow down?*

"Today is our early day," said Emily, not remotely out of breath. "I hope we can unload the tubs Jonas delivered before the locals start coming in. Sometimes Plain folk are worse than tourists with heeding posted store hours."

When they turned the corner, Grain of Life bakery loomed into view. Nora whispered a prayer of gratitude that she hadn't fallen down dead on the side of the road. "I love Thursdays, when people drop by for coffee and a few cookies, if not for full pies," she said, silently hoping Elam would be one of those people on his way home from work. Nora hadn't seen or heard from him since last Friday at the singing. He'd been sweet and attentive while roasting her hot dog just the way she preferred, but when she realized he had been drinking and confronted him about it, the evening had been ruined.

Had anyone else down by the bonfire suspected his condition? She cringed at the thought. She couldn't help but be grateful that Violet had already left the get-together by then. Elam's drinking had caused him problems in Maine. At least he promised to stop for her sake, before it caused problems for both of them in Paradise.

"I hope the ice didn't melt in the cooler." Emily's worry broke Nora's daydreaming as they unlocked the door and entered the bakery.

Nora began opening windows. May was much warmer in Missouri than at her last two addresses. "It's only been a couple hours since Jonas delivered the totes, and we packed the pies in plenty of ice."

"*Jah*, true." Emily flicked the switch for the propane refrigerated display case. "The Amish love cream pies in warm weather even more so than *Englischers*. I think it's because Plain women don't often bake pies that must be kept cold."

Nora laughed. "I doubt they'll last long enough to spoil even without refrigeration. What type did you make?"

Emily dragged the cooler across the floor from the back porch. "Coconut cream, lemon meringue, and chocolate cream pies— three of each. I'm raising my price to eight dollars this year to see if anyone will pay it. The cost of sugar and butter keeps going up."

"I would charge nine if I were you. Why not see what happens? You can always drop the price if they sit in the display case ignored." Nora carried in the rest of the plastic bins of fruit tarts and pies. She neatly arranged them on shelves with prices marked on each one. She had just finished wiping down the countertop with spray cleaner when the bell jangled.

"Exactly ten o'clock," crowed Emily. "What did I tell you about eager beavers?"

Nora glanced up and froze. Solomon Trask entered the shop and swept off his hat. His flyaway hair stood on end from static electricity like a white cloud.

"You're an early bird, Sol. Our first customer of the day." Emily pulled a clean apron over her head and walked to the counter.

"*Guder mariye*, Emily, Nora. Do you have any cream pies?" He twirled his hat brim between his fingers.

"Three different kinds." She pointed down into the display. "But I reckon I know which one you want. How is Violet? I didn't have a chance to see her last Sunday."

The minister's face turned beet red. "She's fine and sends her regards with compliments on the peach pie you left." He looked as uncomfortable as a chicken in a coyote den. After a few moments of shuffling his feet, he bent down to study the contents of the shelves. "Ah, there they are. How much for the coconut cream?"

Emily hesitated for half a moment. "Nine dollars."

"All right, I'll take two. But first I have a matter to discuss with Nora, if you don't mind."

"With me?" croaked Nora, sounding like a frog.

"*Jah*, if I may interrupt your work."

Because she wasn't actually *doing* anything, Nora walked to the counter on leaden legs.

"I met your friend who also moved from Maine—Elam Detweiler." Sol paused as though she needed time to place the name to a face. "I visited him yesterday at the farm where he rents a room. He has acquired several habits not in keeping with our *Ordnung*. I'm worried about the man's future in our community."

"Elam hasn't taken the kneeling vow yet," said Nora, gripping the edge of the display.

"That is true. I'll say no more about him because it's not my desire to spread gossip. But you are Violet's friend—is that not so?" He stroked his long beard.

"It is," she declared. "I like her very much." Fear bloomed in Nora's gut. She'd finally found a true friend. Would Violet be taken from her so soon?

"*Gut* to hear. That's why I'm cautioning you not to let the actions of others taint your reputation."

Emily put an arm around Nora's waist in a show of support. "Let's hope others will judge Nora by her own deeds."

Solomon wasn't daunted by the challenge. "I hope for the same, Emily, but I've lived long enough to witness what happens when young women run with the wrong kind of men. She might one day wish to court others, but they may spurn her."

"Elam isn't the wrong kind," said Nora, finding backbone she didn't know she had. "He's simply spirited and independent and wants to discover the world before he settles down."

Solomon Trask seemed to age before their eyes. "Perhaps you're right and he'll join our district eventually. But in the meantime, he isn't to drive my Violet anywhere, whether in car or buggy. I won't have her life put in danger. Do you understand?" His voice took on a sharp edge.

"I understand," she said in a barely audible voice.

"Don't misinterpret me. You are welcome in our home and I encourage your friendship with Violet. But she isn't to be part of any threesome for outings or events with that Detweiler man." Several seconds spun out in the warm bakery. The women stared at the preacher while he now remained calm and unruffled.

Nora crossed and uncrossed her arms. "Your daughter was first to welcome me to the community. I will always be grateful to her, besides thinking she's one of the nicest people I've ever met." She swallowed the rest of her comment. *Violet must take after her* mamm *in personality and temperament.*

"Shall I box up the two pies now?" asked Emily on her way to the cash register. "That will be eighteen dollars."

Sol stood rooted to the polished wood floor as though unsure how to proceed. Nora backed up to the table. Surely he wouldn't beat the issue of her friendship with Elam into the ground.

He cleared his throat and tucked his hands under his suspenders like a statesman from Colonial times. "Emily, if the job is still open, I accept the offer on Violet's behalf."

Neither woman spoke. They appeared to have been struck dumb.

"Have you already hired someone else?" he asked after a few silent moments.

"*Nein.*" Emily finally found her voice. "The job is hers if she wants it, three days per week. I'll write down the hours of operation on a paper." She reached for her tablet and pen. "You just took me by surprise, Sol."

"*Jah*, I imagine so." He focused on Nora. "I don't want you to think I hold Elam's behavior against you. Emily is right. Each person should be judged by their own actions. And you have done nothing to warrant my censure."

"*Danki,*" murmured Nora, unsure why she thanked him.

"And if your offer to pick Violet up still stands, I would be obliged."

"Of course. I pass by your place anyway. And we can sure use her help." Nora's smile widened upon realizing she would no longer have to walk to work.

Sol lowered his chin. "There'll be extra fuss for you. I'm afraid you'll have to fold up the wheelchair and carry it back and forth."

"That is no problem. It would be my pleasure to help." Nora reached for two pies from the cooler case. "Coconut cream, did you say?"

"*Jah*, that's correct. Did you say nine dollars each, Emily? I'll take two dozen chocolate chip cookies too." He dug his wallet from a hidden inside pocket.

"The pies are sixteen and the cookies six dollars for two dozen." Emily appeared to be holding back laughter. "You and Rosanna now qualify for the employee discount." She took his money while Nora boxed the pies and handed him a sack of cookies.

"Good day to you both." He tipped his hat and left with his purchases.

The two women just stood and stared at each other.

"Doesn't that beat all," said Nora.

"Just when you think you have a person figured out." Emily shook her head and watched the door as though expecting him to return.

But Nora started mixing more chocolate chip dough. She was going to bake enough cookies today to allow plenty of chitchat time tomorrow.

# SIX

*That fountain in his day*

Solomon debated how to spend the rest of his afternoon. He should hurry home before the coconut cream pies turned runny and warm, but one piece of district business still remained. He needed to stop at the Huffman farm to see how they fared. The husband suffered from kidney disease and remained weak after frequent dialysis treatments. Mrs. Huffman had recently given birth to their seventh child. A son would have been nice to take over the farm someday, but instead God delivered another daughter to the couple. Just for a moment, he wished their *Ordnung* allowed the practice of birth control in unusual circumstances. This would be another mouth to feed for a man who couldn't provide for the mouths he already had. But Sol banished the notion. His fellow district members would have to pitch in until a kidney became available for transplant and John got back on his feet.

Spying the bag of cookies on the seat, he turned his horse into the next driveway. The *kinner* would love a sweet treat while their *mamm* took care of more practical dietary requirements. As the buggy jostled up the rutted and potholed lane, Sol noticed he wasn't the only visitor to the Huffman farm. A small bus had parked cockeyed on the lawn, and its occupants were pouring out like bees from a hive. And, like insects, people dispersed in every direction, each one carrying a camera.

"Oh, no. Not again," he muttered. Sol parked in the shade of a leafy maple and climbed down with his sack of cookies. He would check on John and Deborah, make a list of repairs or chores needing immediate attention, and distribute the treats. He could still be home before the whipped cream topping sunk into the coconut cream filling.

Whatever business these *Englischers* had wasn't his business... until a teenager ran up and took his photograph. "See here, miss," he called. "I want you to destroy that photograph this instant!"

The girl peered over her shoulder, surprised, as she walked back to her parents.

Sol marched to the knot of adults chatting under a tree with two of the Huffman youngsters. "Did you hear me, young lady? I want that picture of me exposed to the light." He shook with fury at the rude disregard of his culture.

The girl's father held up a hand. "Simmer down, old-timer. My daughter didn't mean any harm. She'll erase the photo, no problem. Say, are these kids your grandchildren?" He pointed at five-year-old twin sisters. "We shared some gumdrops we bought at the store in Sturgeon. They sure love them."

Solomon blinked. "They most certainly are not. I'm a minister of this district, and we do not permit pictures to be taken."

"Why is that?" asked the dad. "I'm just curious."

"Because you're creating a graven image of my likeness with that." He pointed to the camera in the girl's palm.

"Sort of like American Indians?" she asked. "You don't want your spirit captured in photos?"

Sol shook his head. "I don't know anything about American Indians. I can't speak for them. We're Amish, and I ask you to respect—"

"Sure thing. Watch this," the teenager interrupted. "I'll erase the picture as quick as a bunny. It's easy with a digital camera." She held out the contraption while pushing a series of buttons as though he would be fascinated with the process.

"Because you're their pastor, maybe you can help us out," said the dad. "We would love a tour of the farmhouse, and these two kids act as though they don't speak English."

"That's because they don't, not until they start school." In *Deutsch*, Sol told the sisters to stop taking candy from strangers and go inside the house. Off they ran, holding hands.

"Well, I'll be. That explains it." The man acted as though he'd solved a mystery.

Solomon's patience was waning. "It doesn't explain what you're doing here or why the bus stopped in the first place." He wiped his brow with a handkerchief as sweat dampened his hat band.

"Oh, of course. Brown eggs and goat's milk cheese. We spotted the sign and asked the driver to stop. Our wives are up at the house right now buying dairy products. My daughter wanted a tour of the place. She's writing a term paper on divergent religious sects." He pulled a wallet from his back pocket, smiling at the girl with pride. "We're prepared to pay whatever you think is fair. How does ten dollars a head sound?" He began extracting money.

Sol exhaled his breath in a whoosh. "I will try to clarify the situation. You may not take a tour at any price. This isn't a tourist farm. You may not snap any more photographs of anything. And for the record, we don't consider ourselves 'divergent.' Good day to you."

He stomped off toward the house, but not before he heard the father mutter, "Cranky old guy, isn't he."

Inside the kitchen Sol found Mrs. Huffman slicing a brick of cheese, while English women were talking up a storm. Their children wandered around, peeking in adjoining rooms. "Do you need help, Deborah?" he asked.

"*Ach*, Sol, you're a sight for sore eyes. I can't think straight. Please take people's money and make change while I wrap up the cheese and box the eggs." Deborah's face was dangerously flushed due to her stress level and the kitchen's temperature.

Sol cleared his throat. "Ladies, if you've already made your purchase, please wait on the porch. Mrs. Huffman can use some air." He pushed open a window while an *Englischer* slid up the pane on the opposite side of the room. Then she picked up her bag and herded the children out the door. Within a few minutes all the customers had their cheese, eggs, and correct change. Blessedly, the bus soon pulled away, leaving behind a blast of diesel exhaust.

"Where is John?" Solomon pulled out a chair for Deborah.

"In the front room, resting." She lowered herself wearily. "I have a fan blowing on him. He's still too weak to get out of the hospital bed." She fanned herself with a scratch pad.

"Where are your older daughters?"

"In school. They are almost done for the year."

Sol poured a glass of water and handed it to her. "Keep them home tomorrow. If they miss a few days, it shouldn't make much difference. I'll talk to their teacher and have her stop by if necessary." He peered through the open window. "Should I take down the road sign so folks don't stop to buy cheese?"

"Oh, no, Solomon. Please don't." She finished the water without pausing. "We need the income our goats and hens bring in." She dabbed her face with the apron and struggled back to her feet. The infant in the cradle had begun to cry.

"I brought cookies for your little ones, but I must get perishables in my buggy home. I'll arrange for someone to stay with you a few days. At least until John gets some strength back. District men will come on Saturday to catch up with chores and repairs around the house."

"*Danki,* Solomon. I'll tell him when he wakes up." She lifted her brand-new daughter into her arms. The *boppli* immediately stopped squalling.

Solomon left by the front door so he could check on his friend. John Huffman was slumbering fitfully, his skin ashen and dry. He didn't awaken even when Solomon touched his arm. Sol prayed all the way home for the man's health to be restored. Only then could the family be free from the intrusion of busloads of tourists.

"Rosanna, Violet?" he called, entering his home thirty minutes later. He placed the pies into the refrigerator.

"*Mamm* is at the neighbor's and I'm out here." His daughter's voice carried through the screen door.

Sol walked onto the back porch and found Violet reading in her wheelchair with a basket of sewing by her bare feet. "You're the one I wish to speak with anyway," he said.

"I'm caught up with darning, so I'm reading a book from my stack from the library in Columbia." Violet looked mildly guilty. "It's too hot to quilt in the front room. There is poor ventilation where we set up the frame."

"It's fine, daughter. I'm not checking on your industriousness. I bought a couple of coconut cream pies at Emily's bakery. They're in the fridge. We might have to eat them soon because they didn't remain very cold."

Violet glanced up from her book. "*Danki.* We can cut one up for supper and give the other to Kathryn's family. They won't go to waste." She turned the page as a bug buzzed around her lemonade.

Sol leaned against the post. "I stopped at Grain of Life, where Nora works."

She cocked her head to the side. "So you said. Thank you for the pie."

"I told Emily that if the job was still open, I wanted to accept it on your behalf." He shrugged off his black coat while she stared at him.

"What did you say?" she asked, barely audible.

"I said you would start work at the bakery tomorrow. Emily wrote down the store hours because they are different each day." He handed her the note with Emily's scrawl.

Violet gazed at the paper as though confused. "You'll let me take a job, with Nora?"

"I am, providing you don't overdo it." Sol draped his coat over his arm.

"Did you spend too much time in the hot sun?" A smile began to lift one corner of her mouth.

"Perhaps so. What say you? I'd like to take off this vest and pour something cool to drink."

Violet struggled to stand. "I say you're the best *daed* in the world!" She stretched her arms toward him and took two steps.

Sol grabbed her before she fell. Her arms locked around him so tightly she could have cracked a rib. "*Jah*, we'll see what you say next week," he said, patting her back. "Work isn't half the fun you think it is. Now sit down and conserve your energy. Nora will pick you up at twelve fifteen tomorrow and forty-five minutes before each day's starting time. Be ready when she drives up and don't make her wait."

"*Danki*, Papa," she said, muffled against his shirt.

"Just try not to get fired on your first day." He pried her arms loose, lowered her to the chair, and headed inside as his eyes filled with tears.

It wouldn't do for his *dochder* to see him weak and emotional.

*ᐧᐧ*

"Whew, it's a hot one today." Emily glanced over her shoulder at Nora. The girl was twenty paces behind her and panting like a spaniel. "It's not much farther. Can you make it home from work or shall I hitch up the wagon to come fetch you?"

Nora lifted her hand in a feeble wave and caught up to Emily at the roadside mailbox. "Let's see what treasures the postman delivered." Emily flipped through the stack. "A bill from the county for land taxes and one from Dr. Spears for Jonas's broken finger last March. He caught it between pallets at work. Flyers from the mall in Columbia. Goodness, they stretch far and wide to attract customers. The Randolph County newspaper and two *real* letters—one for me and one for you."

Nora, who had been holding herself up with the mailbox post, straightened. "Is it from Amy?" she asked, reaching for the letter. "I can't wait to hear the news. It's been so long."

Emily read the return address before surrendering the envelope. "*Nein*. It's from a Lewis Miller at the Harmony General Store in Harmony, Maine." She waved it before Nora's nose.

Nora plucked it from Emily's fingers. "*Danki*, but I do recall what town I lived in last. Lewis's family owns the organic cooperative market. My sister will sell produce there as soon as she has vegetables to harvest." Nora ripped open the envelope.

"If my memory serves correctly, isn't that the third letter the mysterious Lewis Miller has written to you?" She tried to read over Nora's shoulder. "He must miss you something fierce, even though you've never actually mentioned his name."

Shifting just enough to block Emily's view, Nora scanned the single sheet of paper. "Life is dull in Maine. There's not much else for him to do but write to me. And he's not mysterious."

"He's not informing you about a sale on muck boots available for immediate shipment?" Emily loomed again over Nora's shoulder.

Nora stuffed the letter back into the envelope. "You are shameless when it comes to privacy. I think I'll read this in my room, not that I don't already know what's inside." Her expression changed from teasing to sorrow.

Emily stepped back. "No, your room will be too warm to relax in. You've had a hard day. Why not grab a soda from the fridge and sit under the grape arbor? It should be cooler on the north side of the house by now. I promise not to spy with binoculars." They walked side by side up the drive.

"I don't know why I'm being secretive about Lewis. It's no big thing." Nora kicked a stone in her path. "He...sort of fell in love with me last year when I moved from Lancaster to Maine with my sister and her fiancé. Amy and John are very happy there."

"But you were not."

"It isn't a good place for single people. There are too few residents to allow much selection for courting." Suddenly Nora burst into giggles. "Goodness, I make romance and falling in love sound like shopping for dress fabric or groceries at the IGA."

Emily slowed to Nora's turtle pace. "This Lewis Miller wasn't the bolt of cotton broadcloth you had in mind for a mate?"

Nora's eyes took on that look of sadness again as she shook her head. "But he was very nice to me, even when I didn't deserve kindness."

"So you didn't like his appearance? What was the matter? Too short, too tall...or perhaps he had little hairs growing from his ears? I hated to see that when I was courting."

Nora couldn't help smiling a little. "I never know when you are pulling my leg, Emily. But either way, his looks certainly weren't the problem. Lewis is very handsome, with eyes as blue as a June sky. I just couldn't imagine myself married and living in the apartment above the store or in the log cabin behind it." Nora grabbed onto the handrail and used it to pull herself up the stairs.

"A real log cabin? That sounds romantic." Emily skipped up the steps and opened the door.

"For some maybe, but snow reached the cabin's windows in winter. Thick, heavy icicles hung down from gutters almost to the ground. Lewis often had to break through them to get outside. It would be like living in an igloo. I just couldn't see myself spending my life there." Nora followed her inside and headed for the refrigerator.

Emily shivered, despite a room temperature in the low eighties. "I wouldn't enjoy that either, but I find the story rather sad, like one of those novels set in an English castle. The son of the duke must marry an heiress, but he's head over heels in love with the poor-but-worthy governess."

Slumping into a chair, Nora popped open a soda. "I've read enough of those to know they seldom turn out well."

Emily reached for the pitcher of tea. "I've read a few recently that ended happily. What does Lewis want from you in the letter?"

Nora extracted the sheet a second time and read. "He says one of his sisters got married, one got engaged, and that the bishop tripped in a gopher hole and sprained his ankle. The bishop will stay up north until his foot heals. Thomas must assume his preaching duties on Sundays." She took another long pull of root beer.

"That's it? Only catch-up news?" Emily lifted her eyebrows.

Nora met her gaze. "He wants me to come back, or at least permit him to come *here* for a visit. And he says he tried desperately to forget me but found it to be impossible. There, are you happy now?"

Emily's jaw dropped. She waited for Nora to break into laughter or chime, "Just kidding." But she didn't. Instead the young woman's melancholia seemed to grow as she slumped in the chair like a rag doll. "You're serious? He said that?"

"I am. Read it yourself if you think I'm making it up." Nora pushed the letter across the table.

"I don't think I need to." Emily sat down across from her. "Goodness, this really is like that Heathcliff person, out on the lonely moors pining after his beloved Catherine. Is that what Lewis wrote in his first two letters?"

"Pretty much, except the local news was different."

"What are you going to do about him?"

Nora shrugged. "Nothing. What can I do? I live here now, and I never want to move back."

"But he offered to come to Missouri, at least for a visit." Emily pressed the cool glass to the side of her neck.

"What good would that do? I'm courting Elam, who also *never* plans to return to the Northeast."

"And how's that going?" Emily sounded as sarcastic as possible.

Nora pinned her with a green-eyed glare. "It's too soon to tell, but I'll keep you posted as you have an inquiring mind."

Emily tapped her front tooth with an index finger. "That's right. It's too soon to determine how things will turn out with Elam. So why not invite Lewis to see the Show-Me state?"

"And where exactly would he stay? He knows no one here but me. And I'm already mooching room and board off you."

"Don't be ridiculous. You've been working like a dog in the bakery, just as I predicted. Either allow your friend a vacation destination or let me start paying you a salary."

Nora rubbed her eyelids. "Speaking of dogs, you're like one with a bone once you get a notion in your head."

"That's what Jonas says! Has he been gossiping behind my back?"

"He doesn't have to. I'm very perceptive."

"You really think so? Because I think you're missing the forest by watching only one tree. What's your answer?"

Nora stood and tucked the letter into her apron pocket. "I'll think it over and let you know. Now, don't you think we should start supper?"

Emily smiled at the woman's spunk. "*Nein.* I'll fry the pork chops and boil some noodles. I already have turnips and carrots steamed. You go take a nap in the hammock. You'll need a cool head to think straight."

Once Nora had carried her soda outside, Emily pulled the defrosted meat from the refrigerator. Then she remembered she'd received a letter from Maine too, from her sister. The timing of Sally's warning couldn't have been better.

> *Dear Emily,*
>
> *Thomas told me to mind my own business and stay out of the romantic affairs of others. He's right—I probably should. But I'll put off turning over a new leaf until tomorrow and meddle one last time. By now, Elam must have reached Paradise. He left word your community would be his final destination. I pray every night that God would place a burden on his heart regarding his worldly habits. In the meantime, it's Nora I worry about. Amy's sister is a fine young woman, but she's also flighty and easily influenced by others. And by others, I refer to fly-by-night Elam.*
>
> *Nora told me she would resettle in Missouri for a fresh start in a new land. But she also told Amy she was following her heart.*
>
> *Anything you can do to offer a voice of reason would be appreciated by her loved ones in Maine. We are a long way away. We pray that God and you won't let Nora wander too far from sight.*
>
> > *Your loving schwester, Sally*

Emily exhaled through her teeth. *Is that all you want me to do, Sally? Simply keep Nora from ruining her life? Why not ask me to make it rain, or perhaps stop the sun from rising tomorrow?*

❧

Nora carefully lowered herself into the hammock and set it swinging. She loved hammocks. They made her feel hidden and protected from the world, but they really were rather unsafe. If you moved too recklessly, it could easily flip over and dump you unceremoniously onto the ground.

Much like life in general, especially in a small town.

Did folks in Rome, Paris, or Kansas City have to worry what others were thinking every minute? Probably not. But here, like in Harmony, a woman needed to somehow control people's perceptions of her. And Emily Gingerich certainly fell from the same tree as Sally Detweiler. Emily all but ordered her to stop seeing Elam and start courting Lewis.

As though a gal could control whom she fell in love with. But was she in love with Elam? She'd thought so back in Maine, but in Missouri he frightened as much as attracted her. Despite her worries as to who might be watching or listening to their conversation, Elam offered the one thing she sought: He made her feel special, that she was somehow unique among a sea of fish…or in this part of the country, among waving sheaves of grain in the field.

Individuality wasn't a sought-after trait among the Amish. They were taught from the cradle that no one should set themselves above others. Competitiveness, whether in sports, handiwork, or physical attributes, was discouraged. Everyone was special to God—and His favor should be the only favor sought. Yet Nora had a problem with that idea. She wanted—no, *needed*—to feel that she stood out from her siblings and friends. Because so far she never had. Amy possessed superior domestic skills, such as cooking and sewing. Younger sister Rachel stopped traffic with her beauty. And little Beth? That girl sang like an angel and could even read music without having been taught.

Elam had been drawn to her adventurous spirit, her willingness to walk to the precipice and look over the edge. They were kindred souls, but was that love? How could a person discern true love from human gravitational pull?

Lewis Miller had never been on a precipice in his life. He'd never ventured outside of Maine. His talk about wanting to travel to Paradise was just chatter. He possessed no wanderlust, no desire to sail a boat or take a train ride or walk barefoot through warm sand along the beach. Yet something about him made him hard to forget. Lewis sought a wife to work beside him in a store that would someday be his. To take buggy rides in the moonlight that went nowhere and then turn around and come back. To walk back roads strewn with leaves that would remain *exactly* the same for another week or month or maybe until next year. To become his wife and bear his children in a town of two dozen families.

"Ugh," muttered Nora. In sheer exasperation she kicked her legs, an unwise move. The hammock flipped over, catapulting her into the tall grass below. Her soda spilled, her letter fell into a muddy patch, and she skinned her leg on a rock. She needed to stop mulling over these men as though they were a great mystery of the universe. Grabbing her things, she got up and marched toward the house, brushing off her skirt along the way.

When the screen door slammed behind her, Emily called from her position at the stove. "Feel better? Did the nap refresh you?"

"Quite the opposite. I've given myself a headache from too much thinking." Nora washed her face and hands.

Joining her at the sink, Emily plucked a leaf from her hair. "Must be nice to have two beaus. Many girls would love to have just one man interested in them."

Nora dried her hands on a checkered towel. "It's not nice at all. I'm scared witless I'll pick the wrong one and ruin my entire life. Or worse, I'll dawdle and procrastinate and they'll both lose interest. I've never been good at making decisions." She released a weary sigh.

Emily hooted much too loudly, another characteristic she shared with Sally. "Then don't choose. Invite Lewis to visit and court both of them. Let God sort out the matter for you. Maybe it will be neither and the love of your life will arrive on the next bus from Columbia."

Nora laughed in spite of herself. "Do you really think God cares about whom Nora King courts?"

Emily's eyes widened. "I know He does. If He cares about the smallest sparrow, He cares about whom you will someday marry."

She reflected on this for a long moment. "Do you need my help with supper?"

"I told you before, no. Go write your letter, Nora. Let the chips fall where they may."

"What chips?" she asked heading toward the stairs.

"I have no idea, but I heard an *Englischer* use the expression in my shop and I liked it."

Nora smiled all the way to her room. Emily had the best attitude of any woman in the world. She would do well to emulate her. Sitting at her desk, she drew a sheet of stationery from the drawer along with her favorite pen and began a long overdue letter. Even if she never saw the man again, she shouldn't neglect answering his letters.

*Dear Lewis,*

*I'm happy about your sisters' news but sorry to hear about the bishop's ankle and Thomas's increased workload. As for me, I love living with Sally's sister and her husband. I have my own room and few chores because the Gingerichs do not farm. Emily hired me in her bakery three days a week. I've learned to make a decent pie crust and respectable cookies. And I enjoy waiting on customers and seeing their faces as they buy sweet treats.*

*But I'm sure what you're interested in is your offer. I have
talked with my hostess, and she insisted you stay here should
you visit. They have several spare rooms. I would like to see
you, Lewis, but I make no promises. I am courting Elam
Detweiler, but we've reached no understanding of any kind.
If these terms are acceptable, you can take the train to St.
Louis and then a bus to Columbia. We can arrange a hired
van to bring you the rest of the way. I'm sure you won't be
disappointed with a vacation in Paradise. This is a lovely
part of the state of Missouri.*

*Truly yours,*
*Nora King*

She folded the paper, jammed it into an envelope, and scribbled down his address before she lost her nerve.

*Won't be disappointed with a vacation in Paradise...*

What was the matter with her? The area mainly had farms and more farms. The shops and cafés were little different than those back in Harmony.

*If these terms are acceptable...*

She sounded like an English lawyer, not an Amish girl writing to a former beau. Nora attached a stamp and placed it by her purse to mail tomorrow, hoping that she would soon find the mind she apparently had lost.

# SEVEN

*And there may I, though vile as he*

Emily fried the bacon until crisp but not burned. She melted cheddar cheese over the mushroom-and-ham omelet just the way Jonas liked it. While Nora buttered a stack of toast and set jars of peach jam and apple butter on the table, Emily carried the skillet to the center of the table.

Jonas entered the kitchen while still fastening his shirt. "Goodness, *fraa*, that's a lot of food for a workday." He settled into his usual chair.

"The lumberyard doesn't open until ten o'clock. You have time to eat a hearty breakfast before you leave." Emily filled three mugs with coffee.

"Are you trying to butter me up or fatten me up with your good cooking?" He lifted his plate to be filled.

She cut a large wedge of eggs and slid it onto his plate. "The former, I suppose. I'll be gone for most of the day in Columbia. Some folks arranged a hired van for today, and there is room enough for me."

"On a Monday—the washday?" He sounded aghast. "How could I permit such divergence from Amish tradition?" He quickly consumed two strips of bacon while his dimples grew ever more apparent.

"I must be a bane to your existence as deacon," said Emily. "But Nora has volunteered to do the laundry while I'm gone, so any passersby will see shirts and sheets on the line as usual. Our reputation in the district should remain wherever it stood before." Emily made an egg sandwich using two slices of toast. "Are you sure you don't want to visit Columbia with me?" she asked Nora. "You've seen little other than this house and the bakery since you arrived."

Nora sipped coffee but mostly pushed her breakfast around with her fork. "I'll go the next time Violet has a doctor's appointment. That will be soon enough." She ate a tiny bite of eggs.

"Where are you headed in Columbia?" asked Jonas. He followed Emily's example and built an omelet sandwich. "You're not going to that giant mall to have your toenails painted blue, are you?"

"I certainly hadn't planned on *blue*." Emily winked at her *ehemann*. "My library books are overdue. I want to return them before I owe a fortune in fines. And I love the library's reading room. They have local histories and newspapers from everywhere that can't be checked out. You must look at them there." She finished her sandwich with two more bites, drained her coffee cup, and filled their travel mugs from the pot.

Jonas rose to his feet too. "Want me to drop you off somewhere?" He set down his half-eaten sandwich long enough to shrug on his coat.

"*Nein*. The van will pick me up at the end of our driveway in…" She consulted the wall clock, "about five minutes."

"I'll see you when you get home, then. Enjoy your day in the city, but remember I'll be inspecting those toenails before bedtime." Jonas buzzed a kiss across her *kapp*.

While Nora giggled, Emily blushed to the roots of her hair. "*Danki*, Nora, for doing the wash," she called, following Jonas out the door. "Maybe I'll check out one of those happy-ending romances for you. After all, they are *fiction*."

Within ten minutes, Emily was riding with six chatty Amish women to the capital of Missouri. And within the hour she sat at a polished oak table in the quiet solitude of the library—her favorite place in the English world. How she loved to read—novels, magazines, national newspapers, books filled with inspirational devotions, even self-help books of every ilk. Somebody had written a guide to help people with every facet of life, from learning how to knit, paint watercolor landscapes, or grow heirloom perennials to dealing with disease, rebellious teenagers, or potty-training. Most of the books had little usefulness in Plain lifestyles, but last year Emily had read *How to Run a Small Business* to her great benefit. Most of all, she loved to read biographies of famous people, such as Jesse James and Abraham Lincoln, or stories of the founding and settling of America, especially the westward expansion of pioneers into Missouri. Their daily struggles for survival paralleled the Amish quest for a simple existence.

After paying her fines, Emily browsed the stacks, fingering the bindings as though petting a favorite animal.

"Here you are, Mrs. Gingerich," said the librarian, appearing around a corner. "I found some books I think you'll like and marked a few pages with interesting articles." She handed Emily two thin volumes. "They are both regional histories from the reference department, so I'm afraid they can't be checked out."

"Thank you. I'll take a look right now. I have a few hours before the van comes back for me." Emily accepted the books with a gracious smile.

"With all of the movie theaters and lovely parks in Columbia, I'm thrilled you choose to spend your time in town here." The young librarian smiled warmly before going back to her computer monitor.

After settling down at a table, Emily opened the first book, *A Regional Account of Audrain County*. Because she was a fast reader and the book was full of photographs, it wasn't long before she reached the first page marked by the librarian. With growing fascination, Emily read about an extinct settlement of Old Order near Centralia.

In 1898, a group of Amish had come from Iowa looking for cheaper farmland. They were more liberal than their conservative brethren back home and thus devised a new *Ordnung* in their new state. Soon the residents were beset with extremes in weather lasting for years, alternating between unrelenting drought followed by periods of excessively wet conditions with continual flooding. For nineteen years the community tried unsuccessfully to survive in a hostile land. Finally, the last two families gave up in 1917 and moved elsewhere. For the next thirty-six years, Missouri had no Amish population until a few families moved from Iowa, determined to try again.

Emily sat transfixed by what she'd read. Bad weather was one thing. Every farmer in every state suffered crop losses due to weather from time to time. But nothing but one disaster after another for almost twenty years? That was something altogether different. God didn't seem to want the Iowa Amish moving to Audrain County a century ago and changing their rules. They had suffered year after year until they moved back or died off.

She stuck in her bookmark and thought of Solomon's sermon about Noah's neighbors. Because of their wickedness, God had unleashed a giant flood of water and wiped them out. He may have established a covenant with Noah's descendants to not destroy the whole earth again, but apparently that didn't include flooding in Centralia, alternating with ground-parching months of no rain whatsoever. Emily picked up the book and finished it within an hour and a half. After checking the wall clock, she wrote down page numbers of articles in the second book for her next visit to the library.

"Thank you," she said, returning the histories to the librarian. "Those gave me something to think about."

"At least we know recent natural disasters haven't been something new to central Missouri." The librarian peered over her glasses. "Bad things have been happening here for a hundred years."

Emily smiled, even though it took some effort. The news was grim. She couldn't wait to tell Jonas what she'd read. Would he pass along the story to the ministers and the bishop? Did Solomon Trask already know about the Centralia Old Order settlement? Is that why he felt the district needed to shape up? Maybe he had already heard about a community who left their conservative roots behind and started over with more liberal ways.

Across the street in the coffee shop, Emily joined the Amish ladies chatting and grabbing a bite to eat before the van ride back to Paradise. Everyone shared tales of medical examinations, chiropractic adjustments, or shopping trips with carefree animation. Emily sipped her latte in silence. She wanted to mull over the newfound information before discussing it with fellow district members. It was easy to dismiss history as irrelevant to their lives today, but those who couldn't learn from the past were doomed to make the same mistakes over and over.

Apparently, every one of Noah's warnings had fallen on deaf ears as well.

❧

Jonas finished his last dregs of coffee as his buggy rolled into the parking lot of Gingerich Lumber. Several men working the yard lifted gloved hands in greeting as they unloaded a tractor trailer of pressure-treated wood. The sun was shining, a cool breeze blew from the west, and overnight showers were predicted to help gardens and farm fields. *It will be a good day.*

Unfortunately, his initial intuition proved false.

His English foreman, Ken Stewart, cornered him the moment Jonas entered the office. "I had to take men from the sawmill to fill the morning orders, boss. Deliveries needed to be made and the loads weren't ready."

Jonas scratched his nose. "I know the regular crew doesn't start until nine on Mondays, but Elam Detweiler was supposed to be here by six to pull orders."

"'Supposed to be' being the key words." Ken rolled his eyes. "That guy has been late to work more often than not. I've spoken to him three times already and told him that if there was one more occurrence I would take up the matter with you."

"He's been late frequently?" Jonas, never a man to react hastily, slowly processed the information.

Ken nodded. "Every time he's scheduled to start before the rest of the crew. He says he arrives on time, but I can tell by what he has done it's not the case."

"He *lies* to you?" asked Jonas, not hiding his surprise. It was rare for an Amish man to bear false witness. Most took the Ninth Commandment seriously, even those who hadn't joined the church yet.

"I believe he does." Ken locked eyes with Jonas, shifting his substantial weight from one foot to the other. "He can't seem to adjust to the idea of a time clock, either."

"I'll take care of this. Thanks for moving men from the mill to pull orders." Jonas picked up the ledger of deliveries for the day and the list of scheduled pick-ups. Then he went in search of his tardy employee. He found Elam in the outdoor racks of two-by-fours. He was loading an order onto a wheeled cart.

"Elam, we need to talk." Jonas matched his tone of voice to his current mood.

The younger man peered up from under the bill of a Cardinals cap, apparently fond of hats that advertised St. Louis baseball. "What's up?" he asked, lifting another stack of lumber.

"Put down those boards and come here." Jonas loathed speaking to a person without their full attention.

Elam brushed off the palms of his leather gloves and approached with his usual swagger. Somewhere he had acquired the walk of a rodeo rider. "Here I am."

"A Sturgeon carpenter is coming for that order in a few minutes." Jonas hooked his thumb toward the wheeled cart.

"Yeah, that's why I'm hurrying." He slouched against an upright post.

"All the more reason you should have arrived to work on time." Jonas didn't blink as he met the other man's eye.

Neither did Elam. "Who says I didn't?"

"My foreman told me you didn't. It's his job to keep track of those things. He also said this wasn't your first time late. You've had several warnings."

Elam broke the stare down and glanced up into the racks. "I've been having engine trouble. My car keeps stalling and then doesn't want to restart for a while. One guy said I'm flooding the engine." He laughed as though this were humorous. "I really don't know how I manage that."

"I can't help you there since I know nothing about cars. But I need you here on time to fill orders."

Elam crossed his tanned arms while muscles bulged at the bands of his T-shirt. "Everybody else arrives right before the yard opens. Only the tow motor operator and I have to be here so early."

"When I hired you, the only position available required an early starting time. You said it would be no problem, yet apparently it has been a problem on a regular basis."

Elam's brown eyes darkened. "I didn't anticipate this car giving me so many headaches."

"I'm sure you didn't, but I need someone in the first slot who can be counted on. If another position opens I'll move you into it, but in the meantime I expect you here by six every day. Or you could start looking for another job."

Elam's gaze narrowed like a hawk focusing on dinner. "I would have thought family members could be cut some slack."

"According to Ken you've been cut plenty of slack. Men who work construction projects need materials delivered at the *start* of the workday. Whether or not you're family, I have a business to run." Jonas stomped off before Elam annoyed him with any more rationalizations. Men like him were all the same—blaming others for their shortcomings, always making excuses to mask their irresponsibility. Sally's brother-in-law or not, Elam Detweiler was walking on thin ice.

When Jonas arrived home, he was eager to see this wife, enjoy a good meal, put up his feet, and relax. Only one of his three wishes would be granted that night. He'd forgotten about Emily's trip to Columbia for the day, so she wasn't yet home when Nora served supper. Jonas knew he couldn't relax until the van dropped her off hours later. There were too many accidents on Route 63 for him not to worry. Although Nora served a fine meat loaf, buttered yellow beans, and mashed potatoes, his houseguest said barely six words during the entire meal. Her attempt at conversation consisted of "Do you want catsup or gravy on your meat?" He'd never met a woman so quiet.

At last, Emily bounded into the kitchen as he was nursing his third cup of tea. "*Ach,* I'm glad you're still up." She slung a bag of library books onto the kitchen counter.

"You know I can't sleep until you're home. How did you fare with the fines? Must we take out a mortgage against the farm?"

"I paid them two dollars and ten cents. Perhaps they'll name a new wing after me someday." Emily turned on the burner under the kettle.

He clucked his tongue. "Such vanity. The bishop and Minister Sol would never permit the Emily Gingerich Auditorium. You must remain a secret benefactor."

"Speaking about Sol, I thought about him while reading the history of Audrain County." Her honey brown eyes sparkled with energy, despite the hour. "I learned about an Old Order community near Centralia that went extinct—that's the word the book used. Amish folks moved here a hundred years ago and tried to farm, but they suffered crop failures year after year. Either it was too wet or too dry, to the extreme. The last families gave up in 1917 and abandoned their land." When the teakettle whistle blew, she poured hot water into a mug and dunked a teabag vigorously.

"Did the others die? Is that why the book called them extinct?"

She reflected a moment. "Maybe some died, but I think the rest just gave up."

Jonas drained the last of his beverage. He would float to bed on the liquids he'd consumed. "Why did this remind you of Solomon? I don't follow."

Emily brought her tea to the table and sat down next to her husband. "These Old Order people wanted to be more liberal than the district they left behind in Iowa. They came to create a new *Ordnung* in Missouri." She paused, waiting for him to reach some implication.

Unfortunately, he still didn't make a connection. He shrugged in bewilderment.

"Don't you see, Jonas? They were going against God's plan. They didn't want to keep traditional Amish ways. Instead, they amended the rules to suit their own selfish desires. God sent nothing but hardship, forcing them to eventually abandon their farms in the new land."

Jonas knew his wife well enough not to contradict her logic outright. He chose his words carefully. "On the surface a person could draw such a conclusion, but that might not be the case. Sometimes a string of bad years is nothing more than that, not necessarily the result of adopting a liberal *Ordnung*. We can't say for sure after nearly a century and limited recorded information. I know no one *Amish* person kept a written account of their hardships in Missouri. We have only the opinion of English neighbors."

Emily's face puckered into a frown. "But doesn't it make sense as a likely probability? We know what happened in the days of Noah."

"Noah wasn't the only man described in the Bible. Did God judge Saul on the road to Damascus? Did He strike him down for persecuting the early Christians? No, He gave him a new life as Paul, both while on earth and in the hereafter. God's judgment isn't always swift and merciless."

Emily nodded but looked less than convinced. "That's true, but if it's just the same to you, I'll keep researching the surrounding counties. Maybe there were other Amish settlements that died out." She carried their cups to the sink.

"That'll be fine, *fraa*. You do love to read." Jonas headed wearily up the steps to some overdue sleep. *I couldn't stop you from chasing this notion if I tried.*

☙

Nora folded the wheelchair and put it in the back of the buggy. Then she helped Violet get settled on the seat. She took the reins, and with a shake of the harness, the horse left the parking lot of Grain of Life at a fast trot.

"Your third date with Elam," mused Violet. "Sounds like you two are getting serious. Is that why Emily let us leave work an hour early?"

"I do have a date and that's why she released us on the bakery's busy day, but no, Elam and I aren't serious. We barely know each other. One volleyball party and a cookout don't allow much talk time."

"Emily certainly isn't how bosses are portrayed in novels. She's so sweet to me—to both of us. I love working at Grain of Life. Next week she'll teach me how to make bread. *Mamm* will be pleased because I've shown zero interest in learning at home."

"Emily will be able to perch on her stool with a good book, just as she has always wanted." Nora relaxed a little, now that the conversation no longer centered on her date. Her relief didn't last long.

"You two are going to dinner in Columbia, right? That should allow plenty of get-acquainted time. What color dress will you wear? Do you think he'll hold your hand? What kind of restaurant will he take you to?"

Nora sighed, shaking her head. "'I don't know' answers all three questions. Why are you so curious about my date?"

"Because I've never been courted before. No one has even asked to take me home from a singing." Violet focused on young corn, growing in the fields beside them for as far as the eye could see.

Nora could have kicked herself for being so thoughtless. "I haven't been on that many dates either. I've only had one boy court me, back in Lancaster, and that didn't turn out well. Besides, you make little effort to strike up conversations. You're friendly enough with females, but with males you tend to hide."

"Who would want to put up with a girl with these?" Violet slapped her leg braces through her skirt.

"Don't be ridiculous. There's almost nothing you can't do. It might take you a tad longer, but men aren't looking for partners in a relay race. You're pretty, Violet, and sweet, and the funniest person I've ever met. It's time you let people get to know you."

"You think I'm pretty?"

"I do." Nora grasped her arm and shook it.

"My *daed* says I am, but I thought that was only because he's my father."

*Solomon Trask encouraging vanity in his* dochder? *Would wonders never cease.*

"You're *daed* speaks the truth."

Violet filled the rest of the drive with amusing tales from her last doctor's appointment, so Nora didn't have much opportunity to fret about the evening. She dropped off her friend close to the porch steps and carried up her wheelchair.

"Wish me luck," Nora called on her way back to the buggy.

"Good luck. Remember, tomorrow is a preaching Sunday, so don't stay out until sunrise." Violet waved as though they would be apart for weeks.

*Out until dawn with Elam?* The idea set a shiver of anticipation through Nora's veins.

With Emily at the bakery and Jonas at the lumberyard, she had the bathroom for a full hour. She soaked in strawberry-scented bubble bath, washed her hair with raspberry-scented shampoo, and then misted herself with lemon-scented body spray before she dressed. Elam would think he was going out with a bowl of fruit, but the fragrances made her feel feminine and desirable.

Her hair had barely dried before she heard his car spinning gravel in the drive. Nora swiftly wound it into a bun and pulled on a *kapp* just as his boots stomped up the steps. She opened the screen door before he could knock. "Hi, Elam. You're right on time."

"Wow, look at you in that pretty blue dress. And you smell nice too." Elam sniffed the air and produced a bouquet of daisies from behind his back. "I bought these, although I considered pillaging my landlady's garden." His grin stretched from ear to ear.

Nora stuck her nose into the flowers. "They're beautiful, *danki*. I'm ready to go." She stuck the bouquet into a jelly jar of water and then picked up her purse, remembering to also to grab an umbrella because of a light rain that had begun to fall. She tried not to stare at Elam's long, straight hair tucked behind his ears, his blue jeans, or his soft chambray shirt open at the neck. He looked about as handsome, and as English, as anyone she knew.

"Anxious to leave before the Gingerichs get home?" he asked. "Suits me fine. I'm not eager to run into Jonas until Monday morning. Funny, isn't it? You work for one Gingerich and I work for the other." Elam held the umbrella down the walkway and swept open the passenger door gallantly.

"How is your new job at the lumberyard?" Nora stepped into the car as modestly as possible.

"Good, up until last Monday. The foreman has been causing trouble. Jonas said he'll fire me if I don't get to work on time."

Nora braced herself as the Chevy accelerated onto the pavement. "Have you been late?"

"Only because of old Betsy here." He patted the steering wheel. "But it's not her fault. A buddy at the lumberyard said I shouldn't pump the pedal when I turn the key. That sends too much gas to the engine, causing it to stall out. Then the car won't restart until some of it evaporates. I should have figured that out from using chainsaws." He sighed as he slicked back a lock of hair that had fallen into his eyes. "Anyway, that guy is coming over tomorrow to change the oil and tune things up. Betsy will be purring like a cat once we're finished." He caressed the dashboard affectionately.

"On the Sabbath? That sounds like work to me." Nora rubbed her collarbone as though she had indigestion.

"It can't be helped. Sunday is the only day neither of us works. My other day off is different than his. I need the car fixed to keep my job, Nora."

She watched the passing scenery, not wanting to argue during their first fifteen minutes together.

"Did I mention how pretty you look?" Elam tugged one ribbon so hard he pulled her *kapp* off her head. He pressed it to his nose and inhaled the raspberry scent. "Mmm. Even your bonnet smells good."

"Give me that," she demanded.

"No one will see you in Columbia. Why not leave your head uncovered for one night? In fact, I would love to see your long hair. Why not take it down?"

She stared at him, wide-eyed and aghast. "Have you lost your mind? I could never do that!"

"But you haven't joined the church yet. Technically, you're still on *rumschpringe*."

"*Rumschpringe* or not, I'm still Amish, and Plain women keep their heads covered." She yanked the *kapp* from his fingers and pulled it on. Noticing his disappointment, she tried to make light of the situation. "How would it look? In this dress and apron with hair down to my waist? *Englischers* would think I'm an imposter playacting at being Amish."

Elam slanted a wry smile. "We could easily remedy that. We'll drive past a discount store on our way to the restaurant. I could buy you jeans, a T-shirt, and sandals. Then you can wear your hair anyway you wanted. And you could change back into your dress before you got home."

Nora pivoted on the seat. "It sounds as though you've given this some thought. But no, I'll just stay as I am. Don't you wish to be seen with someone Plain?" Color flooded her cheeks.

"It's not that at all," he said, reaching for her chin. "I think you're gorgeous, Nora King, however you're dressed. I just thought you might want to be adventurous."

Funny how adventurousness was no longer appealing now that she had the perfect opportunity. "What kind of food will we eat?" she asked, changing the subject. At the rate he was barreling down the freeway, they should arrive any minute. His high speed frightened her, because the drizzle had escalated into a downpour.

"A man at work recommended a Mexican place. Its name means 'three horsemen' in Spanish. I have directions." He patted his shirt pocket.

Nora began chatting about the bakery, but before she could share too many stories, they pulled into the parking lot. Elam came to her side with the umbrella and snaked an arm around her waist. All the way to the arched entrance she felt cherished and protected by his attentiveness.

Standing guard near the door was a life-sized ceramic horse with a fancy-dressed rider holding the reins. "Pretty, no?" he asked.

"Pretty fancy, I would say." She couldn't imagine what that size decoration had cost.

At the tall desk, a pretty hostess greeted them with a smile. "Table for two?"

Elam nodded, while Nora asked, "Where are the other two horsemen? I only saw one outside." When the girl looked confused, she added, "Your name means three horsemen."

"Oh, that. The owner only ordered one display. He's as tight with décor as he is with our paychecks." The hostess shook her shiny hair. "This way, folks." She led them to a dimly lit booth.

Nora studied the huge menu to no avail. "It's too dark in here to read."

Elam moved to her side of the booth. "Don't worry. I'll order for both of us." He was sitting so close she could smell his bath soap. When the waitress arrived, he ordered an inordinate amount of food.

Nora tried a little of every dish and discovered she loved guacamole, didn't care for tamales, and could eat corn chips with mild salsa all night. They ate and laughed and talked, and then ate more until she thought she would explode. Suddenly, two drinks in odd-shaped glasses appeared before them. "What are these?" she asked, as unease tickled the back of her neck.

"The mandatory drink in a Mexican restaurant—margaritas." Elam carefully lifted one and took a long swallow.

Nora studied the glass. "What's on the rim?"

"Salt. Give it a try." He took another gulp.

She sipped and scrunched her face. "Goodness, that's sour. Does it contain alcohol?"

"Yes, but not much." Elam moved her glass closer.

"*Nein.* I don't want to drink and neither should you. You're driving tonight." She pushed the glass away.

Elam studied her with one eye. "One drink won't make me drunk."

"I'm sure that's what all drunks say." Her words flew out without care for the consequences.

He stared at a painting of children batting at a paper cow in the booth. "All right, Nora, as you wish." Pushing his glass away, he rose to his feet. "I'll go pay the bill and then meet you at the door." Without waiting for a reply, he strode off in search of the waitress.

Nora walked to the front of the restaurant on weary legs, trying to forget his attempt to ply her with alcohol. On the way home, they made polite conversation about the weather and the St. Louis ball team. Just when she thought the evening might turn out pleasant after all, Elam showed his true colors. He parked his car in the Gingerich driveway under a tree but made no move to get out. Nora turned on the seat to thank him for the delicious Mexican meal. Suddenly, he grabbed hold of her face and kissed her hard on the mouth.

"Stop, Elam." She tried to pull away, but he locked his arm around her back, drawing her close without lessening his grip on her chin. He kissed her again, harder and deeper than before. Not for the first time, fear churned her belly, along with the spicy food.

She struggled against him, pushing against his chest with all her strength. "Stop!" she demanded.

Suddenly, he released her and Nora fell back against the door. "It was just a kiss, Nora," he muttered, surprised by her reaction. "Not the end of the world."

"I know what it was, Elam Detweiler, but maybe I didn't want to kiss *you*." Nora pulled the handle and almost fell out into the rainstorm. Slamming the car door behind her, she bolted into the house. She didn't stop running until she reached the safety of her bedroom. She leaned back against the door and closed her eyes. Only then did her emotions well to surface like a bubbling kettle. And Nora didn't know whether to cry, or shout, or fear for her life.

# EIGHT

*Wash all my sins away*

## Sunday Morning

Solomon Trask gazed out the window at dawn into the heaviest downpour he could remember. Rain pounded the metal roof like drumbeats, while the air was thick with humidity. He dressed carefully for preaching in his black coat, pants, mustfa vest, and starched white shirt, knowing his clothes would be damp by the time he reached the service. At least the hosting family lived only a few miles away.

"*Ach, ehemann,*" moaned Rosanna. "The hem of your coat has come loose in the back. And with this weather, I'll have no time to mend it before church. Our mare always walks turtle slow in heavy rain."

"Who can blame her when neither man nor beast can see ten yards ahead?" Sol straightened his collar. "Don't worry about my coat. I'll be sure to face the congregation all day long. No one will be the wiser." He sat down at the kitchen table and bowed his head.

After a silent prayer, Rosanna fixed him with a glare. "I wish you would let me buy new fabric. It's about time we replaced that coat. I'm starting to patch the patches from the underside."

Sol poured cornflakes into a bowl. "Let's wait a bit longer. I prefer we use the money for Violet's therapy. Those legs of hers are getting stronger, no?"

Before Rosanna could answer, their daughter rolled into the room. "I heard my name. Are you two saying good things about me?" Violet pulled herself up to the table and reached for the box of cereal.

He smiled at her fresh young face. "What other kind could they be?"

"Do you think it will be a light crowd at preaching?" she asked. "It didn't stop raining all day yesterday or all night." Violet poured milk in her bowl. "Do you think the Gingerichs will be there? I can't wait to see Nora."

"Might be a sparse turnout if there's flooding. The routes we'll take, as well as the deacon's family, should be fine, but roads in low-lying areas could wash out. Eat up, *dochder*, so we can leave."

Violet and Rosanna hurried through breakfast, donned their black capes, and climbed into the enclosed buggy, where Irvin and his wife, Susanna, waited in the backseat. Sol's other children from adjoining farms would drive their own buggies. As his *fraa* predicted, Nell pulled slower than moss growing on a rock in the shade, delivering them to the Yost farm barely at the appointed hour. Everyone was already inside the barn and seated on the long benches. After the opening hymns and prayers, Sol walked to the front to deliver the first of two sermons.

Clearing his throat, he gazed over a crowd half the normal size. "*Welcum*, and bless you for venturing out on a day such as this." Thick humidity hung in the air, and buckets had been scattered across the floor to catch steady drips from the leaky roof. The windows rattled in their frames as the wind buffeted the barn.

"In the book of Exodus," Sol began, "we learn that Pharaoh oppressed the Israelites mercilessly. God instructed Moses to lead his people out of Egypt, but when Pharaoh refused to release them, God delivered ten plagues to the Egyptians." Sol paused as a crack of thunder startled his flock. "The first plague turned the Nile to blood, killing all of the fish and polluting the drinking water. The second plague unleashed a swarm of frogs that overran their homes. Pharaoh asked Moses to remove the frogs, and when God complied, the king went back on his word.

"The third plague sent lice and the fourth sent flies, yet Pharaoh's heart remained hard. The fifth killed the Egyptian cattle yet spared the cows of the Israelites. The sixth brought festering boils to cover the faces of every man, woman, and child. A hailstorm on the land of Egypt was the seventh plague. It rained hail mixed with fire, destroying crops and livestock everywhere except in the land of Goshen, where Moses' people lived."

Sol scanned the congregation, meeting the eyes of those who didn't avoid his gaze. Everyone sat very still, listening with rapt attention. "Once again Pharaoh showed signs of repentance and made false promises. Moses entreated God for the hail to cease, but Pharaoh still wouldn't release the people. Next God sent a plague of locusts to eat every plant and flower not already destroyed by hail. The ninth plague brought unrelenting darkness for three days. No one could see the hand in front of their face. Yet Pharaoh kept the Israelites in bondage, knowing his own people were starving.

"With patience exhausted, God sent His death angel to every home in Egypt to slay the firstborn of each family. A giant cry arose throughout the land. God told Moses' people to sacrifice a male lamb for a feast and mark their doors with its blood. The death angel passed over those homes, sparing their offspring. When Pharaoh's own son was killed, he finally released the Israelites from bondage in Egypt."

The district sat spellbound without a cough, clearing of the throat, or shifting of benches. They stared at Solomon, horrified by God's wrath.

"Because the king was stubborn, every Egyptian suffered. Only when sorrow cut close to home—his own son—did Pharaoh see the foolishness of challenging the God of Moses." Solomon paused and drew breath. He struggled to select the right words to relay his timely message. "It has been raining without cessation for two days. Some may make light of this—no big deal. Others may say it could be a sign that *we* have displeased the Lord. I cannot say for sure, but I ask you to examine your hearts—every man and woman here. Are there sins you have ignored? Have we grown lackadaisical about maintaining the *Ordnung* in our homes? Are we becoming worldly like the *Englischers* we do business with? God misses nothing. We might be able to keep secrets from one another, but we keep no secrets from Him."

If a pin had dropped in the Yost barn, everyone would have heard. No one moved. All eyes remained locked on the minister.

"Unfortunately, it took blood, frogs, lice, flies, disease, boils, hail, locusts, darkness, and the death of the firstborn Egyptians to get the Egyptians' attention. Will we be so thickheaded about transgressions in our own lives?" Solomon stepped back and unclenched his fists. "Root it out, I say to you. Repent of whatever you're guilty of and live by the laws that have served our people for hundreds of years." He clamped his jaw shut, having done his job. No need to browbeat them with the sermon. He returned to his place on the men's side to await the other minister's message, not noticing the pale, stunned expressions on people's faces.

Later on the drive home, Solomon Trask felt he'd served his district well. Yet his wife and daughter were uncharacteristically silent. They neither discussed his sermon as they usually did, nor asked questions about certain points they might not have understood.

*Did I sound accusatory rather than cautionary?* he asked himself. *Have I distanced those I intended to draw closer to the fold?*

Yet events in Audrain and Randolph counties during the next twenty-four hours only solidified Solomon's convictions. For the rest of that day and night, the rain continued, flooding roads and cellars, washing away precious topsoil, and destroying the corn and soybean crops…just when both had been off to auspicious starts.

᳇

If Violet asked one more question on their way to work, Nora thought she would scream. How do you tell your best friend you would rather not discuss your disastrous date? Violet yearned for details.

"What did you eat?"

"What did you talk about?"

"How close did you sit on the ride home?"

Nora yielded only in that she enjoyed the Mexican food and they both had talked a lot about work. She didn't mention Elam had tried to ply her with alcohol or that he'd gotten fresh with her while parked in the driveway. Her shame over his behavior lasted for days. When Violet's father had referred to sins people were hiding, Nora thought she would melt into the floor. Memories of mistakes she made in Lancaster returned—mistakes she could never rectify.

How could she admit she had foolishly surrendered what should have been saved for marriage? Thinking she was in love, and that the man courting her was in love with her, she'd lost her innocence, her dignity, and her self-respect on one regrettable summer night. What Christian man would want her now?

"Planet Earth calling Nora King," said Violet, breaking through Nora's fog.

"Sorry, I was daydreaming." Nora glanced over at her passenger.

"About Elam?" Violet sounded hopeful.

"I was thinking about Pennsylvania. What did you say?"

"I asked what you and Emily baked yesterday."

"Pies. Six different types, so today we'll make bread and cookies." Nora relaxed as conversation changed from Saturday night to how Violet had spent the past three days. She and her *mamm* had cleaned, cooked, and done laundry at the Huffman house to help the new mother and bedridden father.

Once they entered the bakery, Nora built a fire in the stove and opened every screened window. Violet wiped down shelves and unloaded the totes into the displays. Grain of Life was ready for business when Emily arrived twenty minutes later.

Emily preferred walking to work for the exercise and reached the shop not remotely out of breath. "Look at this place. You could eat off the floor and we're all set up." Slipping on a clean apron, she flipped the sign to "Open."

"My first batch of oatmeal pecan cookies will be done in ten minutes, but I strongly recommend you use a plate to eat," Nora said, smiling at her cheery employer.

"I've assembled twenty pie boxes and made new signs." Violet beamed from her front counter post. "We're prepared for the onslaught."

Customers, mostly Amish and locals, showed up throughout the day in a steady stream but didn't overwhelm the shop. Emily was able to bake multigrain and whole wheat bread while Nora baked twelve dozen cookies, enough to hold them until Saturday. Unfortunately, the last batch remained in the oven too long and need to be scraped from the cookie sheet.

"Is something burning? I'd heard this was the *best* bakery in Paradise."

The booming male voice sounded oddly familiar to Nora. She had been concentrating on her overdone cookies and not heard the bell above the door. Peering up, Nora met the gaze of Lewis Miller—her former beau from Harmony. "Lewis!" She dropped the spatula and approached the counter. "What a surprise."

"A pleasant one, I hope," he said. "You did write and invite me to visit. Or don't you recall?" He folded his arms against his black coat. "Maybe you send out so many invitations, it's hard to keep track." His blue eyes danced with delight.

Nora wiped damp palms down her apron. Despite having sent a letter, being face-to-face with the man she once thought she'd marry left her weak in the knees. "*Nein*. I recall inviting only one person—you." She approached cautiously and offered her hand, which Lewis pumped vigorously.

"I'm happy to hear it. Now, what's your price for burnt cookies? Surely you can cut an old friend a deal." He held her hand a few moments longer than necessary.

"Ahem." Violet cleared her throat with exaggeration. "Have Emily and I blended into the pastries or have you simply forgotten us?" She straightened taller in her chair.

"Excuse me. Lewis, this is my dear friend, Violet Trask." Nora placed both hands on Violet's shoulders. "And this is my mentor and employer, besides my friend, Emily Gingerich. She is also Sally Detweiler's sister." Nora encircled Emily's waist with her arm as she joined them at the counter. "Ladies, this is Lewis Miller from Maine."

Lewis swept off his straw hat and bent low. "Violet, Mrs. Gingerich. I'm pleased to make your acquaintance. I had prayed Nora would meet nice people in Missouri. I see that prayer has been answered."

"*Welcum* to Paradise. And call me Emily, especially if you're planning to stay with us during your visit. Before you argue, you should know we have no hotels or inns or bed-and-breakfasts in town. Even the nearest campground is fifteen miles away."

Lewis clutched his hat to his chest. "I wouldn't dream of declining your hospitality. I spoke with your sister before leaving Maine. Sally described your cooking as memorable."

Emily's laughter filled the shop. "Memorable could be either good or bad, so that sounds exactly like something my sister would say."

While they exchanged friendly banter, Nora focused on Lewis's hands. Where were the ink stains from keeping his father's ledgers? She remembered his hands as large but not as calloused. Had he been working his *daed*'s fields as well as the store? Last year his face had been full and round, with a hint of remaining baby fat. Now his jawline was sharper, while his chin dimple had deepened into a cleft. She shook her head to stop staring. "Emily and Jonas have plenty of room," she said with every gaze on her. "Where is your bag?"

"Bags," corrected Lewis. "They're on the porch. I didn't want to take up valuable shop space."

"How long will you be here? A couple of weeks?" asked Violet.

Lewis trained his cornflower blue eyes on her. "Oh, no. I intend to stay a while. My *daed* gave me a leave of absence from my job, replacing me in the store with a cousin. I don't need to return until September to help with the harvest." His focus drifted from Violet back to Nora.

After this bombshell, Nora felt the floor tilt beneath her feet. Lewis would be in town for *months*? When she'd invited him, she imagined a week—two at the most. "It must be nice to be able to take long vacations," she murmured.

"It's no vacation. I intend to look for work so I won't deplete my savings account. If anyone knows of any job openings, I'd be appreciative." He turned back to Emily. "Now that you know my plans, does your offer of a room still stand? I'll gladly pay room and board, of course."

Emily began bagging up an assortment of cookies. "Of course it does. Your first two weeks will be Gingerich hospitality, and then Jonas will set a fair weekly rate. You can discuss that with him."

"You traveled all this way to see Nora and will remain the entire summer?" Violet's words dripped with admiration.

Tiny laugh lines formed around his mouth as Lewis smiled. "The truth is, Violet, I have a definite goal to accomplish in Missouri. And I'm not leaving until I'm successful."

Nora had to force her legs to walk back to the table. "Let's see, you said you wanted this burnt batch? How does a dollar sound for the dozen?" She shoveled the crispy cookies into a brown paper sack.

"Nora King, we do *not* gouge customers on their first day in town. We wait at least till their second visit to Grain of Life. Give him those at no charge." Emily stood with both hands on her hips. "How did you get here, Lewis?"

"A taxi brought me from Columbia. When I noticed the sign for the bakery, I had the driver drop me off. I figured I could walk the rest of the way to your house, even with luggage."

"You're not walking anywhere. I have a brilliant plan." She took the bag of cookies from Nora and handed it to Lewis. Then she put another two dozen is a separate bag and handed it to the blushing Amish girl standing next to her. "Nora, you and Violet may leave now. The baking is done for the day anyway. Drive Lewis to my husband's lumberyard so he can apply for a job. You can put those cookies in the company break room. Jonas mentioned he still needed to hire another man, and Lewis looks strong as a bull."

"Like Paul Bunyan," piped up Violet.

"Or at least his blue ox," Nora said, smiling for the first time since he arrived. She turned to Emily. "You think Lewis could work at Gingerich's?"

"*Jah*, why not? After the lumberyard you can drop Violet off and take him home. Lewis can unpack and get comfortable in his new room. Show him around. Maybe he would like to relax after the trip, especially if Jonas wants him to start work right away."

"*Danki*, Emily. I am in your debt." Lewis pulled out a cookie to sample. "These are delicious, by the way."

Things were moving too fast for Nora. She swallowed down a surge of anxiety as she fetched their purses from the cupboard. "If you're sure you don't need us this afternoon…"

"I can leave too?" asked Violet. "What an adventure."

"Life generally is, often when we least expect it to be." Lewis's cryptic words hung in the air as the three of them left the shop. While he folded up the wheelchair and helped Violet into the buggy, Nora retrieved the horse from where she'd been grazing. She needed five minutes to decide which confusing emotion to focus on—panic or pure joy.

❧

Elam Detweiler rubbed his eyes to make sure he wasn't seeing things. He stared across the sawdust-strewn floor of the showroom where Gingerich Lumber sold hardware, metal work, hand tools, and other equipment. A tall, powerfully built Amish man talked to Jonas near the office door. When he turned, Elam recognized the face of Lewis Miller. What on earth was the Harmony shopkeeper doing in Paradise?

He tossed his clipboard of loading bills onto the desk as a disturbing memory resurfaced. Lewis had briefly courted Nora back in Maine. When Elam had questioned her about their relationship, she had dismissed the idea, insisting that the frigid north held little appeal for her. Afterward, Nora had helped him buy a car and kept his confidences regarding his plans to leave. She'd let him kiss her in the henhouse. They had taken a late night buggy ride while his brother's household slept, none the wiser. And she secretly drank a beer with him at a community pig roast. But that was the old Nora, before she'd become all buttoned-up and standoffish.

Funny how she had acted boldly in ultraconservative Harmony, but here in Paradise, where the bishop actually permitted *rum-schpringe*, she'd turned into a gray-haired old biddy. She worried about everything from driving too fast to hiding every strand of hair under her *kapp*.

While Elam watched unnoticed across the room, Jonas and Lewis shook hands, both men wearing smiles. Then Jonas introduced Lewis to Ken Stewart, the foreman. That could only mean one thing—Lewis had just been hired—but it didn't explain why he had come to town. In six long strides, Elam closed the distance between them.

"Lewis Miller," he said. "As I live and breathe."

Three pairs of eyes turned toward him. "Hello, Elam. It's been a long time, no?" Lewis stuck out his hand.

After a moment, Elam shook. "What's going on?"

"You two know each other?" asked Ken, scratching his chin.

"Of course. Harmony is a *small* town." Elam's inflection on his former residence reflected his low opinion.

"Jonas hired me to work the counter. I'll wait on customers and write up phone orders." Lewis looked pleased, standing there with his hands tucked beneath his suspenders.

"Is that right? On the day shift?" Elam directed his question at Jonas without hiding his irritation. "I thought any openings for a late start time would be mine." He sucked in air through his nostrils.

Jonas shrugged his shoulders. "You mentioned your car had been repaired. If it's running fine, you should have no trouble getting to work on time. Lewis, on the other hand, drives a horse and buggy. A delayed start would serve him better." He fixed Elam with a cool stare, as though daring him to argue.

Elam considered his options. Gingerich paid a decent salary in a county with few employment opportunities. He'd just caught up with back rent but still owed his friend for the car parts he purchased. After a moment's hesitation, he nodded. "Yeah, that makes sense. Besides, the earlier I start, the sooner I get out of here."

Ken checked his clipboard. "Is your paperwork caught up, along with organizing the orders to be pulled tomorrow?"

"All ready to go, boss." Elam looked at the foreman, not the newest employee, but Lewis appeared to be studying him with great interest.

"In that case you can punch out." With the matter settled, Ken turned to discuss something with Jonas that Elam couldn't hear. Then the three men walked into the office. Lewis acted as though he owned the place instead of having worked there for fifteen minutes.

Elam punched out at the time clock and collected his thermos from the break room. Someone had set out a bag of cookies from Grain of Life, probably Jonas. After helping himself to four, he walked outside into bright May sunshine. Just as he reached his car, he spotted Lewis climbing into a nondescript buggy. How did he manage to buy a rig so fast? But that question paled in importance compared to why he had come to Paradise in the first place.

Elam's mind whirred in turmoil during the drive home. Knowing only one person who could answer his questions, Elam took a quick shower, put on clean clothes, and drove to the home of Jonas and Emily Gingerich. Maybe his boss would invite him to share supper with the family. Then he could spend time with his girl, patch up their minor misunderstanding, and get information about Miller.

The woman he was looking for was exiting the barn when he drove up and parked in the shade. "Hey, Nora," he sang out, springing from the car.

"Elam, what are you doing here?" She looked and sounded downright flabbergasted to see him.

He caught up to her on the path to the house. "You're not still sore about last Saturday, are you? I'm sorry I got a little frisky after our date. You looked so pretty that I temporarily forgot my manners." Elam jammed his hands into his back pockets.

Nora clutched her purse to her chest. "*Jah*, I'm still upset. Just because you bought me dinner doesn't give you the right to take liberties."

Elam was both confused and disappointed. Nora had kissed him back home without hesitation and expressed no remorse. But he had no desire to make matters worse. "It won't happen again, I promise, but let me ask you something." He paused long enough to swat a mosquito on his neck. "Why do you suppose Lewis Miller is in town? You remember him, don't you—the shopkeeper's son?"

"Of course I remember him. I'm not addlebrained. He came to Paradise to see what all the fuss was about. The way your sister-in-law talks about Missouri, it's a wonder everyone in Harmony doesn't show up." Nora's lips drew into a smile.

That wasn't the anticipated response. Lewis's arrival didn't remotely surprise her. "You *knew* he was coming?"

"Well, *jah*." She clutched her purse tighter. "He wrote me a letter to say he would."

"Have you seen him yet?" A spark of anger began deep in Elam's gut.

"When he stopped at the bakery. Emily asked Violet and me to drive him to Gingerich's to see about a job."

"That was *you* waiting for him in the parking lot?" The tiny spark fanned into a blaze.

She nodded. "I drove Violet home first and then Lewis." Nora glanced nervously over her shoulder.

"Drove him where?" Elam practically shouted the question.

Nora lifted her chin and narrowed her gaze. "I brought him here. Emily invited Lewis to stay."

"Doesn't that beat all? Emily never offered me a room, and I'm related to her."

She set her jaw in that new exasperatingly haughty pose. "You'll have to take that up with her, but right now I must help make dinner. My chores won't get done by themselves. Good day to you, Elam." Nora pivoted and sprinted toward the house.

*Good day to me?* She sounded like a checkout girl at the grocery store. Elam stared at her retreating back until the screen door slammed behind her. Then he jumped in his car and peeled down the driveway just as Lewis appeared in the barn doorway. This matter wasn't settled—not by a long shot. But considering Nora's odd behavior, he needed to cool off and plot his strategy carefully.

# NINE

*Dear dying Lamb, thy precious blood*

Emily let the curtain drop back into place before Nora reached the porch steps. What did that Elam Detweiler want on a Thursday afternoon? Nora had said little after their date, and that in itself spoke volumes. She certainly wasn't walking on clouds either on Sunday or Monday as young women usually did while being courted.

Now Elam postured in her side yard with clenched fists, towering over the young woman as though he had ownership rights. But she stood her ground, not cowering or backing down from his intimidation. Whatever they discussed had sent Elam back to his car in a hurry, while Nora ran to the house as though chased by a pack of wolves.

*Or maybe just one.* "Is everything okay?" Emily asked when her flushed and breathless houseguest entered the kitchen.

Nora walked straight to the kitchen sink and began to wash. "Elam wanted to know why Lewis came to Paradise. And apparently he didn't like the fact Jonas hired him." She dried her hands on a towel.

"Do you think he'll cause trouble at the lumberyard?" Emily watched the girl's reaction carefully.

"I don't think so, but it is rather shocking that Lewis traveled so far. I think Elam felt jealous, especially as Lewis will be staying here."

"Jealousy is a very destructive emotion. Much harm has been done because of envy and jealousy."

Nora wrinkled her nose. "He'll get over it. Anyway, no one knew where Elam was living when he moved here. You couldn't have invited him if you'd wanted to."

Emily might have commented on the unlikelihood of *that* prospect, but Lewis strolled in the back door just then. "May I come in, Mrs. Gingerich?" He set down two suitcases and swept off his hat.

"Of course you can. And call me Emily, or I'll take a wooden spoon to you."

He turned a lovely shade of scarlet. "I feel right at home already."

Nora hung up the towel while stealing surreptitious glances at him. "Should I show him upstairs and around the farm, Emily?"

"*Nein.* I'm home now, so I'll do it. Why don't you pick tomatoes and lettuce for a salad? Then you can start frying the pork chops."

"See you at supper," Nora murmured to Lewis on her way out the door.

"I look forward to it." His smile revealed more than just relief at having reached his destination. Emily had seen that expression before—*Englischers* called it "the look of love."

"Let's get you settled in your new room first." She led the way as Lewis followed with his luggage, ducking his head at the entrance to the stairwell. She swept open the door to the second guest room and waved him inside. "Here we are. Just holler if you don't find what you need in the blanket chest or linen closet." She pointed out the location of both. "One bathroom is at the end of the hall, and a second is off the kitchen. My, you're a large man," she added unnecessarily. He certainly knew how tall he was.

"*Jah*. Because my parents only had one son, they thought he'd better be big." Lewis blushed each time he made eye contact with her. "May I set my bag on that?" He pointed toward a trunk by the window.

"Of course. Jonas made that chest. It's filled with baby clothes for our future *bopplin*." Emily backed toward the door. "Would you like to rest before dinner?"

"No, I'm not tired, but I would like to make myself useful. I rubbed down your buggy horse and gave her grain and fresh water. Do you have other chores for me? Or maybe Nora might need help in the garden." His blue eyes twinkled.

"Aren't you a sly one, Lewis Miller, angling for a way to spend time with her."

"My family will assure you there's not a sly bone in my body. What you see is what you get." He sat down on the bed. "I'll be straight with you, ma'am. I'm here because I'm in love with Miss King. I made my intentions clear back in Harmony, but she didn't like our long winters. Maine isn't for people with thin blood or those easily bored. After she left, my sisters tried fixing me up with every single woman from sixteen to thirty-five. But despite their noble attempts, I couldn't get Nora out of my head." His laughter sounded sad rather than amused. "So I've come to win her back from that rascal Detweiler, if there's any possible way." He slapped his palms down on his knees for emphasis.

Emily blinked. "There was nothing sly about that declaration. Your motives are crystal clear."

Several moments of silence spun out as each carefully evaluated the other. "You say you have sisters but no brothers? What would happen if Nora agrees to court you but refuses to move back North?"

"I've thought about that. I talked to my father before I left to make sure he understood why I'm here. He said because two of my *schwestern* are married and their husbands enjoy working in the store, he would have enough help." Lewis rose and walked to the window, somehow deducing which offered the view he cherished. "*Daed* wants me to be happy, as long as I bring my bride home once a year to visit." He gazed down on the garden below. "I can't imagine marrying any other woman."

Emily joined him to watch Nora plucking ripe tomatoes from the vine. "My goodness, look how many vegetables she already has picked. Certainly such a skinny girl will need help carrying the basket to the house." Emily winked at the earnest young man, who wore his heart pinned to his Plain blue shirt.

Lewis sprinted across the room but paused in the doorway. "*Danki*, Emily, for taking me in and for listening to my pitiful tale of unrequited love."

"You're *welcum*. But I wouldn't be so sure about the *unrequited* part. The jury's still out. If it makes you feel better, I'm rooting for you."

Hope filled his face. "Then how can I possibly fail? You won't be sorry you backed my horse in this race. Now I'd better get downstairs before she tries to lift that heavy basket." He bolted down the steps.

Emily watched Nora and Lewis in the garden for several minutes. They danced around each other like wary coyotes, barely making eye contact—he, so tall and powerful; she, so petite and thin—and both painfully shy. Emily had always possessed a certain intuition when it came to people. It was something she inherited from her *grossmammi*. It told her Lewis was a good man, without pretense or swagger, whereas she wouldn't have trusted Elam even without Sally's warning. No one sat on the fence this long. By now he should have decided whether or not to remain Amish. A man afraid of commitment offered little to Nora. Elam was playing a game of manipulation, but she was too naive to realize it. Unfortunately, wisdom often didn't arrive until people were long past courtship.

Emily abandoned her window vigil and walked to where Lewis had left his bag. Setting it on the floor, she raised the lid of the trunk to look inside. She saw little quilts, booties, tiny *kapps,* and baby accessories—painful reminders of her heart's desire. For years she had sewn clothes in her spare time for when God graced her and Jonas with *kinner.* A vice tightened her ribcage when she spotted one tiny garment. She'd embroidered a duckling on the front of a sleeper—an unnecessary embellishment, to be sure. Today, seeing the yellow duck nearly made her weep. She closed the trunk lid carefully, not fingering her handiwork as usual.

*In God's own time.* Jonas's words haunted her like a melody.

"Your will be done," she whispered, choking back tears.

She replaced Lewis's suitcase on top of the trunk as her mission became clear. If the opportunity presented itself, she would play matchmaker between her houseguests. Nora should forget about Elam—a man with little intention to commit to her or the Amish faith. Emily had grown fond of Nora, just as her sister had taken Amy under her wing back in Maine. Nora still needed a *mamm...* or at least a guiding hand. Until God provided her with another maternal outlet, she would assume the responsibility. But Emily knew she'd better tread carefully. That twenty-two-year-old fireball might not like being bossed around at work and at home too.

❧

Nora concentrated on supper, grateful that Emily and Jonas kept the conversation lively. She devoured two pork chops instead of her customary one, a large baked potato, and two servings of salad. While Jonas learned about Maine and Lewis found out about Missouri, Nora prayed for divine guidance. *Things are happening too fast*, she thought for the sixth time that day. Lewis's arrival had shaken her world, despite the fact she had invited him. She hadn't anticipated he would seek employment and stay until the fall. She refused to consider that Lewis was here merely because he cared for her.

Didn't her heart belong to Elam? Isn't that why she'd traveled fifteen hundred miles from her sister's home? So why had she resisted a simple good night kiss?

Until she made up her mind, maybe a diversion was a good idea.

"I noticed fields under water," Lewis said, taking another potato from the bowl. "Have you had heavy rains of late?"

"*Jah*. Last weekend the skies opened up and dumped more rain on Randolph County than we've seen in a long time, washing out most of the corn crop and soybeans. Wheat and oats were better established and should recover if we get enough sunshine."

"Will you still have time to reset corn and beans?" Lewis rubbed a hand across his clean-shaven jaw.

"We have a longer growing season than up North, so we'll replant, providing the land dries out in the next couple of weeks." Jonas selected his third chop from the platter.

"We don't grow wheat in Maine. No oats or rye, either, but beans and corn do well. We usually get three cuttings of hay."

"Lancaster County, the breadbasket of the East, ships grain up to Harmony," said Nora, breaking her silence. "Lewis's family grinds it using horsepower and sells it in their co-op." Warmth spread though her blood as his blue gaze fastened on her.

"I remember each one of your trips to our store," he said. "Do you still have your sweet tooth? I filled every extra space on the shelves with lemon drops, chocolate kisses, caramel bullseyes, and cinnamon fireballs."

Emily leaned toward Nora. "Have we learned your weakness, Nora? Your deep, dark secret?"

"I'm afraid so. I've loved candy since I was a little girl." Feeling heat rise up her neck into her cheeks, Nora wished the topic would change back to farming.

"Now I might be able to bribe you into washing windows." Emily winked while slicing an apple pie.

"Bribing won't be necessary." Nora grew nervous under Lewis's perusal. "Do you need help with dessert? Why don't I pour coffee?" She jumped up, feeling his gaze follow her to the stove, to the refrigerator, and back to the table. "Is something wrong, Lewis?" she asked, setting down the pot and mugs. "You seem to be studying me."

He cocked his head. "Nothing's wrong, but I remember you as taller. Did you wear high heels back in Maine?"

"Not that I recall." Nora poured milk in her cup. "You look different too. Maybe you changed after I left, or maybe the state of Missouri agrees with you."

"My first day certainly does. Time will tell regarding the future." Lewis accepted coffee from her and pie from Emily. "*Danki* for the delicious meal, Emily, but I should pay toward my board before I eat you and your husband out of house and home."

Emily spooned a dollop of Cool Whip onto his slice. "Not for two weeks. My terms were clear."

"Let my wife fuss over you for a while, Lewis. She enjoys it." Jonas grinned at Emily over his mug.

Suddenly, Nora needed to be away from their hosts for a while before she blurted out the wrong thing. "Would you like to see the rest of the farm?" she asked. "After you're finished, of course."

Lewis devoured his dessert in five bites. "I would love to. That is, if no one has chores for me."

Jonas dabbed his mouth. "Not on your first day. Go enjoy your walk. Tomorrow on our ride to work we'll figure out how you'll earn Emily's delicious cooking. Because my *bruders* tend the fields, neither of us have farm chores. I'm the entrepreneur in the Gingerich family."

Lewis stood and pushed in his chair. "I once read that word in a book. I understood the meaning but didn't know how to pronounce it. Now I know how to describe myself—an *entrepreneur*." He met and held Nora's gaze.

A shiver brought goose bumps to her skin. Either she was coming down with a virus or her old friend now affected her in strange ways. Nora grabbed her shawl from the peg and reached for the doorknob.

But he beat her to it and swung the door wide. "Allow me." Together they walked from the overheated kitchen into the cool evening. He didn't take her hand or stand too close, yet she seemed aware of every movement he made.

"Are you happy to have found a job so fast?" she asked, draping the shawl across her shoulders.

"I'm overjoyed. I never expected to be hired *and* housed by Sally's family. I pictured myself sleeping in someone's hayloft and showering with a garden hose. I'm in your debt, Nora, if you had anything to do with my good fortune." He tipped his hat brim.

"I might have mentioned you're not a kleptomaniac or an ax murderer."

His laughter roused birds from a nearby fence. "I've missed your sense of humor. Harmony returned to its somber self without you. By the way, Amy and John send their love. She's still sewing curtains for all the windows in their new house. She'll tell you the rest of her news in a letter, so I won't spoil the fun." Lewis paused where the dirt path forked into two directions.

Nora liked his newfound talkativeness. In the past Lewis had struggled for things to say. "To the left leads to endless pasture-land," she said. "The path on the right takes us to the Gingerich pond, and beyond that, the river."

"Definitely to the right. Pastures look the same everywhere, but I'd love to dip my toe in Paradise water. I'll bet it's not half as cold as Maine's."

"This will be my first time too. I've been learning to bake and working long hours. I haven't had much leisure time. You might notice some improvement in my culinary skills." With an uncontrollable urge, Nora picked up her skirt and ran down the path, not stopping until she reached the pond.

Lewis kept pace easily with his long legs. "Does that mean you're better at rustling up grub? Isn't that how you say it out West?"

"It does and it is," she said, laughing. They kicked off their shoes and socks, rolled up hems and splashed into the shallows. "Goodness, that feels good," she cried, holding her skirt above the water.

He waded along the shore toward a rickety fishing dock. After boosting himself onto one end, he offered his hand. "Need some help?"

"No, I'll take the easy route." Nora climbed the bank and walked onto the dock from shore. "You seem more relaxed than you were last summer," she said, settling down beside him.

"That's because I am. Crossing multiple state lines has given me more confidence." He leaned back on his elbows, gazing over sparkling blue water.

"What happened to the starched New Englander who refused to walk me home without a chaperone?" Nora hoped humor would mask her anxiety.

He cocked his head. "That guy stayed in Maine. The new Lewis Miller is ready to take on anything...or anyone." He watched her from the corner of his eye.

Her nervous giggle fooled no one. "Are we talking about someone in particular?"

He straightened to a sitting position. "Nora…you know why I came."

She gulped while her mouth went dry. "Three or four months does sound long for a vacation."

"To tell you the truth, this was a spur-of-the-moment decision. I missed you something fierce after you left. Then things Sally said made me curious about what's so all-fired great about Missouri." He watched as two mallards approached the water. Beating their wings furiously, they landed with a noisy splash. "But I'm not here to play games or beat around the bush. If you're already promised to Elam Detweiler and intend to marry him, just say the word. I'll stay long enough for Jonas to replace me, do a little sightseeing, and buy my train ticket home. I'll be happy for the change of scenery…and for one last chance with you."

Nora ran her tongue over dry lips. "As I explained in my letter, Elam and I are courting, but I've made no promises. I still like him, but certain things haven't changed from how they were in Harmony." Uneasiness and shame swept over her. Why was she gossiping about someone she professed to love?

In slow-motion, Lewis lifted her chin and turned her face, studying her while she held her breath. "Hearing that makes me happier than my new job, a place to live, and good meals all summer. I'm asking only that you court me as well. Give me the same chance you're giving Detweiler. By midsummer you will have made up your mind. If you choose him, I'll buy you a wedding gift and catch the next bus back to St. Louis."

"I don't see why not, since I'm undecided about my future." Nora smiled tentatively, waiting for him to kiss her or draw her into his arms. After all, they were alone and that's what Elam would have done.

Instead, he jumped off the dock into the shallow water. "Fair enough. We'd better start back. I don't want to oversleep on my first day of work." Lewis offered both his hands.

"No, I'm not ready for bed. I want to stay for a while. You go ahead."

He hesitated for a moment. Then he strode up the bank and didn't glance back.

Nora sat until almost dark, but lucid thoughts or wise intuition refused to come. She felt more confused than ever. Lewis Miller was like a cool drink of water on a dusty afternoon. In so many ways he was the better man of the two. So why couldn't she forget about Elam Detweiler once and for all?

❧

Jonas awoke with a jolt. His troubling dream lingered for several moments until he shook away its last residue. He'd dreamed two stray dogs were fighting in his yard. Every time he tried to break them up, one or the other bit his hand. It didn't take a psychiatrist to figure out what had triggered the nightmare. He rose as quietly as possible to not wake Emily, slipped on his robe, and padded downstairs. He might as well start the day because he would get no more rest.

Downstairs, Lewis sat at the kitchen table with his head bowed. Whether the man was deep in thought or in prayer, the aroma of coffee was a welcome greeting. "You're up early for someone who just finished a cross-country trip."

Lewis's head snapped up. "Too much on my mind to sleep. At the store we serve complimentary coffee to our customers, so I often brew a pot throughout the day. I hope you don't mind that I made myself at home in your kitchen."

"Don't mind at all. We give it away free at the lumberyard too.

If the secretary doesn't notice the empty carafe, I'll expect you to come to the rescue."

Lewis poured two mugs and handed Jonas one. "No problem. I'm anxious to learn the ropes. That's why I couldn't sleep more than four hours. Considering all your generosity, Jonas, I want to earn your trust and confidence."

"Today is Friday—our busy day with Amish customers. On Saturdays we're packed with *Englischers*. There's no other hardware store around for miles. Robert, who you'll meet this morning, will train you. He has complained about needing help for a long time. Thursday is his normal day off. I'm hoping you'll catch on by then and will be able to manage alone. For now, your day off will be Wednesday—the same as mine—since we're riding together. We're closed on Sundays."

Lewis poured milk and sugar into his mug. "Our co-op sells hardware, hand tools, and sheet metal, including roofing materials. I learned how to estimate quantities and costs for homes and commercial buildings. And I'm not shy about asking questions for anything I don't know."

Jonas arched an eyebrow. "In that case we should get along fine. I assumed the Harmony General Store only sold candy, crafts, and sewing supplies, not construction materials." He carried a pan of blueberry muffins to the table. "On days my *fraa* works at the shop, she leaves baked goods for breakfast. On Mondays through Wednesdays, she'll cook us a hot meal of bacon and eggs."

Lewis's color heightened. "Bread and butter would be enough for me. I don't want your wife fussing over me."

"Whatever I eat, you'll eat. Emily only fusses when and if she chooses. And if she chooses, there's no stopping her, so don't worry about it."

The younger man nodded, ate three muffins, and set his plate in the sink. "I'll hitch up the buggy and wait for you outside." He grabbed his hat and coat.

Jonas packed the sandwiches and fresh-baked cookies Emily made last night into a soft-sided cooler and followed him out the door. He appreciated a man with initiative—someone who didn't wait for every sit-down-or-stand-up command. So far, Emily's idea to hire him at the lumberyard looked better and better. On their way there, Lewis didn't fill up every minute with useless chatter. He asked some questions about local customs and traditions, listened carefully to the answers, and then watched the passing scenery.

Even though Lewis was as subtle as a mule in the kitchen regarding Nora, Jonas respected that aspect too. When he'd been courting Emily, he'd had to hold off other suitors with a pitchfork until she agreed to marry him. But as much as Lewis impressed him over the likes of Sally Detweiler's brother-in-law, Jonas decided not to form an opinion of the superior beau for Nora. He felt young people should sort out romantic concerns without interference. Once he arrived at the lumberyard, however, that conviction became impossible to maintain within fifteen minutes.

Jonas introduced Lewis to Robert and left the two together for training. When he entered his office to catch up on paperwork, his foreman was waiting inside with a stack of inventory reports and a sour expression.

"What's the matter," Jonas asked. "Nothing biting on last night's fishing trip with your son-in-law?"

"I caught two smallmouth bass right at sunset. My wife plans to fry them up for tonight's supper," Ken said as he leaned against Jonas's oak desk. "The fishing was fine. My irritation began in the yard this morning. I came in early to make sure Detweiler was here."

Jonas lowered himself into his swivel chair and leaned back. "Was he late again?"

"Nope. He was right on time, but I heard him bad-mouth the new guy while unloading a semi." Ken sighed with exasperation. "He told the Amish men that Lewis comes from an odd district where they marry their first cousins, aren't allowed to talk to *Eng-lischers*, and the bishop arranges the dates for courting couples."

Jonas righted his chair. "None of that is true. My wife's sister lives in Miller's town—she's friends with her English neighbors, and the bishop does *not* tell them who to marry. Besides, every Amish *Ordnung* forbids marriage between cousins."

"I figured as much but I wasn't sure. I simply told him 'more work and less chatter.' Everyone immediately became very industrious."

"Do you want me to speak to him?"

"Let's wait while I keep a keen eye on things. I just wanted you to know that for an Amish guy, Detweiler has some rather anti-Amish opinions." Ken dropped the pile of finished orders into the basket and headed back to the yard.

For the rest of the morning, Jonas tried to concentrate on his ledgers while wondering if this had been Emily's plan all along. First she'd talked him into hiring Detweiler. Then she convinced him to take on Miller and invited him into their home. She had to know both men were interested in the same woman—Nora King.

*What could possibly go wrong with that idea?*

While Ken kept an eye on Detweiler, Jonas watched Lewis. The man worked hard, learned quickly, and interacted with customers with friendly attentiveness. He didn't follow them around pressuring their decision. Instead, he waited patiently to answer questions or write up an order. Lewis possessed an easy rapport with *Englischers*, which most Amish men lacked. Jonas could only hope that Ken would straighten out misconceptions among the employees, while Jonas would introduce him to the rest of the district. Being the deacon had some advantages. If he took Miller under his wing, few would believe tall tales spread around by a fence-sitter.

That evening, when Jonas stopped at the mouth of the drive,

he felt tired down to his toes. "Why don't you take the buggy to the barn," he said to Lewis. "I'll get out here for the mail and walk the rest of the way."

"See you in the house." With a wave, Lewis drove straight for the barn.

Jonas loved scanning through the stack first and would read any business correspondence on the porch. Any bad news sounded less loathsome as he rocked in his favorite chair. A small white envelope addressed in Solomon Trask's spidery handwriting caught his attention...and ruined his Friday night good mood.

"Meet me at the bishop's house Sunday afternoon," he read aloud. "Please bring Emily. Ephraim needs to know about the sorrowful outcome of the extinct Centralia Amish. The wages of sin is death and eternal damnation." Sol's warning loomed large on the paper. "We must take immediate steps to avoid such a fate for Paradise."

Jonas trudged up the steps into the house, relieved to see Emily's sweater and bonnet on the peg. The women were home from the bakery. "Emily?" he called.

She entered the kitchen from the back porch. "Why all the commotion, *ehemann*? Can't a hardworking gal enjoy a glass of lemonade before she starts supper?" Emily reached up to plant a kiss on his cheek.

"Of course, but I wanted to ask you something while we were alone." He lowered his voice so as not to be heard by their houseguests. "Solomon wants you and me to come to the bishop's this Sunday—"

"There's nothing out of the ordinary about that," she interrupted. "We usually visit *somebody* on a non-preaching Sunday."

He shook his head. "Sol wants to talk about the Centralia Amish. And he used the word 'extinct' in his note. How do you suppose he came up with that term?" Jonas stared at her without blinking.

Emily emitted a nervous laugh. "Goodness, Jonas, you know how women love to chitchat at work. I might have mentioned the interesting tidbit of local history I read."

"*Might have?*" He didn't like it when Emily stretched the truth.

She flushed and crossed her arms. "Okay, I did. I talked about the Centralia folk in front of Violet. She probably told her *daed* that night at supper. I didn't know it was a secret."

"*Ach,* it's not a secret, Em, but I don't want to rile Sol up over something that happened a hundred years ago." Jonas filled a glass from the pitcher of water. "We'll see what the bishop has to say, but be prepared to answer his questions."

"I almost memorized everything in that article. Trust me to be accurate." Emily pulled a pan of meat loaf from the refrigerator.

"Accurate, *jah,* but don't add kindling to Sol's smoldering fire." He drank the water in three long gulps.

Emily lit the oven before turning to face him, her brow furrowed with worry. "Sol isn't exaggerating about district members bending the *Ordnung.* I've seen it myself in Grain of Life… young women carrying cell phones who have no legitimate need for them."

Jonas set down the glass. "What else?"

She fidgeted with her apron ties. "Some young men meet on Saturday nights to watch the Cardinal game on television."

His jaw dropped open. "Watch it where?"

"At the home of an English neighbor." Emily began chopping tomatoes and carrots with excessive zeal. "Don't ask me for names, because I don't know all of them, but we have problems in this community you don't want to acknowledge."

Jonas heard footsteps in the hallway and knew Nora approached to help with dinner. "Then you'll have every opportunity to speak your mind on Sunday," he said quietly, reaching for his hat. He left the kitchen to make sure Lewis had found everything necessary to groom the horse.

And because he was close to arguing with his *fraa*—something he refused to do in front of other people.

# TEN

*Shall never lose its power*

Solomon dressed carefully that Sunday. Although there would be no regular church service, he held morning devotions in the front room for his wife, daughter, married children, and their families. After a simple meal of cold food prepared yesterday, the rest of the Trask clan returned home to await the arrival of guests or loaded into buggies to visit nearby friends and neighbors. The off-Sunday was a day of rest, prayer, and socializing.

But it would be no day of leisure for the district's two ministers and the deacon. Everyone would meet at Bishop Ephraim's house. The situation had become too urgent to wait even another day. Learning that Nora wouldn't attend, Violet opted to stay home reading paperbacks from the Columbia library. The elder Trasks bid their daughter goodbye and drove the three miles in silence.

"Sol, Rosanna," greeted Ephraim. "Come in. Tea and zucchini bread await you on the back porch, along with my *fraa*. She's having trouble walking since her latest flare-up of arthritis."

"There's no need for Josephine to get up. We stand on no ceremony in Paradise." Solomon and Rosanna followed the bishop through the kitchen and out the back door. Sol blinked upon spotting Jonas and Emily perched on the glider. The deacon and his *fraa* never arrived anywhere twenty minutes early. The other minister was already present too. "Where is Margaret today?" asked Sol.

Peter grinned. "Home with a cold. She didn't want to spread her germs."

The other minister was younger than Solomon by twenty years. District members never considered age a factor when nominating men to draw lots to serve as preachers. Sound judgment, knowledgeable about Scripture, and being temperate in both mood and actions rated much higher. "Tell Margaret we wish her a quick recovery." Sol and Rosanna settled onto straight-backed chairs.

While Josephine filled glasses with room temperature tea, Ephraim cleared his throat. "Everyone is here. Solomon called this meeting of the ministerial brethren for an urgent matter." As his gaze drifted over the assemblage, he smiled warmly. "And just when I thought life was returning to normal. I give the floor to Brother Solomon."

His jest produced a few chuckles, while Sol straightened in his chair. "Emily brought something to my attention," he said, nodding at the deacon's wife. "A community of Old Order moved to this area many years back. They wished to begin new lives in Audrain County, just south of us. Unfortunately, they didn't leave Iowa solely for better farmland. They came to rewrite their former *Ordnung* to conform to their liberal and lax standards. If they didn't like a particular rule, they changed it or ignored it altogether." Sol paused, noticing he held the bishop's attention. "God didn't look kindly on these brazen people who allowed selfish desires to supplant His Word in their lives." Jonas scraped his heels on the floor, but Sol ignored it. "God sent heavy rains to destroy their crops, while other years He provided no rain whatsoever. The scorching sun parched the fields and turned their grain to dust. They suffered His wrath for almost two decades until the entire community had either died off or moved away…every man, woman, and child. It would be years before Plain folk ventured back to the inhospitable land of Missouri." He grasped the lapels of his coat.

An ashen-faced Ephraim looked at Emily. "Do you have anything to add?"

She folded her hands in her lap. "It's how Sol described. I read about the Centralia Amish in a history book on Audrain, Randolph, and Boone Counties at the Columbia library. Either drought or horrific flooding, year after year."

Jonas placed his hand atop his wife's as he addressed the bishop. "This happened more than a century ago, Ephraim. We have no further information about this district other than a couple of paragraphs of secondhand accounts—"

Solomon snorted. "It makes no difference whether this happened a hundred years ago or a thousand. They disobeyed God and the Amish *Ordnung* and were punished for their sins."

"Do you know which particular rules they found so objectionable?" Ephraim looked from Solomon to Emily.

"I do not," said Sol.

Emily shook her head mutely.

Ephraim ran long, slender fingers through his snow-white beard. "A tragic tale, to be sure." He picked up his glass of tea and drank deeply.

"A *cautionary* tale," corrected Sol. "I believe our district is headed down the same path that leads to destruction."

"But if we—" interjected Jonas.

Solomon held up a hand. "Allow me to finish, Deacon. Then you may have your say." He turned to the bishop. "I have spoken to you before about members allowing *kinner* to be photographed by tourists. And permitting youth to mingle and converse with English teenagers of the opposite sex without adult supervision." He sucked air into his lungs. "I have witnessed people working on the Sabbath to produce overpriced goods to sell to the English. They have dishonored the Lord's Day."

"But you've spoken with these families, is it not so?" asked Ephraim.

"I have, but their determination to earn money is great. They may not have heeded my warning."

Peter spoke for the first time. "I know one of these families. For the Huffmans, the cost of kidney dialysis is also great. Because John has no insurance, the hospital won't continue to treat him without substantial payments toward his medical bill. A man with faulty kidneys will surely die without the regular cleansing of blood."

"Better a man dies a humble and devout death than to live long and then spend eternity in the lake of fire." Sol clenched his fists and set his jaw in a hard line. He wouldn't back down with so much at stake.

The bishop bowed his head for a long moment, thinking or perhaps praying. "I will visit the Huffmans tomorrow. We'll hold fund-raisers and take up a collection. As a district we must ensure John receives necessary medical treatments without placing his eternal soul in jeopardy."

Josephine smiled. "Let's have the zucchini bread. I have baked some with and without nuts."

Sol raised his arm like Moses' staff. "There's more to this. Emily and my daughter have noticed many young women carrying cell phones in their purses. They call each other without a legitimate need for these phones. Gossip does not constitute an emergency."

Ephraim appeared perplexed. "Where do they charge up these phones?"

"I really have no idea. Perhaps with electricity from propane generators in their fathers' businesses, or maybe at the home of an English friend." He spat out the words like a mouthful of wormy apple. "There is too much friendliness with the English. Our young men have taken up watching sports on a neighbor's television. Probably relaxing in recliners with their feet up, munching popcorn, and rooting for their favorite team."

Rosanna touched Solomon's sleeve but he ignored it. "From our association, the English don't adopt our simpler ways. Instead, we mimic their competitiveness and materialistic values, where God is no longer first in our lives. Look around, Ephraim. If you don't take decisive action, we'll soon see power saws, boom boxes, and Cardinal ball caps at the next barn raising."

The bishop paled, as did his wife. "Apparently, my poor health has prevented me from serving diligently. I will remove the blinders from my eyes and observe for myself if we are, indeed, falling away. And I shall speak to the congregation this Sunday about cell phones and television shows and whatever other bad habits we've acquired lately. God's Word is law. I will remind our district of the Ten Commandments and what will be the fate of those who flagrantly disobey." Ephraim placed a palm on the worn Bible in his lap.

Solomon rose to his feet, bowed to the bishop, and nodded at the other brethren. He knew this old-fashioned, formal gesture was unnecessary and annoyed the two younger men, but he believed the old ways were best—when the Amish had separated themselves from the world, whether from other fellow Christians or godless heathens. Only with strict adherence to their *Ordnung* without exception would they ever find the true paradise for which their town had been named.

"Where are you going?" asked Josephine. "You and Rosanna haven't had refreshments yet.

"*Danki*, but we must be on our way. I don't like leaving Violet alone for long periods of time." Solomon took his *fraa's* arm and helped her to her feet. With a frown Rosanna dutifully followed him off the porch toward their buggy, knowing full well Violet could manage just fine by herself.

&#8494;&#8272;

When a man declares his intentions as Lewis had, a girl naturally would think he would take the opportunity to spend time with her. But Nora hadn't seen hide nor hair of him all day. With Saturdays busy at lumberyards and bakeries, they both had to work yesterday. Last night during dinner, Lewis talked about his first two days on the job, proud of what he'd mastered while laughing over what would take more time to learn. He wasn't shy with Emily or Jonas, and he certainly ate his fair share of fried chicken, baked beans, and sliced tomatoes, and yet he had said little to her other than "Please pass the cornbread." Nora had lingered in the kitchen after doing the dishes, hoping for an evening buggy ride or a walk to the tall pines. After sweeping the floor twice and wiping down the countertops three times, she finally gave up and went to her room.

Lewis had disappeared after supper and didn't return with Jonas after evening chores. Even after Nora's late night bath, there was no sign of him. *Did he climb the oak tree outside his bedroom and crawl in through the window?* Why would a man interested in courting avoid her like this?

Today they had the perfect chance to get reacquainted when Jonas and Emily left to visit the bishop after devotions. Because their trip was for district business, not socialization, neither houseguest had been invited to tag along. When Nora heard the Gingerichs would be gone all afternoon, a surge of anticipation raced up her spine.

That anticipation had been for naught.

After wolfing down a bowl of cold cereal, Lewis headed for the barn, even though Jonas had already tended to the horses. Considering it was the Sabbath, Nora had little to do but wait for her beau to return. A few hours later, she heard the buggy clatter down the driveway just as she set a cold lunch on the table. *Where on earth is the man headed? He's only been on the job two days and has gone to no social events. Who would he know in Paradise?*

Nora looked at the sandwiches, marinated vegetables, and homemade applesauce with little appetite. She had no taste for the lemon meringue pie she brought home, either. Wherever Lewis went, she hadn't been asked to accompany him. *Is courting always this confusing? What was the big declaration down by the pond all about?* Nora kept watch at the window and tried to read the inspirational romance Emily gave her. But, unfortunately, the Gingerichs returned from the bishop's before Lewis and neither seemed inclined to talk when they walked through the door. Emily and Jonas ate a sandwich and left the room, never inquiring about the missing buggy.

The elusive Lewis returned shortly before dark. While he took care of the horse, Nora nursed another cup of tea. By the time he stepped into the kitchen, she'd read the same page for the third time.

"I didn't expect you to still be up," he said. "It's late."

"I was curious as to where you went today. Did you already receive an invitation to someone's house?"

He laughed with good humor. "*Nein*, I'm afraid I haven't made any new friends in the district yet." Lewis hung up his coat and hat next to hers. "I borrowed Emily's buggy and drove around to familiarize myself. So far I'd seen only Grain of Life and Gingerich Lumber." He leaned his tall frame against the counter.

"Why not sit down and tell me what fascinating sites you discovered?" Nora twiddled with a *kapp* ribbon.

"I found two carriage shops, a sorghum mill, and two cabinet makers. I also found the town of Clark, whose heyday appears to have passed. Rather sad, no? Perhaps the *Englischers* didn't support the local businesses. Just about every one of them is shuttered and abandoned. The town seems ready to blow away with the next strong gust of wind."

"I'll have to take your word for it as I haven't been there yet." Her trembling fingers gripped her mug as though strong gusts buffeted the kitchen. "What else did you see?"

A grin filled his face. "I discovered an honest-to-goodness restaurant in the town of Sturgeon—rather like the deli you were fond of in Harmony."

"Is that right?" Nora opted for a tone of nonchalance, remembering she'd never gone to that diner with Lewis, only with her sister. "Did you get something to eat?"

"No, not today, but I asked if they would be open on Tuesday. Not only will they be open, but on Tuesdays they offer a dinner special of stuffed peppers and mashed potatoes, along with two additional side dishes." He wiggled his eyebrows. "And I must add they have an impressive list to pick from."

"Sounds delightful." She smiled at his enthusiasm for food.

Lamplight shone in his eyes, deepening them to a rich shade of sapphire. "They also had a large assortment of pies in their spinner rack, in case you're curious about the talents of Sturgeon bakers."

With her napkin, Nora dabbed a bead of perspiration from her lip. "Grain of Life isn't worried about competition, but I will mention your fondness for stuffed peppers to Emily. She grows row after row of green, red, and Hungarian hot peppers in her garden. That restaurant must have imported theirs from Florida. It's still too early for ours." She sniffed.

Lewis closed the distance between them, stopping across from where she sat. He leaned forward and placed his palms flat on the table. "I bring this up, Miss King, not only to explain my absence, but in preparation to ask you out...on a real date, as the English call them. Would you go to dinner with me on Tuesday evening?"

A strange paralysis seized Nora. For several seconds, she could do nothing more than stare at him. "In Sturgeon?" she asked ridiculously.

He smiled at her. "That's where the Crossroads Restaurant is located. Because you don't work either Tuesday or Wednesday, and Wednesday is my day off from the lumberyard, neither of us will have to get up before dawn the next day."

"That's what you were doing? Planning an outing for us?" she asked in a tiny voice. Elam had never invited her anywhere unless it involved one of his schemes.

"Well...of course. Now what do you say, Nora, yea or nay? Tomorrow *is* a work day, so I need to hit the sack."

"Yea, or I mean *jah*—yes, in English." She pushed herself to her feet.

"Glad to hear it. See you tomorrow at supper. *Gut nacht.*" Lewis jogged up the stairs to his room.

After Nora heard his door close, she floated on air up to hers. He had asked her out. He was serious about courting her after all!

❧

It was all Nora could do to get through Monday's laundry and then pie-baking on Tuesday. When Lewis and Jonas drove into the yard after work that afternoon, she was dressed in her prettiest sage-colored dress and pacing the floor.

"What are you so tense about?" asked Emily, entering the kitchen to start supper. "You knew him back in Maine. I thought things hadn't worked out."

"It was Harmony that didn't agree with me, not Lewis. Everything is different now that he's here in Missouri."

Emily rolled her eyes, pulling out a head of cabbage. "Okay, but stop pacing the floor. You look ready to pounce the moment he walks through the door. Why not wait on the front porch? He'll need to shower before you leave."

Nora exhaled with relief. "Good idea. I don't want to become all sweaty while you boil cabbage and noodles." She hurried down the hall before the men reached the house.

Twenty minutes later, she and Lewis were driving down the road on a perfect early June evening. A light breeze carried the scent of freshly cut hay—sweet perfume to the hearts of farmers—and cooled her overheated face. Lewis kept up the majority of conversation by pointing out three schoolhouses, a cabinet shop, a metal supplier, and a cemetery he'd found two nights ago.

Nora relaxed—something she seldom did around Elam. Lewis put her at ease, even if he didn't possess Elam's magnetic appeal. However, inside Crossroads Restaurant, situated close to the main route to Columbia, she found appeal of a different sort. Several pairs of eyes turned in their direction when they entered the diner. And each of those faces wore a bright smile.

"Good evening." Picking up two menus, the hostess nodded at Lewis. "We're all ready for you, sir."

Nora gasped when the woman led them to a table set with a white tablecloth, linen napkins, bone china plates, and crystal goblets. Two tall tapers burned from a gleaming silver sconce. She glanced around the diner. Everyone else was eating supper with ordinary plates, paper napkins, and plastic cups without the benefit of a tablecloth. No candles illuminated any other meal. "Why are we the only people getting the fancy treatment?" she asked once the hostess left.

Lewis pulled out her chair. "I suppose because no one else is on a first date." After she was seated, he sat down in his own chair and draped the cloth napkin across his lap.

"How much extra will this extravagance cost?" she hissed under her breath. "Did you forget we're Amish?"

He shrugged while scanning the menu. "Nothing beyond the price of our meals. These nice people were tickled to make the evening special for us. Even Amish people are allowed to be romantic during courting." Lewis leaned across his dinner plate. "My *daed* bought my *mamm* a potted orchid while they were courting. She had admired one at a garden shop. Can you imagine an orchid in Maine? It didn't last a month, but my mother cherished it until it curled up and died." Lewis set down the menu. "I took the liberty of preordering the stuffed peppers. After all, they are on special." His left dimple appeared. "But you may select your own side dishes."

Nora scanned the daily special sheet, conscious of the attention they had attracted. "I'll take green beans and the cinnamon baked apples." When she set her menu on the edge of the table, he covered her hand with his.

"Relax, Nora. Worry about nothing but enjoying supper in Sturgeon, Missouri. Life is short—over with in the blink of an eye. Let's make the most of tonight."

"Okay, I'll do my best."

And so she did. They ate delicious food on elegant china and chatted about their trips across America. They smiled and laughed and enjoyed each other's company. Not once did he behave embarrassingly bold toward her. Not once did she fear for their reputations in her newfound community.

Along with the check, their waitress presented them with a giant cupcake. "For your dessert, compliments of the owner," she said. Someone had written "good luck" with white icing across the rounded top.

That night, in the charming Sturgeon diner, home to local *Englischers* and Amish folk alike, Nora's world shifted on its axis.

Nothing was different in her life and yet, somehow *everything* had changed.

۶۲

**Wednesday**

The hired van carrying Violet and Rosanna picked Emily up promptly at seven thirty. She had decided to accompany the Trasks to Columbia for the day while Nora stayed home to bake cookies for Grain of Life. While Violet received her physical therapy on her legs, Emily planned to spend the day at the library. She had a lot of research to do if this thorny issue between Jonas and Solomon was ever to be settled.

Jonas had barely spoken to her on the ride home from Ephraim's last Sunday, apparently peeved she'd revealed district cell phone use and television viewing. But wouldn't withholding the information be the same as lying? Honestly, she didn't know if she'd done the right thing or not. *Take the log from your own eye before worrying about the speck in your neighbor's. Isn't that what Jesus had taught us?* And Emily's life was hardly sin-free.

When the van dropped her off, Emily found peace and quiet for a few hours in the reading room. As fond of Violet as she was, sometimes the girl's chatter and bizarre sense of humor got on her nerves. Nora adored Violet's quick wit, but lately Emily found her quips disrespectful and almost rude. *There I go again—judging another person instead of leaving that up to someone more qualified.* As Emily entered the air-conditioned, tranquil world of books, periodicals, and computer stations, she pledged to immerse herself in history and not allow a single judgmental thought intrude.

However, the second regional book set aside for her by the librarian turned out to be anything but a pleasant diversion. Emily propped her reading glasses on her nose and pored over the history of Boone County. Anxiety and a dull sense of foreboding grew with each passing minute. In Centralia in 1982, twenty-eight homes and businesses burst into flames when a backhoe hit a natural gas line regulator. According to the account, hot water heaters and furnaces spit flames like blowtorches. The mayor of Centralia declared a state of emergency. One woman cooking lunch had been warned by her son and they escaped the house minutes before the furnace blew up. "It was the hottest fire I ever saw," she declared. Pilot lights on stoves shot flames into the air. Smoke billowed over the community for hours. "First one house blew up and after that it was bang, bang, bang in a chain reaction," stated the chief of the volunteer fire department. A man interviewed said one of his sons lost his house while the other's insurance business was leveled. "It seemed fire was everywhere you went." One hundred twenty-five firefighters were called in from surrounding towns to battle the inferno. The Red Cross set up shelters for the newly homeless in two churches, surprisingly unscathed.

Emily slipped her marker in place and closed the book. Five people had been injured, including a woman who had suffered a heart attack, but miraculously no one lost their life. Twenty-eight homes had either exploded or burst in flames, and not one person died? Had God meant this to be some sort of warning?

She turned next to a story of epic brutality during the final year of the Civil War. A Missourian named William T. Anderson joined a group of guerrilla warriors led by William Quantrill. Although Southern sympathizers, these cavalry raiders operated beyond the sanction of the Confederate Army and became famous for terrible acts against their enemies. They tortured and mutilated prisoners, showing no mercy to those who sided with the Northern cause. In 1864, Anderson, nicknamed Bloody Bill, led his gang of bushwhackers into Centralia, looting and terrifying the residents. During the raid, they blocked the tracks of the Northern Missouri

Railroad and forced a train to stop. The group robbed the civilian passengers and killed twenty-two Union soldiers, many of whom had surrendered. Some of the executed soldiers had been scalped.

Emily pressed a hand to her chest. Again, tragedy had descended on the town of Centralia. She skimmed the next few paragraphs. After Anderson had been shot by militiamen, soldiers found a silken cord that contained fifty-three knots, presumably the number of men he killed. Human scalps were discovered hanging from the bridle of his horse. Emily's skin began to crawl when she read of the horrific treatment of Anderson's body after his death. She slammed the book shut.

Both sides had been guilty of godless acts of cruelty.

Emily walked to the women's room and splashed cool water on her face, trying to rid herself of the disturbing images triggered by the account. What had happened to Bill Anderson as a child or young man to harden his heart and blacken his soul? Refusing to read anymore war stories, Emily leafed ahead to the third and final bookmark.

The last article notated by the librarian involved other Plain settlements. The Centralia community in Audrain County hadn't been the only one to disappear in Missouri, not by a longshot. A Hickory County Amish settlement went extinct in 1882 after continuous crop failures, financial losses during the Civil War, lack of congregational growth, and rough neighbors. During the war, both Union and Confederate troops preyed upon the Amish by confiscating their grain and cattle. And at least one case of pies had been purchased with counterfeit money.

*Pies? With everything a baker must worry about, now she must wonder whether or not the currency handed over the counter was real?*

After a few minutes, a more disturbing thought took root and began to fester. *Lack of congregational growth*…did that mean few or no babies had been born to these people? The Amish usually had large families. What could have caused a low birthrate other than God's displeasure?

Emily stacked the books and returned them to the front desk. She would read no more today. Was this the reason she and Jonas had no *kinner*—because God's wrath prevented her from conceiving? She hurried outside into the blinding sunshine. After the air-conditioned building, the heat struck her like a slap to the face. She shielded her eyes against the glare and spotted a bench across the street, a place to wait until Violet and Rosanna returned for her. She had much to mull over and even more to pray about if she were ever to atone for her past transgressions.

# ELEVEN

*Till all the ransomed church of God*

When Solomon sat up in bed the following Monday morning, he gasped for air as needle-sharp pain rendered him breathless. Every once in a while if he slept in the wrong position, his lower back spasmed in protest. He should see the chiropractor in Middlegrove again, but he hated to take time away from his district or spend the money—more so the latter than the former. The less cash he wasted on himself, the more he had for Violet's treatments. What if her doctor suggested additional surgery on her legs? Even if they arranged a payment plan, surgeons expected half the amount up front. Thus, he reached for the aspirin and glass of water from his bedside table. He would take three tablets today instead of his usual two and pray for relief.

Rosanna's side of the bed was empty. His dear *fraa* must be already up and preparing breakfast. Even though all his children had married and moved out except Violet, washday still proved long and tedious. Violet would press clothes at her knee-height

169

ironing board, but washing and hanging outdoors remained Rosanna's chore.

One thought strengthened Sol as he staggered across the room to dress. The bishop had followed through with the decision reached at their meeting last week. During yesterday's preaching service, in a clear and booming voice, Ephraim enumerated the Ten Commandments delivered to Moses on Mount Sinai. He stated the laws as written in Scripture and repeated them in common, everyday *Deutsch* to make sure no one misunderstood. Then he read the entire wording of the second Commandment about graven images. "The law includes 'any likeness of anything in heaven above, or that is in the earth beneath,'" explained the bishop. "No one should photograph you or your *kinner*." He gazed over his devout congregation before elaborating on number four: "'Six days shalt thou labor and do all thy work.' If God could create heaven and earth in six days, surely we can get *our* work done in the same amount of time."

Solomon had been especially pleased when Ephraim cautioned against becoming too worldly. "Phones are to be used to conduct business or in case of an emergency. Period. There should be no idle chatter on telephones. Such nonsense can wait until the next social event. And television viewing or radio listening is *verboten* by those baptized into this church."

You could have heard a pin drop. Many nodded their heads in agreement, while a few looked disappointed. "Better disappointment now than eternal suffering later on," Sol muttered on his way downstairs. He winced with each step.

"*Ach*, Solomon. Is your back bad?" asked Rosanna, frying sausages at the stove.

"My back is bad, *jah*. But it will improve after the first bite of your breakfast." He sat down clumsily, trying to hide his misery. "Eggs today?"

"*Nein*." She focused on the spattering grease as she removed links with her tongs. "Sausage and French toast."

"Where did you find a Frenchman or woman in Paradise so early on a Monday?" Sol pressed his back against the chair. Slouching only aggravated his pain.

Rosanna carried the platter of meat and two plates of crusty, bright yellow toast to the table. "Who would have guessed such a serious man would have a sense of humor?" She kissed the top of his bald spot before sitting across from him.

After they bowed their heads in prayer, he said, "I picked up the trait late in life from my *dochder*. Speaking of whom, where is our youngest?" Sol spiked a sausage with his fork.

"In the living room. I believe she's unhappy about something, but I don't know what." Rosanna cut her toast into small bites.

The minister briefly considered his options. "Violet Trask, stop your nonsense and come to breakfast!" His words echoed down the hallway. Sol seldom raised his voice in such a fashion, but considering his back, he wasn't about to search for the girl. And his *fraa* needed to eat her meal in peace.

Within a minute his daughter rolled into the kitchen up to her usual place. "I told *mamm* I wasn't hungry."

"Then you can drink a cup of coffee and watch us eat."

Violet pushed up and transferred herself into a kitchen chair. She reached for the coffee pot to fill her mug as the scent of breakfast proved irresistible. "Please pass the toast and sausage," she said to her *mamm*. "I will eat something after all."

"What are you sulking about?" Sol asked. "Out with it, and don't say 'Nothing.'"

Violet pulled off her prayer *kapp* to scratch her head. Several auburn curls sprang loose. "People were talking yesterday after church. They were wondering how Bishop Ephraim heard about the cell phones and watching ball games on TV." She tugged her head covering back on, leaving several copper tendrils askew.

Sol frowned. "What difference does it make if I'm the one who informed the bishop? Our *Ordnung* must be upheld."

Violet lowered her fork to her plate. "It makes a huge difference to me. People will figure out that either Emily or I told you what we heard or saw at the bakery. What if Amish folks stop coming to Grain of Life?" Her forehead creased with worry lines.

"What if they do? You'll still have local *Englischers* and those ever-increasing tourists." Sol stabbed another link of sausage from the plate. "Then perhaps business at your *aenti's* bakery will improve."

Violet swallowed down a mouthful of French toast as though it were dry instead of moist and tender. "*Daed,* I love it when Plain folk stop in. Some of them stay to talk with me. I enjoy having friends again like I had in school."

Rosanna slapped another piece of toast onto Violet's plate "Everyone likes you, *dochder.* People always mention you have a good sense of humor."

Violet peered up, her brown eyes round and moist. "That's just what they say to you, *mamm*. Only recently have I felt that people actually like me. Nora helped me break from my shell, as she calls it." She glared at her plate. "I don't want anything to hurt the progress I've made."

Sol drank half his cup of coffee. "Stop being foolish. Your imagination is running away with you. Besides, a preacher's job is to minister to his flock. You don't see me telling you how to make piecrust, do you?" He dabbed his mouth with his napkin.

Violet reached for his arm, clutching the sleeve of his coat. "Please, Papa. A couple of friends who linger to visit are single men my age. They see me as a woman capable of earning a living by cooking and baking, besides being friendly and talkative and humorous." She shot Rosanna a wry smile. "I feel normal for the first time since I fell from the barn loft. I might still have a chance to court and marry and have my own children someday. I hope they don't stop visiting our bakery just because they also enjoy an occasional baseball game."

Solomon opened his mouth but shut it just as quickly. He was speechless. Never had his daughter asked for anything like this. Coconut cream pies and packs of wintergreen gum had been the extent of her desires.

*How could he grant such a request with the position he held?*

*How could he not?*

"I don't know how to answer you, *dochder*. I must think and pray for guidance." He awkwardly patted her head as though she were still eight years old.

One tear ran down her freckled cheek as Violet nodded.

"Mercy me!" exclaimed Rosanna. "We have more urgent problems than business at the bakery right now."

Sol turned his attention to his *fraa* at the back window. "What is it?" A chill swept over him as the color drained from Rosanna's face. She clutched her throat as though gagging on a chicken bone. Despite his back spasms, he hurried to the window.

"What are those, Solomon? Are they grasshoppers?" she asked. They stared at the wheat crop, being inundated by a swarm of insects.

"Locusts, I believe." While they watched, the swarm swelled, darkening the sky as though they were experiencing a rare solar eclipse. Sol pushed up the window. They listened to the cacophony crescendo. Locusts alighted on his son's wheat, remaining long enough to devour the head of grain before moving on. The swarm hovered over the field like a summer thunder cloud, advancing slowly but methodically along.

Finally galvanized to action, Sol and Rosanna ran out the door toward the field. Solomon's two sons had also spotted the vermin and abandoned their chores. Irvin and Mark and their wives, along with Sol and Rosanna, ran up rows of wheat shouting and waving hats in the air. Even Violet beat on a pot with a wooden spoon from the back porch, trying to scare off the insects. In the end, the seven Trasks accomplished little but to drive the swarm

into the next farm's field of oats. Rosanna met Sol at the end of
a row that had been picked clean. Irvin and Mark hiked through
the fields to inspect the damage, still waving their hats at lingering grasshoppers.

Suddenly, the air filled with an even louder racket as an enormous black cloud of birds arrived. The giant flock of crows
descended upon his field, landing on crops with a great fluttering of wings.

"It is the wrath of the Lord!" declared Sol. "Whatever grain the
locusts miss will be consumed by the crows."

"Look, *ehemann*." Rosanna pointed at the surreal scene unfold-
ing before their eyes. "The birds are eating the bugs, not the wheat.
Have you ever seen anything like this before?" She gazed wide-eyed
as the flock of birds cawed, cackled, and devoured the locusts.

Putting an arm around Rosanna, Solomon pulled her close.
"Not once in all my sixty-five years."

ॐ

Nora loved Fridays at Grain of Life for several reasons. First, she
got to sleep late because the bakery didn't unlock the doors until
one o'clock. They stayed open until seven p.m. to accommodate
local *Englischers* running afternoon errands and those on their way
home from work. Second, Emily, Violet, and Nora usually shared
packed lunches before starting work. A grove of trees behind the
shop provided cool shade for their picnic. They would swap news
or tidbits of gossip they forgot to share the previous day. Emily
always had district updates, while Violet's tales frequently centered
on news from one of her sisters or something she'd read in an English newspaper. Unbeknownst to Solomon, his elder daughter sub-
scribed to the Columbia paper and passed the issues along. Violet
loved stories of any kind, even if she didn't know the people. The

third reason? Friday evening was the usual night for Amish social gatherings. If there was to be a cookout, bonfire, or hayride, someone would stop by the bakery and extend the invitation to Violet and her.

Then maybe, just maybe, Lewis would take them. The past ten days since their romantic dinner in Sturgeon had been a roller coaster of highs and lows. Despite both of them having the next day off, she'd spent hers in a hot kitchen while Lewis helped Jonas's brothers attempt to salvage the wheat field. Usually she saw him only at supper each night with the Gingerichs. During meals Lewis behaved with the upmost reserve and decorum. Occasionally, he referred to her as Miss King, even though she had sat with him in the porch swing three different evenings after supper. She felt like marking notches on the doorjamb. Considering the turtle pace of the courtship, it was a good thing he planned to stay until fall.

The bizarre act by Mother Nature had dashed their plans to go fishing from the dock. When the skies filled first with swarms of locusts and then flocks of crows, everyone in Randolph County canceled their outings. While she and Emily baked on Wednesday, Lewis and Jonas assessed crop damage on the Gingerich family farm. Then they drove around the district, viewing the destruction to the other farmers' oat, rye, barley, and wheat crops.

Who could imagine cute little grasshoppers would eat so much?

And who could have predicted hungry crows would devour enough locusts to prevent a complete loss of the grain harvest?

It was all Violet and Emily wanted to discuss while they ate their sandwiches, chips, and fruit. Of course, Violet's *daed* was fraught with anxiety over the implications. Nora had to admit that only in Bible stories had she ever heard of such catastrophes.

Emily wrung her hands. "I don't know what to think," she moaned. "Jonas tells me not to worry, but when I witness an honest-to-goodness plague, how can I not?"

Nora ate her bologna sandwich stoically. *Didn't Jesus teach us not to be afraid?* Despite crop losses, she doubted anyone in Randolph County would starve due to locusts.

Not that her concerns were any worthier for fretting. Her stress involved being courted by two very different men. During her evening with Lewis, she decided with certainty he was where her heart lay. But what would happen to Elam? He had the notion she'd come to Missouri because of him—which was, in fact, more truth than fiction at the time. And since then she seemed to be his last connection to the Plain world—a slender thread to his former life and birthright. Elam Detweiler, although dressing more English than Amish, hadn't found acceptance within the fancy lifestyle. No one could live for long perched between two worlds, yet that seemed to be where he remained. Without her, would Elam's reclusiveness increase or his drinking escalate? Nora shook off the grim notion as Emily poked her arm.

"Stop daydreaming. It's time to open the shop." Emily rose to her feet and brushed crumbs into the grass. "I don't pay you gals big bucks to lounge around my picnic table."

Violet burst into laughter. "You pay Nora nothing and me very little."

"Save your breath," teased Emily. "Fridays aren't the day to discuss pay raises. I only discuss them on Monday nights between two and four a.m." Emily hovered next to Violet as she struggled on crutches to reach the back door.

Nora carried in and set up the wheelchair. "I don't need a raise. What's there to buy in Paradise anyway?" She switched the window sign to "Open."

"If you come with me to Columbia next month, I'll show you an assortment of candy at the mall to rot every one of your teeth." Violet limped to the chair and lowered herself with an audible sigh of relief.

"That sounds like a wonderful idea," said Nora, switching on the fan.

Because the day was very hot, they would do no baking. Their supply of pies, bread, and cookies would just have to suffice. Throughout the afternoon, the women tended customers, updated accounts, inventoried supplies, and wiped down shelves. At six o'clock, as all three were ready to wilt, the bell above the door jangled. Perched on her stool at the back table, Nora didn't glance up with the routine sound.

"Nora, you'd better come up here," called Violet.

Nora swiveled to see tall, broad-shouldered Elam Detweiler in the doorway. He sported a ball cap turned backwards, a scruffy beard, a T-shirt under another plaid shirt, and snug blue jeans. She hadn't seen him since they exchanged strong words in the Gingerich yard—the day Lewis had been hired.

"Hey there, Nora," he said in his husky, deep voice. Elam directed his smile solely at her, despite the other two women in the room. "Remember me?"

Nora walked to the counter. "Of course. Do *you* remember Violet and Emily?" She angled her head toward her coworkers.

"Good afternoon, ladies. You're both looking lovely as usual." Elam offered a forced smile at the two. "I wondered if I could speak privately with Nora for a moment." He pushed up his hat with one finger.

She shuffled her feet on the polished wooden floor. Since Lewis came to town, she no longer wished to see Elam, but something about his hopeful, solemn face resurrected memories of Harmony when he'd been her only friend in the world. Not knowing what to do, she glanced at Emily.

"Take a walk outdoors," said her boss. "I wouldn't want the Department of Labor showing up for not providing break time." Emily adjusted her reading glasses on her nose.

"All right. Just for a few minutes." Nora slipped off her apron and left it on the counter. When Elam opened the door, she followed him into the blistering summer heat. Although not air-conditioned, the bakery remained livable due to screened windows and battery-powered fans. They walked to the shady trees behind the shop, where she'd eaten lunch a few hours earlier.

"I'm not afraid to admit I've missed you, Nora. I still think about our date in Columbia. Didn't we have fun that night?" Elam cocked his head to one side. "I shouldn't have come to Jonas's all hot under the collar. I don't care whether or not Lewis works at the lumberyard as long as we're together." His soft words drifted on the warm air like a caress…and took Nora by complete surprise.

"But we're not *together,* Elam, and we never have been. I did enjoy myself at the Mexican restaurant—up until you bought us alcoholic drinks and tried to get fresh when you dropped me off at home." She stepped back, uncomfortable with his proximity and spicy scent. He wore some sort of men's cologne.

His handsome face blanched. "I regret ordering the drinks, especially since I don't seem to handle alcohol well. And I shouldn't have tried to kiss you. Both were big mistakes." He had never sounded more sincere. "Are you courting Lewis Miller now?" His question was barely a whisper.

"I went out with him once, but I don't want to get serious with either of you." Nora felt shame about minimizing her relationship with Lewis, but she saw little advantage in hurting Elam. The man had few friends in Paradise—very much the way she had been in Harmony.

Elam brightened and pulled off his hat. A thick lock of hair fell across his forehead. "In that case, give me another chance. Let's start over, and I'll do things right this time. I have a soft spot for you, Nora King. Surely you must like me better than that duller-than-spoons shopkeeper."

The little hairs on Nora's neck rose like porcupine quills. "Have you forgotten *I'm* a shopkeeper?"

"Only temporarily, until I win you over. Then we'll move to my new apartment and you won't have to work in this sweatbox. What can you find to talk about with Miller—the exorbitant prices of baking ingredients?" Elam hooted maliciously. "Or maybe the best way to get nasty stains out of white aprons?"

Nora's nostrils flared. She felt like a goat preparing to charge a fence. "Maybe Lewis and I discuss how we enjoy being Amish and, unlike you, wish to stay that way. I'm not interested in your English apartment in the city."

"That's because you've never tried things my way." His eyes narrowed into a glare.

"And I don't plan to. Your intentions are clear, Elam, but so are mine about remaining Amish. I tried courting you and it was a disaster. I'm sorry you stopped in today for nothing." Nora tried to step around him, but he blocked her path.

"I pegged you wrong back in Harmony. You're exactly like your sister Amy."

He reached for her arm, but she shrugged away. "Well, *danki*. I'll take that as a compliment."

"You'll regret this, Nora, long before you trade one boring store in for another."

Her patience had dwindled to nothing. "Whether or not I end up with Lewis, I don't want to spend another five minutes with you, Elam Detweiler. Now kindly forget we ever met!" Shaking with fury, she stomped back to the bakery.

An unfortunate ending for a former friendship—one she had cherished after first leaving her Pennsylvania home. But if you back a stray cat into a corner, sooner or later she'll bear her claws.

❧

His landlady's covert glances were wearing on Elam's nerves.
Each time he entered the house, he had to walk down the hallway and through the Petersheim kitchen to come and go from his
first-floor room. How he longed for the basement quarters with
an outside entrance he'd had at his brother's house in Maine. Not
that Elam missed spiders lurking on the walls or his clothes damp
from the humidity. Privacy was the only thing he missed about
Harmony, except maybe his sister-in-law's fried chicken...and
his two cute little nephews. Harmony's conservativeness hadn't
been a good fit for him. Here in Paradise, he was pretty much left
alone, except for Mrs. Petersheim's surreptitious glances and her
husband's thinly disguised questions: "Given any more thought to
getting baptized, son? A service will be coming up in a few weeks."
Or, "I'd be happy to accompany you to a horse auction. Getting
rid of that gas-guzzler will go a long way toward being accepted in
this community."

He didn't want acceptance.

He no longer drank alcohol inside their home and carefully
kept his car parked out of sight of the road. The Petersheims should
be satisfied with that and leave him alone. They were nice enough
people. Ruth Petersheim let him use the propane washer and dryer
at no charge, and she often invited him to share supper with the
family. But Elam always declined. There was no sense getting
chummy with folks he would soon leave in his dust. When hunger
got the better of him, he ate a bowl of leftovers from their refrigerator after they went to bed. Usually, he drove up to Columbia and
bought packaged food to keep from starving. When his stockpile
ran out, Elam relied on the vending machine at Gingerich Lumber, along with the free coffee and baked goods.

Austere living, while saving most of his pay, was part of his
master plan. He'd spotted reasonably priced apartments on the
northern outskirts of Columbia. Because Randolph and Audrain

Counties had few rentals, he would have to commute back and forth to work, but his saving account would allow him to buy furniture and appliances for the apartment—everything a woman needed to feel at home.

Too bad the only woman he pictured on his new sofa was Nora King. And she'd just told him to get lost. *When had she become so pretty?* Putting on a few pounds at the bakery had done wonders for her figure. Nora had been bony when she arrived in Harmony, barely able to keep rooted in a stiff wind. Funny how he'd never imagined sharing an apartment with her before. But lately, he hadn't been able to think about much else. Despite her pronouncement at the bakery yesterday, he remembered her sweet soft lips on his more than once. She'd surrendered to his kisses in Maine, enjoying them just as much as he had.

*"You're a dog in the manger, Elam."* His *grossmammi*'s words still haunted him, even though the woman was long in her grave. That might be true, but this dog needed to get rid of the stray who wandered into Paradise with his sights set on Nora. It galled Elam that Lewis lived under the Gingerich roof when he was no relation whatsoever. It was no use fantasizing about Nora as long as that stock boy was still in town. If Miller were to hightail it back home in disgrace, Nora would change her mind about the two of them. She wasn't a woman to spend life alone.

With irritation, Elam glanced down at the gas gauge on his way to the lumberyard. He would have barely enough to reach the gas station after his shift. Living out in the middle of nowhere had many disadvantages—no restaurants, no bars, no gas stations, no movie theaters, or anything else to do for recreation. The sooner he and Nora moved from this one-horse town the better. In Columbia, he would find plenty of better places to work than Gingerich Lumber.

Elam parked in the employee lot and punched his time card

right on time. He headed toward the break room for coffee and bakery items. On Saturdays, Jonas usually brought in day-old cookies. But the foreman circumvented Elam's plans.

"There you are, Detweiler. We have no trucks to unload this morning, so I want you to add a coat of waterproof sealer to the roof. It's supposed to be dry for a few days. Bob and Jack will pull the morning orders."

Elam blinked, his smile fading to a scowl. "Spread black tar on the roof? You picked *me* for the job? Why don't you make that new guy do it?" He hated to even mention his competition's name.

Ken glanced up from his clipboard. "Robert is training Lewis on the computer today. The buckets and rough-napped roller are in the supply room, along with muck boots and gloves. Be sure to wear goggles and don't roll it too thinly." Ken flipped the page on his clipboard and began to walk away.

Elam needed only a moment to recall tarring his grandfather's barn one summer…the heat, the smell, the flies buzzing around his head. And, no matter how careful you were, you always got tar on your skin. "I hate that particular job. Why don't you ask one of the *Englischers?*"

Halting in his tracks, Ken glared over this shoulder. "Because I'm asking you, Detweiler, so get moving or consider this your last day." His beady eyes narrowed, giving him the appearance of a weasel.

Elam stalked to the supply room with clenched fists and thoughts running through his head not part of any Christian upbringing. After tucking his pant legs into tall rubber boots and donning the elbow-length gloves, he grabbed goggles and the first load of materials. It took four trips up the ladder before all of the cans of sealant were on the roof. During his final trip, he spotted Lewis Miller bent over a computer monitor in Jonas's office. Sitting next to him, Robert rested a hand on Lewis's shoulder as though the two were old pals.

Typical of when someone senses they are being watched, Lewis glanced up to meet Elam's gaze. With a bucket of tar in each hand, Elam felt like the lowest man on the totem pole. Miller forced a smile. Or was that a mocking smirk because he'd won favor with the bosses…and with Nora King?

For the next five hours, Elam swabbed on the thick sticky goo, spreading the coat as best he could. As predicted, flies circled his head, sweat from the relentless heat ran down his face and neck, and when he absently scratched a mosquito bite, he streaked his cheek with tar. Seldom had he endured a more onerous morning in twenty-two years of life. At eleven o'clock, when he climbed down the ladder for his lunch hour, he met Ken Stewart on his way up.

"Good, you're taking a break. Why don't you eat this in the shade by the picnic tables?" He held out a large paper sack. "That way you won't track tar inside the store. I bought you McDonald's on my way back from Moberly—two Quarter Pounders with cheese, a large order of fries, and a chocolate shake. I know how men your age can eat. There are two bottles of water in the bag too." Ken laughed as though one free meal made everything hunky-dory between them.

But now wasn't the time to settle scores. Elam was starving. After a small bowl of cold chili last night and no breakfast, he could practically eat the Styrofoam containers. "Thanks for lunch," he muttered, pulling off his gloves. He carried the bag to an empty table and devoured the food in record time. Before returning to the roof, he used the outdoor facilities instead of the indoor restroom, ratcheting up his sense of alienation from the other employees, both Amish and English.

The afternoon contained more of the same oppressive heat and backbreaking labor. By the time Elam finished coating every flat surface late in the day, he was in a foul mood. How dare Lewis come to Paradise and ruin everything for him? If he'd stayed where he belonged in the Great White North, the free room and board at the

Gingerichs' would have been Elam's, along with the position inside the showroom. And Nora would still be his girl. He needed to send Lewis scurrying back to Maine like the cockroach he was. With him out of the way, she would forget her straightlaced convictions. With patience and gentle coaxing, any woman could be seduced.

Elam shucked off his boots and gloves in the supply room and cleaned tar off his arms and face as best he could. When he approached the time clock to punch out, his temper had reached its boiling point. He almost missed the perfect chance to solve his problems in one fell swoop.

*Almost*...but never let it be said that Elam Detweiler didn't seize opportunities handed to him on a silver platter.

# TWELVE

*Be saved, to sin no more*

Lewis tried his best not to get too full of himself, but at the moment, he was one happy man. When Robert mentioned he would learn the computer today, Lewis had felt sick to his stomach. Typical of everyone Old Order Amish, his formal education ended after the eighth grade. Of course, a smart man never stopped learning throughout his lifetime. He'd been trained by the best Amish bookkeeper in Maine to handle the accounts at his *daed*'s cooperative market and general store. But keeping ledgers wasn't the same as imputing data into a computer.

By the end of the day, Robert had taught him the rudiments of a program called Excel and then slapped him on the back. "Good work, Miller. Before you know it, you'll be a techno-geek."

Lewis didn't know what that meant, but he accepted the compliment with a bit of pride. "Thank you, sir. I'll be happy to fill in for you whenever needed." They shook hands, wished each other a happy Saturday night, and left to collect their belongings. Lewis had just retrieved Jonas's gelding from the paddock when he spotted several Amish young men headed his way. His good day was about to get even better.

"Hold up there, Lewis," said one. "I'm Josh, and this is Albert and Seth."

Lewis grasped the gelding's bridle to keep him from prancing and nodded at each man in turn. He recognized them vaguely from the lumberyard, but all three worked in the sawmill. "How's it going?"

"*Gut, gut.* We heard you're new to the area and staying at the Gingerichs'." Josh wiped his forehead with the back of his hand. "Tonight there will be a bonfire and hayride at my house. Do you want to come?"

Lewis considered. "Much as I'd like to, I don't know if I can. Might be too late by the time I get home from work. Where do you live?"

"Not far away. Around the corner and halfway down the next road. We live in the same district as Jonas and Emily...your new district. Jonas can give you directions."

"Sounds *gut,* as long as I can borrow Emily's buggy again. I haven't had a chance to buy my own rig."

"I might be able to help with that when the time comes," Seth said. "My *daed* breeds and raises Standardbreds. He has several horses for sale along with a few buggies—used, but still in fine shape."

"Stop with the sales pitch," said Josh with a grin. "It's Saturday night. Let's talk hot dogs roasted over an open fire, buttered corn on the cob, and desserts the girls spend hours making just to impress us."

All four Plain men laughed.

Albert clapped a hand on Lewis's shoulder. "Don't worry. Because tomorrow's a preaching Sunday, we'll break up early. What do you say?"

Lewis tucked his hands beneath his suspenders. "I say *jah* and *danki*. Is it okay if I ask a young woman to come?"

The sawmill workers hooted. "Where did you move from, Miller?" asked Josh. "Of course it's okay. What would a hayride and bonfire be without single young women to talk to?" He received arm punches from both Seth and Albert.

"What should I bring?" asked Lewis, already backing away.

"Just yourself, but that young lady of yours can bring anything she wants as long as it's sweet." Josh waved his hand as they headed to their buggies.

Lewis mulled over Josh's words while hitching up the horse. *That young lady of yours.* How he loved the sound of that. Nora had agreed to court him, but he had no exclusive claim on her affections. Would she someday become his bride? Where would they take the kneeling vow, committing themselves to God and the Amish church? And where would they make their home after the wedding—here among acres of flat, wind-swept farmland, stretching for as far as the eye could see? Or back home in his beloved Waldo County, Maine, surrounded by the family and friends he'd known his entire life? One thing was certain. He loved Nora and refused to consider that she might pick Elam over him. But in the end, if she chose Elam he would behave honorably. After losing her parents, Nora deserved happiness with whichever man captured her heart.

Jonas reached the buggy just as Lewis untied the reins from the post. "I see some Amish men paid you a visit," said Jonas. He set his empty lunch cooler under the seat and took the reins.

"*Jah*. They invited me to a social tonight." Lewis tried to tamp down his excitement. "A bonfire and hayride."

Jonas steered the horse out of parking lot onto the pavement toward home. "Is that right? I suppose you said *nein*, not wanting to sit on bales of scratchy straw. Then there's all that smoke and flying ash at bonfires to stink up your clothes and irritate your eyes.

I wonder why they don't call them 'strawrides' since they seldom use bales of hay."

Lewis studied his boss from the corner of his eye. "You and Emily sure were blessed with the same sense of humor."

"It was a match made in heaven." Jonas shook the harness to pick up the pace. "Do you plan to invite Nora?"

"The moment we get home. I hope she agrees, considering the late notice after a long workday."

"She's probably desperate to relax. I know Emily shakes a bull-whip at those girls."

Lewis laughed as he pictured her standing over Nora and Violet with a whip. For a devout deacon of the church, Jonas had an exceptionally wry wit. "I'm sure the whip is more for show than any real motivation." He slouched on the bench and pulled down his hat, as though preparing to catnap. But instead of sleeping, he planned how to approach Nora. Maybe he would sneak up on her in the garden while she selected the perfect ripe tomato for supper. Perhaps he would find her on the porch swing, lost in the drama of one of her novels. Or maybe she would be on the fishing dock, catching some afternoon sunshine on her cheeks. Before Lewis finished his perfect strategy, Jonas turned into their gravel drive.

"Let me tend the horse while you look for Nora," said Jonas. "If you're going somewhere tonight, I suggest you not dillydally."

Lewis waited long enough to obtain directions to Josh's before entering the house. While imagining where he would extend the invitation, he hadn't considered the most likely place—in a hot, airless kitchen. Nora stood frying meat at the stove. Sweeping off his hat, Lewis crept into the room. "Nora, could I speak to you a minute about something we might like to do together?"

She turned to look at him. Her face was sweaty and blotchy, her head covering wrinkled and askew, and her apron looked as though she had used it to strain tomato juice. A pot of something pasty and white boiled over onto the enamel surface of the stove.

"Ah, you might want to turn down that burner," he said, pointing.

"Dear me, the rice!" With a pot holder she pulled the pan from the burner and lowered the heat. "I never know how high to set the flame—too low and the rice stays hard; too high and you have a mess on your hands." She tucked a damp lock beneath her *kapp*. "You wished to ask me something?"

Every ounce of courage mustered on the way home vanished. The woman of his dreams stood before him, hot and exhausted from a long day of waiting on customers. Now she was cooking dinner for the Gingerichs in a hot kitchen. What she probably wanted to do was put her feet up after supper and listen to crickets until she fell asleep in the chair.

Nora perched one hand on her hip. "Well, did you forget your question already? It must not have been earth-shattering." She turned back to flip pork chops in the skillet.

"I didn't forget," he said, running his tongue over dry lips. "I got an invite late in the day. Some fellas told me after work. One of them, Josh, is having a get-together at his parents' house." His voice cracked like a fifteen-year-old's.

Nora lifted her brows. "I met Josh once and the girl he's courting."

"Sorry about the late notice, but would you like to go to a bonfire and hayride…with me?" Lewis swallowed hard. "Tonight?"

Nora pressed a finger to her lips. "Let me think a moment…. *jah*, I would love to go." She contemplated less than three seconds. "I'll ask Emily to finish supper while I shower. Maybe you could shower upstairs? It's lovely having two bathrooms in the house, no?"

"No need to ask me anything." Emily strode into the room and pulled Nora's soiled apron over her head like a magic trick. "I'll finish up in here. Go get ready. The last time I checked, a person is only young once." Leaning over the stove, Emily lifted the lid of the saucepot. "Goodness, what is this sticky goo? It looks like wallpaper paste."

Lewis didn't wait to hear Nora's answer. He bolted up the steps to grab fresh clothes and claim the bathroom before something changed her mind.

❧

For a few minutes, Nora just stood under the shower spray, letting cool water wash away the day's residue. Her fatigue disappeared along with the scented soap bubbles down the drain. She would spend the evening with Lewis. It would be their second date. And with that thought, she barely noticed when the water chilled as someone ran the shower overhead.

As she toweled her hair and dressed in her favorite rose-hued dress, she thought about the ruined rice and spattering grease. Why did Lewis have to witness her poor performance in the kitchen? Why wasn't he there when her piecrust turned out flakier than Emily's? Or when customers at Grain of Life raved about her chocolate chip cookies, insisting they were moister than anyone else's? Instead, he saw her damp and disheveled, boiling rice into wallpaper paste.

Yet apparently it hadn't made a difference to him.

Nora believed a woman should excel at *something* to be worthy of a man's love, or at least prove herself organized, efficient, and resourceful. She'd demonstrated none of those traits to Lewis in Maine, and here she hadn't had much opportunity. But he seemed to like her anyway, just as she was. That realization lifted a burden from her shoulders, one as heavy as a plow blade. Her *mamm* once said each person is unique and special in their own way. Lewis had turned empty words into something meaningful.

When she left the steamy bathroom fifteen minutes later, he was leaning against the doorjamb with his arms crossed. "Ready to go, Miss King?" he asked. Strength and energy practically radiated from his skin.

"Don't you have to hitch up the buggy?" Her breath caught in her throat.

"Jonas already switched horses for us."

"Didn't you want a bite to eat first?" Nora felt as though it was the first day of school.

"Whatever Josh sets out will be enough, don't you think?" Lewis grinned and bobbed his head toward the door.

A mournful train whistle sounded in the distance, distracting her. "I should take something for the dessert table and not show up empty-handed." Nora rubbed the backs of her fingers.

"Goodness," interrupted Emily. "You're not thinking of baking *now*, are you? Take the cupcakes I made for tomorrow and stop being so afraid." Emily thrust a Tupperware tote at her. "Lewis promises not to bite." She made a clucking noise, like a chicken.

"*Danki.*" Nora grabbed her sweater and purse.

"Are you afraid, Nora?" he asked, once they reached the buggy. "I'm curious to know what of."

She waited to respond until inside the vehicle. "I don't know. Maybe that you'll discover the true me and won't like her." With his hat brim low, she couldn't read his expression.

"Why don't we fix that? Tell me about yourself. Start with growing up in Pennsylvania. What were you like in school? I'm guessing you were the teacher's pet."

Nora relaxed against the bench and talked of her sisters and grandparents and her beloved farm in Lancaster. He shared details of his youth while growing up with four sisters. "It's nice here in Paradise, *jah*?" she asked. It was their first lull in the conversation. "Couples are allowed to court instead of being constantly supervised."

He thought for a moment while someone's dog barked from a nearby front porch. "*Jah*, it's nice here, but for better reasons than that." Lewis patted her arm. "It will be nice to have several hours alone to get better acquainted. Then all your hidden, loathsome tendencies will undoubtedly come out."

She smiled. "The Gingerich sense of humor seems to have spread to their boarders. That's a good thing." Suddenly, the dog from the porch bolted across the yard and barked a happy greeting. Recognizing Daisy, Nora realized they were passing Violet's house.

Her best friend...who might not know about tonight's bonfire.

A woman who longed to socialize with people her own age.

A selfish thought flitted through Nora's head and then vanished. "Stop, Lewis. Please turn up this driveway. I know we just talked about spending time alone, but I'd like Violet to join the fun. She's my best friend, and she doesn't get out often enough."

Lewis tipped his hat back and pulled the harness hard to the right. "I don't mind. Sounds like you're a nice woman—despite your opinion to the contrary."

Violet Trask took no time to decide and only five minutes to get ready. Her brother walked her out to the buggy, stowed a cake pan in the back, and helped her step up. When Violet climbed into the front seat, she shoved Nora so hard she practically landed in Lewis's lap.

"I could sit in the backseat," offered Nora.

"*Nein.*" The other two answered in unison. "It's a bit snug, but we fit," said Violet. "That might be a different story after I hit the dessert table."

"What did you bring, Violet?" asked Lewis, leaning over Nora.

"I grabbed two loaves of pumpkin bread my *mamm* plans to serve tomorrow. I'm hoping one of my sisters baked today, or I'll have to break into Grain of Life for half-priced leftovers."

"Stealing on the Sabbath?" Nora tilted her head to the side.

"Of course not. I'll have Emily deduct the price from my check and owe her money on payday. But you two continue talking as though I'm not here." She ran two fingertips across her lips. "I'm happy just to tag along."

"And we're happy to have someone to break the ice, so to speak. It takes the pressure off Nora and me."

Nora peered at him from the corner of her eye. Elam had resented it whenever Violet accompanied them and would never have said something sweet. She relaxed against his side, amazed by a man both strong as a bull yet tenderhearted.

"Nora was about to reveal what she'd been like in school in Lancaster." Lewis bumped shoulders with her as a prompt. "I guessed she was the teacher's pet."

"I'll bet she was a tomboy." Violet bumped Nora from the other side.

"You're both wrong. Amy was the teacher's favorite. She always had the correct answer and caught on to everything quickly. My younger sister Rachel was good at volleyball and kickball and softball too. And she's so pretty the boys didn't mind if she asked to join their game. I have yet to discover what makes me unique in the world." Nora shrugged as best she could on the crowded seat.

For two seconds the buggy was dead silent. Then Lewis and Violet started to speak nonstop, as though competing to banish Nora's misconceptions. Several terms were thrown out, such as best cookie baker, nicest friend in the world, prettiest complexion in Paradise, and patience of a saint, along with humble, cheerful, devout, trustworthy, and kind to animals. The volume reached din level.

"Stop, please," pleaded Nora. "I get it. You both like me so that it makes up for any shortcomings. Well, I think you're both pretty special too." Impulsively, she grasped Violet's hand and reached for Lewis's.

He wrapped his fingers around her small hand to complete

a three-way handshake. "Whew, I'm glad we got that settled since we're almost to Josh's."

Up ahead, Nora spotted flames and sparks from the bonfire shooting high into the sky. She froze, momentarily unaware of conversation or anything else. Again, the sight, the smell of wood smoke, the voices raised in excitement transported her back to an evening more than a year ago—the night her parents perished in a house fire. Nora's stomach churned while her heart rate increased two-fold.

Lewis tightened his grip on her fingers. "Relax, Nora, and breathe. All is well. It's just a fire to cook hot dogs and marshmallows. You're safe with me." His soothing words broke through her anxiety.

She inhaled and exhaled until her heart stopped slamming against her ribcage. "I'm better now, *danki*," she murmured.

"We're here," crowed Violet as Lewis parked in the line of buggies. "Set up my wheelchair, please, so I don't slow down this parade by trying to walk. Let's head straight to the barn with our desserts. I have no intention of getting my clothes smoky smelling."

"That is a great idea," agreed Nora. The three found Josh, Albert, and Seth inside the barn, carrying full plates to the picnic table. Hot dogs, burgers, and corn had already been cooked and were piled high on plates, so they didn't need to venture down to the fire. They fixed their supper and joined Lewis's new friends. Violet ignored her food and struck up an immediate conversation with the man across from her. Later, when Josh announced it was time to load the hay wagon, Lewis offered both girls a hand.

Violet shook her head. "I'm happy as a clam right here. You two run along." She turned her attention back to Seth. "We're discussing breeds of horses, of all things, which I happen to be fascinated with."

Nora bit back her laughter as they exited the barn. "Did you know your friend was interested in horses?" asked Lewis, helping her into the wagon.

"I believe it's a *brand-new* fascination." Nora peered around. Few sitting spots remained except for a cozy bale in the back row.

"How about that one?" he asked.

"It looks stable enough, with no great danger of falling off." Nora sat primly on the straw. But once the wagon started to roll, Lewis snaked his arm around her waist. The team of high-spirited Belgians turned down a dark lane, away from the barn and bonfire. Soon courting couples snuggled close to gaze into the panoply of constellations overhead. "I can't remember a lovelier evening." Leaning against his shoulder, Nora sighed with contentment.

"Something else we agree on," he whispered. Lewis's breath smelled of peppermint and tickled her ear.

Memories of Pennsylvania tragedies vanished, along with insecurity about her future. This was turning out to be the best night of her life so far.

Just as a crescent moon broke free from the clouds, Lewis turned her face toward his. "I'd like to kiss you, Miss King. But if you allow such a liberty, it means you're officially courting me and me alone. So think long and hard before you agree to such—"

Nora had had enough idle chatter. She arched her neck and kissed him first, brief but squarely on the lips.

He smiled as she drew back. "You call that peck a kiss? This is what I had in mind." Lewis kissed her in a fashion no one would describe as a peck. Then they settled back against the wagon slats to watch the passing fields, cloaked in shadows.

Nora's heart began to race for the second time that evening, but not due to grim memories of her loss.

These heart palpitations were for a different—and entirely delightful—reason.

❧

**Sunday**

When Solomon entered the house hosting the preaching service, every spot on every bench was filled. No one had stayed home with a cold or bellyache from an overindulgence of one sort or another. Clusters of men and women talked with far less exuberance before the service began.

Strange, what a plague of locusts could do to the attitudes of believers. Men who normally mumbled raised their voices in hymns of praise from the *Ausbund*. Women who usually craned their necks to observe each other bowed their heads to listen meekly to opening Scripture readings. When Solomon was asked to preach the first of two sermons, he took his place before the congregation, filled with the fervor of his youth. He glanced at the women's benches and spotted the kind eyes of his *fraa* and the hopeful gaze of Violet. They depended on him for guidance. Sol then observed the men's side of the room and caught a nod of encouragement from Deacon Gingerich. Jonas sat next to the newest entry into their Plain community, Lewis Miller. Jonas and the other younger minister looked to him for leadership. Sol hoped he was up for the challenge.

"By now we have assessed the damage done to our crops by the locusts," he intoned solemnly. "And we have taken steps to salvage whatever we can of the next harvest. Maybe we inquired about bank loans to carry us through the lean months ahead, or we might have decided to sell livestock or equipment to pay future bills. I hope we have given as much attention to the spiritual message of the bizarre event." He paused for a moment. "There are some who will say the locusts were nothing more than a freak of nature, just like the heavy rains and flash floods last month were simply bad weather. But the faithful recognize so-called natural disasters for what they truly are—acts of God, due to His displeasure. The Old Testament is filled with examples of God's wrath. We must wipe out sin and return to lives of isolation and devout contemplation, as intended by our forbearers. Only then can the curse levied on this part of the state be lifted."

Murmurs and mumbling rose in the back of the room, but Solomon paid them no mind. "Pray for forgiveness!" he shouted. "Pray for direction! And pray that God shows mercy on our town of Paradise. His power is absolute. Nothing is beyond His scope, not the wind, not the rain, or any creature large or small."

Solomon clutched his Bible to his chest. "We must pray not less than three times a day so our children will be spared His wrath. Let's look to the book of Daniel for a perfect lesson today." He cleared his throat and organized his thoughts to be as concise as possible. "While the Israelites were held captive in Babylon, King Darius appointed Daniel chief of his advisers because he was the favorite. This action infuriated the other counselors, and they schemed to snare Daniel in a wicked plot. Because it was Daniel's custom to kneel and pray to God three times a day, the evil men devised a new law. Any man caught praying or honoring anyone other than the king would be thrown into the lion's den. King Darius signed the decree into law without realizing the implications. When the other advisers spied and caught Daniel giving thanks on his knees, they brought him before the king. Darius realized he'd fallen into their trap but felt helpless. After Daniel was thrown into a pit of ferocious beasts, Darius prayed that Daniel's God would save him. The next morning, when soldiers removed the stone sealing the pit, Daniel climbed out unscathed. The Lord had sent an angel to close the lions' mouths. King Darius rejoiced and issued a decree that everyone should worship the God of Daniel. Then the king threw the evil schemers to the lions, where they were quickly consumed...along with their wives and children."

Several women gasped audibly, while a couple of *kinner* started to cry.

"Let us bow our heads in prayer that we will turn from our evil ways before it's too late."

Every head, young and old, bowed. Solomon prayed for his district with the zeal of the ancient prophets. Dark days required a firm hand from a minister who would neither vacillate nor hesitate if this area were to break free from the curse gripping Missouri for years.

# THIRTEEN

*Ever since by faith, I saw the stream*

Emily walked from the preaching service in a daze. It seemed as though Minister Sol had directed his message at her. Everything he said weighed heavily on her heart. Daniel had fallen to his knees three times each day to give thanks for God's blessings. Surely, his workday in the king's court had been busier than hers, running a small bakery only open Thursdays, Fridays, and Saturdays, yet Daniel never neglected to pray. Although she prayed before bed, when was the last time she had started her day in the same fashion? Always busy, always in a rush…as though baking batches of cookies was more important than her eternal soul. And her silent prayers before meals were little more than "Thanks for the food." *When was the last time I initiated a personal conversation with my Maker?*

Suddenly, Emily felt a soft touch on her arm. She raised her head to see Margaret, the wife of the young minister, at her side. "Stirring words today, *jah*?"

"Whew, that's for sure." Emily peered around the room. Men were moving the benches to the backyard. Afterward, the benches would be stacked in the wagon and taken to the next family to host the church service.

"Let's get out of their way. We can help set out lunch."

Emily and Margaret joined a queue of women carrying bowls of salad and platters of meat, cheese, and bread from the kitchen to tables in the shade. Young girls mixed giant jugs of iced tea and lemonade. Soon the men formed a line to fix sandwiches, while the women followed soon after. Throughout the simple meal, Emily noticed that most people remained subdued and left shortly after the Morgansteins' yard had been cleaned up. She sighed with relief when Jonas suggested they do the same.

"Ready to go?" he asked.

She nodded. "Let me find Nora and collect my potato salad bowl."

"Lewis will bring her home later. They want to drive around the township a bit." Jonas squinted into the sun.

"Sounds good to me." Emily practically ran to retrieve her side dish. She joined him at the buggy before he could finish hitching up the gelding. While waiting, she dabbed her face several times with a handkerchief and fanned herself with her apron.

"Something troubling you, *fraa*?" asked Jonas, once they were rolling down the drive.

"Certainly I'm troubled. Aren't you? I didn't know all the details about Daniel and the lions."

Jonas tipped his hat back. "*Jah*. It's sorrowful the wives and *kinner* of the evil advisors suffered the same fate as the men. I suppose that's what is meant by 'sins of the father.'" He settled back, loosening his grip on the reins.

"You're not upset by the sermon?" Emily faced him on the bench.

Jonas barely reacted. "I don't like women and children being eaten alive any better than you, but I cannot question the sovereign authority of God."

"I'm not talking solely about the book of Daniel, Jonas. Aren't you upset by Sol's conclusion?"

He finally looked at her. The lines around his eyes deepened into a complex web. "What conclusion would that be, *fraa*?"

She stared at him. "That we have only ourselves to blame for the terrible events happening in this part of Missouri."

"We, meaning the Amish of Paradise?" His tone remained calm. "The *Englischers'* crops were also heavily damaged by the recent floods and horde of grasshoppers. Are you saying the English must suffer because of us? Sort of like the unfortunate family members of the king's advisors?"

She blinked, unnerved that he asked that with no greater concern than enquiring for the time of day or her menu for supper. "Not necessarily, but for some reason these counties have attracted evildoers and thus have drawn God's wrath in retribution."

Jonas stared at her as though she were speaking Chinese. "These counties?"

"Please, *ehemann*, stop repeating my words or this will take all day. You aren't aware of the horrible things that have gone on in Randolph, Audrain, and Boone Counties. Not just the woebegone group of Old Order from Iowa a century ago, but many other strange events and acts of unspeakable cruelty." Emily pressed her sweaty palms on her knees, trying not to sound smug. "I have studied the history of this area while you have not."

"Then perhaps you will enlighten me," said Jonas with his signature composure.

She explained to him about the Centralia gas explosion, including every detail of the disaster she could remember. "Can you imagine if the pilot light on our propane hot water tank or stove suddenly shot flames like a blowtorch?"

"I cannot." He rubbed his jaw with the back of his hand. "But it sounds to me as though the Lord showed mercy that day. All those houses exploding and burning down and, thankfully, no one died? God is good."

Emily certainly agreed, but her story didn't have the effect she intended. Next she repeated the heinous saga of Bloody Bill Anderson's activities during the Civil War. She hadn't yet reached the despicable way his dead body had been treated when Jonas raised his hand.

"Enough, Emily. Don't allow those images to fester in your mind. They'll serve no purpose other than to disturb your sleep with bad nightmares. War brings out the worst in human behavior. It has corrupted many Christian lives throughout the ages. Look no further than the Crusades. Let us pray mankind will lose his taste for war." Jonas craned his neck out the window to follow the flight of a red-tailed hawk on warm air currents. In no way did his heart seem as burdened by Solomon's sermon as hers.

"So you don't think the plague of locusts was a sign from God? Are you one of those who'll scoff and say it's simply Mother Nature acting up?"

He remained silent for a moment. When he replied he appeared to be struggling to keep his voice even. "There is no 'Mother Nature.' All nature is the handiwork of the Lord, but I don't believe all disasters are punishments due to His dissatisfaction with us. He created the earth and then left it in our control. He gave us free will to make decisions, and unfortunately man has not always chosen wisely. We have squandered our resources and polluted His majestic creation beyond repair, according to some *Englischers*. We've driven thousands of species of life to extinction with our greed and carelessness. That's probably why the locust and certain bird populations are out of whack."

Jonas pulled on the reins as they picked up speed downhill. "But Sol's advice is sound. We should pray daily to be delivered from ourselves. These may well be the end-times prophesied in the book of Revelation—a book I cannot begin to fully understand."

His stoic reserve was Emily's undoing. She burst into tears. "How can you sit there so relaxed? I fear God's judgment is upon *us*—you and me—because of my mean spirit."

He covered her hand with his. "What are you talking about?"

"Our childlessness. The fact I can't conceive. It's due to my past sins."

"What sins are those?" he asked. A hint of apprehension crept into his voice.

"I'm impatient with people who can't make up their minds. After preaching, I sometimes sneak food in the kitchen instead of waiting for the men to eat first. Often my mind wanders during the bishop's sermons to what I intend to pick from the garden or whose house we'll go to after church." Tears streamed down her face. "I secretly covet Nora's slim figure and Violet's ability to add sums in her head without paper and pencil. And I've been known to spread gossip more times than I care to admit. Once when—"

"Em, stop. You're becoming hysterical. Wipe your face and blow your nose." He handed her a handkerchief and waited until she composed herself before continuing. "You think these sins are why we haven't been blessed with *kinner*?"

"I'm convinced of it."

"Every Christian falls short of Jesus' example. Unfortunately, it's in our nature to sin since the Garden of Eden."

"That doesn't excuse it."

"Of course not. We must confess and never stop trying to live a more righteous life. But if God only blessed sinless people with babies, I'm afraid the human race would have died out long ago with the other extinct species."

Again his calm voice irritated her, yet she didn't know exactly why. "I can't take this matter as lightly like you can, Jonas. Solomon is right. This district has slipped into bad habits, including me. And until we take steps to change, horrible things will continue to happen in Paradise. And I will never know the joy of becoming a mother." Emily crossed her arms and stared out the side window as her tears flowed again freely. She turned her back on her beloved *ehemann*. He was too lackadaisical about sin, too forgiving. She needed to heed the dire warnings raining down on them, literally and figuratively, before her child-bearing years were over.

෨෬

Jonas had never been so happy to greet Monday morning in his life. Never had a Sunday afternoon and evening dragged on so interminably. After their discussion during the buggy ride home, Emily had turned moody and sullen. If he came to the front room with his newspaper, within a few minutes she took her book to the porch to read. Later, when he ventured onto the porch with his Bible to catch the evening breeze, she retreated like a scared rabbit back into the house.

Whatever she'd hoped he would say he hadn't said.

Whatever solace she needed from him he hadn't given.

But Jonas couldn't agree with her conclusion that God was smiting the people of Missouri. This was not the God he knew. Why should Christians dwell in Old Testament stories of failed tests and subsequent judgments? Not when His Son came to earth expressly to show them how to live their lives. Jonas preferred to study the psalms, the proverbs, the miracles performed by the apostles, and, of course, the parables told by Jesus. Through His teachings, the way was clear. Difficult but clear. However, Jonas knew better than to argue with his strong-willed wife. Her heart would soften and the forgiveness she readily extended to others would eventually include her. Then she would realize that we need not question God's motives, but wait patiently for life's mysteries to unfold. Even so, Jonas was pleased to hear the crow of his brother's rooster at dawn, granting him a temporary reprieve from Emily's cool treatment.

During their ride to the lumberyard, Lewis kept him entertained with his enthusiastic assessment of Paradise. "Did you know, Jonas, that there are eleven sawmills in the area? Just imagine, *eleven*," he repeated.

"I didn't know that. I never counted them before."

"And Nora and I drove by at least eight schoolhouses. You know who would make a great teacher? Violet Trask," he answered, without waiting for Jonas's guess. "She is very patient and funny—both good attributes for a teacher, don't you agree? We passed several farms for sale too. Some with decent-looking houses that wouldn't take much time or money to fix up."

Jonas finally gave up trying to insert comments into the conversation. He enjoyed listening to the young man's viewpoint on his hometown. After Lewis ran out of landmarks and interesting facts to expound upon, Jonas asked his one and only question: "Are you thinking of moving permanently to Missouri?"

Lewis lifted a boot heel to the wooden slats. "It's too soon to say, but life holds plenty of twists and turns, no? I try not to plan too far in the future."

"Sounds like good advice for everybody." Jonas slapped him on the shoulder as they drove into the Gingerich parking lot. "You go inside so you don't punch in late while I tend to the horse. If I'm late, nobody can fire me."

Lewis hopped down and sprinted to the employee entrance. Jonas put his gelding into the back paddock, marveling at what a blessing the young man from Maine turned out to be. His good mood faded, however, the moment he walked into his office. Ken and Robert were waiting with grim expressions.

"Good grief, is something wrong all ready? It's not even eight o'clock." Jonas poured a cup of coffee from the small office pot.

Ken closed the door, signaling news other employees shouldn't overhear. "Robert called me at home on Saturday night. You and I had already left before he made the discovery. I didn't bother you yesterday because I thought it could wait until this morning. We couldn't have done much on a Sunday anyway." He shifted his weight from one leg to the other, while Robert looked equally nervous from his position by the window.

Jonas lowered himself into his chair, hoping to ease the tension in the room. "We're all here now. Why not get whatever is bothering you off your chest?" He took a long drink of strong black coffee.

Robert took over the narrative from the foreman. "I had paperwork to finish Saturday night before heading home because I'd been tied up training Lewis all day. I collected the cash and checks from the lumberyard register to tally for my nightly bank deposit. Then I went to get the receipts from the showroom cash drawer." He paused to scratch his ear.

"Go on. Spit it out." Jonas grew impatient as Robert danced around the news.

"Well, the checks were there, but no money whatsoever. And I know for a fact Lewis and I both made cash transactions while working the front counter."

"What happened to them?" Jonas took another sip.

"I haven't a clue. During the afternoon we closed the showroom register and set out the sign directing customers to use the outdoor checkouts. I needed to train Lewis on the computer in your office because the software is different than on the floor."

"And you locked the showroom register?"

"Of course we did." Robert scratched his ear again with more energy.

"You or Lewis?" asked Jonas, about to lose his patience.

"I told Lewis to. I'm sure he did. That kid is nothing if not thorough with details." Robert pulled off his Gingerich Lumber ball cap—a gift for English customers who purchased more than fifty dollars' worth of merchandise.

"The trouble is, boss, that nobody has a key to that cash drawer other than Robert, the *new hire* Lewis, and you," Ken said. "I don't even have a key. There's no sense having too many floating around to get lost or stolen."

Jonas noted the foreman's emphasis on "new hire" as though new equated with untrustworthy. Yet Jonas also trusted Robert implicitly. The man had worked for Jonas since he'd opened the sawmill, using a lean-to for a store and office. *So who does that leave?* Jonas jumped to his feet. "All right. Call Lewis in here and let's see what he has to say."

Robert left the office for a few minutes. When he returned, Lewis was at his side, fresh faced and unflustered. Either the man was innocent or he should pursue a career in the theater. Robert closed the door and returned to his spot near the window.

Lewis remained in the center of the room, glancing from one man to the next curiously. "What's going on?" His focus landed on Jonas.

"After you and everyone else left Saturday, Robert discovered that money was missing from the showroom cash register."

Lewis's face was blank. "How much?" he asked after a moment.

"All the cash. Probably close to a thousand dollars. We won't know the exact amount until we review each purchase made that day and subtract those by check or credit card."

Then, as realization dawned, Lewis's upbeat demeanor faded. "And you think *I* took the money?"

"No, I do not." Jonas answered without hesitation. "I can usually read people fairly well, and I don't think you would take as much as a second donut from the break room."

Robert cleared his throat, drawing Lewis's attention. "The trouble is, only three keys exist to the drawer—yours, mine, and Jonas's. And I sure didn't steal anything." He leaned his substantial bulk against the sill.

Lewis's complexion paled to the color of skim milk. "I can't explain this, Jonas, but I would never rob you. You and your wife have been as kind and generous to me as my own parents...and besides, it would be breaking a commandment." He raked a hand through his thick brown hair. "Besides, I am now officially courting Nora."

His voice cracked, and for one horrible moment, Jonas feared he might cry.

But he straightened his spine, clenched down on his back teeth, and glanced from one man to the other, waiting.

"I don't know about anybody else, but I have a suspicion who might have pulled this stunt." Ken almost spat the words.

Jonas cut him off with a wave of his hand. "We are not going to throw around baseless accusations." He turned toward Lewis. "Do you remember for sure if you locked the drawer before going to my office on Saturday?"

"I think so, but I was still jotting down notes in my spiral tablet." Lewis flushed a bright pink. "I can't say for certain one way or the other, but if this happened because of my carelessness, I'll work off every missing penny."

Jonas shrugged, with his hand already on the doorknob. "Let's all get to work. Don't speak to anyone about the missing money. No one," he emphasized. "We'll keep our eyes and ears open for a while. The real thief might resent getting no glory for his misdeed and start dropping hints to his friends."

Robert and Ken exchanged a brief but pointed glance. Jonas's intuition told him the two *Englischers* would prefer he fire Lewis on the spot, or at least transfer him to a position without access to money. But he knew Lewis would never recover from such a blow to his character. He would quit his job and move out of the house tonight. Jonas refused to hobble anyone's future based on circumstantial evidence, no matter how conclusive it appeared to be. "Everyone back to where they belong," he repeated, louder than before. "We have a business to run."

His three employees filed out without another word or backward glance. Jonas was left with a mountain of paperwork, a bad feeling in the pit of his stomach, and the undeniable reality that he had a thief on the payroll.

❧

Their boss truly got her money's worth from her employees on Thursdays. The bakery didn't open until ten o'clock, two hours later than on Saturdays, but Violet worked her tailbone off the whole day. And Nora? Between baking pies and cookies, helping Violet wait on customers, and running back and forth to the shed for more supplies, she resembled an unfortunate hen being readied for the dinner table. As Nora walked Violet to the buggy after closing up shop and stowing the wheelchair, she grabbed her friend's arm several times to steady her.

"Would you stop babying me?" Violet huffed. "I can walk. My legs are getting stronger every day."

"Then why are you staggering as though you're drunk?" Nora lingered close by, ready to catch her friend.

"I'm exhausted. Aren't you? This heat drains the life out of a gal."

"Totally agree with you there." When they reached the buggy, Nora put an arm around Violet.

But she shook off the assistance. "Back off, missy. Let me do this myself. How will I improve if you and *mamm* keep hovering?"

Nora moved away to steady the horse as Violet limped up to the steps. With one hand on the handle Jonas had installed and the other on the buggy's frame, she pulled herself up. But with the cumbersome leg braces, her body remained immobile in the doorway.

"A little push would be nice."

Still hanging onto the reins, Nora stepped behind her friend. "With pleasure," she answered and delivered a hearty shove to Violet's backside.

"Oof!" she sputtered. "There we are, all inside." She shuffled her feet and plopped down on the bench. After straightening her skirt, she grinned at Nora as she climbed in from the other side. "I almost flew right out the other door." Both women laughed uproariously as Violet yanked Nora's *kapp* askew.

"I believe in putting forth my best effort." Nora drank deeply from her water bottle and flicked flies from the horse with the long-handled whip.

"Why don't we get moving before the three of us melt?" asked Violet after a minute of sitting in the hot sun.

Nora lifted her chin. "Only if you promise to spill the beans about last Saturday night. Otherwise we'll stay until you're ready."

"Whatever do you mean, Miss King?" Violet reached for a soda from their cooler bag.

"Don't play coy with me, *missy*. You pried every detail from me about the hayride—from where each courting couple sat, to what Lewis and I talked about, to where the wagon took us…as well as a full description of both kisses." With the last item, Nora dropped her voice to whisper. "You know everything about the hayride except for the exact location of stars and planets in heaven above."

"I do wish you had taken better notes regarding the sky." Violet smiled, sly as a fox.

"And then you peppered me about our buggy ride around Audrain County on Sunday, even though you've lived here your entire life and have seen everything I described a hundred times." Nora tugged Violet's *kapp* to the side.

"It's always good to hear things from a fresh perspective. Could we go home, please?" Violet pulled a hanky from her purse and blotted her perspiring face. "All right, I'll tell you, but I didn't want to jinx things by blabbing too soon. And don't tell my *daed* I used the word jinx—he doesn't like it."

"Then I suggest you start talking." Nora released the brake and shook the reins. With the buggy finally rolling the breeze felt wonderful. "All I know is by the time Lewis and I returned from the hayride you, your wheelchair, and Seth Yoder had disappeared. Someone said you went down to the bonfire for marshmallows, but Lewis and I couldn't find you anywhere."

"Maybe you didn't try the path to the river." She smirked behind a raised hand.

"Violet Trask, you and Seth snuck off *alone* from the get-together?" Nora couldn't believe her ears. "You two just met!"

"Don't make such a big deal about it. It was all in fun. Seth was telling me about the horses his family raises. And he mentioned several are saddle broken because he and his *bruder* like to take trail rides into the hills or down to the river." Violet rolled her eyes with great exaggeration. "I asked, what river? I've lived here my whole life, and there is no river close to Josh's house." She fanned herself with a piece of cardboard.

Nora steered the buggy to the side of the road as a car passed. "Go on."

"Seth said he would show me. Then I asked if he happened to notice I use crutches or a wheelchair." Violet laced her fingers together and cracked her knuckles. "He said climb into that chair and we'll go for a ride."

"Goodness, girl, you move fast."

"At my ripe old age, a woman should. Well, the lane was hard-packed dirt, not gravel, so Seth had no trouble pushing me, especially as he's probably the strongest man in Missouri."

Nora sprayed a mouthful of water onto the horse's rump. "Is that so?"

"The *river* turned out to be more of a creek or stream, but I didn't care. After all, Seth is one fine-looking man…if a person takes the time to notice such things."

"And I believe you took the time." Nora giggled as though they were schoolgirls on the playground. "How exactly did you get home Saturday night? I was worried until I saw you in church the next day."

"You must learn to relax, Nora. I got home in Seth's buggy…his courting buggy. My *mamm* almost dropped her dentures."

Nora issued a sound halfway between a dog's bark and an owl's hoot. "He asked to drive you home in his *courting* buggy already? What else? Should I pick out fabric for a bridesmaid dress? Wedding season will be here before we know it."

With Nora's teasing, Violet sobered. "I hope he really likes me and doesn't just feel sorry for me."

"Don't be a ninny. A person might fetch pie or lemonade out of pity, but nobody would take you home unless they were interested."

Violet whistled through her teeth. "That's what I thought, but it's good to hear it from someone else. The whole idea seems too good to be true, like that last bizarre dream before dawn. Then you wake up and you're still in the same old nightgown."

"Trust me, my friend. You're not dreaming." She pinched Violet's arm for good measure as a car honked its horn.

"We're on the side of the road. What's wrong with that guy?" Violet craned her neck to see out the side window.

Nora spoke soothingly to the nervous horse as the red car slowed and stopped up ahead. An odd sensation settled in her gut as a man climbed out and walked in their direction. "Elam Detweiler," she moaned.

"What does he want?"

A shiver ran up Nora's spine, despite the afternoon heat. "We shall see." She pressed down hard on the brake.

"Hey there, Nora, Violet." Elam swaggered toward them. "Lovely day, ain't so?"

"What do you want, Elam? We're both hot and tired and anxious to get home."

"Is that any way to greet an old friend?" He grasped the mare's harness. "I'd like a word with you—a private word, if you don't mind." Elam doffed his cap at Violet.

"You don't have to, Nora. We can just be on our way." Violet's expression and tone of voice permitted no confusion regarding her opinion of him.

"It's all right. This won't take long." Before she could reconsider, Nora jumped down onto the sticky blacktop. "Five minutes in the shade, no more." She pointed at a cluster of trees by the fence.

Elam hopped the drainage ditch and trailed her through tall weeds. "It shouldn't take longer than that," he said, close on her heels.

Once she reached the ancient maple, Nora turned and crossed her arms. "Well, what is it?"

"For starters, why are you so nasty toward me? I've done nothing to deserve such un-Christian behavior from you."

Nora glanced around, mildly ashamed. "I'm sorry if that's how it seems, but I've made my feelings toward you clear."

"You gave me the distinct impression you would date *both* Miller and me. Then all of a sudden I'm not getting my chance to make things right with you. That's not fair." He purred with deliberate sweetness, like a cat begging for a lap to curl up in.

"I don't want to waste your time because I've already made up my mind." She mimicked his saccharine tone.

"And you picked Miller over me? I would have thought you had more spirit than that."

"Then you would have thought wrong, Elam. Lewis is better suited to my new Missouri temperament. I seem to have grown stodgy since turning twenty-one." Nora flashed her prettiest grin.

"Oh, that smile. It does me in every time." Elam reached out and took hold of her chin. He paused. Then without warning, he leaned forward and kissed her.

Nora stumbled back against the tree, shocked and frightened. "You've got no right to—"

Elam grabbed her face again and pressed her against the tree trunk with his body. His mouth covered hers in a searing, painful kiss.

Without hesitation, Nora reared back and slapped his cheek hard—an unfamiliar response she hoped never to repeat. "Don't ever do that again!"

Elam rubbed his face gingerly, stunned by her action. "That hurt, you little varmint. All I wanted was a few kisses, nothing you haven't already given Miller by the bucketful."

"You and I are not courting, Elam, and we never will be. Leave me alone, or I'll tell Jonas or the bishop or…or the sheriff if I have to." Nora shook with fury.

Elam's gaze narrowed into a glare as he rubbed his cheek. A red blotch rose where her palm had connected with skin. "I was wrong about you. You're no different than the rest of these boring folks. Except you're going to be sorry you ever crossed me." His eyes held an evil glint.

"Get away from her, you creep!" Violet shrieked at the top of her lungs while waving the long-handled whip above her head. She helplessly stood in the buggy doorway, unable to get down into the roadside brush.

Elam glanced at Violet with contempt and then back at Nora. "You mark my words, Nora King."

# FOURTEEN

## *Thy flowing wounds supply*

Because his first knock went unanswered, Solomon rapped again on the door, harder. "Violet, have you fallen in there? Did you pass out from all the steam?"

After a moment his daughter called out, "I'll be out in a minute, Papa. I'm trying to hurry."

"Trying to hurry," Sol muttered, setting into a kitchen chair. "She's been in there an hour, Rosanna. How long would it take if she proceeded at a *leisurely* pace?"

His *fraa* patted his back as she brought him a cup of coffee. "I think she's *en lieb*, *ehemann*. A girl wants to look her best."

He snorted. "If she walks out wearing cosmetics or smelly perfume, she will take another bath before leaving. Who is this young man worthy of our *dochder*'s attention?"

Before Rosanna could reply, the bathroom door opened and a blast of humid air wafted into the room. Violet limped to where he sat, shifting her weight from leg to leg with improved mobility.

Her young face was free of makeup, and she smelled solely of Ivory soap. Violet leaned to kiss his cheek. "You know very well who's picking me up for the singing—Seth Yoder. It's been two weeks since our last social event and I've missed him terribly. I wanted to scrub my skin with the loofa sponge until it glowed." She limped toward the window.

"And *you* know very well what Scripture says about a woman's beauty. Don't be vain and prideful about your appearance." Sol drummed his fingers on the table, while Rosanna finished preparing their supper.

Violet parted the curtains to peek down the driveway. "Those verses refer to wives, not women who haven't snagged a husband yet." She tied her *kapp* ribbons behind her neck to get them out of the way.

Sol's mouth dropped open. "*Snagged a husband*...you're not fishing in a rowboat with a rod and reel. I expect you to behave in a demure, reserved manner."

Violet glanced at her *mamm*. "Because Seth looks nothing like a trout, I'll leave my net and bait at home. In fact, I'll pretend I barely like him."

"See that you do and come home early. Tomorrow is a workday at the bakery."

"*Jah*, I know. We open at eight o'clock." Violet peeked out the window again.

Sol's irritation rose with her impertinence. "Remember not to sit too close in the buggy, so there will be no accidental touching. Don't share the same snack plate. And don't whisper private messages. Anything you have to say to Seth should be heard by everyone." He leaned back in his chair. "And the two of you should never be alone. Stay in a group of young people at all times. Don't wander off and give folks something to wag their tongues about."

For the briefest of moments, Violet glanced over her shoulder with a startled, anxious expression. Then she walked without her crutches to the sink.

"Sit down, daughter. Aren't you having a bite to eat with us?" Rosanna stirred fresh tomatoes into a pot of chili.

"No, *danki*. I'll eat after the singing."

"Sweets aren't food," said Sol. "You'll end up with a bellyache. What time are Lewis and Nora and Seth Yoder picking you up?"

Violet scrubbed her hands as though she just finished shoveling out the hog pen. "Seth will be here any minute, so I think I'll wait on the porch with my wheelchair."

Rosanna carried the pot to the table, setting it on an iron trivet. She ladled chili into bowls without paying much attention to their conversation.

Solomon mused on his daughter's response with growing bewilderment. "Seth? Are you saying the young man is picking you up first and then your friends?"

Violet's hand turned the doorknob. "Papa, your supper is ready. Don't fret about me. We'll be very careful and home early." She sang her reply more melodically than a nightingale.

"Sit down this instant!" he thundered. "How dare you try to keep the truth from me? Why isn't Seth stopping by the Gingerichs' first?"

She limped back to the table and lowered herself into a chair. "Lewis must help Jonas's brothers harvest the hay because they're shorthanded."

"And Miss King?" Sol crumbled crackers into his bowl.

"She's been fighting a migraine for days. She plans to take a couple of ibuprofen and go to bed early." Violet kept glancing at her mother, perhaps hoping for intervention.

"In that case, *dochder*, you're spending the evening with us, rocking on the front porch."

Her large brown eyes rounded into saucers. "You can't be

serious! Courting couples have been coming and going alone for years in this district."

"Only those who have announced their intention to marry in the fall and have received approval from the bishop."

Alarm contorted Violet's features. "I do believe he's serious about me," she said softly.

Solomon burned his mouth on his first taste of supper. "Bah, too soon to tell. If Nora isn't going, you're not going either."

"But, Papa..." Two tears slipped from the corners of her eyes.

"Enough. I refuse to discuss this further." Solomon straightened in his chair. "Have you paid no attention in church whatsoever? These could be the end-times we're living in. Our community is being tested, and so far we've not covered ourselves in glory. My family should set an example of proper Christian behavior, not stretch the *Ordnung* to fit their own will. Our rules need to be more rigid, not less, if we hope to stem the tide of horrible events." Spittle collected at the corners of his mouth as fury got the better of the minister.

Violet sobbed, the way she had done as a child. "I don't believe...this area is cursed...like you say." Her words came in fits and starts. "It can't be true...God loves us and forgives...our transgressions."

Sol shook his head as though his hearing must be faulty. "You question my understanding of Scripture? Or my authority in the church? In this family?"

"*Nein*. I don't question your knowledge or your authority, but I disagree with your opinion." She wiped her face with her sleeve.

Rosanna approached Violet's chair with a cold, wet washcloth. "Calm yourself, *dochder*." She placed the washcloth on the table and a hand on her shoulder.

"My insight isn't my *opinion*. It's based on studying the Bible and the signs for years. Did you not see the plague of locusts that covered the sky like an enormous black cloud, devouring acre after acre of grain in the fields?"

"*Jah*, I did, but I also saw the giant flock of crows that ate enough locusts to save part of the harvest." Regaining her composure, Violet met Sol's gaze. "If God sent the locusts, then He also sent the crows. It doesn't seem as though He's unhappy with us to me."

Sol stared, stunned speechless by her effrontery.

Rosanna reached for both of their hands. "We're losing our tempers, something we never should do. Let's bow our heads in prayer that peace and cooler heads would be restored to our family."

Solomon complied with his *fraa*'s advice, as did Violet.

Two or three minutes elapsed before the Trasks lifted their chins. Sol was about to speak to his daughter when they heard a knock on the porch.

Violet pressed the cold cloth to her streaky face and puffy eyes while Rosanna opened the door. Seth Yoder stepped inside the warm kitchen and swept off his hat. "*Guder nachmittag*, Minister and Mrs. Trask. Hi, Violet. Are you ready to go?"

With both palms flat on the table, Violet pushed herself to her feet. "I can't go with you tonight, Seth. My *daed* feels it's not proper." She wiped her neck with the rag.

He peered at Solomon. "Have I done something to appear untrustworthy?"

"*Nein*, it's not personal, young man. If Miss King were attending, then Violet could accompany you, but she cannot go unchaperoned."

The two young people exchanged a glance. "Maybe Nora feels better by now," said Violet. "Could I ride with Seth to the Gingerichs'?" Her voice lifted with hope.

Sol looked at Rosanna and sighed wearily. "Because it's less than two miles, you may go. But if Nora's headache isn't gone, Seth must bring you straight back."

Seth nodded his agreement and retrieved Violet's crutches from the corner. "I will. You have my word."

"See to it she uses the chair and doesn't take a tumble on uneven ground."

"I will, and she won't."

"And don't forget tomorrow is a workday for my daughter."

"It is for me too, Minister Trask." Seth opened the door for Violet, who ambled through on crutches with amazing speed and dexterity.

As she passed him, Violet brushed a kiss across his cheek. "*Gut nacht*, Papa, and *danki*."

"Don't forget what I said," he murmured.

"I couldn't. Not in a million years."

❧

"Nora, time to get up."

Nora buried her head beneath the pillow. *How can it be five thirty already?* She'd barely slept a wink since her headache returned with a vengeance. How she wanted to stay home last night, curled up on the sofa with a cup of peppermint tea. She hadn't seen Lewis at all yesterday because he had eaten both lunch and supper with Jonas's brother. But after one look at Violet's desperate face, Nora knew she couldn't refuse her request. So she had swallowed two ibuprofen tablets, grabbed a bottle of water, and accompanied Violet and Seth to the singing, where voices sounded even more off-key than usual.

Seth truly liked Violet, despite her friend's skepticism. Any man willing to chance Solomon Trask becoming his father-in-law must be serious about a woman. But getting up before dawn with the dull malaise of a lingering migraine, Nora wished she wasn't such a loyal friend.

"Nora, are you up?" Emily's impatient voice carried up the steps.

"*Jah*, I'm coming." She washed her face and hands, dressed, and bound her hair into a tight coil beneath her *kapp*.

Downstairs in the kitchen, Emily bustled around like a hummingbird. "There you are. You must hurry and eat something. It's late."

"What's the rush? It's not even six o'clock." Nora poured a cup of coffee, savoring the aroma as much as her first sip.

Emily loaded the cooler bag with water, fruit, and sandwiches. "It's almost seven. Your clock must be wrong. Lewis hung around hoping to see you, but he finally had to leave for work." Emily handed Nora a blueberry muffin wrapped in a paper towel. "Eat this on the road. We still need to pick up Violet."

"I must have forgotten to wind the alarm." Nora downed the coffee, practically scalding her throat. Her hand shook as she refilled the travel mug. "Did Lewis say anything else?"

Emily grabbed her purse, sweater, and their lunch, double-checked that the stove burners were off, and marched swiftly out the door. She said over her shoulder, "He asked if it was custom in Missouri for courting women to attend singings alone."

Nora picked up her bag and pulled the door closed behind them. She hurried to catch up. "What did you say?"

"I told him not usually."

Nora's face flamed. "Didn't you explain about Violet and Seth?"

"No, I didn't. You'll have to straighten that out by yourself. You shouldn't have gone if you didn't feel good." Emily climbed into the waiting buggy and released the brake.

Nora jumped up as the wheels began to roll. "Violet really wanted to go."

"She should have waited for a singing when you all could attend. Young people act as though social events are the most important things in the world."

Nora slumped on the seat, silent on the ride to the Trasks. What could she say? *Don't you remember being young once? Couldn't you have smoothed things out with Lewis?*

This wasn't a good day to oversleep.

Unfortunately, Violet didn't notice Emily's mood as they drove to work. The girl rattled on about who baked what desserts, who was or wasn't courting whom, and just about everything Seth uttered throughout the evening, whether particularly witty or normal banal conversation.

"Goodness, Violet," moaned Emily, several minutes into the narrative. "Don't you know any topic other than Seth Yoder? You've only been courting three weeks."

Nonplussed, Violet gazed at their boss. "We could talk about registered Standardbreds or the horse auction they have outside of Columbia. I plan to go later this summer with a man who shall remain unnamed." She burst into peals of laughter.

From the backseat, Nora tried to contain Violet by placing a hand over her mouth.

Emily clucked her tongue. "Your poor *daed* has his hands full with you," she muttered under her breath.

All three women sighed with relief when they reached Grain of Life. Unfortunately, there would be no slow start to their workday. Three cars were waiting in the parking lot for the bakery to open. After Nora helped her inside, Violet readied the store deftly from her wheelchair. Emily turned out the horse into the fenced area, while Nora carried in totes of pies baked last night. With a steady stream of customers all morning, they had no chance for conversation, whether on Emily-approved subjects or not. By one o'clock, they ran out of every variety of cookies. Nora started mixing batches of molasses crinkle and oatmeal raisin. Those cookies had barely cooled when a vanload of tourists arrived to purchase every last one.

It was close to two before they enjoyed their first lull. With the baking done for the day and the parking lot empty, Nora pulled sandwiches and fruit from the cooler.

"Whatever you can share is fine with me. I'm starving." Violet rolled up to the work table. "I left without packing a lunch, not eager to cross paths with my father this morning. He's still not happy I rode a mile and a half alone with Seth. *A mile and a half?* No one can get into mischief in that short distance." She giggled while Nora cut a turkey sandwich in half.

Rising to her feet stiffly, Emily dropped her sandwich onto the waxed paper. "I'll eat later. I want to make sure my horse has enough water in this heat."

Violet waited until the door closed before she whispered, "Did a bee crawl under her *kapp*? Why is Emily in such a bad mood?"

Nora pondered while she chewed. "I'm not sure, but she seems irritated that I went to the singing without Lewis. I got the impression she feels we should have stayed home, listening to the crickets on the porch."

"We'll do plenty of that when we're gray-haired." Violet chomped into an apple. "But there is something I need to discuss with you, something important."

"Violet Trask, we were together last night, then on the way to work, and all morning. You're finally getting around to this?"

Her mouth drooped into a frown. "This isn't a topic I could talk about in front of Seth or Emily. Now that we're alone, I'm not sure where to begin." Violet set down the apple.

Nora fought off a frisson of anxiety. "We're friends. Just tell me."

"Do you remember when Elam stopped us after work a couple weeks ago?"

"Of course, I do. I ended his misconceptions, once and for all."

"*Jah*, but do you recall his parting words?" Violet began tearing her napkin into shreds. "He said 'You're going to be sorry you ever crossed me'."

She stopped eating. "An idle threat. He was angry about being rejected. His male pride had been bruised. Believe me, Elam has probably focused his dark eyes on another gal by now, maybe an *Englischer* this time."

Violet shook her head. "He's making good on his threat, Nora, causing trouble behind your back."

An undefined unease took root and grew into full-blown fear, bordering on panic. "Spit it out already. You're scaring me with all this dillydallying."

"Elam is spreading stories among the Amish at Gingerich Lumber…stories about you. And some men were repeating those lies at the social last night, after the singing finished."

Nora thought she might be sick. "What kind of stories?"

"That you're…easy. That you have loose morals. That any man can get some without trying too hard."

Her words were little more than faint whispers, but they struck Nora like slaps to the face. "*What*? That's not true! Elam got fresh on our way home from Columbia and I told him no. He got fresh again the day he stopped us and I slapped his face." Nora trembled as shame from past deeds came home to roost. "You were there. You saw that I didn't encourage him."

"*Jah*, that's what I saw and I believe you. But I'm not the one you need to convince. There's more. He said you snuck out with him at night in Maine and drank beer at parties in his buggy, unbeknownst to the hosts. And that you helped him buy a car on the sly from his *bruder* and kissed him willingly."

Nora felt the oppressive heat of a bakery in summer close in, cutting off the air. She felt faint, while her dull headache ratcheted into a migraine. She struggled to stand. "I need to step outside a minute."

"Is it true?" A stern voice sounded from behind them. "Is any of it true?"

Nora and Violet turned to see Emily in the doorway, shocked and angry.

"Some of it. But I can explain my behavior—"

The bell above the door jangled, drawing everyone's attention.

In marched a gaggle of women, talking and laughing as though life held no cares or worries.

"I will listen to your explanation later, but not now. Start baking more cookies, and Violet, see to our customers." Emily strode to the sink to wash with military-erect posture. She wore no smile—neither for the tourists, nor for them for the rest of the afternoon.

Nora measured out sugar, flour, shortening, and sweet chocolate chips with a practiced hand. She stirred to mix the dough and dropped spoonfuls onto her baking sheet with expert uniformity. But while she baked cookies, she dwelled on the lies Elam was spreading throughout the district: *He said you snuck out with him at night in Maine and drank beer at parties in his buggy, unbeknownst to the hosts. And that you helped him buy a car on the sly from his* bruder *and kissed him willingly.*

Except those tales weren't lies. They were true, every last one of them.

❧

Emily felt much older than thirty-two years when they closed the bakery that Saturday night. Overhearing Violet's words weighed heavily on her heart. She must do something. Nora's reputation was dissolving faster than a meringue pie left in the sun. When she had agreed to provide a home for the young woman, she had accepted the responsibility that had been her sister's. But it was more than that. Emily truly liked Nora. She reminded her so much of Sally during her *rumschpringe* days, before Thomas Detweiler married her and took her away from Paradise…and from a past too wild to be forgotten. *Maybe the area is cursed as Solomon contends. Weakening our resolve and character until we fall so far from grace there's no way back.* It might be too late for her, but Emily vowed to save Nora King, if only from herself.

"I'm glad we don't have preaching tomorrow," said Violet as they climbed into the buggy. "I'm so tired I could sleep standing up like a horse, even wearing these leg braces."

Emily stowed the wheelchair in the back and untied the mare from the hitching post. "You both worked hard today. *Danki,*" she murmured.

"You're *welcum,*" replied her two employees in unison. Then they settled back in silence for the ride to Violet's house.

Emily couldn't remember them ever so quiet, but the silence provided time to plan her approach. Unfortunately, brilliant insight still hadn't arrived by the time Nora helped Violet to the porch and returned to the buggy.

"*Danki* for not talking about Elam in front of Violet," said Nora as soon as they rolled away from the Trasks'. "I don't want to burden her with my problems." Nora gazed off at the passing scenery.

"Does Elam bear false witness against you?" asked Emily.

"*Nein.* Most of what he said is true." Nora's voice was flat and expressionless. "I did drink beer because I was curious about what it tasted like. And I let him kiss me twice because I was curious about that too. But only kisses—we went no further than that."

"Did you sneak out to see him?" Emily focused on the open road ahead.

Nora's young face crumpled with misery. "*Jah*, I took a late night buggy ride while my sister and Sally's family slept soundly in their beds. And once I followed him to see where he was going, but he didn't know I had until later."

"Why would you do such things?"

"Because I was bored and unhappy in Harmony."

Emily sniffed with disdain. "Did you help deceive my brother-in-law?"

Nora began to cry but kept her voice controlled. "*Jah.* I helped

Elam the evening he bought a car, which he hid from Thomas in an abandoned barn. And I knew he was planning to leave Harmony, but I didn't tell anyone."

Emily swallowed down the taste of disappointment. "Why would you do such things to Thomas and Sally? They took you in and provided a home, as Jonas and I have done."

Nora stared at her hands in her lap, as tears fell on her apron and dress. "Because I was a spoiled little girl who had lost her *mamm* and *daed* that spring. I felt sorry for myself and didn't care about anyone's feelings but my own."

The admission caught Emily by surprise. "That doesn't sound like you. There must be more reason than that."

Nora waited several moments before replying. "I fancied myself in love with Elam. And in love with his freedom and lack of restraint. I wanted that and was convinced my future would be with him. It took little encouragement for me to follow him to Missouri."

"And once you got here?"

"It wasn't long before I realized he didn't love me. I simply *amused* him." Her inflection dripped with scorn.

"Yet you continued to see him. You chose to court both men as though you couldn't make up your mind." Emily added an unnecessary huff for punctuation.

"A man can test the waters during *rumschpringe,* so why not a woman? I wanted to know the affections of two men, to feel sought-after and special. Like Elam, I wanted to be carefree and not tied down until I chose to marry." Without lifting her head, she spoke with conviction.

Emily bristled at her stupidity. "Is that how you feel now—carefree? I don't know why it's different for women than men, but it just is. Girls can't behave that way even during *rumschpringe* without being branded as loose, which apparently is what has happened."

Nora emitted several gasps, struggling to draw breath into her lungs. "But I never gave myself to Elam—it was only two kisses. He's making it sound worse out of spite because I refused to see him anymore." Suddenly, her head jerked up as though realization finally took hold. Nora faced Emily on the bench. "I've never deceived you or Jonas. I've neither snuck out at night, nor drank beer since arriving in Paradise." She hugged herself, with arms crossed over her chest. "Since I'm baring my soul in confession, I also kissed Lewis—once after our dinner in Sturgeon."

"Why?" Emily pulled the buggy to the side of the pavement.

"Why what?" Nora's sorrowful demeanor turned confused.

"Why did you kiss Lewis? Were you feeling sorry for yourself that day? Maybe the customers had been rude or maybe I worked you too hard in the shop?"

"No, of course not—"

"Then why did you kiss him? Were you curious how Lewis smooched compared to how Elam kissed? Who, I would imagine, has had more practice," she added wryly.

"*Nein*, Emily. I kissed Lewis because I care for him. I've come to love him." She whispered the words as though the briar thicket might be listening. "Although apparently I came to that conclusion too late, considering the damage Elam has done." Her focus returned to her folded hands while tears started anew.

"Maybe all is not lost. You should write to my *schwester* and Thomas to apologize for your deception. Then tell Lewis the truth about your past behavior in Maine. He may know more than you think. Speak with one of the ministers or Bishop Ephraim whether you should confess your sins during church. Although I don't think it will be necessary because you've done nothing against our *Ordnung*." Emily heard an audible sigh of relief.

"But there are greater things at stake, Nora. You're risking your eternal soul. You must leave *rumschpringe* behind. Take the classes and join the church as soon as possible. Get baptized and dedicate your life to serving the Lord. God will forgive a contrite heart, but people love to gossip. Only actions will prove you're not the same woman you used to be."

"Folks will believe Elam?" asked Nora. "But he's not a member of the Paradise district. He drives a car, dresses more English than Plain, and has never gone to a single preaching service."

"All true, but the natural human tendency is to believe what you hear. No one knows *you* very well either to dismiss his assertions. And partial truth lends credibility to everything he says."

Nora shrank inside her clothes. "Will Lewis believe him?"

"I don't know, but I would talk to him if I were you. Tell him everything. You have no choice."

She just sat there—not agreeing or disagreeing, which struck Emily as odd. *If she truly loves Lewis, wouldn't she be anxious to profess her innocence?* A charge of promiscuity usually rang a death-blow for a man with marriage on the mind.

"If he'll still have you, perhaps you two should marry and return to Maine as soon as possible. Plan to make your home close to your families." Emily shook the reins and guided the horse back onto the road.

"Maine? Why would I have to move back?" Nora arched her back like a startled stray cat.

"It was the best choice for Sally. She married Thomas, left behind her reckless past, and now has two fine *kinner*." Emily clamped down on her molars. "This section of Missouri isn't kind to those who have fallen from grace."

"What do you mean?"

"If Sally and Thomas had stayed in Paradise, they would be childless—the same as Jonas and me."

"You can't believe a couple's address determines their fertility." Nora issued a statement, not asked a question.

"That know-it-all attitude is why you're in hot water now. Never listening to counsel and acting from your own pride and willfulness. *Jah*, I do believe it. This county is cursed except for the truly righteous. And there are few of them around anywhere." Emily glanced at Nora and softened. "Go back to Harmony and start fresh. Make the necessary adjustments. Don't forget that Elam Detweiler lives here now. If you and Lewis stay, you'll never live down your shame. And that's on top of the wrath of God."

If the look on Nora's face was any indication, Emily's warnings had finally hit their mark.

# FIFTEEN

*Redeeming love has been my theme*

Nora climbed down from the buggy feeling sick to her stomach. "Shall I take care of the mare?" she asked.

"*Nein*. You start supper—something quick, like hamburgers, baked beans, and succotash." Emily shook the reins and the horse headed to the barn.

Nora felt as though she walked underwater wearing tall boots filled with stones. *How foolish I was to think my past wouldn't catch up with me. How can I possibly deny Elam's accusations to Lewis? Although I never lost my virtue to Elam, I'm hardly white as snow.*

Inside, she washed up and began frying hamburger patties in a cast-iron skillet. The smell of sautéing onions and peppers whet her appetite. Once she set the pan of burgers in the oven to stay warm, she placed pots of beans and mixed vegetables on to simmer. Deciding on a last-minute salad, she hiked to the garden to pick a bowl of spinach and scallions.

"You're a sight for sore eyes."

Nora straightened to see Lewis leaning against a gate post. His sleeves had been rolled above the elbow, revealing his muscular arms, while his blue eyes sparkled like the pond at dawn against his summer tan. Her heart swelled with love that would never be hers. "Tough week, Mr. Miller?" She resumed picking salad.

"Indeed it has been, Miss King. I've never been so glad for a week to be over. And as much as I love to hear the ministers' fiery sermons, an extra hour of rest tomorrow couldn't come at a better time." He closed the distance between them in two long strides.

When she looked up, he stood right behind her. "Extra sleep will be nice." Accidentally, she tugged spinach up by the roots instead of breaking off the tender leaves.

"Need some help?" He planted his feet on either side of a row of green beans.

"I'm all done." She clutched the colander to her chest and hurried toward the gate. "As soon as I wash these greens, supper will be ready. I suggest you get cleaned up."

Before she could duck under the arbor arch, Lewis grabbed hold of her. "Give me just a minute, Nora." He dropped her arm the moment she stopped. "We barely spoke all week and haven't seen each other except during supper. Will you walk with me tonight or maybe take a buggy ride?"

For an instant, a bizarre thought flitted through her head: *Why, did you hear rumors that I was easy?* She shook off her hatefulness like a horsefly. "We're both tired, Lewis. You said so yourself. Why don't we talk tomorrow on the porch after morning devotions?"

"No, this can't wait another day. And we need a bit of privacy. So will it be a walk to the pond or a ride to the schoolyard? I'll push you in the swing if you say please."

Another memory returned—this one poignant and melancholy of her *daed* pushing her on the backyard tire swing. He was smiling and laughing, as delighted as she. Nora closed her eyes tightly to concentrate on the present. "All right, a walk to the pond. No buggy rides where people on front porches can see us."

"As you wish, but how about some protection from gopher holes lurking dangerously in the tall grass?" Lewis offered his right elbow.

"No, *danki.* I...I must hurry inside." She took off running, heedless of hidden gopher holes. She was more harmful to herself than any outside threat. Inside, Nora found the table set and Emily at the stove, frowning.

"Good thing you set the burners on low or everything would be burned. Should I call Jonas for supper? How long will the salad take you?"

"It'll take only a minute to rinse the greens." Nora held the colander under a cold stream of water, not looking at Emily.

Without a summons Jonas wandered into the kitchen, flipping through a stack of mail. After a short perusal, he tossed all but one small envelope on the counter. "A note from Minister Trask. I'd recognized his slanted handwriting anywhere." Jonas slit open the envelope with a butter knife.

Nora carried the skillet of burgers and fried onions to the table as Jonas's face turned dour. "No visiting with my parents and family tomorrow. We've been summoned to the bishop's house again by Solomon. He wants us to come by ourselves—without our guests." His gaze flickered over Nora at the counter, and Lewis, who had entered from the back mudroom.

"I have some overdue letters to write," said Lewis, drying his hands on a linen towel.

Nora divided salad into four bowls. "I have letters to write as well."

Emily set the bottles of dressing and catsup down with a clatter. "These are difficult times, *ehemann,* requiring sacrifice from everyone. A checker game with your *bruder* in the shade can surely wait another week." Sarcasm dripped from each word.

Jonas tossed the notecard onto the pile, sat down, and bowed his head. After their silent prayer he stared at Emily, more confused than angry. "Have I done something, *fraa,* to warrant your disapproval?"

Lewis and Nora exchanged a nervous glance, and then they began devouring their salads.

"*Mir leid,*" she apologized. "It's been an exhausting day. We'll talk later." Emily poured ranch dressing over half her plate, even the baked beans.

Neither of the Gingerichs, nor their houseguests, ever ate supper so fast. Emily began clearing plates the moment Lewis swallowed his final bite of burger. Nora jumped up too, to scrape her beans into the slop bucket destined for the neighbors' hogs. While she washed and dried the dishes, she could see Lewis pacing the porch like an expectant father-to-be. Setting the iron skillet on a stove burner to dry, Nora pulled off her apron and fled from the house. The cool breeze on her face felt wonderful.

Lewis caught up with her six paces down the path. "Whoa, slow up there. This heat and humidity has really shortened tempers, no? The sooner it rains, the better."

"Rain might make no difference whatsoever."

"I imagine you're not referring to the weather or crops." Lewis kept pace at her side, close but not touching.

"Let's not beat around the bush. I gather you want to talk about Elam." Nora slowed as they rounded the barn, beyond eyesight of the house.

"There's something going on at work I think you should know about."

"Violet mentioned that Elam told—"

"Wait, Nora," he interrupted. "Violet doesn't know about this, so let me continue."

She halted near the fence and grabbed a fistful of chicory. *Could he have not heard Elam's allegations?* "Go on," she said.

"Money was stolen at work a couple weeks ago. I must not have locked the cash register and someone noticed. Elam is the only one I can think of who would steal and then implicate me." He also reached down for a feathery weed. "Luckily, Jonas doesn't believe I'm a thief and decided to see what happens."

"Emily never mentioned this to me."

"Jonas wanted no one to know, not even her. He thought the guilty party would start boasting about it to his coworkers. Besides, the rumor mill can easily convict an innocent man…or woman."

Nora felt her face growing warm, despite the cool breeze in the shade.

"Like Jonas figured, Elam couldn't keep quiet for long. He bragged to the men about buying a used bass boat and outboard motor for a thousand dollars—the approximate amount missing from the drawer."

"That doesn't prove anything," said Nora, not sure why she was defending Elam.

"True enough, but he asked the foreman three times when he planned to fire me. I intend to confront him on Monday about this and the other devilment he's been up to." Lewis tickled her chin with a long-stemmed wildflower.

Nora grabbed the weed and threw it into the brush. "So you've heard the rumors?" She fought back a surge of heartburn, either from the fried onions or stress from her future crumbling before her eyes. She pressed both palms against her stomach.

"I've heard. It would be hard not to working at Gingerich's. Unfortunately, men gossip almost as much as women—almost, but not quite." He tucked a *kapp* ribbon that had blown across her face behind her ear.

Nora stepped back from the tender touch of the gentlest man in the world. "Do you believe what Elam says about me?"

"I do not." Lewis answered without hesitation. "And I told the gossiping men to drop the conversation or I might forget I'm a calm-natured pacifist about to join the Amish church. Everyone took me at my word. We'll see how Detweiler reacts on Monday. But I won't have him sullying the reputation of the woman I love and intend to marry." He lifted her chin with a finger.

For half a second Nora gazed into his eyes and saw nothing but love and acceptance there. Yet despite that and the guilt and shame ruining her digestion, she couldn't bring herself to tell him the truth. "You should do no such thing. I won't have you fighting or threatening him on my behalf. Those who choose to believe him will do so regardless. By confronting him, you'll jeopardize your job as well as your standing with the bishop. And for what?" Her voice cracked with emotion. "I know Elam would never admit he stole. And he won't recant his accusations about me." She batted away a bead of moisture forming on her lip. "It's enough that you wish to defend my honor, Lewis." *My honor?* The false words burned in her throat as tears flooded her eyes.

Far away, some *Englischer* honked his car horn, perhaps at a dog that wandered too close to the road. Overhead, sparrows and wrens chattered high in the tree branches while settling down for the night. And inside her chest, Nora's heart pounded so hard she feared a rib might crack.

Lewis waited, patient as always, to see if she would say more. "Because you insist, I won't confront him about you, but I will ask how he paid for a fishing boat when his car had just been in the shop for repairs."

"Agreed. Are we looking at the pond tonight or not? It will soon be dark." Nora tried to step past him, but he blocked her path.

"The pond can wait. Is there any truth to Elam's gossip?" Lewis gazed to the left where a deer and fawn had crept from the thicket to nibble wind-blown apples on the ground. A muscle tensed in his neck, betraying tension equaling hers.

"Some of what he said is true, but not all. I'm not proud of how I behaved while a guest at Thomas and Sally's."

"Considering we might become husband and wife this fall, don't I have the right to know fact from fiction?"

Nora shifted her weight to the other foot, drawing the doe's attention. For a second, the animal and woman locked eyes—both terrified, but for very different reasons. Then the deer nudged her baby, and they sprinted back to the protective cover of the brush and woods beyond.

How she wished her safety could be so easily restored. "No, Lewis. Despite whatever rights you feel you have, I won't discuss my past." Nora swatted a mosquito feasting on her arm. "It's too buggy tonight to go to the pond. I'm heading to my room to read instead." She turned and walked away—waiting, hoping, praying—for what? For him to declare, "I love you no matter what you did? I want no one in my life but you?"

But no one followed her as she approached the barn. And no declarations of everlasting love carried on the evening breeze. As she had been while fleeing Maine, and also when leaving Lancaster County, Nora King was alone in the world.

$\infty$

Lewis watched her go with a sinking feeling in his gut. Separation from his home and family, learning a new job with *Englischers*, being accused of robbing the cash register—all paled compared to Nora turning her back on him. *Doesn't she love me? Was this trip to Missouri the foolish, desperate act of a lonely man? Why can't she tell me the truth about her past?*

He wandered down to the pond in the growing gloom. Dusk brought forth impenetrable shadows on both sides of the path, while hordes of biting insects took flight from the shrubbery. A three-quarter moon rose above the trees, casting a shimmery glow on the water. Now and then, fish broke the surface as they leaped into the air for an evening snack. Lewis stared at the murky

pond—which concealed the depth, quality of water, and nature
of the bottom and shoreline. A creature might wade in for a cool
drink, expecting a sandy foothold and clean water, only to become
entangled by thick water hyacinths or mired in oozing mud where
living things would soon meet a premature, toxic death. Was this
also the nature of a woman's heart—deceptive, ensnaring, and ulti-
mately destructive?

Fatigue was making him overly dramatic—like an *Englischer*.
Lewis picked up a flat rock to skim across the surface. Once, twice,
thrice it skated across the water until it sank to the bottom—a normal, natural pond bottom, without insidious green monsters hoping to drown hapless deer.

Nora was no green-eyed monster either. She was a spirited
woman who would rather forget past mistakes. Lewis believed she
no longer cared for Elam. If anyone had captured her heart, it was
him. He could live with her errors in judgment. He could even
accept she'd been in love with another man. But he couldn't accept
her refusal to tell the truth. Marriage was a lifetime commitment,
and life usually was long and filled with pitfalls. Without honesty,
there could be no trust. And without trust, love would soon wither
like young plants in the hot sun. He'd heard that beauty fades and
passion wanes, but trust nourishes love like a gentle rain. That was
the kind of marriage his parents had. And that was what he wanted
for himself with Nora, but their future was up to her.

When Lewis smacked his cheek for the third time, he abandoned the mosquito grove and headed back to the house. A sole
kerosene lamp burned on the kitchen counter, signaling that Emily
and Nora had gone to bed. But Jonas sat at the table, nursing a cup
of coffee. An Amish newspaper and his Bible lay nearby, unopened.

"Won't that caffeine keep you awake tonight?" asked Lewis,
opening the refrigerator door. He selected a can of orange soda and
joined his host and boss.

"It's doubtful I would be able to sleep anyway. Too much on my mind." Jonas met his eye, looking older than his thirty-five years. "Why is your face bleeding?"

"I scratched at bug bites, trying to figure out my life."

"How did that work down by the pond?" Jonas clutched his mug with both hands.

"About as well as it has in here." Lewis stretched out his long legs. "But at least you didn't lose a pint of blood."

Jonas's laughter rang hollow in the quiet room. "Elam's causing trouble for you and Nora, isn't he?"

"Only if we let him, but I refuse to give him that satisfaction." He drank several long swallows, savoring the sweetness.

Jonas studied the flame sputtering behind the clear glass shade. "Like I thought, Elam has been bragging to his Amish friends. He told Josh you would pay the price for stealing another man's girl. That soon you'll be heading back East with your tail between your legs." He locked gazes with Lewis.

Lewis fought back a wave of anger. "No one can steal another person's affection. Either you have their love or you don't." He finished the can of soda.

The older man nodded, stroking his beard. "I heard something else too. Elam invited some English friends out on his power boat tomorrow afternoon. He plans to trailer it to Mark Twain Lake and go fishing."

Lewis blinked. "You heard about his new boat?"

"I did, but we can't prove he used Gingerich money to buy it. Suppositions are all I have, and I won't act on assumptions. But I know *you* didn't steal from me. I knew that right away."

Lewis exhaled and ran a hand through his tangled hair. "*Danki* for your trust, Jonas, but I regret causing problems at the lumberyard. If you like, I'll look for another job."

"No, you will not." Jonas thumped his empty mug on the table. "You're not going anywhere. At least, not over this. As early as tomorrow evening, the matter will be out of our hands. Josh and

Seth have talked to Solomon Trask about Elam's threats and about him buying a boat, so we shall bide our time. Put it out of your mind for now."

Lewis struggled to his feet, tired beyond description. "It's not what Elam says or has done that's troubling me, but I appreciate your confidence and concern."

"*Gut nacht*, Lewis." Jonas slipped on his reading glasses and opened his worn Bible.

Lewis wearily climbed the steps, suffocated by the heat in the stairwell. How he wished he was back home in Maine, where summers were cooler and far less complicated. Just for a moment, he wished he'd never chased this pipe dream into the flatlands of Missouri.

❧

Solomon shifted on his chair, his back spasms worsening with each passing minute. No breeze stirred the curtains in the airless living room. His grandchildren squirmed on the couch, while the eyes of his daughters-in-law had glazed over long ago. Violet watched him from her wheelchair, while even Rosanna's face pleaded for an end to the morning devotions.

"In conclusion," he said, "I'll read Revelation sixteen, verses five and six: 'You are just, O Holy One, who is and who always was, because you have sent these judgments. Since they shed the blood of your holy people and your prophets, you have given them blood to drink. It is their just reward.'" He snapped shut the Bible. "Today, I go to the bishop's home for an important meeting with the ministerial brethren to decide the fate of our distressed district. I hope you will pray for the proper solution to our woes." He gazed over his family as they bowed their heads.

Perhaps they prayed for a summer shower to bring relief from the oppressive heat. Maybe they prayed for no interruptions during their afternoon nap in the hammock. Or perhaps they merely prayed for devotions to conclude, releasing them to the cool shade outdoors. Sol would never know. His wife, daughters, sons, their spouses, and grandchildren filed from the room as soon as he uttered a final "Amen."

Only Violet remained, pale and anxious in her wheelchair. "What will happen today, Papa? Something awful? You read from the book of Revelation as though anticipating disaster." She rolled closer to him, not toward the door to the porch.

Sol reached out to pat her head as though she were still a little girl. "I seek to avert calamity with my actions. Don't be afraid, *dochder*."

"Shall I go with you to offer support?" She clutched his hand tightly.

"*Nein*. You stay here and pray for your friends and family. God listens to the pleas from innocents such as you." Solomon turned to find his wife, leaving Violet in the stuffy front room. Within minutes, he and Rosanna climbed into their buggy and were on their way. Irvin raised his hand in farewell from the porch.

After they had both been lost in thought for miles, Rosanna tried to lift his spirits. "Things are often darkest before the dawn."

"Dawn might not be coming soon for the Amish of Paradise," he murmured, more to himself than her.

If the mood inside the meeting was any indication, the minister had prophesized correctly. After the wives left to sew in another room, Bishop Ephraim wasted no time with pleasantries. "I heard there's trouble at your lumberyard, Deacon Jonas. You suspect one of our people has stolen money and blamed another Amish man?"

Jonas cleared his throat. "That's what I suspect, but I have no concrete proof. The man admits no wrongdoing, so I have only theories and conjecture."

"How we must appear to the English—robbing each other and bearing false witness to cover our tracks." Ephraim shook his head sadly, and then he scrubbed his palms down his face.

"It isn't how we look to *Englischers* that should concern us, but how we look to God," said Sol. "It's His judgment we should fear and His reprisals." Three pairs of eyes focused on him. "Elam Detweiler isn't 'one of our people,' Bishop. He's a fence-sitter at best, and, more likely, an outcast from his former community, sent away because of repeated infractions to his district's *Ordnung*. He hasn't been baptized into our faith, nor does he accept our customs or traditions. He's caused problems for the family where he rents a room, concerning his car and use of alcohol." Sol drew in a breath before he fainted from lack of oxygen.

Ephraim, Jonas, and the younger minister, Peter, looked saddened rather than disgusted, the emotion Solomon was experiencing.

"Go on," prodded the bishop.

Sol held up his Bible. "This morning I pored over both books of the apostle John, searching for guidance with Elam. Let me read a passage from First John, chapter three: 'When people keep on sinning, it shows they belong to the devil, who has been sinning since the beginning…Those who have been born into God's family do not make a practice of sinning…So now we can tell who are children of God and who are children of the devil.'" His voice shook with fury.

"What would you have us do, Brother Solomon, with this young man?" asked Ephraim.

"Our only choice is clear. In Second John, we learn: 'Anyone who wanders away from this teaching has no relationship with God… Anyone who encourages such people becomes a partner in their evil work.' We must drive him from our community. The Petersheims should tell him to move out, and you need to fire him, Jonas."

Jonas leaned forward in his chair. "Without proof that he

committed a crime? You wish me to convict him based on speculation?"

"I wish you to pluck a rotten apple from the barrel before it turns the entire harvest wormy. Our young people are our future. Elam influences them with his fancy clothes and fast cars, and now a powerboat." Solomon let his voice rise with agitation. "More of our youth will extend their running-around period and take up strong drink and carousing on weekends. Whether or not he stole the money, the man is a poison to our district!"

Bishop Ephraim held up a hand. "Those are strong words."

Solomon nodded in agreement. "They are, but I haven't reached my conclusion without hours spent in contemplation."

"Couldn't we pray for this young man that he be restored to the fold?" asked Peter with youthful optimism.

"Elam has never been in the Amish fold. He has remained a thorn in the side of his former community and now ours."

Peter stared down at his polished black shoes, deep in thought. Jonas gazed out the window as though distracted by a chattering squirrel in the tree. Ephraim focused on his liver-spotted hands folded atop his Bible.

Solomon knew he must forge ahead. The time was now to make changes that would preserve their existence in Missouri. "Detweiler is not our sole threat. These are dire times we're in. Around us horrible events portend a sorrowful end to the Plain way of life. We need to examine our district for others lingering too long during *rumschpringe*. It's time they take classes and commit to the church. We need to make sure there are no further infractions to our *Ordnung*, and we must reduce our dependence on tourists for income. We should separate ourselves from the temptations of sin—to be in this world, but not of this world. Our community is headed down a path of self-destruction like so many Christians before us."

Sol swiveled on the chair. "Jonas, instruct your Plain employees not to fraternize with their English coworkers. I intend to tell

Violet not to strike up long conversations with bakery customers. Many come to the shop more to spy on our way of life than to fill their pantries with bread and baked sweets."

Jonas glared at Solomon, his face hard and immobile. "And you wish me to instruct Emily and Nora to do the same?" His tone betrayed his opinion of the idea.

"Not Nora, but tell Emily, *jah*. Selling to English locals is one thing, but encouraging the tourists will only hasten our downfall and eventual judgment."

The bishop waved a hand through the air. "Solomon, do not make decisions by yourself. That's why we have four brethren—to reach the best possible solution based on Scripture," said Ephraim.

"I assure you, Bishop, that I have studied Scripture endlessly since our problems escalated—"

"You mean those passages that support your forgone conclusions," said Jonas, opening his hands to show thick calluses. "Have you forgotten the Savior's message of love and forgiveness, of turning the other cheek when wronged? Of not sitting in judgment of our fellow man? That's God's domain, not yours or mine."

Solomon glowered at the deacon. "I haven't forgotten, but I also remember Paul's instructions to Titus: 'If people are causing divisions among you, give a first and second warning. After that have nothing more to do with them. For people like that have turned away from the truth, and their own sins condemn them.'"

Suddenly, Jonas's brows drew together over the bridge of his nose. "What did you mean earlier…not Nora, only Emily?" He rubbed the back of his neck.

He snorted. "Nora King is not my concern because she never joined the church. But if you are wise, Deacon Gingerich, you would send her back to her family in Maine or in Pennsylvania. You are housing a jezebel—a fallen woman—and in so doing, you condone her sinful behavior. You aren't managing your household well according to Paul's instructions to church leaders in the book of First Timothy."

"Enough!" thundered Ephraim with unusual volume and vehemence. "You go too far with your hasty accusations, Minister. If Elam has evil intentions toward others, why would you listen to his slurs against this young woman's character?"

Embarrassed, Sol hung his head, realizing too late that he'd overstepped his role. "You are right, Bishop."

"We will call on this Elam Detweiler to hear what he has to say. He was warned weeks ago, so this will serve as his second warning. We will encourage him to confess his sins on bended knee and join our congregation. If he does, all will be forgotten and never mentioned again. But you're right, Solomon. If the man refuses, he must be treated no differently than a shunned member. We'll ask him to leave Paradise or, at least, have no further association with the Amish."

Ephraim trained his watery blue eyes on Jonas. "Follow your own heart regarding your place of business. But if you choose to let him go, see that he has sufficient severance pay to return to his people in Maine or tide him over until he finds another job and place to live." The bishop stood, signaling an end to the ministerial meeting.

Sol rose to his feet too, nodding at the others. On stiff legs he sought his *fraa* in the front room and they started for home, refusing the bishop's offer of coffee and pie. Paradoxically, he felt vindicated and yet wearier than ever before in his life.

# SIXTEEN

## *And shall be till I die*

Solomon remained on his knees beside the bed twice as long as usual that Monday morning. He had plenty to confess and much to be grateful for. He regretted speaking so harshly about Nora to Jonas. Not only did he need the deacon's support for today's unpleasant task, but his assessment of the young woman hadn't been fair or kind. Since her arrival, she had treated his daughter like a sister. And his daughter assured him Detweiler's claims must be false. Violet was an excellent judge of character and she adored Nora.

His gratefulness stemmed from the bishop and other minister agreeing with him. *What would I have done if they failed to recognize the immediate need to act?* Even Jonas hadn't challenged the bishop's decision to cut off the diseased limb so that the remaining tree might flourish. As Sol struggled to his feet, his final prayer was for guidance and patience. Man could do little on his own, but with divine intervention mountains could be moved. Surely, one wild young man could be sent packing back to the English world where he belonged.

Downstairs, Solomon found Irvin at the kitchen table, finishing a plate of blueberry pancakes. "What happened, son? Did your wife send you away for snoring or for tracking up her freshly washed kitchen floor? It's hard to imagine your house without food for breakfast." He chuckled as Rosanna handed him a cup of coffee.

"*Nein*. I already ate Susanna's eggs with bacon, and now some of *mamm*'s pancakes. Can't play favorites with *two* good cooks in my life, can I?" Irvin patted his taut midsection. "I had to occupy my time until you came downstairs. Or did you forget about today?" He peered over his thick glasses.

For a moment, Sol stared at his eldest son blankly. "Goodness, the hay. I had forgotten you asked for help yesterday." He slumped into his chair.

"I'm short a man since Mark's *fraa* went into labor." Irvin lifted his mug for his mother to refill.

Rosanna placed a stack of three pancakes before Sol, and then she encircled his neck with her arms. "Soon we'll have another *kinskinner*—maybe by nightfall. I'm hoping for a little girl this time." She kissed the top of his head.

"*Gut*, but these things take time, especially as it's their first *boppli*."

"Because it *is* their first, Mark won't leave Ann's side. Can you drive the binder for me? I'll drive the team pulling the cutting blade."

Sol drank long and deep before replying. "*Jah*, but I must leave on district business by three o'clock."

"Then we'd better get the teams ready to go." Irvin sprang up and out the door with the agility of a young man.

Sol ate his breakfast and drank a second cup of coffee before joining his son in the fields with far less energy. Later, after he'd washed, changed clothes, and headed to the Petersheims', his stamina plummeted even further. Jonas had selected today for their visit because Elam had Mondays off. All four ministerial brethren would come after work, each arriving in a separate buggy.

None of them anticipated Detweiler not being home. After they rocked on the porch, sipping Ruth's weak iced tea for two hours, he finally returned. Elam drove up the driveway fast enough to send chickens scurrying for their lives. James and Ruth retreated inside the house and closed the door, aware they shouldn't hear possible reprimands. Solomon, Ephraim, Peter, and Jonas left the porch together and walked across the lawn.

The young man parked his car behind the barn and met them halfway across the yard. "Now I can tell who's who," said Elam. "While sitting like four crows on a fence, you all looked the same." He grinned broadly as though they would appreciate his humor. "Hey, isn't today Monday? Or do I need a new calendar?" An odor of greasy fried food wafted from the paper sack he carried. In his other hand, he held a six-pack of Pepsi.

Briefly, Sol wished the cola had been beer, thus providing an easy entry into their conversation. Jonas got the ball rolling without preamble. "I heard you went fishing yesterday on your new boat."

Elam set the food down in the tall grass. "That's right. I caught a half dozen trout, big enough to fry up for supper, which I just haven't had a chance to cook up yet. So I bought fast food." He nudged the bag with his foot. "My buddies caught the legal limit too. Good fishing on Mark Twain Lake, considering we reached the lake at the hottest part of the day." He turned his ball cap around backward— an absurd custom among the English, in Sol's estimation.

"Boats with outboard motors don't come cheap," continued Jonas. "Josh told me your car recently needed a new transmission."

"Don't forget about the trailer I bought, boss. Gotta have a way to carry the boat to the water." Elam pulled on his scruffy goatee. "You're probably wondering if I'm the one who stole your money instead of Miller."

"I am. Was it you?"

A smirk, not a smile, tugged up the corners of Elam's mouth. "You have electricity running your lights and computers. Maybe you should have invested in security cameras. You'll never know for sure since you won't take my word for it."

"You're right," said Jonas. "I have a hard time believing *anything* you say. That's why I want you to look for another job. I'll give you a recommendation because I have no proof, but I can't trust you. And I don't want men on my payroll I can't trust."

Elam's wry humor faded. "You're firing *me*?"

"Correct. I'll give you two weeks to line something up, plus an extra two weeks of severance pay. But after that, I want you gone."

"Why did you drive all the way here with reinforcements?" Elam nodded at the other elders. "This could have waited until I came to work tomorrow."

Ephraim cleared his throat and stepped forward. "The district is concerned about habits you've developed, son. You've been straddling the fence between the English world and ours for a long time. You're already twenty-two. That's old enough to decide who you want to be."

Something about the bishop's suggestion riled Detweiler. "I'm not your *son*," he snapped. "My dad's been long in his grave. Besides, I know *exactly* who I am. And it's not like any of you."

Sweeping off his hat, Sol thumped it against his leg, but Ephraim raised his hand to control the discussion. "We have noticed that. Maybe I should have approached you formally to invite you to services. You're welcome to take classes in preparation to join our congregation. Once you've been baptized, past transgressions are erased and never talked about again." Ephraim looked from Jonas back to Elam.

"If I join, do I keep my job?" He crossed his arms over his St. Louis Cardinals T-shirt.

"No, my mind is made up about your employment." Jonas stared at the younger man with equal determination.

"Ha!" Elam barked a laugh that cut through the humid air. "I was just curious as to what you would say, Jonas. I have no intention of becoming Amish, either here or back in Maine."

"Then we must ask you to leave the Petersheim household." Solomon could remain silent no longer. "They have young children who don't need your influence in their lives."

"Is that right? James and Ruth know about this?" Elam straightened to his full, impressive height.

"They do," said Sol. "They wish to do what's best for the district."

"My rent is paid up until the end of the month." Elam shifted his weight and leaned toward Sol menacingly.

"You can stay until then or get a refund for the unused portion." Ephraim stepped closer to Elam—a mouse-sized man against Goliath. "No one wishes ill-will toward you. In the end, you'll soon discover it's best for everyone if you find an English place to live and work."

Elam gazed at the elderly bishop—a grandfather twenty times over—and softened. "You're probably right. Paradise has just about bored me to death."

"But sleep on it before making up your mind. Should you decide to remain Amish and become one of us, come see me." Ephraim pulled a note from his inner pocket. "I wrote down the address and directions of how to find my house."

Elam took the paper and slipped it into his jeans.

"But it will be Amish by our rules, not interpreting the *Ordnung* as you see fit," added Solomon. He couldn't resist taking a stand against this potentially deadly adversary.

Elam closed the distance between them. "I knew you never liked me. I don't reckon you like many people. Just be glad your daughter takes after your wife and not you." His sly grin returned for a final appearance.

Peter—a man of equal stature as the bishop—separated the two men with one hand on Sol's chest and one on Elam's. "There is no need to turn things personal here."

Elam walked away, shaking his head. "Time for supper anyway, before my food turns ice cold. I trust you gentlemen can find your way out. Just use the same driveway you rode in on." Hooting with laughter, he ran up the Petersheim flagstone path to the porch.

Once Detweiler closed the door behind him, everyone stood in the yard for another minute. Solomon feared the bishop might censure him for his display of temper, but Ephraim and the others looked every bit as tired as he felt. They shook hands and headed for home...each lost in his own thoughts.

Solomon soon fell fast asleep with his chin lolling on his chest. It was a good thing his mare, Nell, knew the route, or who knew where in Missouri the minister might have ended up.

❧

Jonas bid the other elders good night and climbed into his buggy. What a long drive he faced, alone with his misgivings and burden of shame, despite the Petersheims living only four miles away. He didn't like how he'd risen up against Elam in anger, feeling righteous after firing him. Even if he was a thief, Jonas still should have remained objective and sorrowful that someone would stoop so low to buy a fishing boat. What price for a man's soul? If by some odd twist of fate Elam was innocent, he had just fired a man because he didn't like how he dressed or his mode of transportation.

He had united with the ministers and bishop to challenge this outsider determined to undermine the Amish way of life, yet Jonas felt no kinship with them then or now. The long hot summer was wreaking havoc on their lives. Was it Satan at work? Or did humankind not need outside help to flounder in personal weakness? Jonas didn't believe they must ostracize people or face extinction as a culture. Jesus came with a message of love and forgiveness, of compassion and tolerance. Elam may never find his way back to any Christian faith, but shouldn't they lead by example? Their hostility toward him was more threatening to their faith than the influence of tourists.

Where did the answer lie? Solomon had found Scripture to support his actions and beliefs. But was a heavy hand always the best policy? The *Ordnung* existed to remove focus from the individual and prevent disagreements from tearing apart a community. And Jonas loved his Old Order Amish church. It sustained him, keeping him where he wanted to be—close to the earth, his family, and his Lord. His dilemma stretched far past Elam Detweiler. Solomon had convinced Peter and Ephraim that only rigid thinking and strict enforcement of rules could save them. But save them from what—the next flood or drought or crop-destroying weevil? The three would soon convince the entire district they must sever friendships with neighbors and retreat from *Englischers* as though they carried a deadly virus.

And what would happen to the youth still on *rumschpringe*? Young people were the future of any community. Wouldn't forcing them to make hasty decisions drive many from their ranks? But even Emily agreed with Solomon. She made that clear by blaming their infertility on some unforgivable sin. Jonas didn't believe that. He couldn't believe that. Yet he also realized for the first time he was completely alone, separated not only from his brethren, but from Emily and his family.

*Except for God.* As Jonas meditated on that all-encompassing truth, the despair that had brought him to tears began to lift. Within another mile, his strength returned and along with it came gnawing hunger. When was the last time he'd eaten? Nothing since one sandwich and a pear at noon, seven hours ago?

"Get up there!" he called, shaking the reins. The gelding dutifully complied, lifting his hooves into a proper trotter pace.

After a second growl from his empty stomach, Jonas reached under the seat for his lunch cooler. He found a baggy of oatmeal raisin cookies, baked by his beloved *fraa. No,* he thought, *not by Emily, but by Nora.* He ate them in short order while contemplating the lost lamb from Lancaster. *A jezebel?* Hardly, but he hadn't stepped up to provide the spiritual help she desperately needed. Nora had been confused, or else she never would have followed a man like Elam to Paradise. Even he, a man without any romantic expertise whatsoever, could see those two weren't suited to each other.

Jonas turned into his lane with a plan in mind. He might not possess matchmaking skills, but Emily was good with young people. He would enlist her help with Nora. The task might provide distraction from their problems and, he hoped, bridge the gap between them that had grown into a chasm. Once inside his barn, Jonas jumped down from the buggy and ran smack into Lewis. "Goodness, you almost gave me a heart attack." He clutched his chest.

"Sorry about that." Lewis unhitched the horse from the harnesses with nimble fingers. "I was waiting out here, figuring you'd be tired by the time you got home. Let me take care of your horse." He led the animal into a stall and began brushing his damp coat.

Jonas pushed the buggy into the yard, out of the way. "*Jah,* I'm tired, but I'm also hungry enough to chew on leather right about now. Did you save me any supper?"

Lewis grinned over the stall wall and winked. "I believe there are chicken necks and some lima beans left. Maybe half a corn muffin."

Jonas tugged on a pair of gloves and reached for the bucket hanging inside the stall. "I'll remember that when it's time to hand out raises."

But Lewis pulled the handle from his grasp. "I'll get the water and feed. Emily is waiting in the house."

Their eyes met and held before Jonas turned on his heels. "Much obliged," he said, dropping the gloves on the bench. His kitchen and his *fraa* sounded wonderful, even with only stewed chicken necks and a bowl of beans.

"I thought you would never get home." Emily rose from the table as soon as he opened the door. She had been reading the *Budget,* the Amish newspaper that was mailed to their house once a week from Sugar Creek, Ohio.

"Seemed that way to me too." Jonas hung up his hat and coat and headed to the sink to wash. He splashed water on his face and neck, enjoying the cool relief. "When the four of us arrived, Elam wasn't home. We had to wait hours for him to return from Columbia. But the matter has been resolved." Jonas fell into a chair. Leaning back gingerly, he stretched out his back one vertebra at the time.

"Did you fire him?" She poured him a glass of iced tea.

"*Jah,* with two weeks' notice plus severance pay." He gulped down half his drink.

"*Gut.* Sally's brother-in-law or not, I'll be glad to see that troublemaker gone." Emily pulled a covered plate from the oven and placed it before him.

When Jonas peeled back the foil, he found two chicken legs,

a thigh, and a breast next to a mound of buttered noodles. Not a neck or a lima bean in sight. "*Danki* for keeping my supper warm." Tucking a napkin into his shirt collar, he uttered a brief prayer and bit into a chicken leg. Never had food tasted so good.

Emily handed him a bowl of sliced cucumbers and tomatoes, dressed with oil, vinegar, and garlic. He studied her while she poured a glass of tea and sat down opposite him. She looked hot, tired, and in no better mood than usual for the past week. Wisely, Jonas waited until he finished dinner before broaching his subject. After swallowing the last forkful of tomatoes, he wiped his mouth. "Elam is no longer our problem, but Nora still is," he whispered.

"What do you mean?" Emily also lowered her voice.

"When we agreed to take her in, I'm sure Sally and Thomas expected more than feeding her and providing a place to sleep."

His wife studied him over the rim of her glass.

"I'm the deacon of this district. I should have counseled her and taken interest in her well-being. I've barely said more than 'your pies are better' the whole time she's lived here. She's a troubled woman. Things aren't good between her and Lewis. And he came to Missouri with high hopes of taking home a bride."

Emily cocked her head to the side to listen. "I talked to her the other day and laid down the law," she continued, once certain no one stirred overhead. "I explained that her soul was in jeopardy. She must stop trying to be popular with young men and settle down before she loses her chance for marriage." Emily added an unpleasant *harrumph*, sounding like an elderly widow without a bit of patience with the world.

Jonas peered at the love of his life. "Was that your advice to Sally during her *rumschpringe*?"

The question took Emily by surprise. "Excuse me?"

"Did you deliver an ultimatum to your younger sister, along with an insult and the threat of eternal damnation?"

Emily's eyes almost bugged from head. "*Nein,* I didn't."

"No, you listened to Sally. You were patient with her and not quick to pronounce judgment or issue threats. So why would you treat the younger sister of Amy Detweiler any differently?"

"I don't know. It seemed like the best thing to do at the time." Emily's eyes filled with tears, but her posture indicated resistance still remained. "It's late, *ehemann,* and I'm too tired to debate this with you."

"Perhaps you can pray about it?" he asked softly. "Then maybe further debate won't be necessary."

Emily jumped to her feet, set his plate and bowl in the sink, and hurried up the steps. Never before in their marriage had she allowed dirty dishes to remain overnight. That alone indicated his words may have finally penetrated her thick shell of indignation.

❧

## Tuesday

*"Amy, you and Nora watch over your schwestern. Rachel and Beth are still too little to know they shouldn't get close to skittish mares.*

*Nora gazed over her shoulder at* mamm—*young and thin and smiling as she selected the next tiny dress to hang on the clothes line. Amy took Rachel's hand while Nora clasped Beth's, and together they crept to the paddock fence where a spotted Appaloosa nursed a pair of twins. The colt had brown and white patches like his mother, while the foal was pure white, without marking or blemish.*

*"Pick me up, No-rahh," cried Beth in* Deutsch. *Nora lifted her four-year-old sister as high as she could so that she could also gaze on the miracle of creation in between the fence rails.*

*"Nora."*

*She ignored her sister, content to watch the maternal scene a while longer. The spring sunshine warmed her back, while a cool breeze sent her kapp ribbons fluttering. Yellow buttercups and blue violets dotted the pasture, breaking the verdant expanse of new green grass.*

"Nora. It's time to get up." Oddly, Beth hadn't spoken in their Amish dialect this time, but in perfect English—a language she hadn't learned yet and wouldn't until she started school. Stranger still, a gentle squeeze of her shoulder accompanied the demand.

"Beth?" asked Nora, shaking her head. She blinked, sat up, and then rubbed her eyes.

"Not Beth. It's me, Emily." Her boss perched on the edge of her bed, wearing a worried expression. "You were calling your sisters' names in your sleep. And talking to your mother," she added.

Nora peered around. Their farm in the foothills of the Alleghany Mountains in Lancaster County had vanished. Amy, Beth, Rachel—all still children—were gone too. Slanted rays of sunshine and swirling dust motes filled her austere bedroom on the second floor of the Gingerich home. "I was having a vivid dream of home," she murmured, kicking down the quilt that had tangled around her legs. "Sometimes the pain medicine for my migraines creates intense images that seem so real." Nora scrubbed her face with her hands.

Emily appeared only more concerned. "Are you all right? How's the headache? Maybe I worked you too hard yesterday, baking all those pies and loaves of bread, besides washing clothes. We sure got a lot done." She patted Nora's shoulder gently.

Nora straightened against the oak headboard. "I'm fine. My headache is gone, thanks to the pills and extra sleep."

"*Gut*, because I have two things to tell you." Emily inhaled a deep breath. "One, Jonas and I are going to Columbia in a hired bus. He needs to meet with his banker, and I want to spend time in the library, reading. We'll probably treat ourselves to supper in town on our day off."

Nora's fog had begun to clear. "I thought Wednesdays were Jonas's and Lewis's days off."

"Usually they are, but Jonas decided to switch days for both of them this week."

Nora fidgeted, eager to get up, but Emily had trapped her in the bed. The other side was against the wall. "Have a nice time. I'll surely find something for my lunch and supper. And don't worry about me getting lonesome."

"I won't, because of my second news. Violet is downstairs, waiting for you. She says if you don't get up soon, she'll crawl up the steps and clobber you with one of her crutches." Emily held up her palms. "Those were her words, not mine."

"What? She'll see me at work in two days. Any urgent gossip could have waited. How did she get here?"

"Lewis picked her up. He's waiting in the kitchen for you too."

Nora reached for the balled-up quilt and tugged it over her head. "*Ach,* this is too much. Why have they come? Can't a gal catch up on sleep?" She spoke from under the hot covers. Sweat had already plastered her nightgown to her back.

In one swift movement, Emily stripped the quilt from the bed. "They are here because they are your friends and worried about you. Neither believes a single word Detweiler spews. They want to take you for a buggy ride and picnic to get your mind off your woes. Violet packed a hamper to the brim in case you're gone for days."

"I'll take it from here, Emily." A breathless voice came from the doorway. Violet limped across the bedroom, her braces thumping against the wooden floor. Her face was beet-red and glistening with perspiration, but she smiled despite each painful stride.

Emily rose to her feet as Nora scrambled off the bed. "I would have come down. Emily just told me you were here not a minute ago." Nora put an arm around Violet's waist and guided her to the room's sole chair.

Violet sat down heavily, her braces banging against the chair. "You're lucky, missy, that I didn't carry the crutches up with me." She hiked up her skirt and rubbed an exposed portion of leg.

"Because you would have clobbered me?" asked Nora, kneeling by her feet.

"Without a second thought." Violet smiled and wiped her forehead with her hanky.

"If you can help Violet down safely," said Emily to Nora, "Jonas and I will be off. I just heard the van toot its horn." To Violet, she said, "Good luck."

Both girls nodded and chimed in unison, "We'll be fine."

Emily headed down the steps while the two friends stared at each other. "What did she mean by that—good luck?" asked Nora.

"She knows I'm here to talk sense to a cement-head."

Nora broke into a fit of giggles. "No one has ever spoken to me like that." She shook her head from side to side.

"More's the pity." Violet clasped Nora's arm, her face sobering. "You need to get a grip. That man downstairs loves you. He's pacing the floor back and forth like a dog on a chain. He doesn't believe Detweiler's lies and neither do I. And all the district's *smart* folks won't either. What do you care if a few un-smart people whisper behind your back? In time, it will pass when some other poor soul lands in the spotlight." Violet dabbed her cheeks again as her color returned to normal.

Nora looked at her best friend in Missouri—in the whole world actually, while a lump rose into her throat. "I've never had a pal like you." She threw her arms around the frailer woman and hugged until Violet gasped for air.

"Let a gal breathe, Nora King." Violet extracted herself from the embrace. "And stop sounding like you're dying. Let's hobble down and go riding with Lewis. I packed sandwiches, cold homemade pizza, fresh strawberries—" Her voice trailed off, finally noticing Nora's expression. "What is it? Spill your guts already, because you're scaring me." She thumped her braced leg.

Nora pushed off the floor and settled on the edge of the bed.

"I might not be dying, but I can't face Lewis. He wants honesty, and I'm too ashamed to tell him the truth." She waved her hand through the air to stem potential interruptions. "Elam lied about me and him. A couple kisses were all we shared." She looked Violet in the eye. "But I'm no virgin. I gave in to a boy in Pennsylvania—someone who I thought loved me. He didn't, and I surrendered my virtue for nothing. How can I admit to Lewis, 'No, it wasn't Elam; it was somebody else you've never met?'" Nora dropped her gaze. "I feel so embarrassed. Why did I foolishly think my past wouldn't catch up with me?"

After a half minute, Nora raised her chin. Violet seemed to be desperately searching for a solution that didn't exist.

"Maybe you wouldn't have to bring up Pennsylvania. Just talk about Maine and here," she suggested.

Nora reached for Violet's hand and pressed it to her cheek. "We both know a man as nice as Lewis deserves an honest wife. I couldn't live with myself if I lied to him, and yet I cannot face him and admit I'm a damaged woman. Just like rumor has it," she added wryly, attempting to smile.

"What can I do?" Violet's question sounded weak and child-like. "What should I tell him?" She pointed at the floor in case Nora had forgotten her one true love was pacing the floor below.

"Go down and tell him my headache returned with a vengeance. That's no lie." She closed her eyes tightly for a moment. "Tell him I must pull the shade and swallow more pain reliever." Nora tightened her grip on Violet's small hand. "I'm glad you came over today. Truly, I am."

In that instant, Nora had a blinding revelation—her days were numbered in Paradise. Lewis would soon return to Harmony. Elam would drive off in his red Chevy. And she would have no choice but to move back to Amy in Maine, or Rachel and Beth in Lancaster County. Nora knew she would never have a friend like Violet again. She squeezed Violet's fingers. "You know what? Tomorrow is still another day off. I baked so much yesterday that we'll be in good shape for Thursday at Grain of Life. What do you say we go on a picnic, just the two of us? Girl time—no men allowed. I'll pack the lunch and then find a place to dangle our feet in water, just how you like. Maybe there will even be ice cream involved." She wriggled her brows and grinned.

"I would love that," said Violet, sadness shading her words. "But what should I do with today's hamper and Lewis?" Again, she pointed at the floor.

"Be an angel and share your lunch with him on the way home. Or maybe if you brought your chair, he could push you down to the pond. It's really nice there. Very peaceful."

"You won't accuse me of beau-stealing?" asked Violet. Her true nature was returning.

*Never again in my life will I meet anyone like you.* She helped Violet to her feet. "Not to your face I won't."

"Then it's settled. Let the chips fall where they may where beaus are concerned." Violet ambled across the room, much improved from the rest. At the door she paused and glanced over her shoulder. "Get some sleep. I'll leave your sandwich, pizza, and berries in the fridge in case you get hungry. If you change your mind, you know where we'll be."

Then she was gone and Nora retreated to her bed, still damp with perspiration. She waited until certain they had left before she sobbed like a baby into her pillow.

# SEVENTEEN

*When this poor lisping, stammering tongue*

Emily tried concentrating on Mary Beth's account of her trip to Indiana for a funeral. But after her third time of asking whose relative was the deceased—Mary Beth's or her *ehemann's*—Mary Beth smiled politely and turned to talk to the woman behind them. Emily hated being rude, but she wondered why the women always sat together on trips instead of with their husbands. She so wanted to talk to Jonas, not that a small bus coming back from Columbia would provide much opportunity for a marital heart-to-heart.

She had a lot of crow to eat, as the English would say.

She had much wrong to atone for, as her bishop would describe.

She had been a disloyal, mean-spirited, judgmental wife, and that said it all in any language or culture.

While Jonas arranged financing for some new sawmill equipment, she'd walked to the library, hoping to read more regional history or study the cooking magazines for amusement. But she couldn't concentrate on *Audrain County During the Great*

*Depression* or "A Month of New Casseroles Using Five Ingredients or Less." Her mind kept wandering back to her husband's words: "Was that your advice to Sally during her *rumschpringe*? Did you deliver an ultimatum to your younger sister, along with an insult and the threat of eternal damnation?" He had convicted her without needing judge, jury, or courtroom. With numbing, shameful regret, she remembered telling Nora she should marry in a hurry and move back to where she came from.

With Mary Beth blessedly distracted, Emily peered out the streaky window. After the rain stopped, the clouds parted to reveal a gorgeous blue sky and bright sun. Her delicious Applebee's supper sat heavily in her belly. She hadn't needed the chocolate cake, but Jonas insisted they split dessert. *How did they bake ice cream inside a cake without it melting?* She owed Jonas more than the big half of a high-calorie sweet. At the restaurant, the table for eight hadn't encouraged private chats between spouses. Too many district members sought the deacon's sage advice. Unfortunately, she hadn't been one of them. Emily leaned her forehead against the glass and prayed to be shown the way back to his heart.

With a sudden lurch, she bumped her head on the window, waking up from a nap. Peering around, she recognized the farm of the elderly neighbors behind them. The husband was already hobbling up the aisle, while the wife still gathered their belongings. "Jonas," she called. "Could we get out here too and walk home? The rain has stopped and the evening has cooled off."

He took no time to decide. "Sure thing. I could use some exercise after that dessert you insisted on ordering." Everyone chuckled, well aware of Jonas's fondness for sugar.

Emily grabbed her tote bag of books, gave Mary Beth an impromptu hug, and practically flew off the bus. Their neighbors waved, halfway up the walkway to their porch. Jonas took her canvas bag and slung it over his shoulder. "This is a surprise. I'm shocked you're not tired." He headed toward the back path—a shortcut between pastures and crop fields to their farm.

"We need to talk," she said softly. "I owe you several apologies."

"Will a mile and a half be enough time? Maybe we should take the long way home along the road."

Her heart skipped a beat until she heard his husky laughter next to her ear and felt his arm encircle her waist. "I've been a terrible wife."

"'Terrible' might be too strong a term. Why not use 'mediocre' or 'underachieving, but shows signs of improvement'? I love that description on the new employee evaluation form Ken devised." Jonas pulled her tightly to his side.

"Be serious, *ehemann*. And please forgive the horrible way I've been acting."

He released her waist but clasped her hand. "All right, I'll be serious, but I've already forgiven you, *fraa*. That happened before we left the Yosts' yard. We've been married more than ten years—*good* years," he emphasized. "But couples occasionally slip up because we're human. I'll expect mercy from you if I ever do something wrong." He pinched her side, knowing the exact location of her ticklish spot.

This time she laughed. "I'll try to remember." She pulled him to a stop on the path and then waited until he turned his face to hers. "I want to know your God better, Jonas, not Solomon's," she whispered.

He touched her chin with two fingers. "He is the same God, Emily. He can rain judgment down on His children, but He also graces us with almost inexhaustible compassion. I refuse to dwell on sadness and plight. He created the heavens and earth, everything you see. We cannot understand His reasons when He calls home a young mother during childbirth or a buggy filled with children. Sometimes He allows one person to be cured of a dreadful disease but not someone else. The only absolute I know is that He loves us, and everything that happens is part of His plan."

Emily turned her gaze skyward. "Maybe He'll bring us *bopplin* and maybe not," she said, in a voice barely audible. "But I will trust and give thanks for bringing me a husband as wise as you."

"Pity all the other *fraas* in the world without a Jonas Gingerich to hug in the moonlight on a perfect summer night." He kissed her lightly at first and then deeply, with the tender passion she'd known since the day they married.

Emily found her weariness lifting. "Let's pick up the pace and not dawdle. I want to see if Nora is still awake or abed with her migraine. Lewis brought Violet by today especially to bring that girl out of her depression."

"If you have folks like Violet and Lewis on your side, you need little else." Jonas led the way as the path narrowed around the boggy end of the pond.

"She should have had me guiding her too." Emily shielded her face from low-hanging hawthorn branches.

"It's not too late. It almost never is." He held on to her tightly in the shadowy moonlight.

Emily savored the feel of his dry, rough hand in hers. As they rounded the barn and their house loomed into view, an odd sight caught their attention: A person was taking laundry off the clothes line with light from a lantern. "Who is that?" she asked. "Nora and I did the wash yesterday."

"Considering size, it looks like Lewis. It certainly isn't Nora. Maybe you don't get his shirts clean enough."

Emily swatted his arm, feeling like her old self. "Nobody has ever complained before. Let's ask him what he's about."

"Did you decide it was a nice night to wash clothes?" called Jonas as they approached.

Lewis startled but recovered quickly. "Hello, Jonas, Emily.

How was Columbia? Did you have a nice dinner in town?" He concentrated on folding his trousers and shirts.

"Columbia was fine," said Emily. "Did you forget to throw those in the hamper? I would have washed them tomorrow."

Grabbing the basket and lantern, Lewis walked down the hill. The swinging light cast dancing shadows on the grass. "I need to pack, and I didn't want to put dirty clothes into my suitcase." His voice was flat and unemotional. "It was no trouble, but thanks for the offer." Lewis tipped his hat as he stepped past them.

"Why are you packing, son?" Jonas touched his shoulder.

Lewis halted. When the light illuminated his face, his misery and sorrow broke Emily's heart. "I would have explained on my way to work tomorrow, Jonas, and left a note for you, Emily, but I can't live here anymore. Not with Nora feeling toward me as she does. I intend to ask Josh or Seth if they could put me up for a couple weeks until you hire my replacement. But I'll stay until you do. There's no way I would leave you shorthanded after all you've done for me."

Jonas rubbed the back of his neck, stiff from the bus trip. "Both of them live in big houses. I'm sure they'll have room for you, but where are you going?"

"Back home, of course, to help with the harvest. My father will be glad to have my help in the store too."

"I'll sure miss you around the lumberyard. You caught on quicker to the computer than most Plain men, me included." Jonas and Lewis walked shoulder to shoulder toward the house.

"Stop! Wait just a minute!" demanded Emily, running after them. "What happened today? I thought you, Nora, and Violet were going for a buggy ride and picnic."

Both men stared at her.

"This may not be my business, but I'm sticking my nose in anyway. I probably should have done so long ago." She stomped her foot like an ornery mule.

Jonas stifled a grin as Lewis set the lantern and basket down. "Nora refused to come downstairs or see me at all, not even for five minutes. I waited for an hour. She talked plenty to Violet upstairs in that hot bedroom, but she wouldn't as much as holler out the window to me." He lowered his gaze to the ground. "I've been slow to figure it out, Emily, but Nora's not in love with me. This whole harebrained trip has been a mistake. *Danki* for all your kindness, but I can't live in the same house with a woman trying to avoid me." Lewis reached down for the lantern and glanced at Jonas. "If it's okay with you, I'll put my suitcase in your buggy and take my pillow and blanket to the hayloft to sleep. Then Nora won't have to sneak around like a cat burglar if she wants something to eat or drink." He marched toward the house without another word.

Emily and Jonas shared a helpless look. "There's nothing we can do but give the man some space," he said. "Come sit on the porch swing with me. I'll even rub your feet."

She nodded, knowing that despite the late hour, neither of them would be able to sleep a wink.

Nora listened at the top of the stairwell before creeping down, once she was sure no one stirred in the kitchen. With her headache gone, she was famished. From her bedroom window, she'd spotted Lewis heading to the barn with his pillow and blanket. He probably preferred waking up congested from dust and pollen rather than face her. Who could blame him? He'd come to Missouri to court her. Little did he know she wasn't worthy of his affection.

Peering around the corner, Nora made a beeline for the refrigerator. She filled her apron with Violet's sandwich, cold pizza wrapped in foil, and the bag of strawberries, and then she grabbed the pitcher of milk. Midway to the table, she halted like a naughty child caught in mischief. Jonas and Emily stood in the mudroom doorway with quizzical expressions.

"Food is included with room and board," said Emily. "Don't look so guilty. Although I don't remember buying strawberries, and my berry patch was picked clean long ago."

Nora set the food on the table and fetched a plate and glass, hoping the Gingerichs were just passing through. "Violet left this for me while you were gone. But you two must be exhausted after Columbia. Please don't think you must remain up to keep me company while I eat." She filled her glass with milk, avoiding their eyes.

"We'd like a word if you don't mind." Jonas pulled out a chair for his wife and then sat down, not waiting for Nora's response.

"And I'd like some milk before bed." Emily went to the cupboard for another glass.

Without much choice, Nora decided the running, hiding, and ducking her head had to stop. "Are either of you hungry? There's enough to share." Peering from one to the other, she shook out a napkin for her lap.

"We're not hungry, but we are worried about you," said Emily. "Lewis packed up his belongings and will spend his final night as our guest in the hayloft. Were you unable to patch things up?"

"Lewis came to Paradise seeking someone I am not." She washed a bite of rubbery pizza down her dry throat with a swallow of milk.

"Aren't you ready to marry yet? Do you need more running-around time?" asked Jonas.

"Not at all. I would love to settle down with a man who loves me." She kept her eyes focused on her food.

Emily fanned herself with her apron. "*Gut* to hear, because sometimes what we're looking for is right under our noses." She bobbed her head in the direction of the barn.

"And I love him, if it were only that simple. He wants the truth about Elam, but Elam isn't the problem. I…I was led astray by a boy in Pennsylvania, long before I went to Maine. Maybe that's why Elam appealed to me…a man without high standards might accept a disgraceful woman."

Poor Jonas. He turned a matching shade to the strawberries, receiving far more information than he bargained for.

"Forgive my frankness, but you both deserve honesty after all your hospitality. I'm not a suitable woman for Lewis, despite where my emotions lie." Nora finished the pizza in two more bites.

"If this happened back in Lancaster, you must have been very young, Nora. Sometimes people make mistakes during their youth." Jonas fingered his beard nervously.

"Everyone has, at some point," added Emily. She so wanted to rectify a hopeless situation.

"You're very kind, but you both know this isn't the same as cutting your hair or wearing cosmetics during *rumschpringe.* Besides housekeeping skills, all an Amish girl brings to a marriage is her virtue. It is a gift to her husband."

Emily clucked her tongue. "We also know that isn't always the case. And if we deserve your honesty, so does Lewis. What's keeping you from telling him this? Are you chicken?"

Nora looked her friend and employer in the eye. "Without a doubt I'm scared. To witness his scorn would be more than I can bear. Please don't try to force me." Her voice dropped to a whisper.

"We won't," said Jonas. "But I advise you to swallow your pride and talk to him. Because in part, isn't that what this is—pride? You don't want him to see your human frailty."

Nora lined up the strawberries in relationship to their size. "I suppose, but how does one…rise above their weaknesses?"

Jonas leaned across the table. "Recently I studied the story in the book of Luke when Jesus calmed the storm and saved the apostles from certain death. God is all-powerful. Nothing is beyond His control. Once we surrender, we have *nothing* to fear—not our past mistakes or storms at sea or bugs or birds or changes in weather patterns." Jonas's focus drifted from Nora to Emily and back again. "But by avoiding Lewis, you're denying his chance to rise to a higher level and forgive you unconditionally."

For a minute, no one spoke. Only the ticking of the clock and chirping of crickets broke the silence. Nora stared at the tabletop, fighting back the tears that burned her throat and eyes.

"If you change your mind, he will still work at the lumberyard for another week or so. You can find him there except on Wednesdays and Sundays."

Nora's head snapped up. "He's already moved out?" She dabbed at her runny nose.

"*Jah*, tonight he'll sleep in the barn. Then he aims to bunk with Seth or Josh until he arranges transportation. He won't be returning to the farm, Nora."

"Transportation?" she asked, although she already knew the answer.

"He's going home to Harmony. He came to Missouri not to compare our farms to the countryside back in Maine. He came here for *you*. Apparently, the trip was an unnecessary expense and waste of time in his life."

She choked back her emotions. What did she expect? Lewis to keep pining after her well into old age? "Of course, I'm not thinking straight." She wrapped her remaining supper to take to her room in case she awoke hungry in the middle of the night.

"Say your prayers and go to bed." Emily patted her hand. "After a good night's sleep, the world may look different tomorrow. You may still find your way back to him."

"It's too late, but *danki* for your advice." Nora rose with dignity and pushed in her chair.

Suddenly, Emily's hand shot out and clamped around the younger woman's wrist. With her other hand, she pressed two fingers to the bone just above the vein. "You have a pulse and you're still breathing, so it's definitely *not* too late."

Nora smiled at the Gingerichs. "*Gut nacht.*" She walked from the kitchen on legs barely able to support her weight. "Oh, I almost forgot." She glanced over her shoulder. "May I use your buggy tomorrow? I'd like to take Violet on a picnic because I disappointed her today. I'll pack the sandwiches and fruit this time."

Emily exchanged a look with Jonas. "Sure, no problem. Violet should get out as much as possible. I work you both too hard."

That night while washing her face and hands before bed, Nora analyzed her reflection in the mirror. The young girl who had kissed Elam Detweiler in the henhouse and then helped him run away was gone. Grieving over her dead parents and jealous of a sister whose life seemed easier, she had behaved recklessly, as though she had nothing to lose. The older, wiser woman staring back realized too late that she'd had *everything* to lose.

Nora awoke the next morning with a start. Dreams had once again plagued her sleep. However, these weren't pleasant memories of her Lancaster childhood, but disquieting, dark images of phantoms chasing her through a cornfield. And she didn't even believe in ghosts. Kicking off the damp, tangled sheet, she jumped out of bed and crossed the room. She opened the window all the way against the June heat, yet no breeze stirred the muslin curtains. Although only an hour past dawn, yet every sign indicated another hot Missouri day.

As she showered and dressed, thoughts of yesterday returned to haunt her worse than any fairy-tale specter. Lewis Miller—the only man who truly loved her—was gone. She'd heard Jonas's buggy roll down the driveway before daybreak. Nora had buried her head beneath the pillow until she nearly suffocated. At least she wouldn't have to play a game of hide-and-seek with him. He'd taken care of that by moving out.

Downstairs the kitchen was empty. Emily must be sleeping in—almost unheard of for that ball of energy. While Nora fixed ham-and-cheese sandwiches, chips, and sliced cantaloupe for the picnic, she considered Violet. What a metamorphosis that girl had gone through. *Funny what the love of a good man can do.*

"Don't forget to take some Pepsis in the soft-sided cooler." Emily stood in the doorway, wearing a long white nightgown. With bare feet, no *kapp,* and her waist-length braid trailing down her back, she looked younger than her thirty-three years.

"Good idea. I hope I didn't wake you." Nora loaded a blue freezer pack into the cooler and retrieved an old quilt from the top shelf in the mudroom.

"It's almost ten. Besides, who can sleep in this heat?" Emily pulled a bottle of water from the fridge. "The sky was the strangest color this morning when Jonas was leaving—streaked with pink and orange. More like sunset than sunrise."

"It's a perfect shade of blue now," said Nora, opening the window curtains. "I'll take a towel in case we decide to get our feet wet." She pulled a green beach towel from a drawer and added it to the stack. "Are you sure you don't need me today for baking?"

"*Nein.* Jonas already hitched up the mare. The buggy is waiting for you in the shade, so go have some fun." Emily shooed her out the door.

"See you at supper." Buoyed by the idea of some time with her friend, Nora ran down the walkway.

Violet never made a person wait if there was fun involved. She hobbled down the stairs before Nora could turn the buggy around. Her brother kept within arm's reach in case she stumbled.

"Hand your reins to Irvin," she called. "We'll take my buggy since my *bruder* already loaded up my wheelchair in it. Don't worry. He'll take good care of Emily's mare."

Violet climbed into the open two-seater unassisted, while Irvin shoved her crutches under the seat. Within five minutes Nora had transferred the cooler, towel, and quilt. When she was settled by her friend, Violet handed her Nell's reins and they were on their way.

"Where would you like to go for our picnic?" Nora asked. "Kansas, Iowa, or Colorado? Your wish is my command."

Violet's freckles danced across her nose. "We'll stay a bit closer to home. Head toward Josh's house. You know the way from the hayride. There's a dirt lane that connects Josh's farm to Seth's through the back. Seth showed me a river in the woods with easy access for my chair most of the way. We can sit on a log and dangle our feet in the rushing water."

"A river like the Mississippi?"

Violet's hoots sent birds soaring higher. "More like a babbling brook, but at least it's water in the shade. On a day as hot as this, both will feel like heaven."

"Tell me, Miss Trask. Any news on your three favorite topics: Seth, Seth, or Seth? We have five or six miles to kill."

"Funny you should ask, Miss King, but I do have an update. Did I mention he's taking me to Saturday's singing? And next week he'll accompany me to my therapy appointment in Columbia. We'll have lunch at Red Lobster because I've never tasted lobster before."

"Just the two of you in Columbia?" Nora arched an eyebrow.

"Get serious. Have you forgotten who my father is? *Daed* insists my mother accompany us, but I don't mind. She tends not to say much when Seth and I start talking."

"What choice does she have? Who could squeeze a word in edgewise?"

"I'll ignore that. Did I mention Seth comes over to sit on our porch? He hasn't missed a Sunday in weeks. My sister knits in the rocker if my parents are gone, but Kathryn also knows how to be low-key. Oh, and did you know Seth thinks *my* molasses crinkle cookies are the best tasting in Paradise?"

"That sounds rather prideful, Miss Trask." Nora shook her finger in rebuke. "But I will tell Emily. Either she'll give you a raise or fire you for stealing the limelight from her."

"What's limelight?" Violet stretched out her legs.

"All the attention, but do go on with your update. I want to hear everything Seth had to say last Sunday."

So Violet filled in every blank, adding appropriate flourishes and gestures. By the time they reached the farm lane by Josh's, their faces hurt from laughing. "Let's leave the buggy here and tie up the horse in the shade. It's not far. You can push me the rest of the way."

Nora dragged Violet's wheelchair from the back. "That man is smitten with you. I believe you have met your match."

"And you've met yours, even if you're too stubborn to deal with it."

"Stubbornness has nothing to do with it." Nora opened the wheelchair and hung the cooler on one handle.

"Okay, too chicken then." Violet climbed down from the buggy and ambled to the chair under her own steam.

"You sound like Emily, and we are not discussing this. Either you change the subject and don't bring it up again, or I'm taking lunch down to the river alone. You can sit here twiddling your thumbs for a couple hours."

"Okay, I promise, but I never thought a *best friend* could be so heartless." Violet pretended to pout, while Nora concentrated on finding the smoothest part of the hard-packed path. "Tell me what the ocean is like," Violet asked after a few minutes.

"Don't know. I've never seen it."

"You lived that close in Maine and you never drove an hour east? I can't understand that. If I had your legs, I would have walked if necessary." She shook her head in disbelief. "Twice a year when we see my doctor in St. Louis, *mamm* pushes me to a park along the Mississippi River. I love to watch the small boats, big ships, and huge freighters heading in one direction or the other. I would give anything to jump on one of them and travel to the Gulf of Mexico. I can't imagine so much water."

Nora thought before answering. "You're still on *rumschpringe*, Violet. Maybe you can go before you claim your rocking chair on the porch."

She snorted in unladylike fashion. "You know my *daed*. He would never permit it. He insists I take the classes for baptism and join the church this fall. That doesn't leave much time. Pictures in *Coastal Living* magazine will be as close as I ever get to the sea."

While Nora pushed her friend, working up a sweat and an appetite, her mind concocted possibilities. She also was still in *rumschpringe*. Could she and Violet take a trip down to New Orleans or maybe Grand Isle? She'd talked about this once with Elam, but that seemed like ages ago. "Maybe you and I can save our money and find a passenger boat, so no matter where we end up in life, we can tell our *kinskinner* about our trip down the river."

"My father wouldn't let me go to Columbia with you, let alone to the ocean. I'm shocked he permitted our buggy ride today."

Though she was sure Violet had not meant the pronouncement to sound so harsh, her words stung nevertheless. "Perhaps you'll go on your honeymoon then," said Nora in a shaky voice. She should have known Minister Trask would take her new reputation seriously.

Once at their destination, she slung the cooler over her shoulder and helped Violet down to water's edge. A fallen log provided a perfect perch over the stream. They scooted across on the smooth, worn surface until they were able to dangle their feet in the stream. "Nobody I know would call this a river, but the water sure feels good." Nora pulled out their lunch without changing her comfortable position. "We have ham-and-cheese, chips, fruit, and Pepsi."

"Sounds divine. Isn't this the good life?" Violet took a sandwich and kicked up a froth with her legs.

"Won't your leg braces rust?" asked Nora, biting into a sandwich.

"Nope. They're stainless steel, built to last."

For half an hour, they splashed in the stream and ate in companionable silence. Then Violet dropped her sandwich onto her lap and screwed up her face.

"What's wrong? Too much mustard?"

"Don't you hear that?" Violet sounded terrified.

Nora listened and shook her head. "I don't hear anything."

"That's just it. Ten minutes ago the birds were chirping away. I could barely hear myself think. Now it's dead silent. This isn't good, Nora. I had a bad feeling when I looked out my window this morning. Let's get out of here." She began scooting herself along the log.

Nora jumped down to the creek bed and helped Violet up the slope. "Maybe something scared the birds. There wasn't a cloud in the sky when we got here."

"We've been under the trees. Cyclones come up fast in Missouri, without warning. Get me back to my chair."

"A cyclone?" she asked, picturing the storybook version of *The Wizard of Oz* she'd seen as a child.

"You're in Tornado Alley. Take my word for it and start pushing." The panic in Violet's voice was unmistakable.

Nora did as instructed, but before she could so much as release the brake on the wheelchair, dust in the lane began to eddy around their feet, while the wind picked up and sent their *kapp* strings fly-ing. "It can't be a tornado," said Nora. "There's been no rain or thunderstorms today." Nevertheless, she put her head down and began to push with all her strength.

"It doesn't have to be stormy. Twisters can sneak up when you're least expecting them, usually when it's calm and not windy. Hurry, Nora. Oh, how I wish I had good legs." Violet tried to prod them along with her feet but only slowed their progress.

"Please lift your legs onto the footrests." Nora spoke calmly despite the fact twigs and debris had joined the swirl of dust on the road. Within another twenty feet something struck the top of Nora's head, while chunks of ice clanged against the metal chair.

"Hail!" cried Violet. "This is bad. Let's pray, Nora, for God to save us."

For a moment, Nora stopped pushing. Never in her twenty-one years had she seen hail in summer. Sleet and freezing rain, yes, but not golf ball-sized hail that stung the backs of her hands and shoulders. Ice balls already littered the surrounding pasture, bouncing around like a children's amusement park attraction.

Fearing the unknown, Nora pushed Violet's chair as fast as she could. Then the skies opened with a torrent of rain, soaking them both to the skin within moments. The hard-packed surface of the lane softened into mud with puddles of standing water and riv-ulets of run-off. Violet added sobs to her litany of prayers. The wheelchair hit a muddy low spot and stalled, throwing Nora on top of Violet.

"Please, God, help us!" cried Nora. But the rain and wind drowned out her words. In the middle of crops and pastureland, Nora heard the odd sound of an approaching train, yet they had crossed no railroad tracks on the way here.

"Stop, Nora!" demanded Violet. "There's not enough time. Look," she shouted and pointed at a wall of clouds, dark and men-acing, filled with flashes of lightning. It appeared to grow and separate from the storm front stretching across the horizon. Before their eyes a funnel began at the base of the cloud and swirled ever closer to the earth.

Nora stared for a few seconds, mesmerized, and then galvanized into action. "We must get back to the buggy. There's a culvert pipe where the stream crosses under the road. We can crawl inside." She had read that tidbit of safety advice in a magazine in the bus station. But how she planned to get Violet down an embankment and inside the pipe was beyond her. A maelstrom of rain, hail, and flying debris surrounded them, while the funnel cloud was headed straight down the lane. *It is the end of the world*, she thought even as she continued to force the wheelchair through the mud.

"Please stop. It's hopeless." Violet put her feet down, halting their abysmal forward progress. She grabbed Nora's arm. "You must leave me and save yourself. The road is too far away!" screamed Violet above the roar. "There's no sense in both of us dying!"

Nora wiped wet hair from her eyes. Her bun had come loose, and their *kapps* were long gone. "*Nein*, I won't leave you. You're my friend."

Violet tightened her grip on Nora's wrist. "You're my friend too. That's why I want you to run."

Nora shook her arm free and looked around, ignoring her heart slamming against her ribcage while horizontal rain stung any exposed skin. Frantic, she spotted a deep furrow where a plow probably had gotten stuck last spring. "Get up," she demanded. "We need to reach that ditch."

"That's not much of a ditch," answered Violet. But she rose from the chair and pulled free from the mire, one leg at a time. Slowly, painstakingly, they made their way to the trough and dropped to the ground just as Josh's fence broke apart like a row of matchsticks.

"*Danki* for staying with me," said Violet. Then she sprawled headlong into the muddy water.

"Lord, forgive me my grievous sins," shouted Nora. She threw herself down and rolled on top of her friend. It was the last thing she remembered before a hard projectile hit the back of her head, knocking her unconscious.

❦

"*Ugggh.* Please, get off me. I'm not a fish."

Something poked at Nora's belly and then her shoulder. She shifted her body to the right and opened her eyes. She found herself flat on her back, staring up at a patch of clear blue sky. The cloud wall, the entire storm, had gone. Even the rain had dwindled to a drizzle.

Violet bolted upright and glanced around their frightful surroundings. "The twister's moved off to the northeast."

"And we're alive," said Nora, still lying in cold water.

Violet struggled first to her knees and then slowly to her feet. She wobbled on the wet ground but didn't fall. "You look a mess," she declared after assessing her friend.

"That makes two of us. You're not exactly looking Sunday best yourself." Nora rose to her elbows. "Should we stay here? Will the tornado come back?" Her head throbbed worse than any migraine.

"Not likely. It must have turned directions at the last minute. God saved us," Violet whispered.

Nora labored to her feet. In her long, sodden dress, she wasn't much steadier on her feet than Violet. "I can't imagine any other explanation. I thought for sure we were goners." Holding each other up, the women surveyed the landscape. Hail was rapidly melting. All around lay ruined crops, metal chunks of who-knew-what, remnants of the pasture fence, and smashed pieces of everything common in rural America. Nora picked up the terracotta head of a lamb from a garden planter, the sweet smile on the lamb's face a sad irony.

"My wheelchair has disappeared," said Violet with little enthusiasm.

"I wouldn't be able to push it through this mess anyway. You can wait here while I bring help."

"Nothing doing. I'm walking to the road with you." Violet stepped gingerly over a broken tree branch. "What do you think all those therapy treatments have been for—my exceptional good looks?" She stretched out her hand to Nora.

Nora snaked an arm around her waist. "Good to hear, because we need to get you home fast and into a bathtub. You smell a little funny." Nora pinched her nostrils shut with two fingers.

"Nora King, I've rubbed off on you. You have finally developed a sense of humor."

And with that, the two best friends began the longest walk, through the sloppiest terrain, of their lives.

# EIGHTEEN

*Lies silent in the grave*

Solomon pulled a handkerchief from his back pocket. He and his sons had been raking and baling hay since dawn. They had cut the hay days ago and allowed it to dry under the hot summer sun. Irvin pulled an implement that raked and loaded hay into wagons, while Sol drove one of the wagons carrying hay back to the barn. Mark would feed it through a stationary baler and then load bales into the loft. They had been working hard since dawn with only a short lunch break. The minister was exhausted. Even his boys looked haggard as they swigged from plastic water bottles.

"*Daed*, look at that sky," hollered Irvin from the lead team of draft horses. "A storm's coming. Let's get the horses back to their stalls."

Sol didn't argue. He'd been a farmer long enough to know you could always pick up in the field where you left off, but only a fool took chances in a flat, open space in a thunderstorm. Lightning could kill man and beast many yards from the strike. Or lightning could touch off brush fires, trapping you on the wrong side of safety. As he turned the team and followed his sons, a dark cloud appeared in the southwest, bringing with it bright flashes and rumbles of thunder. The ominous sounds grew closer by the minute.

"We're gonna get wet," hollered his younger son. Mark waved his hat through the air as though at a barrel race, not remotely worried.

His older brother didn't share the casual mood. "That doesn't look good." Irvin pointed at a huge bulge beneath the moving wall of clouds. It resembled the belly of a heifer, pregnant with twins. "Unhitch the teams," shouted Irvin to Mark and Sol. "Leave the wagons and equipment. Let's just get the horses and ourselves to shelter." Irvin issued an order instead of making a suggestion to his father.

For a moment, Solomon felt a surge of annoyance. *I haven't fully retired from farming yet. The boy should show respect for his elders.* Nevertheless, he climbed down and unharnessed the Belgians from the wagon as the wind blew dust into his mouth and eyes. His irritation vanished when the first piece of hail hit his hat brim. Ahead his sons were running toward the barn, leading the other two teams. The sometimes-balky horses needed no special encouragement to leave the fields today. With speed he hadn't known in years, Sol also ran, arriving inside the double doors within moments of his boys.

Irvin had already unbridled his pair and closed them inside a stall. But Mark's Percheron mare stomped her feet and reared, nostrils flaring. Irvin took the reins to calm the horse, while Mark led her mate into a stall. Sol waited his turn, standing in the rain that quickly turned into a full-fledged deluge. It was as though broad daylight became nighttime within minutes.

"Go to Ann and your new *boppli*," hollered Irvin to his brother. "My wife knows what to do in a storm. I'll take care of your horse."

Mark hurried past Sol into the blinding downpour. Irvin managed to calm the prancing mare and herd her through the stall door. He then turned to his father, grabbing the reins from his fingers. "See to *mamm*. I'll confine these two and take cover."

"I'll do this myself," insisted Sol. "Go to your wife and children. Your house is a quarter mile away." He had to shout to be heard over the wind.

"Please, *daed*, go. *Mamm* might need your help getting Violet to the cellar." Irvin's pale face pleaded better than his words.

With the mention of his *fraa* and *dochder*, Sol stopped arguing. "May God protect you." He locked eyes with his son and then ran from the barn. Gusts nearly knocked him off his feet. On his way to the house Sol was pelted with rain, hail, gravel, sticks, and a piece of plastic tarp which wrapped around his head, temporarily blinding him. He felt something warm and sticky run into his eyes and knew he'd been cut. He reached the steps just as the swing broke from the chains and hurtled across the yard. As he traversed the porch, bent low by the opposing gale, his black shutters pulled loose and took flight. Any one of them could have severed his head from his neck. When Sol opened the screen door, it broke from the hinges, knocking him back. He threw it to the side and entered his kitchen, treading over shards of window glass and broken dishes on his way to the basement stairs.

"Rosanna, Violet, are you down there?" he yelled at the top of his burning lungs. Breathing had become difficult from the wind.

"*Jah*, come down, Solomon." Blessedly, the voice of his beloved wife carried up.

"Praise the Lord!" he shouted, unlike his silent prayers before a meal.

At the foot of the stairs stood Rosanna, frightened but otherwise unharmed. She lifted her arms to embrace him. Solomon hugged her with every ounce of energy he had left. "There, there, we're safe down here. Soon the storm will pass." He stroked her head where her hair had come loose into a thick tangle. Rosanna sobbed in his arms.

"What's wrong?" he asked. "Are you injured?" Then in that instant he knew. They were alone in the cellar. "Where's Violet? Where's our girl?"

"Don't you remember? She went on a picnic today because Nora was sick yesterday. Violet fears Nora will move back to Maine." Her words dissolved into wrenching sobs.

Sol sat on the bottom step, dropping his face in his hands. "On, no, not my Violet. She can't be out there in this."

"Don't blame Nora. It was Violet's idea—"

Sol interrupted her with a gentle tug on her arm. Rosanna dropped down beside him. "I don't blame anyone else. This is my fault. The wrath of God has come to Paradise because of me. Violet is in danger because of my lack of compassion and mercy. Oh, Rosanna, what have I done?"

She took his hand in hers, but had no answer.

And there they sat for what seemed like hours, lost in wretched sobbing. But in fact, within fifteen minutes the storm with its accompanying tornado moved from Paradise, leaving behind a swath of destruction Randolph and Audrain Counties hadn't seen in many years.

೧

Jonas Byler stared at the flickering computer screen with a scowl. "Now what?" he muttered under his breath. The computer program had been giving him problems all afternoon. Why couldn't they simply maintain the lumberyard accounts and inventories the old-fashioned way—on long ledgers of yellow paper? Suddenly his monitor whined and then went dark. He checked to make sure he hadn't unplugged the power cord by accident, a frequent occurrence. He hadn't. *If I weren't a pacifist, I might track down the man who invented the computer and...*

He curtailed his uncharitable thoughts when he noticed lights were out in the showroom and hallway. So much natural illumination poured through the office windows that Jonas seldom turned on the electric lights. With a commotion of exclamations, several men ran into the building from the garden area, shouting words he couldn't discern.

One female customer dropped her sacks of potting soil in the main aisle and ran for the exit, dragging her child behind her.

With a sinking sensation in his gut, Jonas jumped from his swivel chair to see what had happened. Ken met him in the doorway, almost knocking him down. "Bob at the outdoor checkout heard a bulletin on his radio. The National Weather Service broke into the ball game to issue a warning. A tornado has been spotted outside of Paradise, moving east, last sighted on L Road and headed this way." Not a drop of blood remained in his pale face.

In that instant two thoughts and one question came to Jonas's mind: *We have no basement. The lawn and garden implements could quickly become lethal weapons. And where are Emily and Nora today?* Grain of Life bakery was a small frame building smack in the middle of flatland. He took a shuddering breath. "Have everyone take cover between the long counter and the interior office walls, away from glass. Flying debris shouldn't reach anybody there. Have them crouch down and cover their heads with their arms. I'm going outside to make sure customers don't get in their cars and drive straight into the tornado's path."

Both men ran in opposite directions. Jonas squeezed by men surging indoors from the sawmill, loading docks, and plant nursery.

"It's coming, boss!" shouted one.

"I spotted it myself, headed right for us," said another. Neither man waited for a response as they ducked down between the wall and the solid oak sales counter.

Jonas held open the door until the last employee filed past before he bolted into the parking lot. Sure enough, a young woman in white capri pants and a pink top sat in her small car as though paralyzed. He ran to the vehicle just as hail began to pelt his head and back. The frozen ice crystals hurt far more than the occasional snowball fights he'd enjoyed during childhood. Jonas reached the driver's side as paper foam cups and dead geraniums eddied and swirled around his feet. Apparently, the wind had overturned the trash dumpster.

"Ma'am, you must get out of the car and come with me." Jonas glanced into the backseat. Wearing an identical outfit, a little girl stared up at him, wide-eyed and terrified. She'd been strapped in snuggly with the seat belt.

The woman shook her head. "I need to get home. My husband will be worried about us." Her hand was on the keys in the ignition, but the car wasn't running.

"And you *will* leave the moment the storm passes, but for now it's safer for your daughter inside the showroom."

It took a moment for logic and practicality to sink in. Then nodding agreement, she jumped out. Jonas unstrapped the child and lifted her into his arms. The three ran toward the back of the showroom as the wind increased in intensity.

Ken opened the door against the gale as they approached. "You're a sight for sore eyes." He tried to pull the door closed, to no avail.

Crossing the littered floor, Jonas heard the infamous roar and the sound of breaking glass just as he shoved the woman and child inside his office. Ken dropped to the floor and braced the metal office door with his back. Covering his head with his arms, Jonas began to pray. He prayed that they all might survive, but if this be his time to die, he asked for forgiveness for his transgressions.

He wasn't the only one praying in Gingerich's that afternoon. Within minutes the storm and tornado were over. The instant the cacophony of destruction ceased, Jonas, Ken, and Robert checked their employees and customers. Everyone survived, and very few suffered injuries—mostly minor cuts from flying scrap metal.

A little while later the woman and daughter in pink emerged from the lunch room. The little girl was sobbing, but the mother smiled. The *Englischer* threw her arms around Jonas's neck and hugged him tightly. "Thank you, Mr. Gingerich. You saved our lives."

He patted her back as a blush crept up his neck. "I didn't do much. Please wait here while I check the parking lot, your car, and the road."

Without argument, she sat down in a clear spot on the floor and pulled her daughter onto her lap. Jonas stepped over broken bird-feeders to walk outside into a sea of destruction. The metal outdoor racks, which had held every dimension of lumber, were twisted and collapsed. The tornado splintered the pressure-treated wood as though it were kindling, carrying much of it away to parts unknown. The plants, shrubs, and ornamental trees were gone, while his diesel-powered sawmill lay in a heap. Most of the workers' cars were crumpled and destroyed, including the sporty compact owned by the lady in pink. The four-wheel-drive trucks and most of the Amish buggies that had been parked in the back grassy area remained unscathed, along with the nervous horses huddled at the far end of the paddock fence. The funnel cloud had hit-skipped its way across the township.

Ken joined Jonas in the yard, throwing pieces of broken lumber out of his way. "My truck is fine," he said, scratching his head. "Why don't I start ferrying people home? I can drive through ditches or fields if need be, but I'd better first clear a path to the road. These folks are anxious to check on their families. I'll take the lady and little girl home first."

"Good idea. I'll give you a hand." Jonas began throwing broken lumber into piles on the side. For the next two hours, he remained until every customer and employee were gone. Because the roads would most likely be impassable for buggies, the Amish men left them in the field and either rode or led their horse home. It would be a long walk, but at least they were alive.

For the first time, Jonas appreciated that his nephew had saddle-broke the Standardbred gelding. The horse barely tossed his mane when Jonas pulled himself astride bareback. He, too, had a long journey to reach Township Route 116. He rode past the former location of Emily's bakery. Little remained except for a debris-strewn parking lot and the huge, black cast-iron cook stove. The monstrosity had been too heavy for the wind to lift. Jonas grinned for the first time since the storm. Emily would be pleased.

But his greatest joy awaited him at home. A few broken windows, some missing roof shingles, broken trees everywhere, and a garden that wouldn't supply much for this year's canning season, but his home still stood. "*Danki, Gott!*" he shouted when Emily emerged from the outside entrance to their cellar.

"Hush now, Jonas," she called. "You know Plain folks aren't supposed to yell." She ran toward him full speed, leaping over branches along the way.

"Praise the Lord!" he shouted. "I'll speak English. Then He won't know we're Amish." Jonas wrapped his arms around his wife and hugged. They fell to the ground laughing and crying and uttering words of gratitude for God's mercy on the Gingerich family that day.

&

Solomon and Rosanna remained in their root cellar long after the storm subsided, praying fervently. Only when their son threw back the steel outside entrance door, flooding the stairwell with sunshine, did they break their meditations. Both blinked several times as though surprised to discover it was still daylight outdoors.

"*Mamm, daed*, are you all right?" Irvin stomped down the steps in this heavy work boots. "We were so worried about you."

Sol struggled up, pulling Rosanna along with him. "We're fine. How are Susanna and your *kinner*?"

"*Gut, gut*. They were already in the basement when I arrived home."

"Mark, Ann, their new *boppli*? Kathryn and John?" Sol squinted as though trapped in darkness for hours.

"All fine. I checked at everyone's house. No injuries."

"And Violet. Is she safe with you?" asked Rosanna, bracing against the upright post. Sol slipped an arm around her for support.

Irvin gazed at his mother in confusion. "No, I haven't seen her all day. I thought I would find her down here with you."

Rosanna began to tremble uncontrollably. She slumped against Sol and wailed, "My helpless baby, out in an open buggy during a tornado."

Irvin lifted his mother into his arms and carried her upstairs to the sofa in the living room. "Violet went for a buggy ride alone?" he asked.

"*Nein*, with Nora on a picnic. It was such...a...nice...day." She spoke in broken staccato between hiccups.

"With Nora?" Irvin repeated her answer as nervous people often did. "She wouldn't be much stronger than our Violet." He ran a hand through his dark hair.

"Violet feared her friend might return to Maine because of the bad gossip, so she wanted to cheer her up." Rosanna buried her face in her hands and cried.

Irvin patted her shoulder tenderly. "Tornados hop, skip, and jump. They could be safe but unable to get home. Downed trees and power lines are everywhere, blocking the roads."

"This is God's curse on our town, like your *daed* warned because our district was disobedient." Rosanna's words were muffled but clear.

"If this be *Gott's wille*, it's due to my disobedience and not anybody else's," said Solomon. "My heart was full of fear and anger. I judged often and harshly." He sank down next to his *fraa* on the couch and attempted to comfort her. But if Violet was lost to them, there would be no consolation for some time to come.

"I'll ride my son's Morgan and try to find them," said Irvin. "His horse is accustomed to the saddle."

Sol's head snapped up. "Don't jeopardize your own life. Those electric lines on the ground could still hold power."

Irvin met Sol's eyes. "I'll be careful. Please don't blame yourself, *daed*. We have yet to witness all of *Gott's wille* today." Then he disappeared out the front door.

After Irvin left, Rosanna retreated to their room to lie down while Solomon wandered the house taking assessment of the damage. The back porch hung at a precarious slant with one end post missing. It had neither a roof nor any of the furniture that had been there this morning. Windows on the western side of the house were broken or missing, but most of the others remained intact. The wind had blown rain and mud into the kitchen and mudroom from the gaping hole where the back door had been. *At last, an appropriate name for the room*, he thought wryly. But all things considered, the house, including his new metal roof of three years, had weathered the cyclone well.

"*Danki* for Your mercy." He uttered the words at first by rote and then with renewed conviction as he walked the farm that had been left to him by his father and his father before him. The chicken coup had been destroyed, yet Solomon counted all twenty-five of

Rosanna's laying hens, scratching around in the dirt. The litter of debris didn't curtail their quest for corn. Most of his barn no longer had a roof, yet his milk cows, Emily's buggy horse, and his plow Belgians were all still in their stalls, unharmed.

*Except for one gentle mare that had been hitched to Violet's buggy.* Standing in his backyard, Solomon bowed his head and wept. He surrendered to his grief and misery as he picked his way to the county road. Sol walked into the sunset, magnificent with vivid colors, stumbling over unseen obstacles, until he reached their nearest neighbor. Sol spotted good news at that farm too. Although the man's crops were ruined, his house and barn remained intact. The *Englischer* stood on a stepladder nailing pieces of heavy plastic over gaping windows.

"How did you make out, Mr. Trask?" hollered the neighbor.

Sol glanced around ridiculously before answering. "My family is safe. House and livestock spared. Barn can be repaired."

"Glad to hear it!" The man shouted and waved his hat as his teenage son came around the corner carrying a sheet of plywood. *A boy a bit younger than…*

Sol had said nothing of his beloved daughter, still missing, or her beloved friend. From every direction he heard sirens blaring and the hum of chainsaws. In dwindling daylight, help had arrived for the injured. And for others, work had begun to repair the damage. Given time, Paradise would one day return to normal. But would life ever be the same for the Trask family? Solomon walked in a daze until a massive sycamore blocked his path. The tree's wilted foliage and twisted branches rendered the road impassable from this direction. He had no choice but to return to his wife and family.

His daughter Kathryn and daughters-in-law had arrived in his absence. They surrounded Rosanna in the downstairs bedroom, murmuring soft words, while his grandchildren watched with apprehension. After seeing that his *fraa* was well tended, Sol retreated to the front porch, dragging a rocking chair out with him. He opened his Bible haphazardly and began to read the first passage he spotted in Proverbs: "The way of the righteous is like the first gleam of dawn, which shines ever brighter until the full light of day. But the way of the wicked is like total darkness. They have no idea what they are stumbling over."

*I allowed the details of observance to distort the true meaning of Christianity.*

Sol prayed fervently that the innocent would be spared judgment. Eventually, he fell asleep with the Good Book still open in his lap. Later, a gentle shake of his shoulder jarred him awake. Sol opened his eyes to see the exhausted face of Irvin.

"What is it, son?" he asked, straightening in the chair. "Did you find the girls?"

The younger man squatted on his haunches near Sol's feet. "*Nein*. I rode up and down the district, but it's pitch dark out there. I didn't see any buggies off the road or any sign of them. If we only knew which direction they had headed it might be easier, but maybe not even then. Most roads are blocked. Very likely they are trapped, unable to get back by any route. In some places the twister did much damage, while other areas are wholly untouched. There's no rhyme or reason."

Solomon patted Irvin's arm. "Go home to your family and eat supper. You must be starving. Nothing more can be done tonight. At dawn we shall start searching anew."

Irvin remained where he crouched, his face pinched with misery.

"What is it?" he demanded. "Tell me, boy."

"When I passed your barn, I found Nell wandering around. She came home, alone."

"The mare is back?" he asked with disbelief.

"*Jah*. She's cut up and scratched, but she has no serious injuries.

Mark is tending her cuts right now and trying to wash caked mud from her legs."

"That's a good sign," Sol stroked his beard and began to rock. "If the horse is alive, maybe Violet and Nora are too. Go now. I'll sit up and wait for them."

Irvin looked bewildered, but soon he rose and staggered off the porch toward home.

And Sol rocked…and waited…and prayed for mercy for an undeserving father.

# NINETEEN

*Then in a nobler, sweeter song*

For the second time that night, Sol awoke from a fitful sleep on the porch. But no family members shook his arm, demanding his attention. Instead, the red and blue flashing lights of the sheriff's four-wheel-drive truck jarred him to consciousness. Stiff from arthritis and bad posture, Sol staggered down the steps to the front lawn. He had reached only the walkway when his daughter, his beloved Violet, climbed from the backseat of the vehicle.

"Papa!" she hollered, in a voice guaranteed to wake any sleepers. "I'm home!"

"You are indeed. *Danki*, Lord." Solomon ran the best he could while Violet hobbled toward him.

"Hold up there, Miss Trask. You've made it this far. Let's not go breaking a leg now." The sheriff steadied her progress with a strong, supportive arm.

"Rosanna, it's Violet," Sol called over his shoulder. "Wake up."

"How can you tell it's me? I'm covered in mud and guck from

299

head to toe." Violet punctuated her question with a loud hoot. "Nora says I smell bad too, but trust me, she is no field of lavender herself."

"I would know my girl anywhere. And we won't worry how you smell right now." He wrapped his arms around her. "Is she injured?" he asked the officer.

"No, sir. The EMTs checked her out at the triage tent and said she's fine. I found her and Miss King on the road, trying to walk home in the dark. With those leg braces they weren't making much progress."

"Where are your crutches and wheelchair?"

"Gone." Violet lifted her finger skyward in a whirlpool motion. "But at least I'm upright and not crawling on all fours." She hugged him tightly around the waist.

"What about Nora? Where is she?" Sol swallowed a bad taste in his mouth for the hasty judgments he had levied against the young woman.

The sheriff pursed his lips, considering. "Are you some kind of authority among the Amish?"

"*Jah*. I'm one of the district's ministers."

"Miss King suffered a gash on her head, but medics think it's a superficial scalp laceration. They stitched her up and gave her a tetanus shot, but she'll require a regimen of antibiotics and need to be watched for signs of concussion."

"They didn't take her to the hospital in Columbia?"

"No, she refused to be transported. And because she's twenty-one that's her prerogative. One of my deputies drove her back to the people she's staying with." The sheriff consulted a spiral notebook. "The Gingerichs."

"He's our district deacon. I'm glad to hear she's well." He tightened his hold on his daughter.

"What did you expect, Papa? Nora and I are cut from rugged Amish stock."

The English lawman gazed at the small muddy woman, barely able to stand and stifled a laugh. "Well, I suppose you would have made it home eventually. By August, perhaps. I'll give you that much." He tucked the tablet back into his pocket. "I'll leave her in your care, Mr. Trask, and be off. There are many damaged houses yet to check for injuries." He tipped his hat and wasted no time returning to his idling truck.

"Thank you, Sheriff, for bringing her home. I am in your debt." Solomon waved his hat.

"Think nothing of it," he called. Then the flashing blue and red lights sped down the driveway and disappeared into darkness around the corner.

"God saved us," whispered Violet. She lifted her face to meet his gaze. "The tornado was headed straight for us, but at the last second it switched directions."

"Let's get you inside and into the shower. Then you'll have plenty of time to tell your story." Supporting Violet's weight, Sol moved them toward the house.

"Nora refused to run for her life even though I told her to. It was hopeless, in my opinion. Then she threw herself on top of me at the last minute." In obvious pain and fatigued beyond measure, Violet dragged one foot in front of the other.

Tears filled the minister's eyes that a woman he wished to shun would risk her life for his daughter. "Your *mamm* will want to hear the details too."

Rosanna had heard his shout and burst from the house in her robe and nightgown, with her hair down her back in a long braid. "Violet, you're alive! My little girl is safe." Rosanna almost knocked the two of them over. She embraced Violet and pressed her head to her shoulder. Violet's muddy hair immediately stained Rosanna's white gown.

"*Mamm*, I'm getting you dirty." She tried to wriggle away without success.

"That's what washing machines are for." After embracing a full minute, Rosanna took Violet's arm to offer support, her composure and reserved nature returning. "I'll bet you're starving…and thirsty. And I'm sure a bath would feel nice." The three Trasks resumed their glacially slow progress to the house.

When Violet reached the base of the steps she began to cry. "Oh, *mamm*, our sweet little mare is dead. We've had her since I was a child. We tied her up under a shady tree by the road, but when we returned after the twister, she was gone." Her cries escalated into near hysteria.

"Stop crying," murmured Solomon. "Nell is in the barn right now. She found her way home and she's fine." Both parents carried Violet up the steps.

"She didn't get sucked up in the twister?" she asked in disbelief.

"*Nein*, she ate a bucket of oats and fell asleep. She'll probably sleep until Saturday." Once they reached the porch, Sol lifted his daughter into his arms, despite her protests, and deposited her on a kitchen chair.

"I'll draw a warm tub of water. Then you will eat and go to bed." Rosanna bustled into the bathroom, content with something practical to do.

Violet propped her head with both hands. "I might fall asleep and drown."

"Not with me in there with you," called Rosanna. "We must wash your hair. Who knows what crawled inside that tangle." Soon, the sound of running faucets obscured the rest of her plans.

Solomon poured her a glass of water, which Violet drank down in long gulps.

"When we got to the road my buggy was gone too—just one broken wheel was left. That's why I thought Nell had died." Her chin sagged despite her cupped palms.

"Knowing how *you* tie off reins," a voice sounded from behind them, "Nell probably broke free after the first peel of thunder." Irvin and Susanna crossed the room in a few strides, with Mark and Ann, and Kathryn and John on their heels. Soon siblings filled the Trask kitchen, eager to welcome home their storm-fighting sister. They surrounded her with hugs and kisses, heedless of her muddy condition.

"Hello, everybody, but where are my nieces and nephews?" she asked. "Don't they want to see the aunt who refused to blow away in a tornado?" Violet drank the second glass of water Sol poured.

Kathryn slipped into the chair vacated by Rosanna. "They're in bed. Tomorrow will be soon enough for that mob to pester you with questions. They can wait until after you're rested."

At the mention of rest, Violet stifled a yawn. "Mama's going to give me a bubble bath, just like when we were *kinner*. And shampoo my hair so I won't drown in the tub."

"I'll feed you supper while you soak," said Ann, burrowing in the refrigerator. "If you weren't so exhausted, you would feel like a pampered *Englischer* at one of those day spas."

"How would you know what goes on in one of those?" Mark sprang up to help slice roast beef left over from dinner.

"I saw a picture in a magazine, and I have a good imagination." Ann loaded enough potato salad onto a plate for three women.

Kathryn set a glass of milk before her younger sister. "How is your friend Nora?" she asked softly.

"The medical people sewed up a gash on her head in a make-shift tent. She refused to go to Columbia, so they gave her a shot and a bottle of pills to take." Violet drank long sips of milk. "They wouldn't give her pain relievers because she might have a concussion. Nora said she didn't have a headache for the first time in days. Imagine that. A clunk on the head can cure migraines. If we had only known sooner." She tried to stand but fell back down. Kathryn and Ann half-walked, half-carried Violet to the bathroom.

Solomon dabbed his eyes again. Summer pollen must be affecting him adversely tonight. "Okay, the rest of you back to bed. Tomorrow will be soon enough for more questions." He resumed the patriarchal role with his offspring.

"Too late for bed, *daed*. Look." Irvin opened the kitchen door, which swung precariously from the top hinge only.

Everyone stared as the sun rose above the horizon, streaking the sky with pink and gold. "Let's hope for good weather. This people of Missouri will have their work cut out for them today."

Mark joined Irvin in the doorway. "And for a long time to come. Who wants to tend animals—and do *everyone's* chores— and who wants to check on our neighbors? Folks might need our help." Sol's sons and son-in-law strode outdoors, arguing as to who would do what.

He carefully closed the door behind them and bowed his head in prayer. *Until I draw my dying breath, I will be grateful to You for preserving my family.*

❧

**Thursday**

Nora awoke to bright sunlight streaming through her bedroom window. Birds chirped in the trees as though nothing had happened the day before. For a brief moment she thought about pulling the shade and going back to sleep, as she hadn't arrived home until almost dawn, but one name sprang to mind and one face was instantly etched on the inside of her lids. Lewis. Was he dead…or injured, still trapped beneath rubble? Or had he already headed to Columbia to catch the next bus back to St. Louis?

*Why stick around when the woman supposedly in love with you had given you the cold shoulder?*

Except she actually was in love with him.

Bolting from the bed, she staggered and nearly fell as the room swam before her eyes. She'd forgotten her head injury. Gingerly, she touched the bandaged spot before swallowing two Tylenol tablets and one of the antibiotics. She'd bathed only a few hours ago, so now she dressed and brushed her teeth as quickly as possible. Within ten minutes she arrived in the kitchen sporting only a minor limp from her assortment of bruises, scratches, and blisters.

Emily stared at her, while Jonas nearly dropped the case of bottled water he was carrying. "What are you doing up?" demanded her boss. "You've only been sleeping about four hours."

Nora clutched the back of a kitchen chair. "About the same length of time for the two of you. Where are you going?"

"*We* didn't get knocked unconscious and then walk miles of bad roads, injured." Emily moved the hampers and several thermoses of coffee to the counter near the door. "You should eat something and then go back to bed, Nora. After we load up food, water, and our first aid kit, we plan to make ourselves useful in the community. People might still be trapped in cellars."

"We've borrowed our neighbor's buggy. We'll take it as far as we can and then start walking." Jonas lifted the first load and carried it outside.

"I have to find Lewis," said Nora. "I can't stay here napping if he might be hurt or…dead. If he's still alive, there's something I must tell him."

Emily's face filled with pity. "There's no point going to the lumberyard. It's closed until further notice. Nobody will be there."

Nora began to perspire, even though the room wasn't warm. "Then where is he?" she gasped. "Why didn't he come home last night?"

Emily shoved bread, crackers, peanut butter, and jam into a cloth tote bag. "He moved to Seth's house yesterday, remember? They only worked half a day and then went home to get Lewis settled in. I'm not sure if they were on the road or already at Yoders' when the twister hit."

Nora swallowed hard. "Then I'll go to the Yoder farm."

Emily pressed the back of her hand to her forehead. "They live on the other side of the lumberyard. You'll never get through." She stopped packing long enough to face Nora. "Give the workers a few days before venturing out for unnecessary travel. Don't forget you suffered a blow to the head."

Nora reflected a moment. "I know you think me silly, Emily, but this is the only thing I've been sure of in a long time. I love him and I must know if he survived the storm, even if he returns to Maine. I know a shortcut to Seth's that will save both time and distance. On my way home, I'll check in on Violet and the Trask family." She walked to the sink to fill her aluminum water bottle. "I promise not to make extra work for rescuers, and I'll help anyone in need along the way."

"Can you ride a saddled horse?" asked Jonas from the doorway.

Nora pivoted around as hope and anticipation began to build. "I can. My father taught Rachel and me when we were young. Amy and Beth would have none of it." She didn't mention she hadn't ridden since she was fourteen.

"You can probably get around on horseback. I'll tie a bag of bandages, antiseptic, and water to the saddle horn of my gelding. Just watch out for live power lines. Don't even try to step over them." Jonas marched off toward the barn.

Emily shook her head. "It's settled then, but be careful. You might not think your life worth much at the moment, but I care very much about you…and so does Sally and your family." She wrapped her arms around Nora in a brief hug, grabbed the last of the supplies, and vanished out the door.

The Gingerichs left home within ten minutes to be of service to their community. Jonas had tied his gelding, saddled and supplied, to the porch rail. Nora followed soon after wearing a backpack stuffed with as much food as it would hold. If the tornado taught her anything, she realized her self-centeredness must stop. She would strive to be more like Emily. The sun would no longer rise and set according to the whims of Nora King.

Her romantic future seemed of little importance as she viewed collapsed houses, damaged barns, and destroyed cars. She prayed for each family she saw as they dug through rubble looking for keepsakes. She prayed every time an ambulance sped by, taking the injured to hospitals in Columbia. And she prayed at the demolished home sites, where no one stirred and nothing remained, that the inhabitants had reached shelters before the tornado hit.

Two hours later, as she passed Gingerich Lumber, she spotted a "Help Wanted" sign in the window. Odder still, that the front window was still intact. Was the notice for Elam's position or Lewis's? She hoped both men would find peace and happiness. Nora stopped only twice more to water the horse from farm ponds before reaching Josh's lane. Remnants of Violet's buggy and shreds of her lap quilt littered the ground where they had tied up yesterday. Violet—what an amazing woman to walk as far as she had without complaining. When Nora rode by Josh's house—untouched by the twister—she prayed for Seth, Violet's beau. The answer to that particular prayer appeared around the next bend in the road.

Seth Yoder stood on scaffolding among the rafters of his family's home with at least four other Amish men. They were replacing a missing roof, while a half dozen more workers handed up materials from ground level. Seth recognized Nora before she could slide gracefully from the horse.

"Wow, look at that! Nora has transformed herself into Annie Oakley of the Wild, Wild West." Seth waved his hat as though enjoying a summer picnic instead of repairing his family's roofless house. "Have you come to help us, Miss King? Or bring word of my dear, sweet Violet?"

Nora laughed, drawing as near as she dared with the piles of ruined materials. "She's fine. The walk did her legs a world of good. Good luck ever getting her back into a wheelchair. How is your family, Seth?" She peered up at the men on the scaffold. The sight of one tall, powerfully built man nailing plywood made her heart clench inside her chest. *Lewis—alive and unhurt. Danki, Lord.*

"We're all fine. My brother spotted the twister early enough for everyone to get to the cellar. Our house lost its roof but the important building—the horse barn—dodged the bullet. No damage, and not one animal as much as tangled their mane or tail with twigs." He laughed from the belly. "Want to climb up the ladder? Or should I send Lewis down there? I suppose you two are glad to see each other."

Nora felt faint, and it had nothing to do with the head concussion.

Lewis finished nailing his piece of plywood and stood, meeting her gaze at last. She shielded her eyes from the glare and stared back, willing herself not to cry. Slipping his hammer into a loop on his tool belt, he scrambled down the ladder, his expression unreadable. It took some time to reach her side with the broken beams and shingles strewn across the yard.

"Hello, Nora. We were glad to hear you and Violet got home safely. I hope that gash on your head doesn't trigger more migraines." His tone couldn't be more lackadaisical.

"You heard about our walk? How could you possibly?" she croaked.

"Seth called Violet's sister on her cell phone this morning. Kathryn reported the ordeal you two had." He crossed his arms, looming large over her. "Why did you come here, on horseback, no less?" Now he sounded irritated.

"I…I had to know you were alive and well."

"I am. Fit as a fiddle."

"I passed Gingerich Lumber. It suffered damage, but it's not a total loss."

"*Gut.*" One word couldn't possibly sound more unemotional.

"I saw the 'Help Wanted' sign and figured it might be for your position. Tell me, Lewis, why are you leaving?"

His eyes practically bulged from their sockets. "Must I spell it out for you?" he snapped, heedless of who might overhear. "Because I'm in love with someone who is not in love with me."

"I *am* in love with you," she snapped back. "That's the other reason I came. But I was ashamed of myself and afraid to tell you what kind of person I am." She spoke low but clear, to make sure he understood.

He glanced around the Yoder yard. Every pair of eyes was focused on them. "Let's talk by the barn. Your horse can probably use a bucket of oats anyway."

Nora stayed silent until the gelding was drinking deeply at the water trough. "I've done things in the past that I regret, things difficult to confess."

"I take it you lost your virtue to Elam?"

"*Nein*...not to him. I...I lost it in Pennsylvania to a boy I thought loved me. But his affections were false, and he soon started courting someone else." She stared at the ground. "I never felt toward him what I feel toward you."

"And you couldn't admit this to me?"

"I thought...I thought you would despise me if I did."

He lifted her chin with one finger. "How could I despise you for something that happened before we met?"

She shrugged her shoulders, while her world hung by a slender thread.

"Well, I couldn't. That's the long and short of it. Now, I'll ask you one more question, Nora King, and I strongly suggest you tell the truth."

Gazing up at him, she nodded because her emotions made speech difficult.

"Do you love me?"

"I do, Lewis. I have. And I always will, without a shadow of a doubt." Nora held her breath.

He rubbed his jawline. "Well then, we'll never bring this matter up again. It's water under the bridge, and it don't make no never mind to me."

"What?"

"I heard an *Englischer* say that yesterday and I liked it. It must be a Missouri expression. I never thought I'd be able to use it so soon." He winked one of his light blue eyes.

"Oh, Lewis." She wrapped her arms around his waist, not caring who saw them. "I'm glad I caught you before you left."

"Why's that?" He stroked the back of her *kapp*, just below the location of the bandage.

"Because I sure wouldn't want to ride that horse all the way back to Maine."

❧

Emily and Jonas drove down Township 116 about a mile and a half to the west before the route became impassable by buggy. Each farm they passed showed signs of repairs under way. People waved from porches, barns, house roofs, or fields. The wind had tossed every kind of junk across pastures and croplands. Even if a crop could be salvaged, countless amounts of debris must be picked out before harvesttime. The only traffic on the road passed by in large pickups with big knobby tires, capable of off-road detours. Each single driver stopped to ask if they wanted a ride or needed food or water.

"People keep offering us assistance instead of us providing help to others," moaned Emily, wiping her forehead with a hanky.

"Our turn may come yet," said Jonas. He pulled the buggy off the pavement under a shady tree, one of the few left undamaged.

An unluckier tree, with roots dry and dying, lay across the road ahead. "We can go no farther." He pulled a tablet and black marker from his duffle bag and began to write.

"What are you making?"

"A sign to hang on the buggy so everyone knows it's mine and not abandoned. We'll take the horse with us. I'll tie whatever supplies we brought to his back. With your mare still at Minister Trask's house and Nora riding my gelding, I'm running low on horseflesh. I can't afford to give this one up too."

"You're one smart man, Jonas Gingerich, turning a registered Standardbred into a pack mule. What if some of his horse friends see him?"

"We can find him a hat and dark glasses." They shared a laugh while loading whatever they could onto the animal. Emily slung the first aid kit over her shoulder, and they soon circled around the fallen tree. As they journeyed in the hot summer sun, Emily wished she'd remembered her sunglasses. Jonas checked at each house to make sure anyone needing medical treatment had already been transported. The uninjured people stood around in a daze, unsure where to begin salvaging useable bits and pieces of their lives. After another half mile, Emily stumbled over a branch and fell to one knee, ripping her skirt.

"I suppose now you'll expect a new dress?" teased Jonas, helping her to her feet.

"It can wait a month or two." Emily rolled her eyes. "But I don't see what use we can be down here. The sheriff's department and medical workers have checked these homes and farms for injuries. We might be wasting our time and shoe leather." She halted finally aware he stopped ten feet back. "What is it, *ehemann*?" she asked, returning to his side.

"We almost walked right by this place without noticing. And we're on foot."

"What place?" Emily gazed in the direction Jonas pointed. She saw an overgrown cut through the woods with two wagon tracks of hard-packed dirt down the middle. "That's probably just a path to a back pasture or woodlot. I doubt anybody lives there."

"I'd heard a family of Swartzentruber Amish moved down here. You know they seldom leave the farm except to attend preaching services. That could be why the lane has overgrown. Look, Emily!" Jonas pointed to a four-by-four post snapped off inches from the ground. "That probably held their mailbox, which now could be somewhere in the next county. Without a mailbox, rescuers wouldn't know to check down that drive."

Emily met Jonas's eye while a sensation of dread spiked up her spine. "We'd better take a look."

"Give me your hand and stay on the path. There could be snakes." Together they ran until breathless before slowing their pace to a fast walk. Poison ivy vines and wild sumac overhung the two-mile lane on both sides. The horse snorted and balked, not enjoying stepping over so many broken tree limbs.

"Let's rest a moment," gasped Emily. She clutched her chest.

Jonas dug out a water bottle for each of them and they drank heartily. The brief respite couldn't prepare them for what was to come. Around the next bend lay the destroyed remains of a frame house. At least they assumed it had been a house, judging by the size and household objects scattered among the debris. A small pole barn forty yards to the rear had suffered damage but remained upright. The outdoor outhouse and separate washhouse confirmed Jonas's suspicion that the residents were members of the most conservative Amish sect. Several hens and one irate rooster pecking through the grass indicated the former existence of a chicken coup.

"Oh, mercy," murmured Emily, surveying the scene. No wall, not one side of the former home remained standing. Only a pile of wood and shattered glass with pieces of cloth marked the spot where a house had been.

Jonas began methodically picking through the rubble. "Be careful where you step, *fraa*. Who knows what lies beneath." He removed lumber one piece at a time and placed it into a new pile.

Following his example, she did the same, selecting smaller, lighter pieces. "Do you think there's a cellar under this?" she asked after an hour of work. "Perhaps folks are still trapped below."

"*Nein*, it doesn't appear that way. It looks as though they built the house on a flat, high spot of land." Jonas started working faster, pulling and tossing boards with both hands, as though he sensed urgency. Haste, however, proved unnecessary when he uncovered two dead bodies—first a man and then a woman in the rubble.

Emily cried when she saw how young the couple had been. "Oh, Jonas," she moaned, holding the *fraa's* cold hand in her own. "May God have mercy on their souls." Tears streamed down her face.

"Go wait in the shade under the trees, Em. Stay with the horse." Jonas spoke softly. "I'll remove the rest of the debris and find enough quilt scraps to cover them. The authorities will want to remove the bodies."

For another minute, Emily crouched beside the young woman and sobbed, still gripping her hand. Then she rose to her feet and staggered away, her face awash with misery. But she didn't hide in the shade until Jonas finished his gruesome task. Instead she circled around to the other side and began removing materials from the back end. "Who's to say they didn't already have *kinner*?" she hollered. "Swartzentruber folks marry young." Emily pulled off lumber and shingles with both fists.

"Just be careful. You could easily break an ankle or cut yourself on glass."

She tossed broken dishes and crockery over her shoulder in a defiant act of frustration until she focused on something odd. She stared, forcing her mind to identify the shape, despite overwhelming fatigue. "Jonas, I think there's an upside down bathtub over here—a big cast-iron tub, not one of those copper kettles. I thought Swartzentrubers usually bathed in their washhouse where they can heat enough hot water. Why would a tub be inside the kitchen, especially in summer? It doesn't look like it blew here. The roof collapsed on top of it."

Jonas cocked his head, and then he dropped the broken headboard he carried. "There's only one reason I can imagine. Stay where you are. Don't move."

"What do you mean?" she demanded. "It looks like one end had been raised up with a brick." Realization dawned. "Oh, Jonas, could it be possible?" Emily could barely draw a breath.

Jonas waited to answer until by her side and they had removed the rest of the trash. "The couple may have placed this tub over a child for protection, not having a basement, and braced up one end for air." He met her eye. "On the count of three, we'll lift up. One…two…"

Upon "three" they raised the cast-iron tub and pushed it back. Underneath sat a small boy, dirty and terrified, gazing at them with round brown eyes. But the child wasn't alone in the cave created by his parents in the final minutes of their lives. In his arms the boy clutched a blanket-wrapped bundle, silent but moving.

"A baby?" asked Jonas.

"May I see your brother or sister?" asked Emily in *Deutsch*. The child thought for a moment and then handed over his bundle. As soon as Emily peeled back the soggy wrapper, an infant began to wail.

*A boppli*…and still alive.

# TWENTY

*I'll sing thy power to save*

**Six weeks later**

Let us know where you want us, Minister Trask," said a voice behind him. "We're here to help."

Solomon turned around to greet yet another English family that showed up to raise the new barn at the Morganstein farm. His jaw dropped nearly to his chest. It was the same tourists he'd met before here at the leather shop and bakery. He had chastised the woman for taking photographs of Amish children and the daughter for being insufficiently attired. Sol blinked and stared before recovering his composure.

"How did you know to come? We put up no announcement in town or in local papers."

"Word gets around," said the wife. "Our pastor at First Baptist told the congregation about it." No camera hung from her neck today. "Just point us in the right direction." She shifted a picnic hamper from one hand to the other.

"Thank you for coming. Women are meeting in the house and setting food that doesn't need to stay cold on the back porch." Sol tipped his hat. "They'll be glad for an extra pair of hands."

"What about me, sir?" The teenage girl timidly peered up from beneath thick bangs. Today she wore very little makeup and a flannel shirt, buttoned to the throat and tucked into her baggy blue jeans.

"Young people are behind the barn. Boys are in charge of getting building materials where they need to be around the construction site, while the girls will see that everyone has enough to eat and drink. Ask for my daughter Violet. She'll put you right to work. She'll be the bossy one, using only one crutch for balance instead of her new wheelchair." Solomon smiled as the girl scampered in the direction he indicated.

The minister turned back to the father. "I appreciate you coming and bringing your family, especially since we got off on the wrong foot." He extended his hand.

"Forget about it. This is a small town. We're all here for each other." He pumped Sol's hand vigorously. "I brought my tool belt and a full supply of energy." The *Englischer* grinned as though this were an outing instead of a long day of hard labor.

"You'll find Levi Morganstein there." Sol pointed to the cluster of men near the barn's foundation. "He'll direct the work on today's barn raising. And thanks again."

"See you later. Save me a seat for lunch. My wife made great barbequed beef." With a wave the man strode off, leaving Sol with watery eyes and a renewed spirit in humankind.

"So many folks have turned out today that Levi will have more than enough hands to raise the entire frame, plus roof the structure by nightfall. God is great," he murmured. He had spared many, many lives that fearsome day when a category 3 tornado cut a path of destruction for miles. All told, only four lives had been lost—two *Englischers,* who had tried to outrun the tornado in their vehicle, and two Plain—the Swartzentruber couple who moved to Paradise a year ago. Both of their children survived and were thriving at the Gingerichs' until relatives traveled from Iowa to claim them.

Sol bowed his head, humbled by the grace of God. Humbled and convicted to mend bad habits that might still linger. He would serve his district and community for the rest of his life a grateful man.

"Am I interrupting?"

Solomon lifted his head to find Jonas at his elbow. "*Nein.* Just giving thanks for the good turnout along with the fine weather."

The deacon gazed around the Morganstein yard. "There are so many folks here we'll be getting in each other's way. I'm going to direct additional cars and buggies to park on the other side of the bakery. There's no more room anywhere near the house." Jonas slapped Sol on the back.

"Another moment, please, before you go." Sol grasped the deacon's arm. "I'm sorry for the way I behaved toward you, Jonas. I've already spoken to Nora, but I wanted to apologize to you and Emily too."

The younger man shook his head. "You were doing what you thought best for the district. Neither of us knew what was coming or how things would turn out. There are no hard feelings." He gazed up at a cloudless sky. "It could have been so much worse."

Sol nodded, knowing Jonas didn't refer to today's weather for the reconstruction. "A miracle, regarding those *kinner*—still alive after their whole house crumbled around them. You and Emily saved their lives."

"Emily hasn't left their sides since that day. She rode in the ambulance, stayed at the hospital for two days of observation, and then completed a stack of paperwork for them to be released into our custody. Children's Services couldn't believe the little boy didn't know a word of English. I figured that's why they rushed through our application."

"Best to keep them in a Plain household. They've been traumatized enough after losing their parents."

Jonas moved closer. "Have you heard anything from the Iowa kin? As much as she wants to do what's best for the little ones, it will kill Emily to give them back. We've had them long enough to grow fond of them." His voice faltered, indicating his wife wasn't the only one who had grown attached.

Four weeks ago Sol had traveled with a sheriff's deputy and the caseworker to meet the children's Iowa relatives. The *Englischers* had asked the minister to accompany them because they feared the Swartzentruber adults also wouldn't speak English. The delegation from Paradise discovered that the children's kinfolk all had large families of their own. The sheriff and caseworker were told that the young couple had inherited the property and thought they would give Missouri a try.

Sol stroked his beard. "I haven't heard anything yet, Jonas. All I know is that the social worker planned to meet with them again before issuing her recommendation to the court. A few days ago she asked me for a statement regarding your suitability for parenthood, and I said no couple would be better than you and Emily."

Jonas sighed. "*Danki*, Sol. We'll be patient and see what God has planned."

Over the deacon's shoulder, Solomon watched a police vehicle pull up the driveway. "You might not have to wait very long. Why don't you see what the sheriff wants? It can't be about us making too much noise. The entire neighborhood is here."

Jonas turned and moved in the direction of the truck, walking as fast as possible without sprinting like a racehorse.

"If it be Your will," murmured Solomon. Then he headed toward the barn to make himself useful.

☙

A dozen reasons could have brought the officer to the Morganstein farm—the most obvious being he was curious about a barn raising. Jonas reached the truck just as the tall man unfolded himself from the driver's side. With a jolt, Jonas recognized the young English social worker in the passenger seat. She'd come to their farm several times to check on Micah and little Laura.

"I thought I might find you here, Mr. Gingerich," said the sheriff, taking off his huge hat. "Looks like everyone in the county showed up."

"Jonas, please. Good to see you, Sheriff Baker, and you, Miss O'Brien." He removed his straw hat.

"You have your work cut out for you today. Judging by the foundation, that's one huge barn to rebuild by sundown." He scratched the back of his head.

"If we don't finish, you know what they say. There's always tomorrow." Jonas peered through the windshield at the caseworker. She seemed surprised by the hubbub and amount of junk still remaining in the yard from the tornado. "Would either of you like something to eat or drink? The women are at the house on one of the porches, Miss O'Brien."

"Why don't you head on up, Terri," suggested the sheriff. "You could observe how Micah has adjusted to the Old Order children of this district. It can count for one of your unannounced visits."

"Good idea. I have a visitation form ready to go." Terri clutched her clipboard to her chest, swung her soft-sided briefcase over one shoulder, and marched toward the house. "I'll see you both later."

The sheriff watched her until she was out of earshot. "I wanted to speak to you privately, Jonas."

The deacon's empty stomach turned over.

"Miss O'Brien has visited the Iowa relations twice more since I went with Minister Trask. To tell the truth, she doesn't seem particularly fond of their conservative sect. She's a city gal. Out-houses and heating water atop wood-burning stoves to take a bath or wash your clothes is too *Little House on the Prairie* for her tastes. She prefers the propane washers, refrigerators, and hot water tanks used by Old Order Amish." He kept his voice soft. "Indoor plumbing is also a big plus for her. I'm not sure what she did when she visited them. Probably didn't drink too much coffee or bottled water." He chuckled good-naturedly.

But Jonas was too nervous to laugh. He was almost too nervous to breathe. "What are you saying, Sheriff?"

"I don't want to raise your hopes before the ink dries on the paperwork, but Miss O'Brien will most likely advise the court to place the children permanently in your home. Unless the relatives have a change of heart and demand Micah and Laura be returned to Iowa, you and Emily will be named their guardians—foster parents for now. In a year you can petition the court to legally adopt them." The large man set his wide-brimmed hat back on his head. "The Iowa kin liked the idea of a childless couple raising their niece and nephew. Like I said, they have a dozen children between them. As long as the kids stay Amish, the fact you're Old Order doesn't seem to be an issue. They would want to visit them, of course, from time to time, and they hope you'll travel to Iowa also."

"Of course we will." Jonas exhaled air he hadn't realized he'd been holding. "Can I tell Emily?"

"Sure you can, if Miss O'Brien hasn't already spilled the beans."

On shaky legs, Jonas walked toward the Morganstein house alongside the sheriff. He ignored the beehive of activity on the new barn where young people scurried to-and-fro, gabbing as much as working as young people loved to do. He stared straight ahead, because somewhere among the throng awaited his wife and new son and daughter. Just as they reached the porch steps, Jonas spotted Emily and the social worker on lawn chairs in the shade. The infant slept in Emily's arms while Micah sat at Terri's feet. The caseworker held a pen over her clipboard, scribbling away.

"Good afternoon," said Jonas, feeling silly about being so formal.

"Join us, Mr. Gingerich. I have a few questions for you too." Miss O'Brien seemed quite at ease under the tree.

"If I'm not needed, I'll get some lunch from the porch," said Sheriff Baker. "I happen to know Mrs. Gingerich bakes the best breads, pies, and cookies in the county." Tipping his hat, he aimed himself toward the buffet.

Jonas pulled up an extra chair with the women. "What do you need to know?"

Terri consulted her paper. "What would happen if you and your wife found out you were expecting a natural child of your own?"

The question took him by surprise. "We would raise them all together, not showing favor to one over the other. Who birthed the child makes no difference to me."

Emily had been watching him from the corner of her eye and nodded agreement. "That's what I said. Love is love. And there's plenty to go around in our household."

"You would be willing to cut your days at the bakery back to just two per week?" asked Terri of Emily.

"Certainly. Violet and Nora work so hard, I'm barely needed in the shop now. And if either woman quits my employment, I have several more who would like to take their place."

"You both keep charged-up cell phones for emergencies?" Miss O'Brien peered at each as they nodded their heads like trained horses.

"And you have access to a vehicle in case of emergencies?"

"Our taxi service is available twenty-four hours a day. And I have English employees with cars I could call on without hesitation."

She pondered for a moment. "Micah's aunt insists they live in an Amish home. And few other Swartzentrubers live here in Paradise. Before you could petition for permanent adoption, I would need financial statements from your businesses. But that's well down the line." The social worker consulted her clipboard one final time before she told Emily the joyous news Jonas had already heard from Sheriff Baker. He bent down to lift Micah into his arms.

Emily closed her eyes and began to cry. Then she jumped to her feet with Laura pressed close to her chest. "Thank you, Miss O'Brien. You won't regret your decision." She kissed the baby's forehead, smiling so broadly her face might break.

"You're welcome, and congratulations to both of you. You'll still see me from time to time, both for scheduled and unannounced visits, but I don't foresee any problems."

"Now would you like something to eat?"

"No, thanks, Mrs. Gingerich. Please tell the sheriff I'll wait for him by the truck." And then she was gone. Jonas and Emily were left with Micah and Laura. And for the first time, the four of them felt like a family.

❧

"Stop staring at them. You'll make Emily nervous." Violet hissed in her ear.

Nora straightened the buffet table for the third time. She pulled her focus from Emily and the skinny woman sitting on lawn chairs. "I'm worried for Emily's sake. That *Englischer* keeps scribbling on her clipboard. What if she says something wrong or that woman sees something she doesn't like?" Nora stirred the macaroni salad again.

"What could she possibly not like?" Violet placed her hand on her hip. "Emily hasn't been apart from those two kids since she found them. She moved a crib and extra bed into their bedroom so they wouldn't be alone. And she even takes them to Grain of Life to watch the rebuilding of the bakery."

"I know, but the English have their own ideas of what constitutes a good home…baby monitors, electric bottle sterilizers, humidifiers. At least Jonas and Emily installed smoke detectors before the county's first visit."

"Remember, those *kinner* are Amish and have a right to stay that way. Come on," coaxed Violet. "Let's go convince our two fiancés that *now* would be a good time to take their lunch break. They can eat with us someplace private." Violet wriggled her eyebrows.

Nora let herself be dragged off the porch, out of view of her boss. "Stop calling Lewis that. You and Seth might be officially engaged, but *my* beau has yet to ask me."

"A minor detail. Everyone knows the only reason Lewis works at Gingerich's and is still in town, for that matter, is because he intends to marry you."

Nora tucked a lock of hair beneath her *kapp.* "Maybe he just likes my plum tarts."

Violet harrumphed. "They're *gut,* but not as *gut* as mine." She punched Nora's shoulder playfully as they reached the work site.

"Miss Trask! Stop hitting people," called Seth. "Or your *daed* will never marry you off. He'll be too afraid for the sake of your unfortunate husband."

"Seth Yoder, come say that to my face if you're brave enough And bring that Yankee Lewis Miller with you. It's time for lunch for hard workers like *us.*" Violet beamed at her beloved up on the scaffolds. "We'll set up over yonder." She pointed at a picnic table by itself, and then she marched toward the buffet.

Nora had no choice but to follow her after making sure Lewis would take his break too. The men ate at staggered intervals to keep progress moving on the barn. Nora got in line behind Violet with two plates. On hers she placed raw veggies, a hot dog, and a portion of baked beans. For Lewis, she selected a double cheese-burger, hot dog, beans, and both potato and macaroni salads.

Violet glanced at her second plate in shock. "Goodness, are you fattening him up for the fall slaughter or for a wedding?"

"That all depends on how long he takes to pop the question," she whispered on their way to the picnic table. Seth and Lewis were already waiting with four glasses of lemonade. Both men grinned when they approached.

"Looks like you got more lunch than me," moaned Seth, comparing the two plates. He feigned disappointment.

Violet arched her neck. "That was due to the 'unfortunate husband' comment. I suggest you be nice or you'll get no dessert." She glared down her nose.

"I'll be sweet as cream, dear heart." Seth winked as he took his first bite of hamburger.

"Much better." Violet straightened her apron and focused her attention on Lewis. "Did you hear where we're going on our honeymoon? You are familiar with honeymoons, aren't you, Mr. Miller?" She fluttered her lashes. "It's a trip a couple takes following their *wedding*."

Nora shrank down on the bench and concentrated on her food, wishing she'd taken more to pick at. Her nudges beneath the table had gone ignored.

"I am familiar with the idea," said Lewis, "but I'm unaware of your destination. Will you visit relatives in outlying areas?"

Seth resumed the narrative. "Nope. We've booked passage on a freighter picking up cargo in St. Louis. They accept eight or ten paying passengers each trip. We'll have a little cabin with a window on the Mississippi River all the way down to New Orleans. Ain't that romantic?" He aimed an adoring gaze at Violet, who blushed prettily.

Their lunch partners stared with sandwiches held midair. "Does your father know about this cruise?" asked Nora.

Violet nodded energetically. "*Jah,* he agreed as long as we dress Plain, drink no wine with dinner, and don't spend much time with the sailors. The ship is bound for Florida."

"Why wouldn't we dress Amish?" asked Seth. "And we'll be too busy to mingle much with sailors."

Nora flushed until her scalp tingled, while Lewis asked, "If the ship's crossing the Gulf, how will you get back. Or haven't you love-birds thought that far in advance?"

"We'll take the bus back to St. Louis. The boat may have room for another couple if there were to be another wedding in the near future."

Nora choked on a bite of baked beans. After a hard slap between her shoulder blades, she was able to address her best friend. "Stop that right now, Violet Trask. You truly are incorrigible." Her voice was hoarse but the meaning clear.

Lewis seemed to be biting his cheek while trying to finish his lunch. When he had swallowed the last bite of his burger, he reached for Nora's hand. "Care to take a short walk with me before going back to work? We'll leave these two to discuss their traveling wardrobes."

Jumping to her feet, Nora pushed their dirty plates across the table. "For your punishment, you can clean up our mess, missy."

They set off toward the Morganstein apple orchard, which they found battered by the storm but still functional. "That friend of yours is one in a million," said Lewis, pulling Nora into his arms.

"I hope she didn't get your goat." Nora peered up at him.

"Nope. And she's right to be impatient for your sake. You're probably wondering why it's taking me so long to propose after we straightened things out at Seth's house all those weeks ago." Lewis held her so close, Nora could barely think.

"It had crossed my mind...maybe once or twice."

"I wrote to my parents to say we intended to marry. I said if they needed me, we would come back to Maine, but if they could possibly spare me, my bride greatly prefers the weather in Missouri—except for tornados, of course."

"Oh, my, Lewis. This is better than I dared to hope. I was all set to move back to Harmony." She blushed and then said, "If, of course, you asked me."

"There never was a doubt about that." He kissed her forehead. "Two days ago I got a letter from my parents. My fourth sister has a serious beau. That's plenty of menfolk to help bring in the harvest and work in the store too. None of the men owns so much land that they can't help my *daed*. My parents give their blessings as long as we promise to return yearly for a visit."

Nora rested her cheek against his chest as she hugged his midsection. "I will miss my sisters, but at least I'll have Violet and Emily."

"Who could leave Violet Trask? Life would seem so dull."

"Shall we go tell them?" Nora turned her face up to his again.

He kissed her lips before saying, "I'll walk you back to the house, but then I need to get back to work. Just don't let the future Mrs. Yoder talk the future Mrs. Miller into a trip to Louisiana and then Florida. We're going to Maine to see our families after our wedding. There's too many for them to make the trip here."

"I wouldn't have it any other way." Nora blinked back her tears as they strode toward the house. However, they had only gone halfway when a familiar face stepped out from behind a tree. "Elam Detweiler. What on earth are you doing here?"

Lewis nodded at his former adversary. "Elam has been helping on the barn, Nora. Nobody cuts joists or rafters as accurately as him."

"Thanks." The two men eyed each other like hawks. "I understand congrats are in order. You two are getting hitched?"

Lewis and Nora shared a smile. "Word travels fast. I only officially asked her five minutes ago."

"Seth Yoder jumped the gun." Elam smirked. "Well, Miller, I will say you are one lucky man." He struck out a hand.

Lewis paused for a moment, and then he shook the out-stretched hand. "I couldn't agree with you more."

Elam turned to walk away, but Nora stopped him in his tracks. "Wait!" she demanded. "You still owe me several favors as I recall. And I'm here to collect."

Elam scratched his scruffy goatee. "Name it."

"You will do *nothing* to interfere with our future happiness in Paradise."

"Done." Elam answered without hesitation.

"Now for the big favor you owe me." Nora looked from Lewis to Elam. "I want you to tell the truth about the robbery at the lumberyard. I won't have anyone thinking it might have been Lewis because we intend to make our home here." She narrowed her eyes into a glare.

Elam stared at her before he nodded. "Why not? I've already made up my mind to see what Colorado can offer a trained lumberjack like me. And I know an Amish man like Gingerich won't press charges." He slicked his finger through his long hair.

"*Danki.*" Nora clasped Lewis's hand and turned to leave.

"One more thing," said Elam. "I left a message for you in Maine that I'll share with you in person in Missouri. Don't let Paradise moss grow up your backside, Mrs. Miller. See some sights. Have some fun before you get too old."

"We intend to do just that." Lewis circled her shoulders with his strong arm.

Nora took one last look before Elam left with his typical arrogant swagger. She felt nothing but pity for him. He was a lost soul, stuck between the English world and the Amish—not fitting in in either one. *Help him, Lord. He needs You now more than ever, even though he's too stupid to realize it.*

"Ready for the rest of our life?" asked Lewis with a grin.

"You bet I am."

❧

## Mid-September

The new bell over the new door at Gingerich Lumber jangled as Nora entered, announcing her arrival.

Two men peered up from the computer monitor on the show-room counter. "Look who's here, Lewis," said Jonas. "It's the bride-to-be with nothing better to do than drive around in the hired van. Welcome to my rebuilt establishment, Miss King. Have you come to outfit your future new home?"

"Not today, Jonas. I had errands in Columbia and thought I'd see the repairs for myself." She pivoted in place. "Your descriptions at the dinner table don't do justice to this place."

Lewis walked around the counter to Nora's side. "Boss, I think I'll take one of those fifteen-minute breaks I'm supposed to have. I believe you owe me at least a hundred of them by now."

"Fine, but don't think I'm not timing the fifteen minutes," called Jonas as they headed out into brilliant autumn sunshine.

Once out of view, Lewis slipped an arm around her waist and drew her close.

"I have two letters from home and couldn't wait to share the news." Nora unfolded a pink sheet of paper. "Amy and John are coming from Harmony for our wedding. And they're bringing Sally and Thomas and your parents. That will just about empty the town. Your *schwestern* and their spouses will tend the co-op in your parents' absence."

"You're joking, right? They know we're coming to Maine in November." Lewis took the letter to skim.

"It sounds as though they're curious about the tornado damage. Also, Rachel and Beth are coming from Lancaster next week. They wrote that nothing would keep them from seeing me on my wedding day." Nora swallowed hard. "My *grossmammi* is mad as a hornet. My sisters are traveling unchaperoned because neither of my grandparents is up to the trip."

"They should be fine on the train." Lewis took the second letter to peruse.

"I believe *grossmammi* has more to worry about than that. After our wedding, Rachel doesn't plan to return to Pennsylvania with Beth. She's on her way to Kentucky to live and work on a chicken farm. Can you imagine, Lewis? *Grossmammi* has asked *me* to talk some sense into Rachel." Nora couldn't hide her joy over her new-found status in the family.

"And why shouldn't she turn to you?" He buzzed a kiss across her forehead. "Any woman who can change the course of a twister can surely change her little sister's mind."

Nora buried her face in his soft cotton shirt. "It wasn't just me…I had a little help from above."

Lewis drew her back to arm's length and lifted her chin with his finger. "Even so, you were pretty amazing that day and all the days after. I look forward to an amazing life with you here in Paradise, Nora, or wherever strong winds blow us."

❧

# Molasses Crinkles Cookies

*Rosanna Coblentz (Old Order Amish)*

3 cups butter

2½ cups white sugar

2½ cups brown sugar

4 eggs, beaten

6 teaspoons baking soda

1 cup buttermilk

1 cup cane molasses (light or dark, whichever your preference)

2 teaspoons baking powder

10 cups flour

Brown sugar

Cinnamon

Mix together the butter and sugars, and then add the beaten eggs and mix again. Dissolve the baking soda in the cup of buttermilk and add that to the mixture, and then add the molasses. Stir in the baking powder, and then gradually add in the flour.

Chill the dough for at least 2 hours and then roll into balls the size of walnuts. Roll the balls in a mixture of brown sugar and cinnamon to taste.

Place on an ungreased cookie sheet and bake at 350 degrees for 10 to 12 minutes, depending on your oven.

# Fruit Tarts

*Rosanna Coblentz*

**2 cups flour**
**½ cup shortening**
**½ cup butter-flavored shortening**
**8 ounces cream cheese**
**Pinch of salt**
**Lemon curd or fruit preserves**

Mix the first four ingredients well with a pastry blender or fork. Form the dough into balls and then press into the cups of a muffin or tart pan and fill with your favorite fruit filling, approximately ½ to ⅔ full (lemon curd or raspberry, cherry, plum, or peach preserves).

Bake for approximately 30 minutes at 350 degrees. Let cool and then add your favorite topping.

*Rosie says, "We like whipped cream, but ice cream is really good too."*

# Coconut Cream Pie

*Rosanna Coblentz*

**Pie Crust** (makes 2 pie shells)
1 teaspoon salt
2 cups flour
2/3 cup butter-flavored shortening
Cold water (just enough to form a ball)

Use a fork to mix the salt with flour and then work in the shortening until the mixture resembles coarse crumbs. Add 4 to 6 tablespoons cold water and mix well. Divide the dough and roll out to fit into a 9-inch pie pan. Place the crust in a pan, crimp the edges, and prick the dough with a fork. Repeat with the other half of dough. Bake until slightly brown.

*Rosie's secret: To prevent crusts from shrinking, place them under the broiler for a few seconds before baking.*

**Filling**
1 pint milk
1 cup white sugar
2 eggs, beaten
2 level tablespoons Clear Gel (moisten with a little milk)
1 tablespoon butter
1 tablespoon vanilla
1 cup coconut, grated and dried

Combine the milk, sugar, and eggs and cook on a medium-low heat. Stirring constantly to prevent scorching, bring the mixture to the point where it almost boils and then add the Clear Gel, butter, and vanilla. Continue stirring until smooth and creamy. Remove from heat.

After filling has cooled, add 1 cup grated dried coconut and then divide the mixture between the two pies shells. Chill and then top with whipped cream and toasted coconut. (To toast coconut, place under the broiler for a couple minutes. Watch closely so it doesn't become too dark.)

# DISCUSSION QUESTIONS

❧

1. Nora arrives in her new community with as much trepidation as excitement. What encouragement does she find that helps her believe Paradise might actually be a good fit?

2. Minister Solomon Trask has his work cut out for him. Why does he find the English tourists such a threat to the Plain lifestyle?

3. Nora originally came to Paradise because of Elam Detweiler. How and why does their relationship deteriorate? How does her character growth doom her feelings for Elam?

4. Why does Jonas Gingerich often feel like "odd man out" in his district, especially with Minister Trask, when both men base their viewpoints on the Bible?

5. Emily's fascination with local history causes friction between her and Jonas. Why does her faith seem to change the more she studies the past?

6. Solomon believes the natural disasters the community experiences substantiate his claim that God has turned His back on Paradise,

Missouri. What changes his mind by story's end and how will it affect his future as a minister?

7.  Violet Trask's physical struggles mirror the emotional struggles of her family and friends. How does this courageous woman influence the lives of Nora, Solomon, and Emily?

8.  Nora's relationship with Lewis is hampered by her lack of honesty. Why does finally letting go of her past mistakes finally give their love a chance?

9.  The hand of God, evident in the devastating tornado, affects Jonas, Solomon, Nora, and Violet differently. How is each of their lives changed for the better?

10. How do Old Testament lessons versus Christ's teachings in the New Testament continue to present challenges to Christians today?

*Don't miss Rachel's continuing journey in*
*Book 3 of The New Beginnings Series*
*by bestselling author Mary Ellis*

# A Little Bit of Charm

ᏸ

## ONE

**Randolph County, Missouri**

"Whew, it's already the middle of September and it's still hotter than blazes."

Rachel looked at her younger sister in horror. "Shush, Beth, before someone hears you. What will the Gingerichs think of us?"

Beth peered up with an innocent expression. "Is 'blazes' a bad word? I've heard daed say 'build a blaze in the woodstove' or 'a blazing sunset.'"

Rachel rolled her eyes. "Just shush on general principles. You'll be on your way back to Lancaster County soon, and then you can revert to your normal self. But let's put our best foot forward while we're still visitors here."

Beth's green-eyed focus turned wary. "What do you mean by I'll be on my way back to Pennsylvania?"

Rachel ignored a question she wasn't yet ready to answer. "Look, here comes the blushing bride and groom." She grinned with a heart swelling with joy and love for their sister.

"Who would ever guess Nora would get hitched to Lewis Miller?" Beth's words were a very audible whisper. "I thought she'd end up with that wily fox, Elam Detweiler."

Rachel shifted her weight to her other foot, which she then placed directly atop Beth's. No other admonishment proved necessary.

Nora and Lewis approached with glowing faces that only a wedding day can inspire. "Well, my dear *schwestern*, did you enjoy yourselves at our wedding?" Nora wrapped an arm around each of their shoulders, drawing them close.

The three-way hug brought a rush of moisture to Rachel's eyes. "Truly, I did. I've never seen you looking so pretty...or so happy." Tears cascaded down her cheeks with the realization the four King siblings would not only be in four different districts, but different states as well.

A couple of years ago they were like any other Old Order Amish girls living with their parents with their grandparents next door. They dreamed of a future around the corner, married to boys they had known their entire lives. But a house fire had changed everything. It took their parents to the Lord and Rachel's two older sisters to where their hearts led them. Amy, the eldest, settled in Harmony, Maine, where her fiancé's brothers lived. Nora, however, didn't find the ultraconservative district to her liking. So when the handsome, fence-sitting Elam Detweiler, Amy's new brother-in-law, took off with his secret driver's license in his bright-red Chevy, Nora followed soon after.

But new beginnings are often hard to predict. Not long after moving to Missouri, Nora's independent streak began to fade. And for the first time she longed to fit in, to be part of a loving, supportive community. If Nora's facial expression could be trusted, she had found what she was looking for in a town called Paradise.

A frisson of anxiety spiked up Rachel's spine. Was she making a big mistake? Would she cause her *grossmammi* grief and worry for nothing? Shaking off the notion, she joined Beth in cleaning up after the wedding meal while the happy couple walked guests to their buggies, expressing gratitude for the gifts and good wishes, thanking them for sharing in their most special day.

Much later that evening, while fireflies lit up the backyard with a thousand twinkling lights, Rachel sat alone on the Gingerichs' porch. Sleep wouldn't come—that much she knew. But she didn't wish to pace the bedroom floor and keep Beth or her gracious hosts awake. She tried to pray, but the only words that came to mind were rote prayers learned as a child. After several silent "Our Fathers," she clenched her eyes tightly shut. *Please, Lord, grant my sister a long life with many kinner and much joy.* Unbidden tears started anew. Her emotions seemed to be a roiling kettle of soup, rattling the lid and threatening to overflow.

"Why are you out here crying?" Nora gently pulled on her sister's *kapp* ribbon before slipping into the rocker next to hers.

"A better question would be what are you doing out here on your wedding night?" Rachel wiped her face and arched an eyebrow. "Don't you and Lewis have some business to attend to?"

A pretty blush rose up Nora's neck. "Don't speak of things you know nothing about." She pinched Rachel's arm. "Besides, I'll join him in a little while. We're both too nervous to sleep much tonight. In a few days we'll move into our new home. It's not much, but it's ours." She rocked with the satisfied assurance of a woman with her life laid out like a well-organized quilt.

Rachel knew no such contentment. Her future looked like an early spring sky—patchy clouds, intermittent rays of sunshine, and the smell of a coming storm. "I wish Beth and I could stay longer to help you pack."

"Worry not. My friend Violet arranged everything for our move and hers before she and Seth leave on their wedding trip to see the Gulf of Mexico. Violet may not be able to run, but she still maneuvers at the speed of light. She absolutely refused to use her crutches at her marriage ceremony. Her poor *daed* kept hovering as though she might fall over."

*Creak, creak, creak.* For several moments, the only sound came from the rolling wooden slats on the porch boards. Then in a hushed tone, Nora asked, "Care to tell me what's troubling you? And don't say 'nothing.' You've been weepy-eyed all day. That isn't like you, Rachel. You know we'll take a wedding trip in November, after the harvest is in. We'll visit Amy and John in Harmony and then come to Lancaster County to see you, Beth, *grossmammi*, and *grossdawdi*."

Rachel debated only half a second. There was no point in withholding the truth any longer. "When you get to Pennsylvania, you may only find one sister." She stared into the darkness as the moon slipped behind a cloud. "I've decided to take the bus from St. Louis to Louisville after I put Beth on the train to Chicago."

Nora stopped rocking. "Who on earth do you know in Louisville?"

"Not a soul. Once in Louisville I'll board a bus to Elizabethtown. Then I'll arrange for a hired van to take me to Charm."

"You're planning to visit Cousin Sarah? But you hate chickens."

Rachel laughed. "I do not hate chickens as long as they are in a pot with celery, onions, and dumplings." They shared a chuckle. "The fact that Sarah and her husband operate a free-range chicken farm doesn't deter me. Kentucky is known for only one thing, and it isn't Rhode Island Reds. The Blue Grass state raises the prettiest horses in the world."

"Prettier than Old Smokey after you braided his mane and tail with ribbons?"

A pang of nostalgia filled her heart. Old Smokey was her father's favorite Belgian draft horse, now relegated to light work with *grossdawdi* in his twilight years. "*Jah*, even prettier than him if magazines and library books can be trusted."

"If you've decided to visit Sarah on your way home, why not take Beth?"

A long minute spun out in the humid evening air while Rachel chose her reply carefully. In the end she gave her sister the short, honest answer. "Because if I find living on a chicken farm tolerable, I intend to stay permanently."

"Whatever for? I know you love horses and have read more

about them than any Amish person in the country, but horses are big business in Kentucky. What would a Plain gal who's never held a paying job in her life do there?"

Somewhere a faraway train blew its whistle. "I haven't the slightest idea. All I know is Lancaster County is a lonely place since *mamm* and *daed* died. I love our grandparents and I'll miss little Beth something fierce, but I can't see myself sticking around anymore than Amy or you could. There are too many sad memories." A lump rose in her throat, threatening her composure.

"I of all people cannot find fault with your plan, but I hate the idea of us spread across the eastern United States."

"Missouri is certainly not the East. Have you checked a map lately?"

"Truly, it is not," agreed Nora with a laugh. She flicked away a mosquito.

For several moments they rocked and listened to tree frogs and crickets fill the air with a late summer serenade. Each of their hearts grew heavier as the irrevocable future closed around them like heavy fog. "No matter where I end up, you will always be my *schwester*," murmured Rachel.

"And I, yours." Nora clasped her hand in the shadows as they savored memories of their shared childhood. Impulsively Nora leaned over and kissed her cheek. "*Gut nacht*, Rachel. I believe I've kept my new *ehemann* waiting long enough." After a nervous giggle, she went inside the house, leaving Rachel alone with her thoughts and fears for the future. When she fell asleep that night, frolicking colts, majestic stallions, and gentle mares filled her dreams, giving her the best sleep she'd had in weeks.

The next day Rachel and Beth accepted tearful hugs and a packed lunch that would feed far more than two, and then they climbed into the back of a hired car bound for downtown Columbia. After paying their driver, they boarded the bus to St.

Louis—a frightening city in terms of the amount of fast-moving traffic. Rachel waited almost until the bus pulled into the terminal to drop her bombshell.

"What do you mean you're only buying one train ticket to Chicago?" demanded Beth. "How do you intend to get home?"

"After I put you on the train, I'll take a cab back to the Greyhound station. I'm traveling by bus to Louisville." Patiently she spelled out the sketchy details as she'd done the night before to Nora.

Beth listened to the explanation without interruption and then wailed, "Fine and dandy, but why can't I go too? I've never been to Kentucky either."

"Because if all goes well, and if Sarah and Isaac allow it, I will stay and work. You're too young to move away from *grossmammi* and Aunt Irene just yet."

"Will you court boys there?" Beth turned toward her on the seat.

The unexpected question caught Rachel by surprise. "I'm not thinking about courting now. I just want to find a job."

"But you're already twenty." Beth sounded aghast.

"That's not that old in this day and age. People are waiting longer to marry."

"Why can't I come with you? If you decide to stay longer than a visit, you could put me on a bus home then."

Finally, the question she had dreaded. "Please don't be hurt, Beth, but I truly wish to try this out by myself." With a shaky hand, she pulled a printed sheet from her purse. "I wrote out directions on how to change trains in Chicago to catch the Capitol Limited to Pittsburgh and then the Pennsylvanian on to Harrisburg. There you'll catch the bus to Mount Joy. It's all spelled out very carefully. It's exactly what we did on the way here in reverse."

Beth shrugged. "*Grossmammi* is going to be miffed, even more so than she was about us attending the wedding unchaperoned."

She shivered, as though picturing their grandmother's seldom-displayed temper.

"True enough. But she knew I was considering it, and I wrote her a long letter to explain as best as I could." Rachel withdrew a sealed envelope from her purse. "Will you give her this when you get home?"

Beth stared at the white envelope and nodded. "*Jah*, I suppose. But maybe I'll just lay it on the kitchen table and hide in the barn until the steam clears. What about Amy?"

Rachel patted her bag. "I wrote her a letter too. I'll post it the first chance I get. I told Nora last night after the wedding. She seemed to understand."

"Then it's all decided."

Her sister's plaintive words of resignation cut Rachel like a blade. She wrapped her arms around her, enfolding Beth in a hug. "You can come visit me once I'm settled. And I promise to come home to Mount Joy too. We'll always be sisters. Never forget that." The rocking bus, the chatter from other travelers, and the scenery passing at breakneck speed all faded away. Rachel was only aware of the skinny fourteen-year-old she held in her arms and how much she would miss her.

"St. Louis," the bus driver barked into the loud speaker.

Everyone jumped up to pull luggage from overhead bins and collect belongings from the seat and floor. Rachel felt Beth shrink by her side. "Don't be frightened. You're a smart girl. You have your directions, plenty of food, and money in your purse. Just remember what *mamm* used to say: 'You're never alone in life. God is always with you.' So close your eyes and let Him fill your heart."

Whether her words did any good, Rachel would never know. Beth was quiet during their walk to the train station and said little as they sat eating sandwiches and fruit, waiting for the next train to Chicago.

Feeling as low as a crawfish on a river bottom, Rachel walked her sister to the turnstiles. She handed her the tote bag of sandwiches and snacks. "Don't lose your ticket. And don't be afraid to ask questions of kind-looking ladies."

"Promise me you'll write." Beth's green eyes were round as silver dollars and just as shiny.

"Twice a week, every week. And Sarah has a phone in her house because she's Old Order Mennonite, not Amish. I wrote her number on your directions. You could always call from the phone shed if you're dying to hear my voice."

Beth laughed. "Most likely twice-a-week letters will fill my need for sisterly companionship. Don't go too sappy on me."

True to the youngest sibling's style, Beth had already adjusted to the change, disappointment rolling off her like water off a duck's back. So Rachel was able to watch her board the train for home without melting into a puddle of sorrow and indecision. Home—Mount Joy, Pennsylvania—didn't feel much like home since the night she'd spotted flames leaping high into the starry sky and smelled the acrid smoke, which had filled her lungs and then her soul.

That night Rachel dozed fitfully in the train station's lounge, per the advice of Jonas Gingerich. There would be more people milling about there than in the bus station, where she returned at first light. She washed her face and hands and brushed her teeth in the restroom. She bought a bagel and cream cheese and pint of cold milk.

By the time Rachel boarded the bus to Louisville, excitement had built in her blood like an herbalist's tonic. She couldn't keep from grinning as they crossed first into Illinois, then Indiana, and finally into Kentucky. She thought even the air smelled different.

She arrived in Elizabethtown by late afternoon and called the number provided by her cousin Sarah. A hired driver, a sweet woman named Michelle, picked her up and drove through Charm before arriving at the Stolls' farm. A historic courthouse with a clock tower soaring into the clouds dominated the town square. Stately elms and oaks spread their limbs far and wide, shading park benches and stone walkways, where elderly men reminisced and young mothers pushed baby strollers. There was a second, new courthouse, along with the sheriff's department, café, furniture shop, post office, pizza shop, and an ice cream parlor. What more did a body need? Two white church steeples loomed above the housetops. Rachel wished she could take a photograph to send to Beth, but, of course, she'd never used or owned a camera in her life.

Charm—the name said it all. Rachel was so eager for a fresh start she almost broke into song.

# ABOUT THE AUTHOR

❧

Mary Ellis grew up close to the eastern Ohio Amish Community, Geauga County, where her parents often took her to farmers' markets and woodworking fairs. She and her husband now live in Medina County, close to the largest population of Amish families, where she does her research…and enjoys the simple way of life.

❧

Mary loves to hear from her readers at maryeellis@yahoo.com

or

www.maryeellis.wordpress.com

❧

## *A Tragedy…a Refusal…a Shunning*
## *Will Their Young Love Survive?*

Amy King—young, engaged, and Amish—faces life-altering challenges when she suddenly loses both of her parents in a house fire. Her fiancé, John Detweiler, persuades her to leave Lancaster County and make a new beginning with him in Harmony, Maine, where he has relatives who can help them.

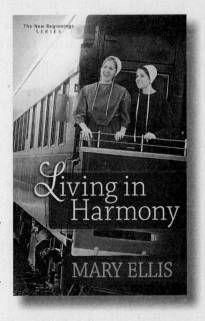

John's brother Thomas and sister-in-law, Sally, readily open their home to the newcomers. Wise beyond his years, Thomas, a minister in the district, refuses to marry Amy and John upon their arrival, suggesting instead a period of adjustment. While trying to assimilate in the ultra-conservative district, Amy discovers an aunt who was shunned. Amy wants to reconnect with her, but John worries that the woman's tarnished reputation will reflect badly on his beloved bride-to-be.

Can John and Amy find a way to overcome problems in their relationship and live happily in Harmony before making a lifetime commitment to each other?

## *Love Blooms in Unexpected Places*

As an Amish midwife, Abigail Graber loves bringing babies into the world. But when a difficult delivery takes a devastating turn, she is faced with some hard choices. Despite her best efforts, the young mother dies—but the baby is saved.

When a heartless judge confines Abigail to the county jail for her mistakes, her sister Catherine comes to the Graber farm to care for Abigail's young children while her husband, Daniel, works his fields. And for the first time Catherine meets Daniel's reclusive cousin, Isaiah, who is deaf and thought to be simpleminded by his community. She endeavors to teach him to communicate and discovers he possesses unexpected gifts and talents.

While Abigail searches for forgiveness, Catherine changes lives and, in return, finds love, something long elusive in her life. Isaiah discovers God, who cares nothing about our handicaps or limitations in His sustaining grace.

An inspirational tale of overcoming grief, maintaining faith, and finding hope in an ever-changing world.

## *How long will true love wait?*

Meghan Yost is bright, talented, and eager to prove to her father, the bishop, that at nineteen she's mature enough to teach in an Amish school all by herself. But just as she gains confidence and assurance, a troubled student challenges her authority and an enthusiastic suitor in the head-strong Jacob Schultz challenges her patience. How can Meghan outgrow her nickname of "little goose" if she can't prove herself to be a capable adult who can stand on her own two feet?

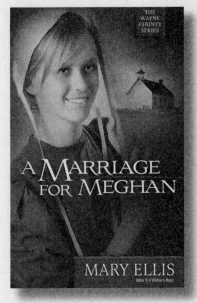

When a series of apparent hate crimes sweep through the district, the sheriff calls in the FBI, and Special Agent Thomas Mast arrives in Wayne County carrying a secret he's hidden for years. Will he come to terms with the past and regain his relationship with God before his career hardened his heart? With more on her plate than one girl can handle, Meghan sets out to help with the investigation, and Thomas ends up working closely with the bishop, who hopes the criminals will be arrested before Meghan finds herself in love with the most inappropriate of suitors—an *Englischer*...

An engaging story of one girl's quest for independence and true love as social prejudice tests a community's faith in a simpler world.

- Exclusive Book Previews
- Authentic Amish Recipes
- Q & A with Your Favorite Authors
- Free Downloads
- Author Interviews & Extras

# AMISHREADER.COM

FOLLOW US:

facebook  twitter

To learn more about Harvest House books and
to read sample chapters, log on to our website:

**www.harvesthousepublishers.com**

**HARVEST HOUSE PUBLISHERS**
EUGENE, OREGON